Michael Taylor is an entrepreneur and well known figure in the North West business community. He is on the board of several organisations and companies and works as an events host and consultant, but his first love is writing. He started out writing about sport, music, fashion, design and culture – but that was in Australia in 1989. He came home to England and became a successful business journalist, becoming an editor by the time he was 30 and winning Northern Business Journalist of the Year four times, Private Equity journalist of the year twice and several other awards.

In his time as the editorial director of Insider Media, publishers of leading business magazines, he built a respected reputation as an investigative journalist, reporting on company collapses and wide scale frauds. In so doing he fought off several libel claims.

He was the author of the monthly Roger Cashman column in Insider which was the best loved part of the magazine, telling truths about business life through the prism of a fictional character.

He's recently started DISCUSS, a debate series for the intellectually curious. In 2012 he co-authored and edited Northern Monkeys a history of northern working class fashion, where he interviewed several entrepreneurs in the fashion business.

In the General Election of 2015 he stood as a Labour Party candidate in Hazel Grove.

Michael lives in Cheshire with his wife and five sons. This is his first novel.

40 BY 40

MICHAEL TAYLOR

Originally published in 2015 by TH Media

ISBN 978-0-9559534-7-7.

Cover illustration: Andrew Swainson

Publisher: TH Media, Derbyshire

Print: Digital Print Media, Cambridgeshire

Dedicated to everyone who
ever helped me understand the world a little more

Cast of characters

Sam Allardyce, football manager, good bloke

Bobbi Armani, entrepreneur, bullshitter

Angela, RC's PA at RC Solutions, quite fit, muppet

Dave Atherton, eccentric entrepreneur

Flamo Ballo, African footballer

Mel Bailey, old bird, private detective

Dougie Barrowman, Isle of Man entrepreneur, great lad

Paul Beck, entrepreneur, great lad

Wayne Bellamy, corporate finance adviser, muppet

Jesu Bravado, footballer, swordsman

Mark Boler, owner Mere Golf Club, great lad

Ben, TV producer, media muppet

Simon Binns, journalist, Crain's Manchester Business

Tom Bloxham, property developer, good lad

Peter Cowgill, entrepreneur, great lad

Sunil Chundapul, Indian businessman

Vinjay Chundapul, Indian businessman

Alec Craig, lawyer, good lad

El Hadj Diouf, footballer

Les Endean, partner in Endean Bellamy Partners

Paul "the Plumber" Davidson – entrepreneur, storyteller

Freddie Derbyshire, lawyer, fixer, good lad

Dave Ecclesthwaite, entrepreneur, great lad

Evil, thug, Chelsea

Tony Ford, entrepreneur, great lad

Dave Foster, property developer, good lad

Brad Friedel, footballer, good lad

Gary Garner, salesman, possibly gay

Chloe, bird at RC Solutions, quite fit, muppet

Julio Grande, footballer, swordsman

Derek Hatton, entrepreneur, good lad

Paul Heathcote, chef, great lad

Hitler, mate of Tosh, thug

Mike Hunt, great lad

Dan Kay, private equity muppet

Brian Kennedy, owner of Sale Sharks rugby

Mark Langford, entrepreneur (RIP)

Aisling Mahon, PR bird

Bernard Manning, comedian. dead

Tony Martinez, swordsman, great lad, mate of Roger Cashmore

Thomas "Tosh" McGeoghan, thug, businessman, old friend of Roger Cashmore

Chris Millar, Taurus wealth manager, likes his food

Vince Miller, compere, good lad

Maxine May, owner of Edge Escorts, hooker

Jon Moulton, businessman, future predictor

Robert Peston, BBC bloke, delivers bad news

Theo Paphitis, businessman, great lad

Morten Gamst Pedersen, footballer

David Rhodes, journalist, *North West Business Times*

Denise Ripley, PR hag

Dave Ritchie, Scotsman, sales bloke at RC

Peter Saville, artist

James Sellars, Taurus, thin one, likes his beak

Samia Smith, actress, fit bird

Sidney Silver, legend, millionaire

Taurus, wealth management advisers

Tony Tighe, PR bloke, good lad

Richard Thornton-Chambers, business partner of Roger Cashmore

Amanda Webb, lawyer, fit bird (on a good day)

Anton Wilcox, arse-licker, employee of RC Solutions

Glossary of technical terms used in the book

AIM – Alternative Investment Market

ASBO – Anti Social Behaviour Order

BTL – Buy to Let

Cat-C - Category C – the highest rating for a dangerous football hooligan

CFD – Contract for Difference

CDO – Collateralised Debt Obligation

C18 – Combat 18 (neo-Nazi thugs)

Dibble - Police

Five – 0 - Police

FSA – Financial Services Authority

FT – *Financial Times* (newspaper)

FTs – Fake Tits

GFE – Girlfriend Experience

IFA – Independent Financial Advisor

ISA – Individual Savings Account

ITK – In The Know

JFDI – Just Fucking Do It

LTV – Loan to Value

MBO – Management Buyout (selling to the muppets)

MBI – Management Buy In (selling to new bunch of muppets)

MILF – Mother I'd Like to…

MIPIM – Massive International Piss-up In the Med – property conference in Cannes

NWDA – Northwest Development Agency (free-spending quango)

OB – Old Bill (Police)

PE – Private Equity

POWs – Predatory Older Women

SIPP – Self Invested Personal Pension

Trade sale – Selling to competitors

TTs – Tupperware Tits

VC - Venture Capital

VCT – Venture Capital Trust

January 2008

Retailers announce they have suffered the weakest Christmas for years. Personal debt levels soar to new a high. Ernst and Young hires more partners to meet 'insatiable demand' of growth companies. Hale Group is bought by an Indian pharma company. The cost of nationalising Northern Rock is priced at £50bn. US banks Merrill Lynch and Citigroup are bailed out by foreign investors for £21bn. Fears of a recession push the FTSE below 6000.

Chairman's trading statement – RC Solutions

The board is delighted to report an increase in profits across divisions. Growth for the forthcoming year is in line with market expectations. Solutions, outsourcing and financial modelling solutions are all performing strongly. Returns from our property investments are stable. Our gearing is manageable and our support from our funders, Bank of Caledonia and Volcanic Bank, remains strong.

The board are delighted to pay a dividend of £8 per share.

To mark the 10th birthday of the company our new corporate social responsibility programme will bring greater awareness of the role of the business within the wider community. The board will be supporting a number of appropriate initiatives in line with these objectives.

"Sick white children. You can't go wrong with sick white children."

How did picking your annual charity become such a ball-ache? It's all so fucking political. And it's the top item on the agenda at our first executive meeting of the New Year, so it must be important.

RC Solutions, my company, Roger Cashmore – RC, geddit? - has adopted a policy of listening to the staff. It wasn't my idea, it was Rick's. My so-called business partner, Rick Chambers.

He has strange ideas about stakeholder democracy, motivation, equity spread and risk. Me? I think it's dangerous talk. We didn't build up this company by taking decisions by committee.

So, I go along with this shite, this charade, this exercise in being a good guy. Letting the salaried masses have their say isn't quite the same as acting on it, but being seen to listen is what the new inclusive way of business is all about, so Rick says.

I know, deep down, what is behind corporate social responsibility and charity. Rick would quite like a gong for services to business and for his charitable work. Either that, or a quiet life with his head down.

It's all about planning for the future. We're selling up and moving on. I've worked out I can net 40 by 40, which sets me up nicely. That's £40m total liquid assets by the grand occasion of my 40th birthday in December 2008.

We're going to accept an offer to buy the business from this outfit called Delphic Private Equity. The deal is sweet for us, £75million, split between me, Rick and the other minority investors.

The clock's ticking on this as Gordon Brown's greedy socialists – the Department of Wealth Prevention - have slapped Capital Gains Tax up to 18 per cent, the robbing bastards. So we're going to have to get this away by the start of April when the tax deadline kicks in so we can get on with the rest of our lives.

Now I don't *actually* give a flying fuck or a rolling doughnut for sick kids and what have you, or whatever charity we choose.

As long as it gets better publicity for my missus, Serena Cashmore, on the occasion of her big night of the year: the RC Foundation Glitter Ball at Mere Golf and Country Club, the epicentre of her world.

Serena, or the tethered goat, as I call her, spends a fortune sprucing up like you wouldn't believe. It's the high spot of her year to be photographed in *Cheshire Life* handing over the charity cheque to some cloying, desperate and overpaid fundraiser with a pathetic specimen of humankind at their side.

And trust me, a sick white kiddie ticks all the boxes.

16

She also thinks it promotes her business and gets her closer to her dream of getting her own television series as the Queen of Tasteful Décor.

For the moment, she's an "entrepreneur". Or at least she thinks she is. I've set her up in this business doing up houses. She calls it "interior ambient solutions". I call it buying stuff you don't need, for people you don't like, for people with no taste.

She goes in and tells these grape-brained bints who've managed to slip onto the arm of some thick-as-dung footballer and tells them what to put in their house. It's really quite unbelievable how utterly incapable of looking after themselves these people really are. She's got an account at Arighi Bianchi that doesn't actually give us any discount, but these idiots think it does.

I've worked out that the whole tawdry enterprise will probably lose us, well me, £100K a year. But even with her taking a decent salary it's still better for the personal P&L overall, as she'll spend that – easily – on shite of her own.

More cars, more dresses, new tits, more stuff for the house, getting her hair done every day, rather than just the twice a week, another new place in Abersoch, or Majorca, or Dubai. So the job keeps her busy, our of the shops and it makes her feel important.

She's learnt to avoid the Dutch and Scandis like the plague, as they're far too intelligent to fall for a caper like this.

No, she sticks to the council estate scrubbers who got lucky, the waxwork dolly birds who, if you let them, would create little outposts of Wythenshawe (or worse still, Liverpool) in the heart of our beautiful county of Cheshire.

One of them bought a gaff with a pool and asked Serena if "they" came round to clean it.

"Sorry, who's they?" she asked.

"The council," came the reply. Unbelievable.

17

Anyway, for Serena, this charity racket is a bit of a personal marketing exercise all of its own.

And that's why we're planning for the 2008 riot now. For the birds, it's all they think about all year. We always try and get a few fit celeb tarts off the telly to come along. Basically, the fitter they are, the harder the wives try. The earlier we can get it out that we've got some nubile starlet that everyone's talking about, then the more likely they'll get their silicon bangers pumped up even bigger. The more bling comes out. The whoredrobes on display would make you gasp. The dresses get sluttier. They make more of an effort. They will do things that even make my eyes water. By the end of the night so air is so thick with competitive tension and female paranoia it's like the set of *Caligula*, Cheshire-style.

And do you know the beauty of it? Do you want to know the beauty of the best night of the year? It doesn't cost me a penny. We sell tables at £2k a pop. I get my best sales guys on it. The ones from a boiler room so pumped up on adrenaline, Red Bull and gak that you can taste the blood in your mouth when you take the junction off the M56 at Sharston and point your satnav in their general direction.

I have this sales motivational technique called JFSI. Just Fucking Sort It. If it worked for me, it will work for them. It works selling solutions and all that techie stuff we do, it works for this as well. I stick a big chart on the wall with a line on a graph etched in red. Fall in the bottom 10 per cent – below that line on the graph, the P45 line - and its goodnight Vienna. At the top is a picture of a Porsche Cayman, the best thing I ever bought for this company (a bright red one as well, nothing subtle here). I parked it at the front and said the best sales person of every quarter gets this for the next quarter. And on it goes. They have pictures of it on the sales floor. Right next to the big fucking bell we have in the middle of the office, which the lads ring every time they make a sale. Then they carry over the magic marker attached to a pulley and a piece of elastic and scroll the numbers up on the white board.

Then there's the mentalist who creams one last sale on a Friday to hit his numbers, knowing he'll be rolling up in a Porsche to pick his kids up that night from his bitch ex-wife and her new fella.

So, for this charity do they target these suppliers, turning the screw on them, these oily little salary men from some law firm, gripped by tension that I might not notice they didn't even try and bid for anything in the auction. Meanwhile, me and my pals crank up the bids for a signed Manchester City shirt, reaching some obscenely horrible sum of money at which I scream to the punters, "come on, this is for the sick kids."

"Sold! For £4,000!" yells the auctioneer, Neil "Ducky" Duckworth, "to Roger Cashmore, a Manchester City football, signed by Brazilian sensation Elano."

Chant it like a mantra: sick kids, sick kids, sick kids. Hospitals, cancer, death. Heartbroken parents. How can anyone not respond to a sales line like that? Pay up, you muppets, pay up. TWO GRAND A TABLE. BARGAIN. Think of the sick kids!

So, back to the big decision and Rick's pointless exercise in corporate democracy. In plain English, who are we going to give a big cheque to this year? What do the busy drongos from accounts and IT and HR all think we should give MY money to?

I slurp down my mug of coffee, ingest the caffeine rush, slam the mug down and shout my morning mantra: "Right, Java installed, let's just fucking sort it."

I survey the scene in this meeting, which has plenty of potential to be dull as fuck. Rick sits at the top of the table. For a "chief executive officer" he's a disgrace. He looks fucked. He tries to smile, but his face is puffed up and sagging. His gut hangs over the edge of the table. When he's listening, he hangs his mouth open to breathe, his striped pink, yellow and brown Paul Smith shirt (which he thinks gives him character and personality) bringing out some of the colour on his purple nose.

I can't believe how much he's let himself go a bit since we were kids. He doesn't go to the gym and he ducked out of the Friday football thing a long time ago, which is just as well because he couldn't score in a barrel of fannies. He's even got one of these poncey Apple iPhone things that all the smarmy twats have got into. Not a proper phone and, from what I hear, they don't even work that well. There's another example of a company that's lost its way.

"Welcome everyone," he says. "This is such a good opportunity for all of us in the business to reflect on our core values and see how we can help those less fortunate than ourselves."

As executive chairman, I offer to lead this one. I've been handed a pile of cards from the office manager, Rick's over-promoted secretary, Geraldine. I give them a shuffle and crack my best sneer.

"Ladies and gentlemen, do we have a violinist on cue?"

Everybody laughs, some more than others, I note. It's my meeting now.

I hand them to Angela to read out for me. She's my secretary, but we've given her the title of "special assistant to the executive chairman". She's a bit obvious-looking in that emergent Cheshire Set kind of way. Straight blonde hair, massive spiky heels, skirt just on the right side of acceptably short. Skin the orange side of salmon pink. Plastic tits, obviously, and if I'm honest, probably a bit underdone. This is something I've never understood. Women get their norks enlarged for one reason: to have bigger ones. The embarrassment, the hardship, the pain and discomfort they go through in order to make themselves more attractive to me, and other men, is something of a turn on, I admit. High heels they can't walk in is one level of commitment, but sticking needles in your face and getting some doctor to slice your tits off and stuff a bag of dodgy plastic in there, just so we notice you a bit more – now THAT'S making the effort.

But why not go for the supersize option? But then I've always held to the philosophy that greed is good.

"Okay Roger, thank you. First one out of the hat, The Big Issue in the North," she says, flashing a big wide smile. I do my best not to notice but the silly cow has had her teeth polished and shined up as well. Probably at one of those new places in Wilmslow, the same one that Rick goes to. How much are we paying her?

I know what I want from this meeting and not only do I want it sorted quickly, I want my outcome.

"Oh dear. Homeless twats. Too scruffy, they'll spend it on wife beater and Buckfast," I say. They laugh nervously at this. Too nervously. But I'm right. You won't get Bryan Robson to donate a pair of his old boots for Ron Wood to buy at auction if he thinks some homeless crusty with a dog on a piece of string is going to get his filthy diseased hands on the money. Not a chance on earth. No debate needed. To this day I still haven't bought a copy off that bloke on King Street in Manchester, just by Boodles. I used to say "already got it mate". I don't even bother saying that now, I just tell him to get a proper job.

"Next".

"BBC Children in Need," she says with far too much emphasis on the "ee" in "need". It's that accent. Not too rough, but clearly still very northern. This is better, but I still don't like it. This is one of those charities where the staff get involved. The very thought of seeing some failing middle manager dressed as Batman makes me think of those sad-sack knobhead custody dads protesting about their bitch ex-wives and pretending they can't see their kids. And they should be working, not baking cakes and taking the team off on bonding trips thinking they might get on telly. No, I don't like that either, the more I think about it.

"I'm sure they'll get along just fine without us," I offer.

"Action Aid for Africa," says Angela with no particular enthusiasm because she knows what I'm going to say, possibly because I puff out my cheeks and roll my eyes in my head.

Anton Wilcox our commercial manager and an arse licker of the highest order pipes up: "We have to be sure we know where the money's going to."

I'm starting to get the hang of this inclusive meeting thing. "Good point, Anton," I say, almost sincerely. "Some General will nick it to buy a new palace. Or tanks and guns to invade the tribe next door."

The rabble, my rabble, my lads, like kicking this African idea to death, and they're getting a bit racist now because they think I'll approve, but I need to move on. There's more ribald laughter. Good, I like this. Rick is sliding into his chair, brooding, and though he knows I can rein in the wild dogs, I don't. He's lost control of this one already and he knows it.

"Mental health hospice," says Angela.

"Nutters," shrieks Gary Garner, another of our commercial boys. He's so far up my arse he can see Anton's feet.

Dave Ritchie, this Scottish low life we hired adds for good measure: "We have to think of the security issue as well. What if one of them attacks Rick or Roger? That wouldn't help our PR."

This is good, this is really good. Because Rick wants pictures when we hand the cheque over. It wouldn't appeal to his vanity to have some hapless mong gurning from the photo, even worse if they threw a wobbly, which I have to admit is pretty much impossible, but I pretend to agree for the purposes of getting what I want.

Ritchie pipes up: "I think Gary knows the bird that works for this charity." He motions with his hands that she's got massive bangers.

"Did you smash it?" says Anton.

"Fucking right I did," Gary chips in, a bit unconvincingly if you ask me. "Filthy bitch she was."

"It'd have to be to have you hanging out of the back of it," I say and they all laugh again. Except Angela, Geraldine and Rick, who are as po-faced as ever.

Anton doesn't hold back, though: "Is that her mate, the Karen one, the slapper who Roger's mate ratted up the arse?" he asks. Adding - ever the diplomat - "he changed lanes without indicating, didn't he Roger?"

I'm just nodding, but there's a bit of a hush when Garner blushes and says, "No mate, that's Karen, my girlfriend, she just moved in with me."

The tone of the meeting has now veered from a lynch mob ready to hack gays to bits, to the Christian Brotherhood praying for the souls of soon-to-be-dead children, to a slightly awkward séance.

Factually though, I think he's right. My mate Tony Martinez, property developer and shagger extraordinaire, did indeed do Gary's new bird up the rusty sheriff's badge. But she wasn't the first or the last to fall for his preying charms.

Angela is by now so anxious I can smell the fear. Women like her just want to be liked by men like me. They seem to gag for our approval every minute of the day. Anything said out of turn, or misunderstood, and you just know, just *know*, it's ruined her day. Give her the nod and the smile and her day is made, she goes home happy and her boyfriend (he's in pensions or something) will get his gold-plated invitation to maul those placcy bangers.

"Next."

No, no, no, no. Someone's suggesting an AIDS charity.

"Who's suggested this?" I demand to know.

"Nigel Brown from sales support," she says, very neutrally, as if she knows she's landed him right in it, but without any kind of encouragement in case she gets caught out for showing any kind of disloyalty.

I'm actually not that bothered, but it's a chance to up the ante and paddle some distance in this meeting. "I didn't even know he was a poof, always seems alright to me."

This unleashes a torrent of abuse and an unwitting stream of foaming hysteria from Ritchie, Wilcox and Garner. "Arse bandit," says one, I'm not sure which because I'm not really listening and I'm motioning to Rick to get this meeting moving along as we've got serious things to do today.

"Pillow biter" adds the other, just daring the other to trump him with "chutney ferret" or some other unimaginative expletive, from which, frankly, the two women in the room are starting to recoil.

"The thought of what those queers do to each other turns my stomach," Gary says, just a little too vociferously.

Sometimes I wonder where we find this rag bag collection of delinquents, psychopaths and sycophants. Then I remember, I hire them and promise them riches beyond their wildest dreams. And the Porsche.

That's what they get when they're here. Word in the recruitment market is you can earn big bonuses and commissions at RC Solutions. As a result it tends to attract the right calibre of cut-throat backstabber. I ask them all a few key questions at interview. If you could have a million pounds right now, but you had to push this button and a Chinaman dies, what would you choose? If the slanty eye gets it, they're past the next hurdle.

Then I move in for the kill. See that Porsche outside? How badly do you want it? What if I said you can have the million, but one of your kids had to get leukaemia?

Admittedly, even for me this is a bit hardcore, but you see the fibre of the man. They have to genuinely struggle to answer that one. They have to weigh up survival rates, how treatable is leukaemia these days? How they could turn it to their own personal advantage? They have to contemplate the bigger picture. Anyone who dismisses the question as abhorrent is not for us.

And do you notice I say lads? Mostly they are lads in frontline sales. We have had a few birds in sales, we had a few right slappers a few years back, but the trouble was they were alright as exercise bikes – quite a few of the lads had ridden them – but it just makes it too complicated.

We prefer to keep chicks in marketing, as secretaries, obviously, and on reception at the front of house. Recruitment here is much more straightforward, they might as well just send in a picture. It's called 'selection by erection'.

And then we have that question about a medical condition for which they are currently requiring treatment? Yes, that's a good one for the birds as well. If they're up the duff then they have to say so. You're not officially allowed to ask them that, but you can ask them about 'condition' and if they are pregnant then obviously we don't employ them. We don't allow flexible working or any of that bollocks and we pay the absolute minimum for mum-leave.

I've absolutely had enough of this and we need a quick decision. Blissfully, Angela pulls out a card from someone who has very sensibly come up with a suggestion to support some hospice for sick kiddies. They even know the name of it. Saint something, God bless. We have consensus. Rick smiles, nervously, weakly and unconvincingly. Even he's pleased with this outcome, so I make the point for him that this is OUR decision.

"I tell you what; you can't go wrong with sick white children," I say it twice for extra effect. And it's true. As long as they haven't been abused, which puts the dinner guests off their starters, you can't go wrong with sick kids. White ones, preferably. The papers love it, the staff love it and you don't

25

feel embarrassed around ill kids and everyone gets to see what a great guy I am.

Charity decisions really shouldn't take as long as they do. And as I twiddle my BlackBerry and pretend to listen to Angela reminding me I'm seeing two birds for lunch in town, we've actually got some hard thinking to do.

She also passes on a message that "Mike Hunt" called again. That's my pal Tony Martinez. She falls for that every time. Brilliant.

We always have time for a laugh. Take last Friday, cold, miserable and this meeting in London is dragging on. By the time I'm getting on the delayed train – first class, of course - it's still crowded, steaming and smelly. Being on a train isn't where I want to be at eight in the evening.

By the time we're rolling through Milton Keynes I'm texting Martinez, then one of the other lads, Bobbi Armani, asking where the party is. I get a reply off Martinez saying he's at some sportsman's dinner with a great bunch of sports lads: Chubby Chandler, Freddie Flintoff, this mate of theirs Paul Beck, Michael "Vaughany" Vaughan and the cast of *Coronation Street*. I text Serena and she's out as well, "with the girls".

Next text, as we're stuck in Crewe for an hour because of signalling problems, I get not a shred of sympathy from any of them.

"This is the best night we've had in years. Shame you can't be here. TM"

"Everyone says hi mate. And I mean EVERYONE who's anyone is here" from Armani.

Another hour later, we've rolled out of Crewe and are parked next to a field. And they're in the Braz now, chatting up birds. Keeping me updated, obviously. Martinez even texts a photo of this fit bird pouting at us.

I call Serena and get nowhere. She's not answering. I text Martinez to ask if she's about.

Comes the reply: "No mate, she just got in a taxi with two black lads."

So I get home and I'm well pissed off. Get the cabbie to take me right up to the house and Serena's there alright with a couple of mates having a drink.

It was a wind up, right. Banter. That's the lads for you.

But that's all for later, for now we have to start to take a bit more cash off the table. Last year we made a killing in net terms but we need to sell up, basically. Me and Rick can't stand the sight of each other; he's still got the hump with me for the office deal we did with my mate Martinez.

As Tony's a mate, and as life's too short not to help out your mates, and as we're all in the business of scraping a living while we can, we did this very sweet deal of our own for new offices. It's another great deal; I moved RC Solutions into some spunky new space in a top new location in Altrincham, which all has to improve their prospects for recruitment, profile, PR and all that. And for committing the business to a long-term deal we got a nice "reverse premium" from the developer to add to our growing pot of gold, that all kicks in on completion as well.

But we didn't even have to build into the figures that our adviser, a dwarf called Wayne Bellamy, has built into the numbers in the IM – or the Information Memorandum, which is a business plan they're currently working on. It's based on chucking a load of numbers in one end and then calculating how much the banks can then pile in with them – the "leveraged multiple" they call it. They're currently looking at valuing our business at 10 times profits, and we've got them fixed on a business plan for a multiple of EBITDAR – That's Earnings Before Interest Taxation, Depreciation, Amortisation. And Rent.

Rick got all carried away with the idea that we should use the dosh from the "reverse premium" to pay for tarting up the new offices, or restructuring our debt. All kinds of mayhem ensued when I told him straight: "I haven't built this business up over the last ten years to pay for your fucking desk and a designer filing cabinet."

What's the point in selling a business and leaving all the upside in there for the next guy? I mean, it's bollocks and he knows it, and there's the other thing, Rick would have handed them a shiny office and no cash. Idiot.

I also own this outfit called Secure Solutions, a research company that does a lot of the stuff behind the scenes that makes the whole thing work properly. It landed on my desk as an acquisition opportunity originally, but I fancied getting my hands on it myself. The administrator needed a quick deal, and basically I didn't really need to trouble Rick with it. I think he was at his gaff in Italy at the time anyway.

Once I'd bought it, it seemed sensible to keep things in the family and tie it into a supply contract with RC Solutions.

Rick got the hump with me because I didn't check with him first, even though it was in the best interests of the company. He seems to think we have to share everything, even though I do all the work. And it's this deal, this messy detail that he gets all precious about, that means we've pretty much fallen out now.

A long time ago Rick twigged that this internet lark had a chance of catching on. We've vaguely done shit around that ever since; sometimes it's tagged as hosted data, at other times it's streaming content. There was a fleeting moment once, about four years ago, when I even briefly understood what it all meant. We also say we provide security software for companies. We set up RC Solutions as a way of selling this to small and medium-sized companies who didn't want to host dirty great servers.

Rick still thinks that's what we do.

Things actually really stepped up when I bought Secure Solutions. It had 12 Russian maths graduates in a shed in Sharston, just round the corner. Their job is to hack into

28

company computer systems and scare the living shit out of the managing directors, or if they can't, just making a copy of their website and turning it into Russian puts the frighteners on. We then sell them a solution that makes the problem go away. Some would call it a hi-tech protection racket; we call it, third generation human interface solutions. We also sell other people's products and make a margin on it. Not a very big one but having accredited supplier status and what have you doesn't hurt the reputation. And the sales guys, who I look after, well, they sell our products on the basis of our range and service solutions and all round ingenuity. Well, that's what Rick thinks.

But here's the real deal. The proper three card trick: Secure Solutions send the clients a data stick with some games and a few other bits of this and that. You won't believe how many senior directors of major companies will download a game and play it for dear life. It also drops a bit of spyware our clever Russian chums have developed, grabs their browsing history and personal banking details. You can guess the rest. Porn. Loads of it. And if they've been looking at even just a tiny amount, then we plant a load more in there. And believe you me, very few haven't, even if they have the good sense to learn the secret formula to a long and happy marriage: Tools – Options – History – Delete All.

It also plants a meeting date in the diary, which our sales boys then call to confirm. Then we get the background on these muppets – home address from Companies House, car details, anything we can find out about their kids, (Facebook is good for this kind of stuff).

Meeting time comes along and we do a demo about the perils of cyber security and what they need to do to protect themselves. They think they've got it all sorted. Then we whip out the dodgy dossier in a plain brown folder. We show how we've got hold of their whole life – and we're the good guys! The bad guys can get all this as well, and they could use it against you. We include a driving licence made out to them (fake of course), a passport application with photos and some credit cards and dodgy bank accounts. We also slip in a few innocuous references to their neighbours, their kids and a copy of some recent internet activity.

It's amazing what our conversion rate is on this kind of thing. Our virus protection software and security stuff is just a white label version of what McAfee and Symantec are knocking out, but who's to know? The sales lads at RC can't believe their luck, they turn up as the knights in shining armour, the clients pay us to make the problem go away, stick them on a rolling 12-month contract, payable by direct debit. RC Solutions takes away those arsey little problems.

Luckily, we're now selling the company just at the right time. The sale process looks like it's cruising towards its happy conclusion. But we still have accounts to settle and people to see. The basic salary and divis that we took out of the business last year cover the car leases (four), the mortgages (two), and the instalments on the client account at the stockbrokers look fine. To do what I really want to do though I need liquid cash, not the promise of it.

We've made enough to offset the losses from Serena's furniture-buying folly and to keep that smile on her face – though Botox played its part, to be fair – but it's still enough to give me cause for concern. There's only so much you can spend on crap. The rest you need to trouser because there's trouble ahead.

And as part of the 40 by 40 plan I've tucked away a nice little nest egg in my bank, the Volcanic Bank, in their tax free outpost on craggy island, the Isle of Man. It's safe as houses, run by the Icelandics – great lads. They've banked a few of our deals over the year – very tasty rates and are always able to stretch that bit more for you. Nice. When you meet them they're like a couple of hairy fishermen, not at all what you usually get. They put me onto their offshore bank in Douglas, where I can stuff away a few of my "alternative" business investments, side projects and gambling wins. The sort of stuff the socialists in the tax office don't need to be troubled with. But we got such a good deposit deal and because the returns from the stock market were so woeful, we thought we'd tuck it up nicely in a bond giving an eight per cent yield. That's about £15m by the way, the last time I looked, the rest is all tied up in RC Solutions, property and a few odds and ends.

This new office in Alty that we moved into is tidy enough and gives the impression we're a quality business, but even with the banks starting to get a bit squeaky-arsed about this we've got plenty of interest in it.

The other reason Rick hates me is I persuaded him to back this estate agency business run by a lad from Alderley. At the time we had a bit of an internet angle on it with some property data-tracking bollocks, but when push came to shove I got bored, as it was doing nothing.

It meant that we had to lay off a load of staff, but the good news is because we ring-fenced the one company, kept it separate from RC Solutions and we didn't put any intra group loans or guarantees in place, just set up special purpose vehicle partnerships to set this up. When we saw it was going tits up we loaded it with all sorts of other liabilities, some suppliers who'd sold us a load of office furniture, leased laptops, internet routers, flat screens. No, they had to whistle for their payment as well. All the lads got some new computers for all our other businesses, like my pal Dave Foster who builds big houses round our way, which we all route through the RC Solutions company anyway.

We slapped it into admin and then we didn't have to pay anything more than the bare minimum of redundo pay or offer anyone any kind of alternative employment within the group. What group? Separate company, amigo. Goodbye.

And this is the thing about Rick; he's a peacetime manager. Despite his expanding girth, he's a lightweight.

When you need someone to fire the bullets he's nowhere to be seen, he gives me zip all credit for anything else we've done, but as I actually enjoy it, I considered it part and parcel of our inimitable double act.

Rick had everyone in the company join Facebook. It was his latest gimmick to embrace whatever was new and cutting edge and was supposed to help with team bonding and sharing news. To be fair I spend a few happy afternoons on the Book of Faces looking at pictures of the girls from school I wished I'd shagged and who would probably like a bit of my pipe now that I've got a few quid. Some of them look grotesque, but some look like they've aged pretty well.

But for Rick it was yet another of his schemes designed for him to come up smelling of roses as the all inclusive modern boss. What a tool. They'd organise parties after work, they'd send out messages to potential clients to arrange viewings of these show homes.

And no-one can accuse me of failing to embrace technology. So when show time came along, 15 December, I remember it well – the same day as the lads' Christmas lunch at the Great John Street Hotel - I thought it would be time to administer a bit of modern management of my own. It's a bit retro to sack them by text – already been done - so when they all logged on to find that Roger Cashmore wanted to "poke them" they had the happy news that the party was over: end of, you're fired. Jog on, losers.

It was mayhem when they found out. No sense of humour these people. Luckily I'd left my Hummer in the garage that day in case it got smashed up and taken Serena's Cayenne, which still has some superficial wounds from a keying. To be fair to us, we at least gave the staff a few shopping days' notice so they could take back all their kiddies' Christmas presents.

But this is why we have to sell. I can take it all in my stride, but Rick takes it personally and it hurts the soft twat to his core. We've basically reached the end of the road on all of this and need to go off in different directions.

So it was hardly a surprise when we started doing our own deals and me taking things to one side. He was free to do it as well, he just chose not to.

Rick offers to drive us from our offices in Altrincham, just off the Washway Road, into Manchester city centre to sign a few documents with the insolvency boys. It irks him that we even have to do meetings like this, and part of him secretly seethes that it was one of my ideas at diversification that has turned on us. But that's business, I tell him. We should focus, he says; focus.

I can't listen to his self pity, so I drive separately. I'm also better at finding car parking places than him, which in a funny sort of way is the root of our relationship. I get things done.

So as much as Rick doesn't like meetings like this, because he thinks it sounds like failure, he misses the point. In America they do this sort of thing all of the time. It's a badge of honour, as long as you don't lose your shirt.

We meet the undertakers, as they don't like me calling them. Sign a few bits of paper. There's no room for humour with this lot. Then, the cheek of it, they start to talk through a few options for some of our other bits and bobs. They've started doing tax appeals and debt restructuring solutions.

They know it's a game as much as we do. They even ask me when I leave if we want to buy anything else as there are going to be acquisition opportunities this year.

By midday I'm desperate to get out and show my face in San Carlo and should get there for one-ish. San Carlo is without a shadow of a doubt the number one gaff for nosebag in Manchester right now. If I get there in enough time I'll get that parking spot on the corner behind Kendals, just before El Hadji Diouf finishes training at Bolton Wanderers and comes into town. It's on double yellows, but it's worth it to show off the new Hummer to whoever is in and it's only £30 if the parking feds get you.

My pride and joy is a H1 Light Utility, which I got repainted in metallic green just to show my commitment to the environmental cause. It has an electric sunroof, which is a waste of time in Manchester. It's got side steps, roof rails, full leather interior and everyone turns and stares, wherever you are. I lend it to pals so they can pull birds and look good, for a favour of course.

It's a damp grey Manchester day but in San Carlo the sun always shines. And today it is buzzing like you wouldn't believe. Breezy bedlam and merry mayhem with waiters flying about like it's the rush hour in Central Station. The Doris on the door knows me by name and always sees me right, I don't need to book, but today I'm being treated and there's every chance they'll cock it up. "Sort me a booth, love," I say and give her my wink.

There's a good crowd around the bar today. I've never been a believer in the value of humility. And neither, clearly, does my old mate Paul "the Plumber" Davidson, who is once again regaling the blokes at the bar with his grand plans. He's holding court while a gaggle of lads sitting on stools at the bar hear his latest stories.

This is the man who fought the law, and won, for a change. He was crucified in the press and accused of being a charlatan. He was down to his brass buttons and now he's back. He was cleared of "market abuse" by the FSA after he took a spread bet on the share price of the company he was floating. Pure genius. And they never made it stick, but it nearly ruined him. Poor bastard. He never stopped smiling either, or telling stories. What a guy. And when everyone else was turning their back on him it was always down to me and a few other lads to stick up for him.

He might dress like a striking miner, but every time I've seen him lately he's had a carrier bag full of £50 notes on him. At first I thought he must have become Mickey Thomas's new best mate, but he picked up the tab for me when we were having a bit of scran in the Alderley Bar and Grill. A couple of days later I was on the train to London and he paid for my ticket. In cash. Top bloke, always liked him. And here he is again, with a new pipe he's invented which he's got a few lads to back him on and he's ready to float another new company, the Fluid Leader Group on the Plus market.

He shows me this business card from Sheikh Faisal Bin Khalid Mohammed Al Qassimi. "He's a member of the ruling family of Sharjah. I'm going to be a billionaire this time," he says. Personally I've never heard of it, but he means business.

A few other lads are already in. Alec Craig is at the bar, a lawyer and another one of the Alderley crowd. He has a group of lads with him, laughing at his stories, some stockbroker and a cricket lad.

"How's it going Craigy?"

"Good, good. Let's have a beer soon. I'll call you."

His firm, Halliwells, have just moved into these unbelievably smart new offices in Spinningfields – or Billingfields as we call it now – he's looking well, obviously been skiing. I predict a bright future for these boys; they have to look the part if they're going to take on the London firms. But that's the thing with lawyers, they always win. In the boom times there's deals to be done and fees to be earned. In a recession, everyone starts suing each other and there's rich pickings being a brief for the insolvency boys.

Speaking of which … there's a crowd of well fed Begbies Traynor lads in the first booth by the door. The insolvency practitioners of this parish are obviously doing very well these days, with all this talk of recession, or a flushing out of the shit as we call it. I've always liked their top lad, Andrew 'Dicky' Dick, who's always good for a tip on the horses and owns a few himself.

At the next booth there's a scruffy young lad in a woolly hat drinking coffee while an Asian bloke with a purple shirt, black suit and a ponytail talks to him. He's obviously some kind of pop star, but I don't recognize him, but even I can work out that the buffoon with the ponytail must be some kind of talent agent. Do people have to be so obvious?

Then in the next one along is Sidney Silver, a legend of the business world, with a few of his old boy Jewish brethren. Always tanned and his eyes always darting around, wherever he is, he's made millions over the years as a wheeler dealer in building up and selling textiles companies. Now he dabbles in property and tech start ups, as you do when the *Sunday Times* Rich List has you into triple figures and it's still roughly half what you're really worth. He catches my eye and gets all his old pals to move along and let him out so he can come over for a chat. Even with two hip operations and three score years and ten under his belt he's a fast mover.

I scan quickly through the crowd of various muppets: accountant, bank lads, lawyers, journalists, idiots basically, sat cheek-by-jowl alongside a few old dears. These are the ladies who lunch: brassy and obvious and they're from Wilmslow or Hale, harder and older and they'll be the Worsley wives.

In the far corner of the bar are four moody-looking lads, all dressed in black with a big older grand-looking bloke with a mane of silver hair and a three-piece pinstripe suit. They've got a bucket of champagne and they're obviously out celebrating. At first sight I didn't think I knew them. But it's all about context and, in this setting, I'm vaguely embarrassed when one of them clocks me. I'm surprised to see him in here, it's not usually his domain, not like it is mine, so I just nod. But, fuck, he's coming over for a chat.

"Mr Cash, the main money man," this brute says in a slightly sing-song way like he's rapping or some such shit. He's stunted, smart and ugly, but as hard a man as I've ever known. He might not be big but when he gets knocked down, he just gets up again. He never stops. He's called Tosh and I know him from back in the day. He never quite thanks me for reminding him he had a scholarship to our fee-paying Grammar School and I used to go to Man United with him before everyone else decided they liked football. He's my tenuous link to the shady side of business. He's as bald as a coot now, but in the early 80s he had a big pudding bowl of a haircut, the biggest flick in the scoreboard paddock at Old Trafford. He was always useful to have around. In the famous words of the Beach Boys, "the bad guys know us and they leave us alone."

He's had a few run-ins with the law; been down a few times, a bit of a grafter, ticket touting, snide gear, knock-off clothes and electrical goods. He was also a hardcore football hooligan at United; he's even written a book about his grafting days after spending a stretch in Sing Sing prison in America. Called *Totally Tosh*, it includes all the scrapes him and his merry band have been in all over the world: Thailand, America, even Leeds and Liverpool. Last time I saw him he'd become a bit of a fixer in his own right and claimed he was going legit and embarking upon a career as a serious businessman. I remember what he said: "Fook me, if you're a millionaire it can't be that fookin' hard."

But his shot at the big time, as far as I know, extends as far as running unofficial travel business for getting lads to United matches abroad. He's rung me a couple of times over the years for tips on avoiding VAT and stuff, but he's gone a bit quiet of late. So while part of me gets a bit embarrassed when he crosses over into my space, other times I'm highly delighted.

I still remember this one time last summer we were on the lash in Panacea, it was late, we were pissed up, we'd been playing pub cricket. You know, one run for a rub against a single tit, two for a lingering stroke over two melons or a knee along the arse. A proper grind is "four" – and it's "six" for a grope AND a grind. But, if some bint gives you a "slap" you're out.

Tony Martinez, property developer, full-time legend and a beast on such occasions, gets quite literally caught in the slips with the careless brush of his knee as this black bird walks past and he makes a foolish attempt at a boogie. Next thing you know her fierce fucking monster of a boyfriend is over in our faces and threatening fire and brimstone, you muthafucka this and that. "My bitch, my girl, you disrespectin' me" and all that gangster bollocks. He's got the full boyz-in-the-hood gear and everything – gold teeth, blinged up all round his neck and as he shows when he pulls over his leather coat to one side, he's only packing a gun...

There's getting caught out at pub cricket and there's getting killed for it. Tony's backing off like you wouldn't believe, hands up, surrender, I didn't mean you no disrespect, the full white flag.

The other mate with us, Bobbi Armani, of some kind of ethnic bent, who was with us, a big shot in textiles, tried pulling the brother card. No joy. "Fuck you, Stan." was the gangster verdict.

"Stan?" I said, wary of playing the pedant card while Mr Gangster was in full flow, but it did throw me a bit.

"Yer man, Paki Stan. This is about your wop mate. Stay right out."

Lucky for me, Tosh was in that night and he knows this mad gang-banger and knows how to talk to him. Calms it all right down, has a word, gets us out, and gave me the nod that says "you owe me". And as we're leaving, Tony tries to claim a six. Saying Tosh was the umpire who overruled her, which technically, he was.

But with Sidney Silver bounding over as quickly as his new hip will let him, it doesn't quite suit the image to have some small stocky thug in a North Face coat done up to the top, sunglasses on his head (in January) and the 1000-yard stare so beloved of Manchester's alternative business community.

I engineer it so I can quickly introduce Tosh to Sidney, who won't even remember, and Sidney to Tosh who won't even care. This is one of those awkward social encounters I'm eager to resolve to everyone's satisfaction. Tosh will have told his moody-looking mates in the corner that I'm his millionaire mate who lives in Alderley, who sees him right for tickets and stuff, otherwise why would he come over. He can't be seen to be had off by me, anymore than I can really afford to blank Sidney just to talk to him.

"Tosh, top boy, top man, legend," I say. I reckon I've got another six seconds. "Listen mate, I'm glad I've seen you, I've got an idea for you, something you might be interested in, give me a call." I thrust a card into his hand, it's my private one with my private line and my mobile on it. He can go away with my card, a trophy, a mark that I'd shown him some respect, even if he already has my number. I get some peace and time to talk to Sidney.

The old fucker makes it over and, ever the genial gent, offers his hand to Tosh with a smile. I use the crowded bar to move Sidney into some space so we can talk and I can start to worry about what I can put Tosh's way in case he ever does call me. It has to be a bit more creative than debt collection, which, to be fair, he's very good at.

"Hello young man, how's business?" he asks, straight to the point.

"Oh, you know it is Mr Silver, scraping a living, getting by."

"That's the spirit," he says, he looks at me with a glint in his eye, like he's waiting for me to say the next thing, like I'm going to amuse him.

"You know what, Mr Silver, it's the burning sky and it keeps a burning bright. That's my theory."

"You keep some very funny company. Who was that rogue you didn't introduce me to?"

And there was me thinking he hadn't paid any attention to Tosh.

"Ah, just some bloke I know," I say, trying to brush it off.

"He's with Freddie Derbyshire, the criminal lawyer, must have been in court today, looks like they're celebrating," he whispers, rolling his eyes in the direction of the corner where one of Tosh's mates is now shouting very loudly and holding the bottle of champagne in their air like it's the FA Cup. I look over at them and notice that Sidney's powers of observation are pretty spot on.

"There's a storm coming Roger, mark my words," he says. "Make sure you're protected," he says. "There are fortunes made and lost in a recession you know, make sure you make one."

Sidney is in a good mood and wants to hold court. "The greatest legal device that this legal system invented for the betterment of capitalism is the pre-pack," he says. "As long as you buy the debt, sometimes at a discount, you can get a business free of all its problems for a bargain price. The administrators are going to be overwhelmed soon, the banks are going to have to repair their balance sheets and will be ready to write down assets. Roger, we can make a lot of money if we're ready, but you're too distracted by all of this nonsense."

He always does this, does Sidney. Baffles me with his tight grasp of detail and law, and business tactics. He never stops. He's exactly the same as he was when I first got introduced to him. He's also the same whether you meet him for breakfast, lunch or dinner. He makes my head hurt, but he's a class act. A money magnet.

"Did you take my advice on pension funds, Roger?"

"Of course I did. Avoid them." Sidney should know, his empire of businesses have pension funds all over the place, he sometimes uses them to lend funds to do other deals. But he knows better than to have a business saddled with the liabilities of paying out to staff who leave anyway. Waste of time, pensions.

"There's a flight to quality, though, eh Sidney?"

"Let me tell you a story. A businessman in America was in a great deal of trouble. His business was failing, he had put everything he had into the business, he owed everybody it was so bad he was even contemplating suicide.

"As a last resort he went to a priest and poured out his story of tears and woe. When he had finished, the priest said, 'Here's what I want you to do, put a beach chair and your Bible in your car and drive down to the beach. Sit down at the shore, put the Bible in your lap, pray and the wind will rifle the pages, but finally the open Bible will come to rest on a page. Look down at the page and read the first thing you see. That will be your answer. That will tell you what to do.'"

This is a typical Sidney joke, and I'm glad Tosh has lost interest and drifted towards his pals.

"A year later the businessman went back to the priest and brought his wife and children with him. He had a Cadillac parked outside, his wife was in a new mink coat. The businessman pulled an envelope stuffed with money out of his pocket and gave it to the priest as a donation for his advice. The priest recognized the benefactor, and was curious. "You did as I suggested?" he asked."

I have absolutely no idea where Sidney is going with this. He does it all the time. But I'll give it to him, he's good at it. He's building up to it, prattling along about the priest again.

"You sat in a beach chair with the Bible in your lap? You let the pages rifle until they stopped? So what were the first words you saw?

"And do you know he said, Roger, you'll love this, tell Richard, it'll cheer him up:

"Chapter 11."

And with that, he peered over his glasses, gave me his big grin and laughed like a hyena. "Do you like that?" he said, nodding, his eyebrows popping up and down.

I laugh along, but I have to say, I do not have a clue what he's on about. He has, however, in all the time I've known him, never been wrong about very much at all. However, he does seem to like Rick for some reason, so it pays to be close.

"Come to my office, it's time we had one of our chats," he says, not so much requesting as informing.

"It'll do you good."

He turns to talk to the barrister bloke and I'm dragged over. For fuck's sake, Sidney.

Tall and grand and with a pinstripe suit with white lines wider than the ones Tosh and his pals have been snorting at some point recently, he casts a big shadow as Sidney nosily enquires as to the cause of the obvious celebration.

"My client here," he says putting his hand on Tosh's shoulder, "a respectable member of the business community is today an innocent man, completely exonerated of the heinous charge of murder and once again I have exposed the utter incompetence of Greater Manchester Police and their lickspittles at the Crown Prosecution Service."

Fuck me, murder! Even that's an upgrade for Tosh.

"Dibble had fuck all on me, Mr Cash. No witnesses, all the phone tap stuff they'd done they couldn't use, and they couldn't match the petrol in my car to the type used to torch the car they found Caveman in because some bottles went missing at the labs," he laughs, still talking in that slow sing-song menace that he's always had.

He looks at his brief, who's smiling at him, probably because he gets him so much business. "The Old Bill were desperate, pal," he says, "this one copper was up as a witness, behind a screen and all that. They ask him to describe me, and he says 'a bully' not, small, bald, white..But 'a bully'...even the beak had to pull him on that one."

I smile and give him the Cashmore wink. "Catch you later."

He smiles, but not with his eyes, and amidst all the bonhomie and the cheering and the noise of a city centre restaurant he mouths to me – "Panacea pay back, Mr Cash. I'll be in touch."

I make a mental note that at no point in all of that performance did he say, nor did his brief, even to me, that he didn't do it. Just that the Old Bill couldn't prove he did.

What a day, charity, insolvency law, Tosh off a murder rap and thinking he's in line to be businessman of the year, and now Sidney Silver's box of tricks.

y the by, I'm being treated to lunch today by these two birds from one of our many PR agencies. I forget which one does what, but Angela put it my diary. It can't be the one who does our charity ball, the golf day and the staff being happy, that's Tony Tighe from Mere PR in Hale, a cheery scouser. No, this is either the one with the old battleaxes who do property, who I will obviously be sacking because that industry is screwed. Or it may be the fitter younger ones who do technology. Then I see them arrive and I see notice two tarts trying to haggle for a good table, with big coats with furry collars, one leopard print, always a winner. Then it's clear that this is the technology outfit, as they are - at a distance - fit enough that you would, even with their winter warmers on.

But, and this is the thing with these women, however good they look, it's also abundantly obvious they know fuck all about how to book a table at San Carlo. The Doris on the door gets Gino, or Mario, or whatever the waiter is called, to show them towards a table in the middle of the floor next to some lad from Royal Bank of Scotland having nosebag with this lad from one of the corporate finance teams at one of the Big Four, who I thought had moved to London.

I remember something Sidney once said: "Why would you go to Ernst & Young for M&A advice? It's like ordering a salad in McDonalds. Or asking a hooker for a hug."

I use it myself, to be fair. Who's to know?

Never mind, but I do think it's a bit like the blind leading the partially-sighted. Plus, I'm keen on the finance lad chipping in with Delphic on some cheap debt when we sell the business and I don't want him listening in, or for him to see me having lunch on the main floor. I need that booth I've been promised, thank you very muchly.

The boy band kid in the hat is getting ready to leave, I notice, so I catch the eye of Marcello, the gaffer, who knows me, to grab that booth before they give it to some lawyer, or, even worse, a commercial property agent.

They hadn't spotted me, so I can now obviously and blatantly upgrade and unseat them from where they were in the stalls and move up onto the stage.

I do air kisses with Denise, the older one of the two (who I now realise I do know quite well, or at least she makes me feel like we do) and a handshake with the younger one, who she introduces me to and who I'm pretty sure I've never met before. As we shuffle into the booth, them either side of me, the younger one, not-Denise, says, "so who's in here today?" her eyes casting around like all the other rubber-neckers on the main floor immediately identifying herself as one of those chicks that reads celebrity magazines.

I'm about to cut her off with a speech about the vapid celebrity-obsessed nature of our screwed-up country and that I know zip all about "celebs" and care even less, when I actually notice what an absolute babe she is. She also has a glorious thick Irish accent, big deep blue eyes, dark hair with a hint of auburn in it and high cheekbones. Once she's taken her coat off I can see that she's got a decent rack, skinny arms, which means she won't have a fat arse either. This is why you hire PR companies, I think to myself.

You can have some grizzled old bloke with stories about the old days, some good younger lads about our age with complex personal lives who'll take you shooting and get you tickets to major sporting events, invite you on golf trips, but when push comes to shove, what's the point in having a PR company that doesn't have fit birds? The owners have cottoned on to this as well. The pitches for this kind of business are getting ridiculous; the main lad or the madam of the rookery gives you the vision and the brand crap. This is always backed up with dubious market research, fancy Power Point slides and trotting out buzzwords about shit like "social media" whatever the fuck that is. But the clincher is the

45

sideshow, the birds they bring along who look like they've stepped out of the pages of FHM or just finished a shift in Long Legs. They drop pencils, flutter eyelashes, cross their legs. Short skirts and cropped tops usually. But tight trousers as well. Sex sells, especially in business-to-business public relations.

The trouble today is the whole Tosh and Sidney thing and the fact that it's winter. She was so wrapped up when she arrived that I didn't notice that she required a little bit more attention than just a chance to laugh at my jokes. And I haven't even dignified her with remembering her name so far, so I'll have to blag it.

"Justin Orange from Take That was in last time," I say. They both laugh, good, I think, I'm onto a winner here, they're both hanging off my every word, because they have to, but they like the patter.

"Yes," I say confidently, "I know his brother, Simon, a really good lad." I do like to shamelessly name drop for good measure, certain in the knowledge that this will impress them greatly. "And some other lad from a band was in here before, sat right here."

Denise grins and Bright Eyes pipes up, politely, diplomatically. "That was Morten Gamst Pedersen," she says.

"From A-Ha?" I ask.

They both laugh again.

"No, he's a footballer, he plays for Blackburn, he's like the David Beckham of Norway, lovely guy," she says, explaining where he lives and all sorts. "He came to the launch of this art gallery we did in the Northern Quarter. Bought this amazing Peter Saville piece."

Jeez, she's cultured as well. Name drops painters and everything. Way out of my usual intellectual range. I have to say, you don't meet birds like this one in the Bubble Room in Alderley, or at Panacea.

46

We order food, or rather I do. I don't even look at the menu, I just ask for a "nice piece of fish" and some of the side orders of veggies. It's a tip I've picked up off some of the big hitters I've met over the years, like Fred Done and Peter Jones. They don't look at menus, they just get what they want. The girls agree with me and have some of the same. And a nice glass of Pinot Grigio. For the record, I know fuck all about wine, but I know when to turn on the lingo. And that never fails.

The trick with anything like this kind of patter is to know a little about a lot. My mates are the masters of this. Martinez has got wine bullshit down to a tee. One time we were at the footy at Blackburn, a night match against United, this waitress breezes up, a teenager, easily.

"Any wine?" Martinez, showing off, orders a bottle of Chablis.

"Red or white?" she asks.

Martinez, looking at me, then looking at this other lad from some bank, says: "red".

Five minutes later she comes back and says we haven't got any red Chablis, but there's plenty of white, will that do? I am sorry." Note to self, when in Blackburn, always order red Chablis.

I bet these two know their pinots from their merlots so I have to be careful not to make a tit of myself. There's enough tit around the table as it is. Denise tries to talk to me as a "fellow entrepreneur", she looks alright for her age, good norks, probably fake, but there's nothing there at all. She's got that contented professional look about her. It's a big signpost saying "back off" before you even think about it.

The other one is different. No mention of a boyfriend. No ring. Not that it matters, especially when Denise starts telling that the by now nameless Irish babe all about Serena's business, as if it's serious, which I'd prefer it if she didn't. And, in case you're wondering, love, she doesn't need her PR doing.

47

I tell them my stock of stories about travelling and doing business aboard. "I went to a meeting at a bank at Zug in Switzerland, the land of peace, prosperity and cuckoo clocks, first thing this geezer does is look at his watch and says, 'ah Mr Cashmore, almost late'."

As I close for the punchline, Denise closes her eyes, cracks a knowing smile and nods benignly, like she's heard this whole routine and patter before.

"Then in Japan, they've got this thing going on with the business card, let me show you, give me yours," I say to her as a ruse to get her name.

She's called Aisling Mahon. Arrrgh. If I'd been listening earlier I'd have heard what her name was; I can't even pronounce this so it gets me precisely nowhere.

I lay down my minimum list of requirements for the year to help me diversify. Without telling them that we're selling up and my 40 by 40 plan, I want to create all the noise in the background, some profile-raising so people know all about me as I get on my next step. I want them to organise my entry, due in next week, for the Ernst & Young Entrepreneur of the Year Awards. I'd be following some other top lads onto that stage as well, I can tell you. When you look at who's been up for this title in the past: Shaid Luqman of Lexi, Peter Bradley of Alta Gas, the iSoft boys; they're all good lads at the end of the day. They get a bit of stick for the odd disqualification, investigation, or insolvency, but that's the trouble with this country. Always knocking down the successful.

I've won my fair share of awards, it's a piece of piss, to be fair. No-one ever checks the figures or anything so we just say how brilliant we are and they take it all in. The one time we didn't win we just got Wilcox to jump on the stage and collect the award before anyone else noticed that the real winner – from PWC or someone like that – was slowly making his way from the back of the room. Class.

48

I also need to be in the rich list again, the *Sunday Times* as well as the local one in the *Insider*. That'll keep her on her toes for now.

"I also need to know, Denise," I pause, just as the food arrives and just so she knows I'm being serious. After all, I'm the client and they do what I want. "I need to know that we're going to be looked after properly. I've had every PR company in town through the door over the years. I'm not being palmed off with a junior; I need to know you're going to look after me."

She nods in comfortable agreement, and says: "That's why I've brought Ash along. She'll be your account director."

Bingo! Ash, Ash, Ash. I don't even have to pretend to pronounce her name correctly now.

Ash, plausibly and intelligently, talks in complete code about brand management, value proposition, lots of ideas for getting me up there in lights. Throws in a few ideas about television. There are a few new formats she thinks will work for me. She says she can use some of her contacts to open some doors. She even suggests a bit more of the charity stuff and some bollocks about "entrepreneurial thought leadership" whatever the fuck that is.

She can come to the ball. She also chucks in that she's able to manage information flow during a time of corporate downsizing, like she's done it before and expects to do it again. She's worked in Ireland for one of those banks that have come over here, name drops that mad man Michael O'Leary at Ryanair and now she knows how to open art galleries and how to get me back where I belong in the Rich List. And she looks very slottable. She'll do for me.

By the time the main course has been polished off and they bring the coffees with those crusty bits all coated in sugary flour, I'm pretty sick with lust at being with these two women. The wine clouds my mind, the booze goggles are firmly on and as they're talking and telling stories I'm picturing a complex and slightly violent threesome where Denise is unleashing all that MILF like fury on a shocked little victim whose innocence melts away into ever deeper depths of depravity.

But it isn't going to happen. Between us we've already stuck a bottle of wine away. Well, I have. I suspect they've been sipping. I'll call my pal Dave Foster, when I tell him I'm having lunch with two PR birds the dirty bastard will be all over this, plus, any excuse to drive my Hummer back to Alderley. He loves it.

Where next you ask? Where does all this go? There are lads I know who would at this point write off the afternoon, get right in this girl's face, order in the next bottle of wine, call lads over for more chat, suggest drinks in somewhere more comfortable (the Lowry Hotel, for example, just a walk away). Let the talk turn from ideas and plans and business to personal opportunities and life ambitions. Talk will turn to passion and seizing the moment, living for the day. It would involve moves and touching and flirting and a bit more wine and would end in her peeling her knickers off in a room, not a suite, not on the first date, and spending an extremely satisfying few hours banging the Irish arse off her. There are also lads, salesmen usually (who can take rejection) who would just go straight for a forceful closing line. To be fair, I don't reckon she's that up for that.

For a start, her boss was clock-watching a bit and when I suggested a swifty at the bar she cut her off sharply, saying "we have to get back to the office." For all the smiles and darlings, I suspect Denise is a bit of a battleaxe.

Don't get me wrong, this isn't a moral lecture on fidelity and faithfulness. Fuck me, I've had birds shacked up in city centre apartments, one for a whole year, just to have as a regular bit of leg-over on the side. She was tasty, mind, but high maintenance. And I've had casuals as well as regulars. I've walked the walk of shame from apartments in the city centre and in places you couldn't find on a map (have you even heard of Cheadle Hulme?) I've been so wasted I've not just forgotten their names in the morning, I've even forgotten the name I told her my name was too. I've paid lap dancers to come to parties with the lads and put on a private show in suites in the Lowry and the Radisson. But I do at least follow a few simple rules.

Number one: don't dip your pen in company ink; fucking the payroll can only ever end in tears, or a tribunal. Two: don't go local, someone, somewhere will catch you out. Three: what goes on tour, stays on tour. Four: never, ever, ever, bone one of your mate's wives. However fit, however bored, however badly-treated they are, this is off limits. And fifth, and finally, don't ever pay for it. Unless of course you're on tour, when tour rules apply and pretty much anything goes.

But these are strange times, and I'm really not sure where nailing your PR girl fits in to all of that, to be fair.

February 2008

Lawyers warn banks to walk away from leveraged private equity deals. UBS writes off $26bn of exposure to the American sub-prime mortgage market. Indian industrial giant Tata moves closer to acquiring Jaguar Land Rover. Lloyds TSB makes profits of £3.9bn, commentators attribute this to a conservative business strategy. RBS records profits of £10bn due to trading in emerging markets

NEWS - The board of RC Solutions can confirm that an exclusivity agreement has now been signed with Delphic Private Equity for a period of five weeks. The offer is subject to commercial due diligence and the directors are recommending the shareholders accept the offer of £75m for the share capital of the company and look forward to an exciting new era for the company.

Let me tell you about the new house we're having done up for us in Alderley Edge. It's absolutely mint. When we bought the place, I said to Serena, you can't argue with a view like that. It has, so the blurb goes, "an elevated position with superior vistas below the Edge and out towards the Cheshire countryside." We were told from the off that the place had "the potential for further modernisation and refurbishment according to the individual's requirements."

Originally, the house was designed in a style known as the Arts and Crafts Movement. The blokes that built it came from a tradition where they were independent designers who were interested in all things medieval. Their founding fathers advocated faithful reproduction of bold forms and colours, I discovered. Like it?

Anyway, we levelled it. We're starting from scratch and doing it properly in what I suppose is a kind of Tudor Gothic look. It's going to have six bedrooms (all en-suite), a gym, a wet room, indoor pool, massive kitchen.

And it's going to have dressing rooms and walk-in wardrobes for us both. I like to look good. In fact, I do look good. Always trim and always groomed. It's my trademark. If you look good, feel smart then you do better business. And what better way to start the day than by looking at me in a full-length mirror?

And it's going to have my own domain, a massive lads' room with a 20-seat cinema for the Monday night football and for showing a bit of porn when we pile back to mine after a few scoops down at The Stag's Head, The Bubble Room or the Alderley Bar and Grill.

Serena's looking after all the interior stuff, obviously, and for now while we're in the old pad round the corner which we'll flog to some footballer when we move into the new drum, which we're going to call Cashmore Towers: a tribute to the power of my name (in fact it's more of a brand now, to be fair).

Make no mistake, this is a serious architectural masterpiece – costing us the thick end of £5m to build, never mind what it took to knock the old gaff down – but the locals have gone proper mental. Which is bang out of order by any possible measure, and harming our chances of being in there in time to enjoy the glorious barbecue summer they keep promising us.

They've had me in front of every planning inspector going, but we've fed them the line about it being an Eco Home. We've slapped a couple of solar panels on the roof, a wind turbine and got the builder to sign a few bits of paper saying it's all sustainable material and what have you. As a ruse it's got the council muppets out of a hole, because we've built most of it already anyway.

Next tactic was they tried to make out our excavations for my lads' room would threaten the Edge itself, and, get this, that my five-a-side football pitch outside would obscure views of the Edge. Well go a different way then. To be honest they have no idea.

After all the work I've done in the community over the years you'd think the Alderley Edge Association would have better things to do than complain about my house and whether it's in keeping with the surroundings. It is, by the way. Have you seen that place that they knocked up on Ryleys

Lane? All turrets and towers? Well, that's a load of tasteless tat, and they're flats! With interest rates so low you've no idea who could scrape together a few hundred grand to move in. At least I'm not riff-raff.

I've also invested literally hundreds of pounds to tidy the area up a bit. A mate put me onto getting a Woodland Creation Grant - which paid for a few trees at the back of the house – and we've tried to protect the locals from certain hazards. We bought the biddies' bungalow next door, which had some land, a duck pond and a boggy field in the grounds. Obviously Serena was worried little kiddies could wander in and drown in the pond, or get stuck in the field, so I got our man to put a fence around it and made it clear they weren't to enter. I was nice about it. You know me, I like a joke, but these in-breds just didn't understand I WAS JOKING when I put up a sign saying "Trespassers Will Be Shot".

The masterplan was to organise some more of these community activities as a crude but rather effective divide and rule strategy. Sadly, our first go backfired. Literally. A few of the lads came over for a duck shoot. I invited my MP George Osborne and a couple of Russian lads with a few quid to throw about, but they said they were busy that day. There we were, popping away, having a great time, feathers everywhere, before the rozzers turned up because the peasants had revolted, some muppet had complained on the grounds of animal cruelty. It was bedlam. There can be no greater indignity for a pillar of the community like me to be explaining myself to the law. But this is not about animal rights. It's obviously just class war.

I then went on a charm offensive that ended up being a bit more offensive than charming. The *Wilmslow Express* completely swallowed my comments about the possible tourist potential of the Alderley caves if the worst happened and the Edge collapsed.

But at the moment it's an island of concrete in a sea of mud. Dave Foster, the lad who's building it, and a mate, has got one of these new paddy banks propping him up – I forget which, but it's got Irish in the name somewhere. That keeps his head above water, plus the entire margin he's making on what we keep paying down. Every time I go on site there's another new problem to splash out for. Every time Serena talks to him she's had another idea about light fittings.

Foster is a good enough lad and he's got a foreman who seems to know what he's doing with a gang of lads who lump stuff about from what I can see.

It's one of the many reasons we're selling RC Solutions this year, the mortgage on it with Bog Trotter Bank is eye-wateringly large, but the interest rate is fuck all. I've got the tuck up money in the Icelandic bank at 8 per cent, but we need that for a rainy day, and we pay ourselves plenty enough to make the payments.

And the six bedrooms? We do not have children. We cannot have children. I do not want children. Serena says she does, and thinks she can't. She goes on about her body clock ticking – I mean, she's only 30. But we've tried everything, so she thinks, IVF, shagging at the right time of the month, more IVF. I've fiddled the bottles that many times, they haven't rumbled that I had the snip. It frees me to go bareback, which I prefer on away trips, and on home runs. Even though it really hurt. My bollocks swelled up like purple turnips and I could hardly walk for a week; had to pretend I'd been kneed in the bollocks playing football. The things we do for a quiet life. Great eh?

So Serena throws herself into all these manic ventures of hers, trying to be a TV star: the acting lessons, the charity work, the social events, the new tits, the house in Abersoch which we've hardly ever used, the place in Majorca, which we've used even less. And the Interior Ambient Solutions business. And then there's this, the new house.

Don't get me wrong, she's alright is Serena, still properly turns heads and all that, and I'm looking at her now and most blokes still would - decent rack (fake, of course), top pins, I mean I wouldn't have married a moose would I? When I first met her she carried off that look that gets me every time: thick black eye liner, pushed-up tits, blonde hair, high heels, a bit of leopard print for added sluttiness. It literally cannot fail to get me going.

Now she's settled into the Alderley crowd she's toned it down a bit. She's gone back to natural brown for a start – but she's a massive cut above most of the slappers we meet on boy's night in town every Saturday.

The life I rescued her from is one of mewling brats, shacked up with a low level criminal, the captain of the football team at school, but basically a brawling psychopath who's gone to seed. If she's lucky. More likely is she'd be pushing a pram around a council estate, smoking 20 fags a day, her weekend entertainment consisting of karaoke nights in some concrete obscenity of a pub every weekend, or once, just occasionally risking a knockabout session with her bloke for daring to go out with the girls.

She knows she's landed on her feet and will put up with pretty much anything. Me, Tony Martinez, Dave Foster and Bobbi Armani know when we go out on a boy's Saturday, when Serena's consoling herself at her busy life down in Abersoch, that we cannot fail. The ego kicks in as you catch the eye of some bint who notices a decent watch, good threads and a toned look after an afternoon on the mountain bikes. These perma-tanned, extension wearing, Blue WKD-swilling slappers are desperate to throw their minge at any passing lad.

"Oi, you one of them millionaires then?" is a classy chat up line next to "you can do me in the bogs if you want," or my personal favourite this: "I'll suck you off in the cab." This is obviously the very height of achievement for these appalling slags.

Serena's a lucky cow and she knows it. Still has muppet tendencies. She's always making out she's the busiest woman on earth, like the rest of us just go to work and look at porn all day and shout at people. Well, just some of the time.

So, here I am, watching Sky Sports News on a wide screen plasma TV screen, a Bang & Olufsen Beovision 7 (some frog called Benzema isn't coming to United). We've got it on in the kitchen diner and I'm drinking a damn fine cup of Lavazza, a large espresso made on the Moda Mio, which we've just got to compare it with the Tassimo. It's retro, but the cute curves and high-gloss two-tone finish in silver means it stands out next to the Alessi kettle, the sleek dark marble tops of the kitchen and the imported bleached white slate floors. We try things out in the present gaff, to see how they'll work when we move into Cashmore Towers.

I've had a good session in the home gym, weights, bench presses, crunches and a steep run up Ben Nevis on the running machine, a Vision Fitness T9800 HRT Full Commercial Treadmill. 4K worth of kit, that!

It has to hurt to look this good and frankly, I look pretty fucking hot if I say so myself. Certainly my Frank Rostron hand-made blue cotton shirt clings to my ripples. Not like a lard arse like Rick who has basically given up.

But it's only 8.30 in the morning and I've got enough to be doing today. Angela is already ringing me asking me where I am, what time I'll be in and telling me people are trying to get hold of me. That's pretty much all she does. Nag, nag, fucking nag.

"Hiya. Are you alright? Working from home are you? Oh I don't know. It's alright for some." As irritating as ever. I wonder if she talks in this whiny drawn-out nasally-contrived way when she's having sex. Does she ask her boyfriend,

Simon, or Tim, or whatever the witless imbecile is called, if you'll be wanting a blow job for yourself?

My day is pretty simple: see some people, be great. One after the other. A couple of lads who'll save me tax, always a good thing.

Then there's football deal we've got going. Foster handles most of that as he's a house builder, knows about greasing the right palms in the planning office and juggling the banks. For a bit of swarthy sophistication I've brought Bobbi Armani in. He loves it. I'm never sure what he actually does for a living, to be honest. He just sort of appeared from nowhere. He spun us this yarn that he's related to the Italian fashion mob; he always reckons he's got a new deal on the go.

He's a tightarse though; always going missing when there's big deals to be done, good at swerving bills. Dodged more rounds than Joe Bugner.

Martinez went down to London with him on the promise of a meeting with some property investors from Dubai he reckoned he knew. Said they'd be staying at his Uncle's house in Knightsbridge, they'd be having dinner at this posh gaff called Nobu with his girlfriend and her mates. You know those trips that sound too good to be true? This was one.

So Martinez bowls over to Knightsbridge in a cab and bells Bobbi Bullshit. There's a problem with his Uncle, but he's got them into a top hotel on Park Lane. Oh, and the meeting with the Ab Dabs has been moved back to the day after, but that they were still on for dinner with his bird and her mate.

Not being shy in the lady department, Martinez doesn't look a gift horse in the mouth. His bird is tasty and her mate is even fitter. During this pricey nosebag at the Nobu gaff he starts getting the footsie under the table and the come on.

He's good at this so, trust me, he knows when he's on to a winner.

He takes her back to his room, gives her one (but knowing Tony, it's probably several). The small hours roll up and he says he wakes up and she's dressed and sat next to him on the bed holding his hand and whispering dirty talk to him. She says, "that was great thanks, lover boy, but I need to go now. And I need my bill settling. It's £1000 for an overnight, but I'll take £500 for what we've done so far."

I mean, fair play to Martinez for fessing up to this, because he rips the piss out of our mate Dave Foster for his brassing. He's only got £100 or so on him and she says she doesn't take credit cards, so he has to go down to hotel reception and get some dosh from the cashpoint.

"Did you wear a blob, pal?"

"Yes, I always do on the first date, or only date," he says.

As for Armani, the meeting with the Arab the next day lasted about five minutes. Barely said anything, just said he was pleased to meet Tony and had no mention of any deal. Armani made up some bollocks that he had no idea the bird was on the game, but played it right down.

Very odd.

Then there's Tosh, who's texted me to say – as he does in his chav speak – "U @ home 4 that chat m8".

I can't be doing with all that teenage bollocks, so I always respond with word perfect replies. It's not done to let your standards slip even in the face of a category C football thug and occasional gangster. "I will be in Costa in Alderley at 11am if that suits. Thanks, Roger."

"Ok" comes the reply. Not "Yes it would be good to see you", or "Thanks". Just "Ok".

I had to think pretty quickly to be true to my promise that I had something for him. He did this book about his life of grafting and fighting. All pretty grim stuff to be honest, but our lads, the Russkis in the data centre, they love it. I got a few of them to take turns in translating it into Russian and putting it onto a spare data stick. One good turn deserves another.

And then there's Sidney to see, for one of our nice chats, this time in his office in Wilmslow. What they both have in common will be a bit of a sulk on about City beating United at Old Trafford at the weekend. I have no idea what Tosh gets up to on match day, but I've been with Sidney in his room in the main stand. Having lunch with him there is interrupted by a constant parade of lads who he's chucked a few quid at. He might be a big shot, tough guy tycoon with a brain the size of a planet, but he's a sucker for a hard luck story and a business idea whoever it's come from. He owns half shares in Salford scrap yards, chippies, bookies, used car gaffs and he even backed this young bird who reckoned she runs a chain of nurseries and old folks' homes. He's proper mad. All of that is on top of him chairing this engineering outfit, a student housing business, some biology software boffins from the Uni and all kinds of green quango bollocks that he keeps banging on about.

But throughout the last month there's been a constant hum to do with the sale of the company with all these spastic advisers, so I'll roll by their gaff for an update later. By any measure that's a busy day. It might also involve dropping round to the office and shouting at some underperforming sales boys on the way home. Then, just as I thought my day couldn't possibly get any better, the lovely Ash texts to say she's got some ideas she'd like to "run through" with me. I think I can find a window, darling.

And while I take all of that in my stride, this is all the kind of order of the day that throws Serena into this manic and breathless whirlwind that gives me a headache.

This is what I think she says:

"Roger babes, I've got the landscape garden guy coming about the pots for the orangery. Then there's a meeting about a new house in Mobberley with that girl that Teresa told me about, she's very excited about the drawings I've done for Cristiano Ronaldo's house. Have you seen my flash drive with it on? I'm going to the gym after that. Meeting a few of the girls for lunch at Players. There's a conference call about that 3D visualisation software licensing with the patent lawyer. What shall we do for dinner?"

The trouble is, this is what I hear.

"Roger darling, blah blah landscape garden guy yak yak orangery. Blah blah Mobberley Big Arse Teresa blah blah blah. Gym yak yak. Lady boy. Yak yak yak blah blah. Witches coven, my name spat out with bilious rage Players. Computer problem. Blah blah. What shall we do for dinner?"

"Yes, very good, cool," I say.

"Roger," she says, "have you listened to a word I've said?"

"Yes, yes, we're going to Heathcotes." I lie. My mate Paul Heathcote is now chasing the same dream and splashing the dosh on some new scran houses as well. I told him ages ago to ditch all that poncey stuff and pile on the quality northern grub. He's certainly taken my advice with London Road, which is just what me and the boys want from our nosebag providers: it's done out in classy beige, glass and chrome with some hanging lamps. They knock out the champagne like you wouldn't believe and the food is ace.

It's Serena's favourite – she loves it, so do her mates, it's the global epicentre of her and her placcy banger fishwife crowd. And the highlight on the menu is the house special of mutton dressed as lamb. It's just as well. Manchester is my playground where I do as I please; this is hers and mine and where my other world shouldn't collide.

Nowhere in that breathless monologue about the shit she does is there a flicker of interest from me. I don't know how or why she puts up with it. I either mask it pretty well, or

64

she's so desperate and determined to impress she doesn't notice.

"Serena," I say, "your hair looks good like that."

She stops, looks at me, and looks like she's about to cry. "Thank you, Roger," she says. "Thank you."

She does look alright, tan still there from Christmas in Barbados. Topped up at the salon she goes to a couple of times a week.

"Yes, listen to this," I say, trying to retell this joke I heard from one of the lads in Ithaca last night. "This bloke comes home and his missus says - 'Hello, darling,' she says, 'do you notice anything different?' 'Oh yes,' he goes, 'you're wearing a new dress.' 'No,' she says, 'I'm not wearing a new dress, I've had this for ages.' 'Oh no, silly me,' he says. 'You've had your hair done.' 'No,' she says, 'I haven't had my hair done.' 'Oh, all right,' he says, 'I give up.'"

She's trying not to laugh, corner of her mouth curling up, though she's had a bit too much of the Botox it's hard to tell, not quite the Leslie Ash, but I can tell the difference.

"Go on," Serena says.

"Yes, yes, she says 'I'm wearing a gas mask,'"

Serena looks confused. "Very funny," she says, trying not to laugh.

"Do you get it," I say, "do you get it? He doesn't even notice."

"Yes, Roger, of course I get it. I'm not completely stupid you know. I suppose that's what passes for humour when you and your mates are all beered-up in Panacea and Ithaca, telling stories about how hen-pecked you all are, bless you all, bless you all," she says.

Bloody hell, what's got her today, must be the time of the month, but then you can never tell with Serena, she's one of those women who spends two weeks with PMT - pre-menstrual tension - and the rest with post-menstrual tension.

Anyway, I say, we've got to sort out the shareholders agreement on her crappy interiors business, which is keeping her busier than normal.

We've got to start planning for the future. The main thing I want to do when I've made my 40 by 40 target is to enjoy life and reap my rewards. Here's where we are with the best laid plans for the rest of the year.

I will own my own football club, ski the best resorts in the world, play golf on all the best courses, visit the best hotels. Shooting parties in Africa on safari where it costs you forty grand to bag a lion, or shooting doves in Argentina (a shoot so bloodthirsty and so easy you end up caked in guts and gunge). I also want to go to all the best parties in world – Rio, Paddy's Day in New York, cricket in Barbados, New Year in Sydney, carnival in New Orleans, find these hedonistic islands off Thailand where anything goes.

And on home turf I'll settle for what the old hands at this, like Sidney Silver, call a "portfolio" career – a few investments and a few cash generating businesses that will keep me busy and make the best of my skills as Cheshire's number one entrepreneur.

You see, I know blokes that have cashed out, done the retirement thing and some of them go mental with the boredom. They make all the money, they have a plan to retire but you still need a job. Brian Kennedy did it, went off to Spain, had everything then needed something else to do and bought Sale Sharks, scraped Ultraframe off the floor and had his lad Stuart Lees holed up in a Travelodge in Clitheroe to sort it out. And why wouldn't you? Life goes on.

Then there's Dave Atherton, mad as a box of frogs, sold Dabs.com for £35m. Last time I saw him he was talking broken biscuits and telling me to read some book about some dead Christian prophet. I do wonder what he's been on, strange lad. I can't see that ending well.

Sidney's big on strategy. At our regular chats, he gives me line after line of quality material to come up with whenever you meet someone who sounds like they know more than you. I like him because he makes me sound well clever.

Globalisation, bond rates, exit strategies. And once you get him onto politics he's awesome. "Why should you even bother going to work if the government take more of the money you make than you do?" Quality.

He plays the tax game well, hiding it all over the show and he's never been rumbled or investigated. He does all this charity and public service stuff – going to meetings and sounding off, which he's brilliant at – and I reckon they just leave him to it. He says it should be up to him how he helps the poor, not Gordon Brown.

Where we differ is on the family. He's always going on about the importance of family and his sons. One of them is alright, but the other is so thick he's got him working managing a property portfolio that doesn't even exist. He pays him a wedge and hopes he'll never notice.

But no, he always asks about Serena. He says I underestimate her. I don't know why? And I never ask him about his Doris, whatever she's called Pam, or Pat, or Val or something.

Long term, very fucking long term, he might have a point. I might even give in to Serena and get a couple of nippers, as long as we have some fit Slovenian nanny to do all the fetching and carrying. Right now it's just more mither than we could handle. They'd just get right in the way.

But we have to get there first. We've been running what our principal financial adviser calls a "triple track process" and now we're at the end of it, we can smell victory. It's basically involved playing one set of muppets against the other.

Here's how it's worked. We got our adviser: Ickle Wayne Bellamy from his own firm in Manchester that he runs with this Orca fat bastard called Les Endean. It's imaginatively called Endean Bellamy Partners, which everyone (and I mean everyone) just calls Bellends. How did they never spot that?

Anyway, they sent a glossy document – an Information Memorandum - to all of them. We even numbered them so they knew there were 28 in circulation; tends to concentrate the mind. Bellamy (who we call Ickle because he's all of five foot four wet through, even with his Cuban heels; a proper short arse) said the buyers don't like that, that he has to keep up the appearance that he's got something special for all of them, just in case they have the chance to throw him a bone. For fuck's sake, I said to the irritating little twat, what the fuck are we running here, an extension of your old pals club, or are you acting for us? As soon as we read section three, paragraph 4 of the 1922 Riot Act he got the message and fell into line. Turns out a lot of the lads around town – like Clearwater and Rothschild – all do this. They just don't want everyone to know it.

For the past six months all the corporate finance muppets - the Bellends are no exception, by the way - have been on at me to sell assets. He reckons the last desperate, spiteful act of the outgoing socialist regime will be to whack capital gains tax up to, I don't know, pick a figure; the more desperate they are, the closer to 50 per cent it creeps. And so they've started with the abolition of what's called Taper Relief; if we own it for a few years and we sell it, then we only pay 10 per cent tax. Good idea, but they're whacking it up to 18 per cent of what you make.

We chose Bellamy because he said he'd do it for a percentage, rather than the fixed fee and the clock watching the so-called Big Four wanted us to do.

Back in the day Endean was a proper player. He'd be the one around town doing all the deals. His Christmas parties were legendary. One year, so the story goes, he invited a dozen top lads, clients and some of his partners to this cat house in the city centre. All the waitresses were hookers, real quality service. Apparently they let you squeeze their arses and feel their tits and everything while they were serving you.

But the real treat came when they'd served up the dessert. Twelve tarts all in, got under the table and gave each lad a blow job. Endean is loving it, roaring with laughter.

Ten minutes later, when a few lads are banging the tables in ecstasy, and a few others are gasping for breath, he calls the girls to order. He then announces that, fun though it was, it was actually the best game of Russian roulette he'd ever played as one of the birds was a bloke: a she-male, a ladyboy. Quality. You've never seen lads move as quick. The one who got his stubby cock sucked by a 'chick with a dick' was Bellamy.

I've never talked to him about it, but it explains a lot. It's an experience that has clearly scarred him for life, as he's developed this nervous twitch which kicks in when he's stressed. On the up side, he's turned into a grafter, a real hard worker. And that was then, and this is now. Deals don't grow on trees and he's keen to earn a few quid for himself and get a slice of a proper piece of action.

So when we got down to it with our sale, we've had three, possibly four different groups running around looking at our auction, so confused they didn't know what time it was.

On one side we had the kids who'd been bullied at school, who now try and cut up rough (private equity to me and you).

Two, the teenage scribblers who've barely started shaving from the City fund managers. They were looking to back our float on the stock market but - get this - it's the Wild West, the Alternative Investment Market where people have a different "appetite for risk". To me and you and the rest of the world, that means there's a lot of shit bundled in there for good measure.

Three, we also got on to these religious weirdos from America who do the same thing as us (in fact, we stole their idea). If you stick a mysterious US trade buyer into an auction

70

and it can go either way; it can frighten the home team off, or spring them into action.

Bellamy also mentions that's he's had interest from some lawyer in London who represents Indian investors. I like his imagination, I'll give him that, and it doesn't hurt to make up a bit of exotic foreign interest. But Indians? Do me a favour. We're not a fucking call centre.

On top of all that, last and by every means least, we strung along these lads in the business who were getting a bit above themselves and encouraged them to put a bid together. Frankly they proved something I always suspected, they think they can do this shit better than me and probably tell everyone else the same thing. They started out by producing a long term strategic review of the business, where they spotted a few things I hadn't, to be fair. As the clock was ticking, we started to notice they were unable to make "important" meetings that I'd arrange at outrageously short notice. Now, they were obviously turning out their pockets, remortgaging their houses, asking their wives' dads, their mates and their pension advisers how they could raid their SIPPs to meet our number. Trouble is, they never could. And when they started to invite banks round for due diligence exercises I threatened to sack the pair of them for gross misconduct and disclosure of confidential information.

But the process has also flushed out a few home truths that have proved useful. In the end they got so frustrated they said they wanted to get out and "do it for themselves". They quite fancied a bit of "gardening leave" until I found out we still have to pay them to stay at home. I don't pay anyone to do nothing, so I told them they could get on the phones in the boiler room and cold call some contacts. They chose wisely and left with fuck all. And do you know what, I can't even remember what they were called. Funny how insignificant details slip your mind.

The American rivals have been a slightly different kettle of fish. They're probably in a bit more trouble than we realised, as their economy is looking pretty screwed at the moment. But it's always useful intelligence and they've borrowed even more in the good times, just as their banks are getting tight. Tut tut. But we keep them in the background, ready to pounce if the City boys and the private equity muppets get too curious and think they can chip the price.

The City malarkey is a massive pain the arse. For a start there's the trips to London where you have to explain yourself to the analysts and funds. What a racket. Look, I can sell. I'm not afraid of standing up and talking shit – I do it all day if I have to - but not to a room full of baby-faced Tarquins. Mind you some of these investment analysts have started employing these French and German birds straight out of business school. Proper tidy pieces as well, but there's no bigger turn off than a woman with an MBA.

I know all the stunts to pull on AIM. I've quietly floated a cash shell on AIM, which has a couple of million quid in it waiting for the right time. When we first stuck it on it was going to be an internet dog food business – Woofwoof.com we were going to call it – which tied up with this idea one of the lads had. We've since had a couple of "strategic reviews" and have renamed it Woof Bay Oil and Gas Explorations and Solutions. The reason being the teenage scribblers at our brokers have gone all cold on internet retail and they're looking for oil. Aren't we all, especially with diesel at £1.40 a litre.

I've told them all about this new product we're beta testing on an oil well site in Newfoundland. It's so hard to get there, apparently, so they're never going to check are they? I could have told them it was in Iraq, or Saudi, but then they'd have started asking questions about how our insurance and security costs don't seem to have been affected. It's kept up the share price and may come in handy if we ever need to up the ante on the deal, or even produce evidence of any actual revenues. No-one's asked yet, but they might.

Which brings us very nicely onto the private equity lads. They still run the best ski trips, to be fair, but they really do have bullshit off to a fine art. They talk about what they do as if it's clever and creative. But as is the case these things are usually best described by a man with two cows. If capitalism is simply, you have two cows, then sell one and buy a bull, this lot take it to another level entirely. Basically, you've bought two cows. Take out a massive structured debt package calculated on ten times the amount of milk they can ever possibly produce in a lifetime. Then hack one cow to bits. Sell off the milk, the meat, the bones, the blood. Squeeze as much milk as you can from the other one, then sell it to one of your mates at some other private equity house with an equally sinister name for twice what you paid for the pair in the first place. Pay off the bank. Go skiing.

Obviously I didn't make that up, I nicked it off some journalist, who probably twisted some internet joke that's been doing the rounds for years. That's how these lazy fuckers work, trust me. We had them all in to have a sniff, made out like everyone was in with a chance. LDC, Icarus, Gresham, Isis, these London boys who don't even have an office in Manchester, which took it outside of Bellamy's comfort zone, I can tell you. But all you have to do is make them think they're missing out and that the new Aston Martin DB 9 one of these lads is driving could also be theirs if only they get a bit of a "carry" on a smart deal like ours, cash out in three years and "happy days".

It's no more complicated than that. They even have computer programs to work it out for them. They talk about backing management teams, analysing real time sector data, but it's all basically about someone reading the paper and counting the numbers on a screen. If they write a cheque for X, then they have to borrow Y off the bank.

73

And do you know the best bit? They don't even pay that much, the bank pays the vast majority. This they call a "leveraged" deal; I call it, like our man with his cows, a massive mortgage. It soaks the company in debt so that it doesn't have to pay tax as technically it makes losses until the loan is paid off. Once it is, these masters of the fucking universe cream it all off the top.

And this lot run their own competitions to get the banks to cut each other's throats to lend the juiciest terms at the lowest rates. They even club together just so they don't have to take it to a credit committee in London, who might kick it upstairs into a special unit. That's their nightmare, that's when they lose a bonus on the way in and just get a miserable 'finders' fee'.

But when it comes off it's like feeding time at the zoo. They'll even get their mate at the bank round the corner, a rival, to make up the difference. They call it staple debt, because this easy money is such a commodity they just staple it to the offer. Unbelievable.

And then they pay the banks off. They call it deleveraging; it's just jiggery pokery and financial engineering. Voodoo economics and playing tricks with money. Which is fair enough as long as it gives me what I want.

Selling a good business that pays me well goes against every entrepreneurial bone in my body. It's the crap ones I try and get rid of, flogging them for the highest possible price before someone works out what's really going on, or just doing a phoenix to wash out the bad debt we don't feel like paying.

For those reasons, and many more, I sort of know what we're doing here. We've bought enough of our own – or stolen, to be fair – that we know all the tricks to drive a price down. The main one is dragging it out. We're at the completion stage now with Delphic; one of the reasons we liked them was this young lad – Toby – who must be 30, but

74

looks 12. All "gosh" and "crikey" and laughs at all my jokes. I think he's desperate to do a deal and we're in complete charge of the process.

There was this one business that was on the block. Some web solutions outfit on Manchester Science Park. There was quite a bit of noise about these lads; won lots of awards, but they couldn't sell it because they weren't making enough profit, the directors were all paying themselves too much and the staff morale was subterranean. Well it was by the time we came to complete. We'd dragged the process on for so long that the uncertainty, the doubt and the fear dragged their performance down. We had meeting after meeting with the directors, and kept asking them for more and more information. We commissioned a due diligence report that asked so many questions they didn't even have time to take a piss, let alone run their business.

The reason they bowed to our every whim was that we'd paid the directors an upfront fee for exclusivity and had dangled such a big number in front of them that I wouldn't have been surprised if they'd offered fellatio into the bargain.

We bought it in the end for £500,000, enough for the directors to go on holiday once they'd paid all their legal fees (you didn't think we were going to pay them out of the business we'd just acquired, did you?) But the trouble was, any more time with us asking for more detail and they'd have collapsed under the pressure. Truth is, we absolutely stole it. I remember like it was yesterday: I asked the bloke we bought it off if there was anything he hadn't told me about. Was there something that would make me very angry if I found out about it later?

He went white, and said he needed to walk around the car park for an hour. When he came back he said he needed to tell me something. He puts his wife's mobile phone through the business. Tut, tut.

When it comes to negotiations, once it gets tasty Rick gets me to come in and make them cry. To be fair, we haven't sold much, but when we buy, we buy well. Very well.

So that's why these other two chancers are here to see me at the house today. They pass Serena on the drive, both of them checking out her very peachy-looking arse. Nice one, fellas. Look but don't ever fucking touch.

These two likely lads are from Taurus Investment Partners. I need them onside to help me keep Gordon Brown's greedy tax elves off the rest of our hard earned money. A couple of mill, that's what we need to have for a longer term punt.

They used to try and set up meetings at seven in the morning, "before the gym" like they had something to prove. I've used these blokes for years, they have, to be fair, put me into some crap over the years. But, by and large, there are enough really good ones to make it worthwhile. They have an investment banking arm that does floats of ever-so-slightly iffy AIM companies, but there's usually a bit of a twist. They brought these two double glazing salesmen to rally our interest into film finance, investment schemes, Venture Capital Trusts all with a tidy tax angle. I don't use them for everything, I got this yank lad at one of the private banks Sidney's introduced me into to roll me into a sweet 10 per cent yielding AIG bond, which is very good, thank you very much.

They're usually pretty good at tipping me the wink when something's going tits up so you can make a quiet exit, or transfer the shares to Serena. They've got a fan club that reads like the local version of the rich list, with a few football lads in there for good measure.

And now they're sinking into the corners of one of my two £15,000 deep brown leather sofas from Arighi Bianchi and drinking my ever-so excellent coffee. We pass through the normal pleasantries. Who's done who, which bank ski trip we're all going on, who's getting divorced, who's off to Nam – Cheltenham - who's managed to sell what.

They're also pretty good at working out how bad things are going to get. The general consensus is the party is over in city centre flats; there are too many crap two-bedroomed flats that look like tiny squash courts, if you're lucky.

I must admit, I've ridden this property rollercoaster pretty well. I've bought 24 of these off-plan from some smarmy developer I met through these jokers. It's a site just over the border from Manchester's shiny new city centre into the badlands of Salford, the bit that's Manchester's car park. I'd missed out on a scheme called The Edge, which has done well, and saw this as the next big thing. It's going to have buyers lined up to take on the risk, he said, even had the valuation work done by these hooky surveyors. They value them high, get an equally dodgy brief to do the same, get a show flat done up in all tiny furniture for the photos so it looks big. Offer the buyers a 20 per cent cashback on the asking price – which is just playing with numbers to be honest - but, as they've been put onto a buy-to-let mortgage company they've set up round the corner who rushes the paperwork through, I'm expecting the completions very soon, which should come in very handy indeed.

But these two Chuckle Brothers are basically telling me that this is going to be a great time to make money, as long as everyone can hold their nerve. They tell me what I already know; Northern Wreck was a blip. What the fuck were they doing letting these Geordie cowboys lend money to the general public to buy their own council houses?

There is some shit coming down the line in the economy, but it will all be a "soft landing" and that the banks are doing a "flight to quality".

They've obviously just both read the same email from the Bank of England Agent for the North West that I read five minutes before – on my BlackBerry - while I was pretending to be listening to Serena.

Chris Millar is fat, posh, smug and not as bright as he thinks he is. He has that well-fed look about him that suggests he knows more than you, but that only he can let you have what he's got if you sign on the dotted line. Anyway, he could do with eating more salad, as he's a bit of a lard arse.

His mate James Sellars is chirpy, skinny, a cockney, laughs at Chris's jokes in all the right places and is clearly brighter than he lets on. Word on the street is he was hawking knock-off watches around Puerto Banus with a chang habit that single-handedly improved the house price index of suburban Medellin for a full quarter. They've cultivated an image of hard drinking and playing the fool and you see them out a lot. In fact, while James is telling some story about some hedge fund bloke from London (a client, he drops in casually) buying a new jet (I noticed what you were doing there, weasel), I think through all the times I saw them last year.

They were at Cheltenham, Ladies' Day at Chester, Man United away in Rome, Ladies' Day at Aintree, Royal Ascot, the Open golf at Carnoustie, a St Anton ski trip. I saw them at the airport when we were off to Banus – they were going to New York on a lads' trip. They were there at every boring dull-as-church black tie business do in the North West of England. And of course, they came to our Charity Ball. Do you think they'd be sat here trying to sell me tax schemes and telling me stories about cockney wanker hedge fund leeches if they didn't? I even saw them in Barbados for the cricket. All of which begs the question: do they ever do any actual work?

But anyway, they have a new investment scheme where you don't have to pay tax, it's as simple as that.

This new one they've got sounds like genius, so I'm waiting for the "but". You buy shares in a quoted company. You immediately gift a chunk of them to charity. Once the price goes up you take the tax out, the charity gets the profit, James can see my expression. It looks too good to be true.

"Rodge," he says, somewhat over familiarly, but he's going to save me money, so I let him carry on.

"Under Treasury rules an individual, or a company, can make a gift of shares to a registered charity and claim tax relief of up to 40 per cent on an amount equal to the value of the gifted shares," he says.

"We're going to float 321m shares we're creating in four newly-formed companies – cash shells – and they're going to be listed on the Channel Islands stock exchange. The shares will then be gifted to charities on the basis that they were worth £1 each."

"Says who?" I ask.

"We do," Chris replies as if it's the most obvious thing in the world. "But for practical purposes they are worthless or of nominal value only," he says, raising his eyebrows in that irritating way know-it-alls tend to.

Sod it, I'm in. A cheeky half mill for starters.

They've also got me into a couple of share buying deals. Basically, and when they explain how it all works, it's just beautiful.

You take out an option on a chunk of shares that are just bound to go up – you pay a deposit on what your take is going to be – a couple of grand on a £20k turn, or so - they call you when it hits a target price. You sell, pay them back, they take their commission, and you cream the rest as margin. It is perfect. It's sweet and it's called a Contract for Difference – CFD. And before the profit touches the sides it's off for a holiday in the Isle of Man. Happy days.

The good news, he tells me, is the smart investors are turning off property and looking for different asset classes to make consolidation plays. When he says this I think to myself, that's quality bullshit that; I even know what it means, and I make a mental note to use it.

I don't like opening myself up too much to these two, but they've given me a few things to think about.

Because I've been concentrating so much on selling the business and making my £40m, I need to put a bit more thought into planning what I'm going to do next.

A few lads who make a few quid like to dabble in the bar and restaurant game. There's the obvious draw of having a place you can call your own.

Chris Oglesby, the Bruntwood lad, has piled in with Paul Heathcote. Now THAT is a good idea. He's got all the property boys in his pocket, he likes fine food and all that. It makes massive sense for him to get together with a chef who knows his way round a kitchen, but is a bit clueless when it comes to making a decent turn. That's what they need.

I've got the chance to sprinkle some of my strategic stardust on the world of football. Again, how the fuck these idiots lose money on owning football clubs I'll never know. Some of the lads around here backed this lad Mark Guterman, who had a punt at Wrexham and frankly I've learned from his mistakes and I've got the taste for it.

Here's my plan. I'm putting a few of the lads together to buy Wilmslow Wanderers Football Club. There's a bit of a field next to the club's ground – Knutsford Road – which we reckon we could get a few houses on.

The vision – and we all need a vision – is to get a few quid off a house builder for the site. That's where Dave Foster comes in handy. We get a boutique hotel on there, fitting for what will be the world's first boutique football club: exclusive, elite and very Cheshire. I've got plenty of signed shirts and photos and what have you from various charity do's. Stick them up in the themed rooms, we could get a few of the local football lads to have their own named suites. Not that you'd be that keen on nailing your bit on the side in the Wayne Rooney Suite, to be fair.

The other part of the masterplan is to stick a fan on the board to appease the Billy Bunters. We'd get Steve "Jacko" Jackson to send Preston North End – and these lap dancing cheerleaders they've got up there, oh yes - up for a friendly and we're laughing.

This is where poor old Guterman went wrong. They fans ended up slaughtering him. Nicknamed him 'the penguin', turned up at his house, scratched his motor, the full package of criminal harassment.

But to my mind, there are two things these lads who put some readies into football get wrong. One, how much money is there swilling around in football? Fucking loads. There are grants for everything: training, facilities, new stadiums, community rooms, kids' pitches, wheelchair access, it ticks all of the boxes for the social inclusion bollocks. You just have to know how to play the public sector muppets.

Number two: who, when they are growing up, wants to work in a sales boiler room like the one I run, getting bawled at by Giant Haystacks on Red Bull? No-one. So we pay them a lot of money, if they're any good.

Now, who wants to be a footballer? Everyone. So how many of them would do it for nothing, just to get in front of the scouts and the links we can pretty much set up with every pro club in the north? Loads of them would. Especially round here; there are so many thick offspring of wealthy families we could set ourselves up as some kind of extension of the private school system. It helps them with those awkward moments at dinner parties. Where's young Tommy these days? Did he find a university that takes kids with no 'A' Levels? No need, he's playing football. We get a few rich kids in the squad, and get the Dads to pay their wages to keep them happy.

No-one has ever tried anything like this before and we reckon, with the wealth of the support round here, we could do something special. Obviously we'd have to win a few games; that's where we'd get a half-decent coach - one of

Fergie's jocko mates or something - and start getting the nod on the lads from academies in shit holes in Africa. Get these kids over to get the team rising through the leagues. Have a proper hospitality experience on match days, none of this spit and sawdust crap they have at football. No, we'll have lappies, blue comedians, the lot. Proper nosebag. Must give Heathcote first option.

I'm so struck on it I'm even getting measured up for a sheepskin coat. Hugo Boss, of course.

I have to fire up one of the motors and head into Alderley to see what Tosh has to tell me about the seedy side of the beautiful game. It's a pleasantly mild morning, faint hint of drizzle in the air, but certainly no reason to skimp on the tin. I get out the scarlet red Ferrari 599 GTB. It's worth a spin to show off to the MILFs, POWs and cougars of Alderley who'll be wasting their day away in Costa Coffee. To liven up the ambience of the high street with a blast of its V12 engine. To show Tosh I'm still doing alright.

Tosh is sat in Costa when I get there, sat in the corner in a dark blue Lacoste jumper, with an Aquascutum shirt underneath. I still have an eye for the labels he wears, even if I long ago graduated upstairs in Flannels and stick to Hugo Boss, Valentino, Armani and Gucci. He's on the phone, a Nokia N95 by the looks of it. He's talking in a peculiar clipped and proper voice and much less of the sounds of Salford. A little less street. I overhear the last part of it:

"Yes, that's right, sir. I'll spell that for you. My name is Thomas McGeoghan. It's quite an unusual spelling, so make sure you write it down."

He spells it out slowly.

"Now, have you got that? I now suggest you type that into Google, it should tell you all you need to know about me. I will be back in touch with yourself at this time tomorrow about the settlement of my client's account. Thank you. Goodbye."

Quality. Right now, the terrified punter on the other end of that phone conversation will be reading lurid accounts of how Tosh the tout has links to doormen, bouncers, private security contractors and his crew of protectors who terrorised the football terraces of England for a large part of the 1980s and then graduated into the fringes of organised crime, culminating into last month's high profile acquittal for a grisly murder involving power tools and petrol. It all serves him very well.

We've got a spot at the back, low key, away from everyone else. It's probably how he prefers to be when he's doing business. It's how I prefer to be when I'm doing business with him, to be fair. It's different when he's in coming out of a court case and larging it in San Carlo, or standing at the door of some Irish bar in an Eastern European city when United are on tour. I think back to all the places and all the cities I've been with this lunatic and here we are in a branded coffee shop in Alderley Edge where they charge £2.40 for what we used to call milky coffee.

Today, the gaff is rammed with a jolly mixture of sluts in tracksuits, the semi-retired and the wheeler-dealers who run their businesses on the hoof.

A lad called Jimmi Barnes is in – great lad, by the way - on his new radio station, Edge FM. One of the DJs down there plays *Lady In Red* for Serena and her mates every morning, just as she's getting on the rowing machine, which keeps her happy. Funny lad, Jimmi. I can never really tell what he's saying, but on the radio he's even better than the legend that was DLT. Clear as a bell. Anyway, we've had the odd chat about different community figures coming on and he wants me to be the "voice of business" on the pre-breakfast show. Good lad.

As for the cougars, they wear the sportswear either because they're going to the gym, or they want you to think they are going to the gym. They wouldn't be here if they had actually been to the gym, because they wouldn't have perfect hair and make-up.

I notice Tracey Friedel, whose husband is the baldy Yank goalie for Blackburn. Good golfer, if I recall; played a round with him at Prestbury. A bit more about him than the usual thick-head footy lads. This is a man who knows everything about coffee, knows all the stocks and shares in the coffee market in the world. Might be worth talking about getting involved in a deal with him.

Anyway, me and Tosh seem to understand each other. He knows I operate in a different league to him, a step above the street hustling and grafting he's done well in, to be fair. But it's real business, not grafter shit.

I help him; he helps me when it cuts up rough. But here's a curve ball for him: an idea from me. "So, mate, remember I said I had something for you? Well, I was looking at that book you did. Well, I like it, but we could take it all to the next level."

"Go, on," he says, looking at me with a blank, stony-faced expression.

I happen to know, because he asked me to check the contract, that he's got precisely £4k up front for this violent "kick and tell" memoir, which one of our lads helped him type up. After that, he's had dribs and drabs of royalty cheques adding up to about £5k if he's lucky. He still has an option on the film rights, but frankly, he's missed the boat on all of that. What, with *Rise of the Foot Soldier*, *The Business* and *Football Factory* and a remake of the *The Firm* all coming up. The last one's a great film by the way; a true classic.

"Tosh, I've got 20 bilingual Russian boffins in a shed in Sharston hacking and programming by day, tearing up in the pubs of Northenden by night. They're bored and brilliant, very handy as well. Do you know what, they're obsessed with anything connected to football, to violence and anything gang-related. All your old shit. They love it. You introduce them to someone from Leeds and they tell them about the fucking Service Crew and how they smashed up Chelsea in 1983.

"By the way, they love your book so much they've translated it into Russian. But look at what I've got for you on this. I think this takes you to another level, and me and you could do a lot of damage. Call it a gift to get our partnership started."

He stares at me for a long time, like he's weighing up what I'm suggesting.

"What are you after? What are you up to at the moment?"

"I'm bored of all this corporate shit, I'm cashing out, I'm looking for new things mate. A bit of excitement. What do you reckon? Me and you, 50-50? Here, have a butcher's at this." And I hand him the pen drive.

He takes it, looks at it. Purses his lips, nods and says he'll have a think.

And do you know what, the only reason I came up with this was because of pub cricket. Fucking hell, eh?

He's into the idea, and I'm telling him how it's going to work, when he interrupts.

"Mr. Cash, to be honest, I had something else in mind. A couple of things, really."

The slower, more deliberate voice from earlier is back.

"I know you probably don't need my debt collection services, but I could do with a bit of advice on the travel front."

He leans in towards me, casts his eyes around as if there would be anyone listening, and talks out of the side of his mouth.

"I'm getting a bit of heat off Dibble. They had my assets frozen."

"Right."

"The European Champions League final is in Moscow. I can get my hands on plenty of tickets, but I could do with getting more into the travel side of it, especially if United get there. We need to make sure we're ready to ship 30,000 over there. We're talking leasing planes, and for that I need to be bonded. And to be bonded, I need a front. Could you…?"

He looks at me with a puppy dog expression. Always strange when an axe-murderer wants a favour.

I'm running through a few ideas and Tosh edges forward. The balance of our interaction is back with me again, and he's all ears. Then, out of my peripheral vision I see this big lad who's caught my eye, some adviser or banker or something. I get this a lot.

Next thing, just as I'm explaining offshore LLPs to Tosh, this bloke bowls up, uninvited. He's got that straight-backed army officer look about him; he's wearing a cord jacket, a checked farmers' shirt and jeans. And he looks pretty pissed off.

"So, you've gone exclusive with Delphic, eh, Cashmore? Nice of you to let me know."

I don't really recognise him. I'm very good at remembering faces as long as the people are useful to me - or are chicks that I'd nail - but beyond that, my life is a constant whirlwind of meeting irrelevant idiots. They blur into an amorphous mass of blah fucking blah.

Here's what I always do when this happens: I introduce him to Tosh. "This is my friend Anthony," I say, hoping he'll volunteer his own name to save my embarrassment.

Instead he says: "A friend of his? Hard luck."

The sort of thing I'd say when I'm winding someone up, but this lad is serious.

"Hi, Dan Kay, Icarus Ventures. This character doesn't even dignify me by remembering my name. No, I've just read that *your mate*," he spits, "your mate has gone exclusive to sell his business to someone else. You'd think he'd have let me know, wouldn't you?"

Tosh's expression is one of absolute disgust. He looks at me as if to invite me to get up and smack him, but to be honest even with a thug like this at my disposal, a Wild West tear-up in the middle of Alderley isn't going to do anything for my reputation round here, sensitive as it is. Kay still looks pretty hostile and I have to do my best to wriggle out of this without losing face in the middle of yummy mummy central.

To be honest, though, at this point I'm sweating like a paedophile on school sports day.

Before I can say anything back, he's right on one.

"Didn't fancy exposing your books to a bit of proper due diligence, eh? You'll never get away with it, you know, not a chance."

Bear in mind we had a massive auction on this deal, but one posh fucker, even an ex-SAS heavyweight who looks like he could rip out your spine and crush your skull in his massive hands, starts to sound very much like another. Some asked more questions than others, some even got to see us; he was obviously one of those who asked tricky questions about revenue recognition and the security of our pre-booked revenue, and who wanted to have a peek at our property leases. We generally binned the awkward squad before the first round, but Bellamy was probably trying to throw him a bone.

"Ha, we'll see," I say, "maybe next time." I try to laugh him off, but he's genuinely pissed off and wants to say his bit.

"Yah, whatever, just poor, poor form that I had to read about it on the *Insider* email rather than you ringing me. Very poor." He adds a jabbing finger to the last barb and I just sit there, hoping he's going to go away without any more of a fuss, and without hitting me.

He walks away. I look at Tosh, and he's still looking at me with a frown and with his mouth open.

I roll my eyes and laugh nervously, trying to give the impression I don't really care.

"Are you gonna let that posh twat talk to you like that and get away with it? I'd fucking knock the cunt out, me. Fucking bang out of order. Who is he, anyway?"

I try and explain to Tosh what's happened - and who he is - and he shakes his head. It's just a game, no big deal.

"Wants fucking sorting, I know that much."

Tosh then reverts to amateur businessman mode and outlines what he wants if United get to the Champions League final; a front to secure a fleet of charter planes - no cash required - but an opportunity to invest in his syndicate if I want, but definitely some support on getting lads out there, and back.

"But if you're a shitter, forget it," he says, rolling his eyes towards where Kay is still standing near the door.

"Look, I'm not going to start brawling in Costa Coffee mate. I'm not scared of him."

I'm properly shaking and take a big gulp from my lukewarm latte.

Tosh has a snarl around his mouth; he's had a smell for violence that he hasn't been able to act upon.

He starts to tell me some long story about Russian football hooligans. "You're not wrong about these Russkis, my friend. They brought it proper on top with us in Moscow in 1998. Mayhem. They don't give a fuck. This lot were proper hardcore. They'd been in the war and were still itching for a fight. They got stuck into us 'cause there were no more Chechen villages to rape and pillage. It wasn't good for business, hardly shifted any briefs that day. Almost as bad as Sunday; all that Munich stuff kept the day trippers away. Fucking washout."

I told you he was sore about the derby result. A match against City isn't the same unless he's had the chance to crack a few heads.

So, Russian book sorted, face saved, and luckily the whole Dan Kay thing went unnoticed by the MILF brigade. But as we get up to leave I notice that Tosh has a stack of estate agents' details under his dark blue Burberry jacket. They're from Jackson-Stops & Staff, Andrew Nowell and Stuart Rushton.

"What's with that lot?" I ask him. "You house hunting?"

"Why not?" he smiles with that sinister grin. "It's a very desirable area."

When you go to Jersey, or the Isle of Man, or Switzerland, they have these 'family offices' behind the brass plates. Obviously these are lads who've made a few quid, but are still active investors and keep a staff going to run their show. It's the nearest equivalent to what Sidney Silver's office is. It's in this suite between Alderley and Wilmslow, so there's room to roar around in the Ferrari for a while first.

Sidney has this old dear who works for him, answering his phone, organising meetings for him, sorting out his annual golf day at Dunham Massey. He's not one of the Mere crowd - not quite his cup of tea – but it's a decent knock. Culturally? Put it this way, you can always get a good tee time on a Saturday and they don't do bacon rolls.

The old bird (Val, or Pam or Pat, I forget), buzzes me up, and I sit down in Sidney's reception. Just to the left-hand side is his boardroom. A bit of a daft idea; I can't imagine he has many meetings with more than two people at a time. There's a long mahogany table, with 12 chairs neatly arranged around it.

He's around; I can smell him. He's not dirty or anything, but he smokes these Montecristo Cuban cigars which you can whiff a mile off. I'm twiddling with the BlackBerry, checking messages, texting Ash about later. Mildly flirtatious, but nothing over the top.

He likes me and Rick because he thinks we were there for him in his hour of need. Basically, we got a call telling us to get down to Southern Cemetery as they were burying his mother. There were all these old Jewish lads crowded around the hole in the ground where they were lowering her in. Sidney looked a right state: tired, unshaven and with his ripped white shirt hanging out of his pants.

Rick was about go up to him and tuck him in when I pointed out that's what they do. As Sidney walked away, tears in his eyes, the crowd parted and formed a line either side. I'd done my homework on what to say (the internet, eh?) and said, "Sidney, may you be comforted with all the mourners of Jerusalem."

He looked up at me, clasped my hands, stared right into my eyes and I knew at that moment I had a friend for life. He muttered something Jewish and squeezed my hand.

But for all this religion and smart business stuff, with Sidney you always have to have your wits about you. He's a daft fucker sometimes. Once, when me and Rick were getting on better, we came to see him and he kept us waiting for half an hour. We were sat gassing away and Sidney had been hiding in a wardrobe. He just jumped out to surprise us. We were talking about birds and football and cars and shit, slagging a few people off (there's usually not much else we did talk about, to be fair). It was a good job we didn't tell any Sidney stories, because there are a few. Thing was, Rick can't quite handle that Sidney likes me more. And so he lays down the Sidney appreciation pretty thickly, while I give nothing away.

This time, though, he just looks busy, "What are you doing in here, Roger? Come on. Come through. How long have you been waiting?"

He sits down at this massive wide-open leather-topped mahogany desk with neat little folders with Post-It notes sticking from the sides. My chair, at the end of this desk, is a solid old leather armchair that seats me a good six inches lower than him. I've been here many, many times before, but I always chuckle to myself at how he's sorted out this seating arrangement so he looks down on whoever has come to see him.

He has the old Doris bring us cups of tea on a tray and in a big old pot; silver spoons, posh biscuits, bone China. You'll be lucky if you get a chipped Man City mug at our gaff, though at least we don't scrimp on the tea; this tastes like there's about one tea bag per pot. Weak as piss, Sidney.

Every meeting has the same structure: a few stock stories followed by a quick-fire round of questions from him to me, despite the fact he doesn't seem that interested in the answer and then gives a long speech about what I should be doing.

I commiserate about City beating United at Old Trafford. "I don't trust this Thai chap, Roger." He's indignant about this Thai prime minister, Shinatra or something, reckoning City are heading for a bit of a crash. "It's all going to end in tears, my friend. Just watch, he's got court hearings in Thailand coming up.

"And their board you know, they've no class," he says. "They may have respected the minute's silence for Munich, but they were dancing on the pitch at the end. Very poor. Class can't be bought you know, Roger. It takes more than money.

"Look at me, I'm 72 now. Manners never cost anything. Taste doesn't come in units, or pieces of jewellery.

"Anyway, how's Serena?" he asks, a dirty grin cracking across his face. He clearly fancies the arse off her.

"That interiors software design will do well," he says. Clearly, she's bullshitted him about some of this crap at some point and he's been too busy looking down her front to pay much attention.

"How's the sale going?"

"Yes, we've gone exclusive with Delphic. Should get the full whack."

Sidney stares at me and pauses, before breaking into a wide grin.

"Then what? What is a young man like you going to do? When are you going to make a real difference and make a mark?"

I cough a little and start to answer him. It's like I'm being interviewed. I say: "All the smart investors are turning off property and looking for different asset classes to make consolidation plays."

"What does that mean, Roger?"

I splutter an attempt at an answer. "What do you mean, Sidney?"

"When I was your age I realised that making money was always going to come easy to me. My mother, she did so much for charities, always helping out. But we needed to understand it wasn't just about what money we could give, but how we can make things better by who we are and what we know. You can sign cheques, run marathons, but what these charities need is expertise. That's real philanthropy.

"I've got a whole forestry regeneration scheme going on, bringing rare species of birds back to the Peak District National Park. These things matter. I've got my charity that's working in deprived communities in Lancashire, putting them to work on social enterprises. There are projects that need help and dedication from people with ideas and energy and resources, which you know all about, Roger."

Indeed I do; I put them onto Ash for some TV programme she was trying to get me into.

"You're facing a choice, Roger. You can mess around with your football team in Wilmslow if you like. Yes, I know about that," my expression must have suggested I was surprised he knew.

"And be very careful you don't spend any of this money you've got coming your way on whimsies. How much will you have?"

I tell him the 40 by 40 plan and he doesn't smile.

"That's it. That's it. You're clever, Roger. But you're just not serious."

Fucking hell. "And what would you suggest?" I ask him, feeling slightly taken aback.

"It's not about that, Roger," he says. "It's not about what you back and what you invest in, it's what kind of person you want to be, what you want to make of yours and Serena's life. Investing is easy money; that's what those two characters you saw this morning will do. It's about stepping up."

I never expect an easy ride off Sidney, but this takes the biscuit. He's got a few cards to pass on to me from these scrotes in Burnley or somewhere, and some bird watching wildlife bollocks.

And here's a funny thing. As I sit at the wheel of my Ferrari fanny magnet, winding my way down the A34 and into Manchester to have an afternoon of flirtatious banter with the lovely Ash and to talk about how she can help me look serious, caring and considerate while helping the lowlife of Lancashire, I have to think that I've met two Man United fans in one day, both with lots to say and not one of them saying a single word about the actual game. Football: bloody hell.

March 2008

Bear Stearns prepares for Chapter 11 bankruptcy, the federal Reserve cut interest rates, house builders predict a disaster if the Bank of England don't follow suit. AOL buys Bebo for $850m. Apple unveils the iPhone touchscreen and invites developers to create customized applications. The Irlam brothers are to share £60m after selling their Cheshire-based trucking group to Stobart Group.

At the end of every quarter I take the team out. And as we run pretty strange reporting periods to confuse the Revenue, they fall at funny times in the year. It's a team bonding ritual that stands us in good stead. The margin by which they've smashed their targets pretty much dictates where we go and what we get up to.

We've done Liverpool (nasty), Blackpool (tacky), Dublin (boozy), Amsterdam (messy) and back in the day we went to Vegas (all of the above). In November, after a terrifying run of orders where we absolutely creamed it, I just rang up this charter company, told everyone to bring their passports to work and we headed for Europe's finest floating brothel, Puerto Banus, for a night of pure debauchery.

Beers on the plane, charlie on the plane, we hit the harbour at ten, had a few sherbets in the Navy Bar. What a place. Wall-to-wall Eastern European and Brazilian birds, most fit as fuck. Except for Garner, who was last seen with this moose (it's called 'going ugly early').

There are no birds from the office on trips like this by the way, just the boys. By the time we're scraping lads off the floor and prising them off the mega-fit Russian hookers in Milady's Palace to get back to the plane for a 7am take off, everyone has a story to tell.

I took one brass in the back room for a hefty €400 (she was a 10 out of 10 to be fair, and has starred in many a wank since). Anyway, anything goes with these dirty slags and she gave me the old trombone. Lovely.

An hour later and she's in the bar all over Wilcox and she's properly sucking face with him, just as that mouth had been around my hairy arse earlier. I couldn't hold it together. Me and Ritchie, who always hangs back, were properly rolling around laughing, Wilcox gets a whiff of what's going on, starts bawling at us. To be honest, I was so wankered I can't really remember. Next thing these Hungarian gangster types are cutting up rough and we're staggering along, pissed, out into the street, still howling with laughter, while the door locks behind us. Next thing Wilcox and Garner are getting a proper shoeing in the doorway.

Because they were soft as shite and didn't give much back, the bouncers just chucked them out into the street.

On the flight on the way back Wilcox was shaking. "We had to fight our way out, Roger. As this monkey attacked me I thought this was going to be such a horrible way to die."

Yeah right, grovelled and begged, more like. That shithouse could crawl his way out of a sewer and come out smelling of roses.

But, none of this gets out when we're home because what goes on tour, stays on tour, even with a story as good as that one.

Rick doesn't come, obviously; most Friday lunchtimes he's off to his place in Tuscany, sitting around eating pizza and getting fat.

The soft fucker tries to have a quiet word about making the quarter session "more inclusive" and that I should make more of an effort to "reflect the diversity of the business."

This was an okay one. I set the bar pretty high as we need to be hitting decent numbers for Delphic to be happy enough that this is all going to come good, but true to form, the boys smashed their targets again.

Which makes me happy because, when we hit, the banks are happy enough with what we're paying them on our facility (or overdraft as the rest of the general public might call it) and they're more than likely to roll it over. Things are pretty sweet with our bank, Olaf and the Icelandics and a couple of local lads from our Jocko Bank.

So, as it was a team do on home ground, we invited the fanny along as well. They take fucking ages to get ready for a start, so we were well on our way by the time they joined us in the Malmaison bar. And then to tick all of Rick's diversity boxes we thought we'd take in a tour of Manchester's gay village, for a laugh.

It's also a good way to test Garner's closet liking for bum banditry by starting in this rough-arsed Man City pub near Piccadilly station, then nipping across the tram tracks and the car park to Canal Street and the gay bars. We get the camera phones and take a pic of Garner with the sign for Canal Street, edging out the first names so it reads ANAL TREET (he wishes). That's going up on the notice board.

After a bit of hilarious chatting up of lesbians and piling into the hen parties we need a bit of proper straight guys' entertainment.

One of the tarts from the office, Chloe, who I'd say was passably fit and has been after getting herself on one of these nights out, reckoning she could match the lads pint for pint, starts asking if we were going to up the pace a bit. Angela eggs her on, having absolutely no idea how far we are prepared to go.

"So what goes on one of these nights out? Show us something dangerous."

I was keen to get on down to the Straight Village by this time, slappers in the Circle Bar, scrubbers from out of town looking to bag a footballer in the Living Room. Much more our scene.

But for the danger they want, we pile into this lappy off Deansgate. We go through the usual routine, get some bird to dance in front of your, sit on your knee, do a bit of grinding. It's alright, but nothing compared to a proper brass house in Banus. And these are usually scrubbers from Oldham, or somewhere. The one I had said she was from somewhere called Failsworth, that's what she said. Quite, I thought.

Angela and Chloe, pissed and a bit randy, reckon the birds in there are nothing special, and asks us, bluntly, what would we pay them to get their kit off. Garner, Wilcox and Ritchie are properly goading them to whip their paps out.

101

Next thing, they only do. I must admit Angela's norks looked better than I thought they would and she's obviously been looking after herself. Chloe, well facially she's alright, but she carries a bit of timber and could probably do with a good session on a treadmill, to be fair. But she's even more game and even more pissed.

The other girls in there, the ones who suddenly aren't the centre of attention, aren't too happy and it's looking like it's about to kick off, when who should come in with a face like thunder than Angela's soft twat husband. There's tears and he's properly throwing a thrombie at her.

"Come on mate, she's just sharing it about. Happens all the time at work," I offer, reassuringly.

What happened next, to be fair, I didn't expect. I've heard of red mists coming down. This kid properly exploded. Except he blamed me. So, he's ranting and raving, Wilcox and Garner are pulling him off, holding him back – "let me at him." Yeah right, pal.

The bouncers have clocked all the mayhem and we're hoofed out. You'd have thought the cold night air might have calmed him down, but Angela was still lashed and was still thinking it's all a laugh. Chloe actually stays in there, still probably gyrating on some pissed-up bank clerk who's stuffing tenners in her big knickers.

So once we're outside, this prick's screaming at me and getting properly angry.

"You've gone too far this time, Cashmore..." He runs at me, swinging a punch as he does. He catches me on the side of the face, but it's a rubbish punch, and I'm sobering up pretty quick as the adrenaline kicks in and everyone else is drawn to the violence and the mayhem. The Friday night crowd spills away from whatever else they were doing, looking eagerly but keeping their distance from just another couple of drunks brawling on the street. I manage to grab him round the neck and buy myself a moment to ponder the whole situation.

There I was in Costa Coffee, two weeks ago with my rough-arsed mate from school. The kid who taught me the most important rite of passage as a 14 year-old: how to kick someone in the face. Pulling their hair, or pulling their coat or jumper over their head, disorienting them, dragging their head down and thwack. And what did I do in front of Dan fucking Kay? Nothing. I fucking bottled it. I shit out.

So I ask myself the four words. WWTD. What Would Tosh Do?

He's wound up and angry. His face is contorted with pure hatred. Every night at home with Angela crying at how I've treated her, yet her strange devotion to me and the company and her job. The ruined weekends and the lack of sex all comes out in this explosion of rage.

But that's his weakness, it's an inarticulate and uncontrolled lashing out. He has no focus and so I have to exploit that. The solution is actually simple, do what he can't. As we grapple, I ram his head into the shutters of the shop next door, pull his suit jacket over his head and give his nut a few sharp jabs with my knee, and as he falls to the ground, helped along by me kicking his legs from under him, I then wade in with the soles of my Patrick Cox loafers, kicking away at this heap on the floor.

As I look down, as someone pulls me back, he's out cold and twitching, his nose busted and his eyes going.

Angela's screaming, "What have you done? What have you done?" From the back someone screams to call an ambulance. Fuck that. The bouncers are attending to him while Wilcox and Garner are pulling me off and I'm pumped up, loaded, feeling brilliant. The adrenaline is pumping. I'm ready to take any of them on. But maybe not the bouncers, who are getting busy.

I'm away like shit off a shovel, calling Ray to bring the space truck around and whisk me back to sanity and Alderley.

There'll be no explaining any of this to Serena. She stays away on quarter days, but there'll be no swift one back to mine for the party people, not tonight. No strippers, no porn, no party. She's off to Abersoch, London or somewhere, I forget.

This is bad, very bad. But in circumstances like this I know who I need to tell this tale to so I make the call and he answers right away.

"Mr. Cash."

"Tosh, I need your help. It's kicked off outside the lappy and I'm getting heat from Dibble. 5-0 are going to be all over me. I need the number of that brief you know."

"Well, well, well." He sounds impressed. Good. "You'll have to tell me about it another time. I'll text it to you. But don't call me again."

Freddie Derbyshire comes good. He's waiting with me at 10 the next morning when the call comes. There's a cop car parked at the gate and Old Bill buzzing me.

We go with them down to Bootle Street in Manchester, and I make a statement saying I was attacked by a drunk man and everything was in self defence. Freddie does all the talking and says we are willing to fully co-operate with the police.

The two coppers stare at as, until one says: "Let's hope for your sake that he wakes up."

My mouth goes dry and my stomach does a plunge dive of about 1000 feet. I grip the corner of my chair and Freddie puts his arm across me.

"Whatever the medical outcome of the assailant's condition, the facts remain the same. My client was acting entirely in self defence."

The coppers run through it all again and Freddie has me sticking to same story: drunk man, upset his wife didn't get a pay rise, attacked me. After an hour of all of this I start to believe him as well. I sound like a saint.

By half-past six the Old Bill have to let me go. They can't charge me with anything. In preparation for any case, Freddie tells them that I'm going to offer to take anger management counselling – apparently it worked in Tosh's favour at his trial – though we aren't even planning on getting to court. You've got to get your defence case in early so the prosecution know they'll have a tough time making the charges stick.

Plus, it's an amusing bit of intelligence to find out that Tosh is a certified nutter and manic depressive and seeing a shrink. Not that I'm surprised.

The Old Bill obviously can't stand Freddie, but they're also shit scared. He runs rings round them and insists they can't question me without him being there. Freedom. I never knew being a criminal was such a breeze.

Sitting in the V-One private jet lounge at Manchester Airport on a Tuesday morning reading the *Daily Mail*, you see evidence of the changing violent world at every turn. The papers are full of more stories about how the footballers and their WAGs have been targeted by robbers. Normally, this would induce gnashing and wailing from the likes of Serena and some of her coven, angry that these talentless bints dominate all coverage of our area and reinforce the weary stereotype that Alderley, Prestbury and Wilmslow are solely populated by the big sunglasses-wearing silicon tit bitches who are, for now, married to football louts. I don't quite get why they're complaining, it certainly keeps her busy.

But there's a few of us normal business lads getting targeted as well, and that's not right. The worst ones are when they do it when the football lads are away playing in some backwater in Austria, or somewhere. So there's Doris, or the foreign equivalent, doing her nails and putting the nippers to bed, or at least shouting at the Polish boiler of a nanny doing it, and BANG! The front door goes in. Balaclava-clad thugs storm the house, with knives and baseball bats and all kinds of shit. She hands over everything she can to get rid. Not the kind of house call you want.

To be fair, you'd expect to see footballers around Liverpool getting turned over - it goes with the territory - but these away day burglaries are getting closer and they're getting nastier.

There's one in the paper here - no names, but it says "leafy Cheshire" - of a bloke tied up in one room, his missus taken upstairs. He gets a proper kicking off these maniacs who say they're going to gang rape his missus. He hands the lot over, cash, keys to his motors, all his watches, all her bling. They even took the art off his walls, his stereo and his tellies. He's making a plea to get them to hand back some photos of his sick kid who died. Horrific.

I call Serena to see what she's heard on the cougar grapevine, which is nothing yet, and give her a tip. She's still none the wiser about my little escapade either, which is how I'd like to keep it.

Apart from the obvious need to upgrade our own security I reckon it could be an opportunity. Get her to offer controlled security in her little curtains and wallpaper bollocks. You never know, it might even make a bit. She reckons she's got it covered but then that's what she's like, never gives me credit for anything.

It's no wonder you need to get away with all this going on.

I'm off with a couple of the lads to this property do in Cannes, MIPIM, as you do. No idea what it stands for, Massive International Piss-up In the Med, from what I can tell. There are worse places to do business in March; we'll get an early kiss of sun as we kill a bit of time before Bellamy whips Delphic into line on our deal, and I'll carry on my plan of how I can be naughty with my 40.

I've also taken on board everything Sidney was saying about projecting the right image. No dicking about on scheduled flights for me anymore. This is the life.

In my posse is Foster, the lad who's building my new house and my good pal Tony Martinez, an animal and a proper expert in the property field. He's got sites all over the show: sheds in Stoke, offices in Manchester, industrial units in corners of those towns you see the BNP going for votes in. He's quietly built up a commercial property portfolio that covers half of south Manchester and a load of sheds over Warrington way. He knows what he's doing and plays the banks off each other. We sold him our old site in Altrincham for retail development, and he cut me and Rick in for a share of the future proceeds. *Ker-ching.*

This is the trick. This is the big one. We can sell stuff to businesses and hawk it around the computer industry forever and a day, but the path to riches is selling shit to sleepwalkers. I mean, think about it, who are the real big hitters, the real loaded players round our way? John Hargreaves of Matalan, Dave Whelan selling shell suits to scallies, the Littlewoods boys. And in property, never underestimate the taste of the general public. The blingier the better; think Trafford Centre, think out-of-town retail sheds. Think John Whittaker. Top man. That's where Martinez has his ticket to ride where he needs a bit of help from his friends.

These two never need any invitation to any kind of bender, though you'd think they'd learn. Foster is currently on his uppers after his wife chucked him out. He talks like the first bloke ever to get divorced. In fact, even now, in this select environment he's bending the ear of some bloke he vaguely knows about the injustice of it, how she won't be happy until he's on the streets, how she's turning the kids against him, how the bloke she's seeing now – some old flame from back in the day - can't write a cheque for £200.

What he doesn't tell are the epic stories of whoring around the world and the extraordinary lengths he'd go to in order to cover his tracks. About the "golf trip to Florida" where the clubs never left the boot of his BMW X5 at Manchester Airport. Instead, they were off in the opposite direction on an extreme form of sex tourism to Thailand and Vietnam, popping Viagra and burying themselves bollock-deep in lady boys and teenage Thai toms, holding orgies where anything and everything goes, screwing and snorting their way through the cesspools of Pattaya and Phuket. He even had postcards sent from some pal in Orlando - dated and stamped - to his wife and kids, as well as a few T-shirts that he ordered online.

No, he doesn't mention that. Neither does he mention his voracious, exhausting patronage of escorts, nor his first name terms with every madam at every cat house between Manchester and Chester. You'd think an appetite likes this would finally catch up with you; oh yes, and how. The 'how' wasn't just catching a nasty scratch of chlamydia off some scrubber; he can't even place which one. No, the greedy fucker wasn't just rutting scabby brasses on an almost daily basis, he still had a bit left for his missus. Talk about spreading your love around. But even he couldn't erase this trace with postcards and cover stories, passing on a particularly nasty dose of the clap after paying some skanky bint a few extra for a bareback session. It's resulted in him becoming estranged from his kids, disgraced, ostracised and bound and gagged over a barrel while his soon-to-be ex-wife exacts ever more imaginative ways to humiliate and vengefully destroy his life.

All told though, it doesn't make him a bad man, does it?

Martinez, on the other hand, is fiercely single. The man who put the eligible in bachelor, who stands on the drive of his LA-style house in Alderley (or his apartment in Manchester's Century Buildings) with a large shitty stick batting off the waves upon waves of blondes, brunettes, gingers, Asian babes, all throwing themselves in his path. Going out to the Bubble Room in Alderley, or to Players in Hale with him is like one of those zombie films, where they keep walking moronically towards a certain slaying, only to be spotted the next morning, walking away like John Wayne. So while Foster is the fanny rat, Martinez is a minge magnet. It's certainly an interesting combination on a night out.

All the big shots have some kind of property angle, and making your money work for you when you graduate into the big league - as I will be doing shortly when I net my 40 by 40 – is what it's all about.

It might be a biggish price on the ticket to get into the property game, but once you're in it's a one-way bet. I mean, they don't make land anymore, do they? So how can you fail to make even more once you're in? For this reason, amongst others, it's as well to make my presence known in these circles and see what opportunities they can chuck my way. In this orgy of arse kissing and forelock tugging there's a big class thing going on in property; lots of old money, lots of ruddy-cheeked, well-fed posh old toffs.

You can get so far with introductions from a few of the boys around town – the agents and low level developers - but to be a proper player you don't want to be seen with an orange boarding card queuing up at Liverpool John Fucking Lennon Airport for a connecting flight to Nice via Amsterdam. The councillors and planners booked the BA flights yonks ago. With our money, lest we forget.

So chipping in for a seat on a private jet can't be beaten. We've got bubbles awaiting onboard, space to swing about and then a chopper over to Cannes. The only way to do it.

It's a funny old week, this MIPIM. When we go to the techie trade shows in Hanover and Las Vegas you have people selling stuff. Over there it's a little bit more complicated than that. You've got all the cities with their stands trying to impress, trying to look busy so they don't get grief for pissing away the taxpayers' hard-earned. And then you've got all the property lads doing what they do best: getting mullered. There are the agents, bottom of the food chain, hanging around like sheep outside Caffe Roma, wondering why they're there. But compared with the penny-pinching in the rest of the corporate world, I have to say property is the last bastion of fun. Whenever you need to fill a table at Sale Sharks or make up the numbers on some curry club lunch, there's always a few willing commercial property lads to bowl along for the ride.

So it's no surprise that this is such a good show. One of the agents even told me they enjoy catching up with their contacts who they only usually get to see across the bar at the City Arms or in Sam's Chop House on a Friday, their own particular dens. The rest of them - lawyers, bank lads, investment fund managers - they all head out there to drink the champagne and chase the women. I can't speak for the architects, but even some of them have been known to like a light ale or two.

But I'm in the lounge at V-One with a few good lads who have a similar approach to travel for this trip. The property lads are all well in with the Manchester leader, Sir Howard Bernstein, and he gets everyone to chuck a few quid in so the city can make a big splash. I'll be catching up with Dave Russell, Tom Bloxham and Oliver Morley when I'm out there. Great lads.

Honestly, though I'm having a couple of meet-ups, it's really just a week long piss-up. I don't even register to go into the concrete bunker on the harbour. What's the point?

We rent a house out-of-town, get a people carrier with blacked-out windows to whisk us between the parties in the old town, Hotel Du Cap, the Martinez and the best night club on the Cote d'Azur, Le Barracuda. Basically, when in Cannes, do as the Russians do.

The slight added complication this time around is the TV crew we've got in tow. After a chat to Sidney's scrotes' charity up in Burnley or somewhere, the lovely Ash has got in with these posh TV kids from a programme they're making called *Slumdog Entrepreneur*. They line up good lads like me who've done well for themselves and get us to help out a few of the poor and bedraggled. Basically, you listen to these povs with half-cocked business ideas to "regenerate their communities," pretend to look arsed, write a few cheques out and look like an all round great bloke. A serious player. We're haggling over the amounts, but I'm up for it.

Ash is explaining what the "social enterprise agenda" is all about and how "empowering communities" is going to be the next big thing that the Tories are well into. Funny, George Osborne - my MP - never mentioned it at the fundraising dinner we went to.

This posh producer, Ben, and a few clueless cows with Berghaus puffa jackets, jeans, Ugg boots and clipboards (who are all well into me) are here because they want to get what they call a few "establishing shots" of me being good looking and successful in Cannes. It was Ash's idea, but as I wasn't about to start shelling out for them to fly down to Cannes to see me in action, they're showing me getting on the plane, hanging out here, then they're getting onto Easyjet, or something, and then meeting up with some French cameraman tomorrow who'll then follow me round Cannes for a day. And what do they want? Just me. Being great.

Ash is parking her smart Irish arse and coming along for the ride. She doesn't know I'll knock the price of her flight off the next invoice, which will cover mine as well. Tidy.

Her boss, Denise, is on the blower to her every half-hour. Obviously we only get one side of it, but the roll of the eyes and the sagging of the shoulders tells a story. "Yes Denise, I'll be writing you a full report of the client benefits and with full line-by-line expenses attached to each client. And yes, I've got the jackets."

Apart from being a bit of arm candy when I'm out and about and not on the lash with the lads, Ash has sorted me out with a few meetings while we're there, as well as some invitations to different parties in between her looking after some of her other clients. I've had her putting it about that I'm up for diversified international investment opportunities, which some of her property agent clients have been lapping up. Denise has saved on shipping by getting her to stuff a consignment of branded yachting jackets into her personal luggage, which is just what you need as the sun beats down at 28 degrees. Cretins.

This may well be the trip where I make my move and put the hard word on her, but she's given none of the signals to go just yet. She just gawps at me with those big bedroom eyes and witters on in that sing-song Irish accent about what she's been up to and still doesn't mention a boyfriend or anything. And right now she's doing a fine enough job blending in with the other fit birds with clipboards that you see whenever they make telly programmes.

They get a few shots of me talking – how flying private is the only way to go. Me and Martinez talking about our watches – his is a Patek Philippe mechanically-wound Chronograph 5170J and mine a Breitling Navitimer (which cost £28,000 from David M Robinson, by the way). But do you know what, these lads look after you. They had me and Phil Redmond, the long-haired telly bloke, flying in a fighter jet at their top customers' day. The Breitling mob only have their own private ex-military fighter display team; how cool is that? And on top of it all, they invite their best customers - or the ones who they think are going to splurge the most dosh on bling - to days like that. If you drop in that the day is almost as good as the Boodles tennis day at Mottram Hall or a champagne tasting at Harvey Nicks, then it sort of ensures they treat you even better.

I tell the telly lot that I've been learning a bit more about the diamond business from reading some woman in some magazine going on about "blood diamonds". By the time I'd even got to the end of that article where she was going on (and on) about conflict diamonds, I was right on the blower to my stockbroker to get me into anything with Liberia and Sierra Leone in it. If this lot are against, there's got to be money made.

I'm on a roll here, as you can tell.

"You might upset the bleeding hearts to start with, but once you've had the ex-professional soldiers in to secure the diamond mines, give the locals a choice to vote for the Party of Corruption or the National Liberation Front for Backhanders. They get the all clear, war's over, and everybody is happy again. Especially my portfolio."

"Is there anywhere you won't invest, Roger?" asks Ben.

113

"Never put your money into a country ending in 'stan'" I say, looking straight down the camera and winking, for extra effect. I'm a pro.

They also ask a me few questions about what I do, who I am, what I think about the tax system, the charitable sector – Sidney Silver's steady stream of bullshit about putting something back serves me particularly well here – so I trot out a few barbs about tax deductions for donations. It's a piece of piss, to be fair.

Once on the plane and airborne, Ash is so excited she's practically wetting her knickers. It's the thrill of a first time (and probably only time) private jet passenger. She's clearly well impressed with the set up, I take it all in my stride and get her to jog on with the business of the day and make her whip out her folder and bring me up to date on what she's been doing for me to raise my profile. Sadly, although she's fit and all that, she still has a lot to learn and I've got to be careful she doesn't embarrass me.

"So, in the words of Al Pacino, 'whaddaya got?'"

She's sorted a site visit next month with the judges for the Entrepreneur of the Year awards. She's done me this brochure about all the changes I've made at RC Solutions. It has about as little relationship to reality as it's possible to have, but that shouldn't matter.

She reckons she can get me on some adverts - airlines, cars, that sort of thing -which sounds promising until she says it's for some Scandinavian airline. FinnAir, it seems, are looking for global ambassadors.

"Why the fuck would I want to go to Finland?"

"They fly over the North Pole to China. They're marketing it as the best route to Shanghai; you get to fly with them," she says. Next.

She's got me a couple of complimentary memberships for these exclusive clubs aimed at lads like me - Quintessential and Paint – which sits nicely in the wallet alongside the Mere Golf Club gold card, but they end up letting any idiot in. I make it clear to her that while this is all well and good, when you're ITK (that's In The Know) you don't need to flash a piece of black plastic to get a table at San Carlo or get a new shirt from Frank Rostron. You get what you want and you just do what you want. I was having this discussion in the sauna with Martinez the other week at the Midland Hotel. We weren't staying there or anything; we just walked in. I mean, who's going to stop us?

This is the problem with the army of hangers-on that even great wealth of the sort that's coming my way brings. They don't get it, do they? Yes, I want free stuff, don't all rich people. Yes, I want cool stuff. But I want blingy, ostentatious and obviously expensive stuff.

So - get this - she says she can get me a Toyota Prius, and that it's a good car because of the lower tax. It costs £240 a year to tax my Ferrari, a car which cost me £198,000. The tax disc, which I don't even buy (Angela has always sorted) costs me less than .001%. She mentions emissions regulations. I have bigger problems, like should I put it through the company? Or should I register it to a private company so I can say Serena "may" have been driving it when I get flashed by a speed camera? So, no, Ash, darling, I won't be getting a Toyota Prius, for free or not. But I'm a reasonable man, and after careful consideration of my own personal lifestyle needs, the carbon footprint, and the look on the faces of the Mere Golf Club boys when I roar into the car park for the Captain's Golf Day, I've decided what I'd be prepared to do. I'd gladly be the face of Hummer. Just Fucking Sort It.

By the time we drop down towards the Mediterranean and follow the course of the Riviera towards Nice Airport I'm already bored of offers and PR and strategy, as well as her stories about whether "Sir Howard" and some Labour guy are going to turn up to some do on a yacht she's stressing about.

I realise I've probably stopped listening to her in the way I stopped listening to Serena. I just hear the noise, the voice, the wittering and wonder what she's like to have sex with.

I wonder if she'd be a demon in the sack, or whether, actually she's one of these prim Catholic Irish birds who wouldn't. She wears a cross around her neck and doesn't flash much cleavage. She looks the part with her big WAG glasses propped up on her head. She might flick her hair and look all smouldering, but she doesn't twirl her ankle or bite her lip like the usual whores do when they look like they're up for a fuck.

She does one at Nice airport to go and tell her journalist mates she's cadged a lift on a private jet with us lot, and I remind her to get it in the gossip column of some magazine. We scoop into the VIP mobster bus – the bags get taken to the house in the hills - then it's into Cannes for the first scoops of the Tuesday afternoon.

The whole place got into the swing of it on Monday, but it never pays to be there at the start. It all adds to the allure of mystery and fuels the idea you've got better things to have been doing.

You can barely imagine what the leather-skinned old biddies of Cannes make of this lot when they're walking their poodles along the promenade, shitting everywhere. They have the film festival, the music market, various TV shindigs and then this lot. Fuck knows what they make of the do that follows this one. Some of the boys stayed down for a few days extra last year just as the porn festival rolled into town, though there's no evidence of what's to come, if you'll excuse the pun. All of these get-togethers are linked by the common bond of middle-aged men selling shit, with the assistance of lots of prostitutes. Some officially, some masquerading as marketing girls.

But next to launching the new James Bond film, or having U2 and Beyonce in town, you'd think the surveyors and municipal clerks of industrial Brit towns must look like a tawdry bunch. You actually couldn't be more wrong. The shitter the place, the more they seem to up the ante on glamour.

Okay, so you can't polish a turd like Telford, or get anyone to "Invest in Bradford", or even to "Think Luton," let alone believe anyone got paid for coming up with "Birmingham: Global City, Local Heart," for fuck's sake. But every lad in town for this is beating a track to check out the action in Russia. The best parties, the biggest boats and, obviously, the fittest tush are all paid for by the taxpayers and oligarchs of Kazan ("Russia's third capital" apparently). At first sight it all has a feel of a spoof bit of marketing for the follow-up to *Borat*.

But for now, sunglasses on, jackets off, shirts unbuttoned to create that relaxed 'working, but on it' look we're just going to get into the flow with a few gentle liveners in the Blue Bar on the Croisette. A few agents from Manchester are about. Some bank lads that Martinez knows and already Foster is on the blower planning on where he's going to swing his pork sword.

We bump into George Downing, a top scouse property lad who asks us what we're doing. "I'm moving into easy money now and getting into this game, mate." We roar with laughter and raise a glass.

He tries to say it's not as easy as it looks, but actually it is, isn't it?

Martinez, already schmoozing a couple of Russian dolly birds and blagging tickets to a party at the Ritz Carlton later that afternoon, starts chiding Foster for his brassing.

"So, you found yourself a cat house?" he laughs.

"Listen, you can mock if you want, but at least I know where I stand. If I want a house wiring, I call an electrician. If

I want a lawn mowing, I get in a gardener. And for the purposes of sex, I also call upon the services of a professional."

We've already created an aura of mystery; everyone wants to know what we're doing here and who we're looking to see. We build on all of this, so the drinks keep flowing and the invites to yachts trickle in. The bullshit flows, the boasts come thick and fast - who's on the brink of this deal or that, who's setting up a new agency and who can do the best job of advising you on your next deal – without even knowing what it is. Amazing.

By the time night falls and we've caned it for a good ten hours of this finely-tuned tour behaviour, we're spilling out of the Barracuda Bar where the thin line that divides Foster's and Martinez's definition of a night on the pull blur the distinctions of what I understand of prostitution. A nod in the right direction, an extra bottle of Cristal and a special show in the curtained-off room for me and for Foster, while Martinez slopes off so we don't see that he gets the same result. I understand from Foster that the technical term is OWO and, while we are Cristal clear as to how we achieved this result, Martinez still lives under the illusion it's as a result of his hard work and drinks-buying.

Wednesday morning, feeling like shit, that little bloke with the jackhammer inside my head drilling for dear life. I'm waking up in the house, it's already 10, I vaguely remember getting in about 6. Ash has been texting already saying she's got my tickets for the King Sturge party, the Manchester do tomorrow night and some concert on the beach with some old punk rockers, the Stranglers, or Stragglers, I think she said (it's that accent). She also gives me a gentle reminder that we're due at a lunch event at the Martinez Hotel to hear about investment opportunities in the UK cities, but to also meet these film crew numpties.

118

It's a good job I look after myself, and can keep my wits about me in the face of these challenging nights out. The night before disappeared in a fury of alcohol and schmoozing. Drooling on my pillow and piecing together the night before, I have broken recollections of the usual sequence of lewd and disgraceful behaviour: insulting some northern politicians, lying to French women about who I am, winding up some snotty London property agents about the northern market for chip shops, bingo halls and re-opening coal mines.

The phone tells me I have two missed calls from Ash. Six from the office, which is par for the course when I'm away on business. And none from Serena, which is probably just as well. There might be answer phone messages but I never listen to them. Waste of time.

I vaguely remember waking an hour or so earlier, by a door slamming and a car pulling away down the drive of the house at speed. The kitchen area is a mass of debris: a pair of Martinez's trousers, champagne bottles, food, crushed cans of beer and a pair of sunglasses missing a lens.

Foster emerges from his pit in his boxer shorts with a young blonde slapper tiptoeing away, carrying her shoes; the classic walk of shame. She's wearing a micro-dress so far up her arse it might as well be a belt. Decent bod.

"Bonjour," I say, adding "taxi," in my very best froggy accent.

"Yes whatever, luv," she says in a throaty Manchesterish twang. "Like, where are we? How am I going to get back to my hotel in Cannes?" Which she pronounces "Canz".

It's 11 and we've got a driver picking us up at 12, but we don't particularly want some tart squeezed in the back with us and, to be fair, she doesn't look like she fancies sticking around. Foster goes to his wallet by his bed and chucks, literally chucks, a pile of Euros at her without even looking at her.

119

"Here you are love, never mind Cannes, you'd get to Paris with that!"

As she scrambles on the floor picking up notes and cursing under her breath Foster gives me a shifty knowing look.

"Where's Martinez?"

"Sleeping," he says, nodding towards the closed door.

"Alone?"

Foster looks sharply at me, with a look that says 'as if', adding, "but I think she left already."

Silly question.

Our big appointment in the afternoon is a special invite-only "showcase" of investment opportunities restricted to big hitters like us. But the reason Ash has been on the blower is that she's got us to bowl over to a buffet lunch and pool party at the Martinez Hotel, which I now vaguely remember was the scene of some quality bullshit last night as Tony told some punters he owned it.

Right now, with the motley crew of northern property muppets milling about, it pretty much looks like an average Friday at Piccolino in Manchester.

Thankfully, the Oakley shades hide my bloodshot eyes which must look like piss-holes in the snow, but a quick Red Bull sharpens me up. I must admit I'm looking pretty good, considering. White shirt, no tie, cream linen Hugo Boss suit, bit of product on the barnet, some of that regenerating eye gel from Philosophy and who can tell I'm wrecked from whatever appalling punishment I put my body through last night.

Ash is there at the foyer of the hotel squinting into the sun with this TV muppet and a French cameraman. I'm getting all kinds of lads chumming up to me, which you have to give Ash some credit for; she's been putting it about I'm a big hitter with money to invest, and she can't help but tell everyone about the private plane trip and the camera crew.

For some reason she's a bit more on edge than usual, probably the TV muppets. The idiot from yesterday, Posh Ben, is hovering around. "Nice flight?" I ask him and he doesn't laugh.

The area around the pool is thronging with punters now. All very politely sharing small talk ("when did you get here? How many of you have come over? Is it busier than last year?") The trick is not to linger too long in a group or you get the full sob story about the Ibis Hotel next to Nice station, lost bags, budget airlines and dodgy taxis.

Patrick Hemmings is here, son of Trevor the racing bloke; well minted they are (Tuesday, just him, seems busier). There's all these agents, lawyer lads, the Hurstwood boys from deepest darkest Lancashire (Sunday, two of us, seems quieter), and more agents. But we're the centre of attention. They're all looking at us. Not many women, just the ones handing drinks out, ticking people off lists and a few politician types on a junket (Sunday, twelve of us, seems busier, on our stand).

This Ben lad has the bright idea of getting a few of the boys to say how they know me, what a good lad I am. Martinez and Foster even manage to keep a straight face while they tell the bird with the microphone and the Froggie cameraman that I'm a visionary and leader in my field. They give their names as Patrick Bateman and Gareth Cheeseman, which goes right over this lad's head. Muppet.

He then says he could do with a bit more diversity. This is what ponces like him say when they mean they want some totty on screen. I know his type. I interrupt this chick with fantastically good tits but suspiciously bad skin who's been talking intently to Foster. After the small talk (Sunday, 16 of us, just nine last year. VERY busy, she says) I ask a favour.

"Listen sweetheart, just say a few words about me. Foster will fill you in."

You'd think it was hard the way these TV monkeys faff about, but it's all sorted in a jiffy. The big tit bird rattles off a few lines about client services and embodying all that she likes about the modern Cheshire businessman, providing her and her team with opportunities. Fantastic.

This has to be it, filming over and I'm off with Martinez over to this yacht moored off the harbour that looks like a floating hotel . Unbelievable. It's where these lads from London have sorted investment presentations.

A hangover never feels quite so fiery in foreign climes, and it doesn't even feel like one at all with the sun on my face, the throng of commerce on the Croisette and the overall buzz of being amongst the beautiful people. It's a long way from sales floors full of raging idiots, from whining from Rick, from nagging from Angela wanting to know where I am and when I'll be back. This is a world of sunshine and dolly birds, of doing what you want and being great all the time. It isn't even about not working, it's about ragging off idiots and doing what you want when you want it.

I'm sat on a motor boat that takes us across to the ocean-going yacht, and am being escorted by a stern faced ex-professional soldier in a black polo shirt and wraparound shades.

"Wouldn't it be great if you could be on tour all the time," I say to Martinez, who's looking edgy and distracted. Sometimes I forget he's running a serious business and has to get in the zone.

"All needs paying for Roger old son, all needs paying for. But yes, basically," he smiles back, holding a look that only a true mate can.

And this is why the 40 by 40 plan is so sweet. This is the life for me. Roger Cashmore, this is your life from now on.

We're welcomed onto this floating palace by stunners, absolutely drop dead stunning Eastern Europeans that look like they've walked off the catwalk in Milan or Paris. Unbelievable. These birds, fit as fuck, must be models, probably hookers, Czech, Russian, don't care. It has to be one of the great propaganda successes of Soviet era communism to keep it a secret that such womanly riches lay waiting behind the Iron Curtain. They pumped up all their boilers and mooses with steroids and had them throwing shot puts, letting us think the ultimate in womanhood lay in Sweden and Holland. Holy moly!

Who would ever have guessed that the best venues for a wall-to-wall tushfest with the lads are in what we used to think of as grey dungeons of doom? And you can't blame the Ivans and Borises for protecting them when they've got a fair percentage of your population who look like this. They have the high-cheekboned, lithe, wild-eyed look, they have that hunger and insanity to do absolutely anything with their God-given assets. So if you were the dictator of a country that had all of this, ask yourself: would you take part in a global new world order that welcomed along westerners who could take away the very best womankind has to offer? Would you invite the world in to observe all of this, and to then see them take all of the best ones away? Would you fuck. You'd build a great big fucking wall and keep them to yourself. Josef Stalin, officially a genius.

But, sad as it is to admit, this lot organising this little investment soiree aren't here to pimp the best babes in town; that might come later, you hope. They're here to offer a few investment opportunities in places around the world. Just as Sidney Silver said, "embrace globalisation, my boy. If I were a younger man, I wouldn't be bashing metal in Bacup."

It's not presentations and sales with these lot, it's discreet chats on an ocean-going liner that belongs to some oligarch with a private army.

First chat we have is about Africa. Uganda, to be precise. Now, to my mind, Africa is a seething lawless mess of a place. It's got AIDS, poverty like you wouldn't believe, more AIDS, bad AIDS in fact. We've all got a few quid in Dubai and look at that place: perfection and paradise. Trouble is now everyone's on the lookout for the next global investment opportunity to make a killing, if you'll excuse the pun. And I do take what Sidney says about embracing globalisation.

In the brochures this lad has handed out there's all the info about a new luxury resort in Uganda. Tastefully, it's called Kensington Heights and, very importantly, it has great big dirty gates around it to keep the beasts at bay. All the banks are signed up for it – it's project-approved by Barclays, DFCU, Housing Finance, Standard Chartered, Stanbic Bank; attractive interest rates; up to 20-year term. Get a decent golf course there and access to decent game shooting and you could be on to a winner.

Rio Ferdinand graces the cover of the brochure with the slogan: "Come, be my neighbour in Uganda," which is ironic, really, because I'm already his neighbour. In Alderley Edge. You see him out and about, here and there. Taking a little of bit of that special Cheshire community feel to the dark heart of the dark continent is a stroke of genius.

But, you have to laugh, Rio has just had his arse kicked by Lord Ferguson of Taggart for organising the wildest Man United players' party yet at the Great John Street Hotel. The whole shooting match: strippers, brasses and, by the end of the night, one of them crying rape. Oh dear. One of the cops was asked what time the alleged assault took place. "Around the time he mentioned he was on loan at Rochdale," he said. Boom boom.

So you have to agree, it's not the best advert, for "come be my neighbour." Not now eh, Rio?

It makes my head hurt how much effort goes into these plans: how, where and what you can go for. The only criteria, seriously, has to be which one can you have the best laugh with. Where are the bigger and better opportunities for adventurers like me?

Next up there's a bull-necked South African telling us the real white hot heat of the globalised revolution is for the opening of a new service centre and programming laboratory in Burma.

"I've been going out there for five years and it's really going places. It's one of those up-and-coming new economic powerhouses where things work with military precision," he says.

"And there are a number of leisure opportunities." He's not wrong and, as if to make the point, there are a whole load of pictures of the Burmese babes. Not half bad. It could be the new Thailand. Foster is practically bouncing in his seat.

There's certainly plenty to think about. They could do with a few more golf courses; worth mentioning it to Mark Boler, could try a branch of Mere in Asia. I'm sure the Afrikaan said the roads aren't up to much once you get out of Rangoon, but there are plenty of contractors who know how to sort that out. It's going to be brilliant once we start looking at the seaside resorts. Imagine Dubai meets Phuket. If Derek "Degsy" Hatton can make it in Cyprus with his Botox clinic and the properties he's flogging, then I have to think we just can't fail on this one.

Then there's some Italian bloke, cool as you like, telling us about a new creative industries cluster in Bologna. Access to labour markets, a creative setting, a legacy of post-industrialisation. I wouldn't be surprised if wasn't lifted off another one we saw yesterday for Munich, or even the crap they're coming out with for Salford Quays now that the BBC are heading there. I'm absolutely sure that no-one reads this stuff.

But these opportunities, these deals, are what it's all going to be about. Not having to bother with Rick and Angela and other assorted muppets. And as if on cue, a call. From Geraldine, who is frosty with me.

"I've got Rick on the line for you Roger. Here you go."

This is another of Rick's intensely irritating traits. He doesn't call people any more, especially if he wants to sound important. He gets Angela or Geraldine to do it for him.

"Roger, we were beginning to think you'd gone on a police hiking trip up Snowdon."

"I don't follow."

"Oh, haven't you heard? The Chief Constable Michael Todd has been found dead on Snowdon. All looks a bit iffy if you ask me..."

126

There he goes again, telling me something I haven't heard. Not that I'm that arsed, by the way. But he was alright, was Todd. We collared him at some lunch do at the Lowry once and he spoke out against speed cameras. Good lad. Popular with the ladies as well. They like a man in a uniform.

"Well I was having a lovely time here until you told me that, Rick, what can't wait until Friday?"

"Angela's handed her notice in. Something about a fight. Geraldine says you beat her boyfriend up and that the police are involved. Roger?"

"Bollocks. It was nothing, handbags and anyway, he started it. He'd been sniffing barmaids' aprons again, there was a bit of a scuffle, and I gave him a slap."

"And what about the police? Roger, we've signed warrants that we are clean and reputable, that this is a good honest business, not some sort of fight club. If you've got charges pending it could ruin everything."

"Pay her off. Money talks. She's probably not going to press charges, because it's my word against his and hers. She's obviously not coming back to work. Pay her a year's money, with a bit more for luck, on the understanding this ends."

"And what am I meant to tell Delphic about all this?"

"They don't need to know. There are no charges."

"Roger. They're hanging on here by a thread as it is. Well, they aren't happy. They're submitting a revised offer and are considering deferring on the full price. They're saying the banking market won't stretch to 10 times profits. So the asking price will be coming down to about £55m. They also think we should use the proceeds from the reverse premium on the property sale to do something called a vendor-assisted buyout, meaning we make up the difference with a contribution to the sale price."

"What's Bellamy saying?" I ask, not unreasonably. I thought he was the master of playing one side off against another.

"Well, Roger, he says he still has some interest from the Indian buyers, but that you don't take them seriously and won't meet them."

So he's even telling Rick about the curry-munchers. He must be believing his own bullshit.

"How can I meet someone who doesn't exist? He just uses that to keep the others interested. Anyway, now it's showtime don't we pay him to tell the Delphic lot to fuck off when it comes to this?"

"Well, technically, no, Roger, we're not paying him yet. Remember? You got him to do it all on a contingent basis. But he says it's just a negotiating position and we should hold out, but that he's busy with other clients as the tax deadline is just a couple of weeks away."

Technically, as Rick says, this is very bad news. Very bad news. We've got a busy dwarf who isn't being busy enough. A posh twat being played by his puppet masters in London, trying to chip the price and get money off me that I can't touch.

"Fuck 'em Rick, fuck 'em. Get Icarus back in to put pressure on them. We can play hard as well."

"Well that could be tricky, Roger. Their guy Dan Kay is nil by mouth in the Alex and pissing blood after he got robbed and beaten to a pulp. Hadn't you heard?"

"I'd heard, something. But I didn't know it was him. Shit, really?"

"Yes, nasty stuff. He's probably going to lose an eye and have permanent brain damage. Thugs tied him up and stole everything. Poor chap. I really liked him as well, really good guy."

Fuck. Fuck, Fuck, Fuck.

"Well what about the others, what about the American trade buyers. Tell me we haven't put all our eggs in this one basket?"

"You mean the American trade buyer that you called an 'ocean going septic cunt'? That one. No, Roger, I'm telling you, out of common courtesy that this is going to get rocky. We may have to defer the amount they pay. Or, if we weigh up the advantage of doing the whole deal before the new tax regime comes in. Then, well, we may have to take a haircut on our exit price. It's something for you to think about on your way back. Either way, you're going to have to treat these guys delicately."

"Yes."

"So what do you think, Roger? Deal or no deal?"

I take a deep breath and try to imagine what it would be like in a life without Rick being smarmy and smart-arsed. Without his showing off about what he knows and what he doesn't. I think about what I would be able to achieve without his weak will, his jelly-backbone and his insistence on negotiation. And compromise. Yet here he is, easing me out of the picture. Adding in extra complications.

I do the maths in my head.

These fuckers delaying until after the tax deadline could end up costing me £8m. Deferring until later also runs the risk of the whole thing falling apart, chipping even more off my 40 by 40. I could hang about and ratchet things up, really turn the screw, hit some big numbers, start selling to smaller businesses on longer term contracts. Get another sales floor in. Get Anton and his boys another Porsche.

Do it later. Do it better.

But I want out. I don't want to hang about. I've got all this to play for; all the things that will get me on that boat over there. That will get me away from Rick.

Do the deal, do it now.

And having someone called Toby playing hardball with me. Fucking Toby. It is too horrific to contemplate. I've still barely got over the humiliation of being faced off in Costa Coffee by a granite-built ex-Para in private equity who right this minute is masquerading as Mr Potato Head in the Alexandra Private Hospital. At least he won't be telling that story around town anymore.

If Angela and dweeb-brain have any sense they'll drop the charges and settle with me, but I'll just have to confront that one when I come to it.

It's stick or twist time on the tax thing. There is no turning back on being taxed on whatever comes my way at 10 per cent. Whether it's £25m now, or £10m, anything we have to wait for is taxed at 18 per cent later. That means we'll have to ramp things up even more on the hacking and the security stuff, probably beyond what even a shed full of Russian lunatics can achieve.

And what about the banks? They're all getting tight. What if Sidney Silver is right? What if there's a credit crunch on the way and the game is over for juicy debt deals? Well, if it is, then the whole show's over for all of us.

And, more immediately, what about my chances of getting a shag tonight? Ash will be winding down later. She's going to Tom Bloxham's party at his house in the hills. If she's got over her grumps from earlier (some other client must have been giving her grief), then she might be up for it. That one with the tits from the hotel might be there as well, she was game as fuck, had that look about her. But this is pressing.

There are a stack of commitments, some are just vanity, some are an alternative to getting me to 40 by 40 by a more colourful route. And sat here in Cannes, by the glittering sea with the palm trees whispering in a cooling afternoon breeze, things start to take shape in my mind.

There's the football club, where a down payment is required, but that's a piece of piss. Then there's Serena's bollocks, I can always pull the plug on that if it gets out of hand. There's the resi scheme – a winner, but possibly a stretch. There's Tosh, the fee for printing the books and his royalty, small potatoes; the house, the payment and the dodgy

130

AIM deals that the Taurus tools have for me. That's just the tip of an iceberg that doesn't involve Rick. That's just what I've come up with despite him. Think what I can achieve on my own. Think what I can achieve when I'm on TV, the businessman of the year, the *Slumdog Entrepreneur* being great.

And then there's always the tuck-up money the Vikings are looking after at eight per cent compound on the Isle of Man.

"Rick, I'm coming back tonight. Let's nail this for once and for all."

April 2008

RBS chief executive Fred Goodwin says the acquisition of ABN Amro gives the group a 'licence for growth'. CBI warns of 11,000 job cuts in financial services. The Co-operative bank loses £31.8m from buying structured investment products linked to US mortgages. Goldman Sachs chairman and chief executive Lloyd Blankfein says he believes the markets are in the late stages of the global credit crisis. Bank of Scotland buys Tulloch Homes for £27.5m

*S*unday Times Rich List — *969: Roger Cashmore (39), the Cheshire technology entrepreneur, is close to selling his technology solutions empire to private equity. He has substantial property assets, offshore investments and sporting interests. With dividends, retained wealth and past salary we value him at £50m.*

There's a crushed can of Red Bull balanced on the edge of the desk. It's been so bent, twisted and compressed it stands barely an inch tall. I look at it for a long time.

The rest of the room is a mess. A mass of discarded pizza boxes, a pile of dirty coffee cups, papers, emptied folders, plates of curled up and uneaten sandwiches from Philpotts, bottles of water, more empty cans of Red Bull, but not crushed as much as the one I'm looking at. There is nothing like a tax deadline to concentrate the mind. With the clock ticking, my loot looking like it was chipped away sharpish, we were, I'll admit, sweating like nonces on school sports day.

But in this room, at two minutes to midnight, we completed the deal. RC Solutions had been packed up, ready to be sold to Delphic Private Equity. If you listen to Bellend Bellamy and his like, these sessions, these completion meetings, where they agree a deal and cream off fees, well, they're like some kind of fucking triathlon. Every time he starts one of his stories about how they worked through the night on a deal, I just say to him, "is that the deal that two lads died on?"

He even tried to get us in the mood by having us all wear silly hats. Two words. Fuck. Off.

It has been, without a doubt, a complete pain in the arse. All this detail and nitpicking doesn't play well with an entrepreneur like me. I like getting things done and have someone else dealing with the bureaucratic bollocks.

We can laugh about it now, but when Delphic came back for the third time (I mean the THIRD time) with another

£500,000 off the asking price they'd already knocked down by a few million as a result of extra assurances they needed on property leases and the like, I had Bellamy by the throat.

To start with, I got wound up by some lanky streak of piss from some big dirty law firm acting for Delphic. You wouldn't know he was on the other side, not when you could see how chummy Bellend was with him. But it was this beanpole who started getting right on my case about financial controls and cash flow forecasts to 2015.

Retiring to another of these tiny rooms, adjacent to the main deal room, I was on the edge of it.

"Bellend, mate," I said, "rather than just showing off over a couple of technical terms and your understanding of some financial rule, could you get me my money. Please."

This is what did it. "Roger, mate, I'm a member of the Institute of Chartered Accountants. I am bound by a code of practice. My instruction is to act in the interest of the board of directors of RC Solutions. Insisting on the terms as you see fit – by shafting the buyers, basically – I am in breach of that. I am also bound as an Institute member to act in the public interest."

So I slapped him. The mist came down, I banged him right in the mouth, then grabbed the little fucker by his shirt collar, grabbing his neck and shoving him backwards over a cupboard full of crockery. The cups and saucers crashed to the floor, the frosted glass partition shook with a dull thud.

In that split second I felt like the most powerful man on earth, again. This little idiot is under my spell, now he's submitting to my sheer physical total power and is in mortal fear. Bellamy's eyes, weary and bloodshot, darted around the room. He, like me, knew this was a line you don't cross. This was Tosh behaviour. This was borderline gangster film stuff, getting what you want through physical intimidation. Something I'd never really had to wield before. Usually I'd just throw my weight around, shout at people and use a wide variety of menacing quotes. It felt brilliant. The hum of conversation and debate from the main room had subsided into silence as I had Bellend pinned against the divide.

To his credit, Bellamy - not a weed by any stretch - was also weighing up the client relationship. This was his one shot. He'd been telling this story all year about the importance of this deadline, and I was his last hope of a fee. All over town, deals were falling over. Owners were either dropping their prices, cacking it that the arse was properly coming out of the market for acquisitions with no-one properly understanding what might be round the corner. They were settling on terms they shouldn't have. For all that I took the piss out him and bullied him with putdowns, Bellamy wasn't a total idiot. He knew he had to make it work. He could edge away from me in the future – I think we both knew that – but the deal would be done.

And I could see from the body language of the lawyers, the other advisers and Rick that they too could see a line being crossed.

The good words first. I will be £8m richer, with the first £4m wired to my bank account. The tax on it (which I'll pay at the end of next January as a capital gain at the old rate) will be £400,000, as I don't have to pay the tax on the contingent element yet, but I will, and there won't be any problems. They just need to see that it doesn't completely fall apart, and there's no danger of that.

I hate paying any tax. I regard it as my money that they're stealing to waste on shite. I try not to think that I could have quite easily bought a new house in Spain with that. But it's better than if I'd sold today, the first day of the new tax year.

A mental tally shows that what I've coined in today, added to my cash pile in the Isle of Man, totals about £19m. Then there's that couple of mill earning decent returns on a bond with AIG; another nice tip from Sidney. The charity tax back thing is going to be worth a couple of gorillas. The buy-to-let property portfolio in Salford is nearly finished, but that's not about income, I'll flip that once it's ready to let.

Now, if I can rein Serena back on the house. We have to sell the present gaff to bridge the difference between what we've spunked on the build and how much the Paddy Bank can stretch to.

I'm reckoning a nice £25m. And that's even before the Icelandic wizards start paying eight per cent compound interest on my nest egg. It's alright, but it doesn't get me that close to the 40 by 40, but as we all know, money attracts money and there are plenty more deals to be done.

But it doesn't end there. I've never signed as many pieces of paper in my life, declarations, assignments, warrants. Promises.

When I got back from Cannes I had decided there and then to go with the lower offer from Delphic; market betas on valuation, they call it. Understanding what you can get away with flogging it for in a volatile climate.

Rick had done an alright job keeping the two banks on board. They were happy to roll over their £9m overdraft facility to the new owners, but then Delphic started talking about renegotiating, asking questions about the interest rate swap we'd sorted out to protect us from the swings and roundabouts of the Bank of England messing us about every month.

Then, without any hint of irony, we get a message from the floor below us at the swanky law firm where we were being fleeced for fees.

At half nine, while he was still shaking from me roughing him up, Bellamy gets a beep on his BlackBerry saying he needs a quick chat. I thought he was going to bin me off, to be fair.

We step outside and he tells me that these Indian buyers he'd been keeping informed were still interested. To be

138

honest, whenever he mentioned them before I thought he was making it up. It's the kind of yarn you spin to string these banker types along. They used to say: "we've had trade interest." Now they say "Chinese and Indian buyers are enquiring."

So, I say to Bellamy, "So where's the Balti boys then?"

"Their lawyers and advisers are downstairs; they've just bought a food processing business in Merseyside, proper knockdown price. They've come to Britain with a decent cash pile of cleared funds ready to invest in UK assets. They're interested in cars, food, textiles, and anything related to IT security and testing. They also said something about wanting to buy a football club at some point," says Bellamy.

"You're fucking joking. What do Indians know about football?"

He looks down at his shoes, like I've crushed him again. He looks up. "Roger, sorry about earlier. I didn't mean to disrespect you. You're the client."

I can't quite believe what I'm hearing. "Yes, alright Bellers. Just don't do it again, alright?" I give him a friendly slap on the shoulder. "So, shall we go for an Indian, pal?"

His face lights up, like I'm properly back with him. He holds out his hand, bonier and smaller than most hands I shake, so I grip it, firmly. He has this jokey habit of engaging his mates in banter when he meets them, and holding their hands for a moment longer than is comfortable. He doesn't try this with me.

Sitting down in the same room that I chinned him in, he runs through the opportunity, this time with Rick present, sweating and wheezing.

The deal is they'll pay half cash, at the same price Delphic had chipped us down to. Most of the upside is contingent, but to be honest we've got most clients in on long term contracts so that's sorted. They want some Indian doctor on the board, a couple of catch up meetings, probably in

139

London. They don't want anyone to leave, but understand that Rick and I are business people who are making other plans. They said they admire the business and they'd like it to be part of their family of companies, but that one of us can leave our executive positions if that's what we want.

"How do we know they're good for it?" I ask, selfishly, but not unreasonably.

"Surely they want me to stay, don't they?" says Rick, pompously, but not unselfishly.

"Right, first things first. They have the cleared funds available now?"

When he gets excited Bellamy sticks a question at the end of his sentence, like some Australian barman.

"In their home city these guys are big players? They own the biggest chain of chicken takeaways in India, they sponsor a major Indian Premier League cricket team, they own a power station, a brewery and even an airline. Sitting in a client account of their lawyers is the cash to do this tonight. They know the tax deadline is looming so they're playing it a bit cute. Subject to the usual disclosures, this looks absolutely mint, guys."

This is pretty far from ideal, but the clock is ticking and I'm not happy. One way or another the price has been chipped like fuck. But at least with this scenario I get a much smaller contingent element than Delphic were edging towards. A split from Rick, guaranteed. Question is, do I want to stick around with a bunch of Indian chicken farmers? And if they want to buy a football club, we could have some more fun along the way. Anyway, I love a curry, me.

"So, Rick, this is it." I take out a 50 pence piece from my pocket. "Heads or tails?"

Twenty years in business, 10 years at school before that. And it comes to a flip of a coin as to who moves next.

I toss the coin at Bellamy and nod to him to flip it.

"Heads I stay," says Rick.

Bellamy lifts his hand from his palm and looks at me. His smile seems to suggest he likes the outcome, but for him it doesn't matter.

"Heads it is," Bellamy smiles, more in relief that he won't have to work with me any more.

I look at Rick's puffy face, his pink shirt with sweat stains under the armpits. He holds out his hand. I shake it. He still hasn't mastered the firm handshake; his hand is flabby and moist. I ponder in a split second the unpleasantness of him and Bellamy shaking hands and shudder as I taste a little bit of vomit in my mouth.

We sign a load of paper, basically guaranteeing everything is tickety-boo and, at my insistence, promising not to disclose the purchase price. Which is, of course, exactly what we will do. Sort of.

The next big important and essential thing to sort out is the press release. There'll be loads of deals getting signed off, but truth be told, I'd quite like a big deal making of this.

So, getting Ash on the blower at this late hour shouldn't be a problem, I've been telling her to stay fresh to get ready to do some work.

"Oh Roger, hi, how are you? How's it going over there?" I still like her accent.

"Alright sweetheart, we've done it. Bunch of Indians bought it off us in the end. We fucked off the private equity lot. Muppets. Make sure you get that message out.

I tell her the next and far more important stuff is a profile piece on me in the *Financial Times* or the *Telegraph*, something bigging up the asking price; I tell her it was £30m by the way, and that I got most of that.

"You need to big me up. Alderley businessman, plans for the future, football, investment, property, you know the script. The next Charles Dunstone...what do you reckon?"

She has this very foxy way of saying 'ah ha, ah ha'. I wonder if she'd mutter that as I was giving her one?

141

"And how are we fixed on the next leg of the telly stuff? What's going on with that?"

She then says the five words that always piss me off, especially from women. "Did you read the email?"

Of course I haven't read the email. I never do. Email is someone else's to-do list; I just ignore most of them. If it's important enough then they'll phone you up anyway. Angela used to print them off for me, but I suppose that's not really an option nowadays.

"Er, I've been a bit busy. What email?"

"Well, we've got lunch with a journalist tomorrow, Simon Binns from *Crains Manchester Business*, then we've got a day of filming with the social enterprise charity up in Lancashire."

"Why do I need an email from you to tell me that? Have you sorted the restaurant? Isn't that what I pay you for?"

"Well Roger, that's the other thing. You don't. Denise is going to stop us working on the account as we haven't been paid yet. She said our accounts department have been sending red letters and it's going legal. Sorry Roger. And yes, I have sorted the restaurant, we're going to Sam's Chop House. I've sorted table 14."

"Oh for fuck's sake, the stupid cow. Tell her she'll get paid. Does she think I've nothing better to do, when I'm in the middle of all this shit, than to pay her for typing a few press releases and setting me up to have lunch with some gobshite journalist? I'll pay you myself out of petty cash when I see you. I'll meet you at Sam's at one, just get the release sorted."

"Yes Roger." Click.

If she wasn't so fit I'd bin for her talking to me like that. The nerve of these women. As for her boss, she is properly taking the piss. 90 days I pay on. Nothing less. How do you think I got where I am?

And that is what happened. That is how we sealed the sale. The truth, which we kind of need to keep buried, doesn't exactly thrill me if I'm honest.

I don't really feel like celebrating, but Bellamy has the champagne out and looks really pleased with himself. The days of heading into the city to toast deals like this is over. Outside all is dead. This isn't New York or even London, it's 3am in Manchester. It's been a long week, but even for a Friday night the pubs are closed, the drunks are stalking the streets and the bars are being mopped.

I'd called Martinez earlier to see if he was happy to be point man and line up the drinks somewhere, but he said he was going to be "laying pipe." I didn't even ask who; I lose track. It's Foster's weekend with his kids and he's obviously whipping himself into a frenzy of excitement before an early start the next morning when he treats them to a Happy Meal in the Wilmslow McDonalds. Oh, how the other half live.

Bobbi Armani was going to be in Brasingamens with Jimmi Barnes and a few of the Alderley lads, chatting up munters and playing pub cricket. But to be honest, the party will have moved on by now and I always end up picking up the bill anyway, especially with something like this to celebrate.

As I drive home, the Braz is all closed up. A few pissed-up tarts in micro dresses and the familiar hunting uniform of false eyelashes, fake tan and lots of bare flesh are tottering on stilt-like heels waiting for a cab to take them back to whichever south Manchester hell hole they're from, ever further away from the dream they'd have any chance of copping off with Cristiano Ronaldo or some bloke from *Coronation Street*.

The lights are on at home too. All of them. Serena, who is none the wiser, usually just wants to know if we are still on track to build the new gaff. And as long as Foster and his pals keep getting the flow of readies from the Bogtrotter Bank, all will be fine and he and I have our little experiment in football to look forward to.

All the doors are bolted and shut and I shout up to her when I get in. Even our bedroom, which she added a new security feature to – some kind of metal shuttering and a lock down mode, connected to a security office, and a panic button – the door is closed.

I shout up to her.

"It's me."

"Up here, babes," she shouts.

She's sat up in bed with her laptop out, looking drawn and ashen-faced. No make-up on and wearing a sweatshirt top and sweat pants. Not my favourite look, if I'm truthful. Surely she knows I've been working, even on a Friday.

"Hi babe, working hard again. I'm so proud of you."

"Yes, we sold it to some Indians. Good deal. Rick's going to tell them all about it on Monday…"

I'm in full flow pacing around the bedroom explaining how Bellamy is a dick, what this lawyer said to me about this and that and I notice she's staring into space and looking very, very upset. And it's not even the time of the month. Surely no-one's blabbed that I've been seen out with Ash, or leaked about the slapper from Oldham I was knobbing last year. Or any amount of gossip that evil people spread about me.

"What's up?"

"I'm scared, Roger. There have been some more robberies. And all of them are clients. Four of them altogether. It's really horrible as well. Masks, baseball bats, demanding money, cars, art, computers. The same gang, the police are saying.

"Every time I hear a creak or a bump outside, or the wind, I jump out of my skin. I can't think straight, Roger."

She starts sobbing into her hands and I put a manly arm around her shoulder.

"And I've got so much work to do," she says through the sobs, waving her arm in the direction of her laptop and a pile of papers, strands of her hair sticking to her soggy face.

"Roger, could I get some help? I just need a hand from some of your guys at Secure Solutions. I've got a massive backlog and I'm sure they'd be able to help."

"Of course, just ring them, tell them I said it was okay. Big strong lads, eh? We'll be alright Serena," I say, reassuringly. "Our security is top notch isn't it? And I'll kill the little bastards if they come here. Who were they anyway? Scallies?"

"Well, they had eastern European accents, but they spoke to each other in English. So they might be just disguising their voices. But, Roger, all of the people had really good, really new, security systems. The ones I've been working on, but it doesn't keep out masked men with weapons."

This is actually pretty shit, to be fair. I tell her how I chinned Bellamy and how I know a few people from round and about who can have a word. I still don't mention the caution from decking Angela's husband, she doesn't need to know about that, or the visits to some anger management counsellor and the £150,000 I've had to pay to keep this sweet, swept under the carpet, a full and final settlement.

But hopefully she feels reassured about my protective abilities.

Sure, no-one wants all this aggro. But emboldened from all of this, I tell her I'm not afraid at all. And she has to believe me, as my own 'personal brand' as Ash would call it, is morphing nicely into local bad boy, millionaire, fixer. No-one would dare. But at the same time it's a distraction you could do without. Maybe we should get tooled up?

"Listen babes, I know it's going to add cost to the new house, but I think we should get a panic room sorted. It's completely secure, has a separate power supply, air con, steel reinforced doors. If we order now it'll be better. I've had a few done for clients."

"Yes, yes, do it, love." Anything to keep her sweet.

I tell her about the deal, the bits she needs to know.

She's looking at me, thoughtfully, pondering something. This is a milestone. I don't sell a business every day of the week, I don't do a deal that has the potential to transform our lives, to secure us a future and to be the bridge from one phase of life to the next. I'm married to her, tied to her, sometimes I have absolutely no idea how I manage to pull this one off. She even took it in her stride that the kid thing wasn't happening, but I'm sure it burns away at her.

I've heard of lads who sell up, cash in and the wives fuck off and take half of it. What a choker. I'm pretty sure Serena won't do any of that, I think. But while she's waiting for her turn to speak – and she's pretending to listen to everything I've told her, give or take the detail of a few million quid missing here and there, she's heard the important bits. Essentially she's getting the new house and financial security.

"What a day. And a few million richer."

She smiles, looks at her laptop and then says, "Roger, be a love, before you come to bed, the dishwasher needs emptying."

On the Sunday morning that the *Sunday Times* covers our story, I make a big point of walking up and down London Road in Alderley, going in and out of the shops, popping in here and there for a coffee, bunch of flowers for Serena, a hello and a few bits and bobs. Everyone's seen it and there's a real spring in my step. It's one of those moments that says I've arrived. You can see it on people's faces as they nod and wave and whisper to each other as I walk down the street.

And this, the attention, and the opportunities that presents, is how it needs to be from now on. No one needs to know I've not creamed the full cash pile just yet, but the opportunities are going to start coming thick and fast now, I can just feel it.

There was a nice piece in the Business section of the *Sunday Times* announcing my sale: The Great £200m Indian Takeaway, listing all the businesses the Indians have been buying up, the lads at Tata, and of course this mob Chunky's. The funniest thing of course is that until Friday night I'd never heard of them. Now the economic success story that's going to transform the British economy is all centred on me and my special corner of Cheshire. Not that I give a toss.

This PR lark is a doddle and I might be paying Ash buttons, but it's working out very nicely indeed and it gives me another brilliant idea. If it works for me here, we need to step it up for the other bits of the growing empire – and for the lads as well.

But on the home front, given that we'd been aiming for this moment for a long, long time, Serena still doesn't seem that happy, to be honest. The scally robbery has shredded her nerves and she's been on pins, not keen to leave the house, fretting over some spreadsheets all weekend and a pile of legal documents to read. You'd think she was running a proper business with all the farting around she's doing. I never

147

realised that spending other people's money on furniture was so complicated. And anyway, wasn't she meant to be paying some lawyer bird at Cobbetts to do this for her?

I have an idea: why don't we get some caterers in and throw a dinner party. A nice strategic event, only invite proper big hitters, you have to be on the Rich List to even get an invite. We've all been to these sorts of affairs before, all part of the networking we need to start stepping up. We can do it for the first weekend we're in our new house, hopefully in August.

We could do without the mither over the robberies, so I give Tosh a bell.

He answers straight away, but the line isn't great. "Mr Cash. How's it going?"

"Yeah, good thanks pal. And you? How was Rome?"

He'd taken six planeloads of fans to Rome for the quarter final in the week, and there was stuff on the news about stabbings, riot police and plenty of the United mob dishing it out as well.

"Tasty as usual, my friend. But good, very good. I'm on my way to Middlesbrough. Always touch and go up here."

I'd just scan read a bit of football news in the *Mail* in Costa Coffee, always on top with the patter, that's me. "Yes bit of a bogey team aren't they? And with Chelsea and Arsenal winning yesterday…"

He snaps back at me. "What do you want? The money arrived didn't it? I can't really talk now, I've got a coach load of lads to sort and a bag full of briefs to knock out."

He has that effect on me. I never quite manage to read him right, or can never quite work out which mode he's in. This being a football day, it's a working day, of sorts.

"I just wondered if you could have a listen out on the street. Serena's in a bit of a state. There's been a few robberies round here…"

I get that sound where the line sounds like it's gone dead.

"Tosh."

His voice is back on the line, but I can't make him out.

"Did you get that? About the robberies?"

"Don't you worry, pal. I'll ask around. Tell your Doris to stop fretting."

He sounds amused by this; I suppose in his world it's a constant threat they learn to live with. I remember him once telling me about some geezer in Worsley who got his house turned over. Daughter and son-in-law given a bit of a shoeing, threatened her with rape and all sorts. Turned out this old lag was a bit of a player in the day, grafting and the like. Tosh and his pals put the word on the street and got all his gear back. The cars were left abandoned outside Salford police station with the keys in the ignition. The jewels, the cash from the safe and the collection of watches were all left anonymously in a pre-arranged pick up time under a canal bridge. Not a word was spoken about it again.

I don't want that to happen to me, so call this one a pre-emptive strike.

"Cheers mate, see you for a beer next week, and good luck at the match today…" but I'm speaking into fresh air as the line goes dead again. Either he's cut me off, or he's somewhere on the M1 and losing his signal.

And what was it he said about the money arriving? I call my everyday bank, a call centre. Some chummy Scottish bloke takes my details and my call, reading out the sums that come in and out of this account, more than he will earn in a year, just bounced from one account to another. A deposit bigger than the value of every house on his street, just arrives and then leaves. In fact, as he tells me the balance it is even bigger than I thought. £768,346. A lot bigger. We can lease a lot of planes with that, and obviously he's going to need all of that for any up front ticket buying for the semi final in Barcelona, and, dare we dream, a final in Moscow against the scousers!

It looks to be going pretty well. Very well, in fact.

You see, this is the thing. Away from the day to day drudge, I have that liberated feeling and the total freedom to follow my nose and make even more. Money follows money.

So, my first day as the former owner of RC Solutions and I'm now the man most likely to turn base metal into gold.

Ash advises me this is all going to sit very well with this kid Simon Binns, a chunky gingerish northern business hack who thinks he's David Frost. He wants to know what I'm up to now the business is sold and what I'm going to do with my investment portfolio.

While he's prattling on, I notice for possibly the first time that Ash looks different than when she first rocked up at San Carlo in January. Better dressed. More confident. She had this journalist bloke right in her pocket. Slipped him the big number, telling him that it was off the record. He loved it. Scribbled it all down.

The geezer at the front of house at Sam's knew her really well, and greeted her like a long-lost daughter. Air kisses and everything. I don't remember introducing her, but she knows him. She twaddles away about how great I am for a bit and, by the time the food's arrived, I've given Mr Journalist the odd quip and told him a few stories about some of the dodgier people he needs to keep an eye on.

For his part, he reckons he's got the inside line on this Iraqi geezer Bashar Issa who's been doing up a few properties and raising money for a film. He always seemed alright to me and I wouldn't mind getting stuck into some of these film tax schemes myself. Must give the Taurus boys a bell.

And Ash's advice on dealing with this lot is to chuck a lot of flattery at them.

"Great article you did," I lie.

"Which one?" he asks, the needy fucker.

"The one in *Crains*," I say. Ash shuffles awkwardly and chips in: "Simon did this piece from MIPIM, I'm sure that's the one Roger meant."

"Yes, that's right. We did MIPIM, great do, loads of wedge knocking about, went to a few good parties. But I had to come home early and do the deal. Quality do that is, pal."

He asks where we stay and Ash says, "it's a gorgeous house at the du Cap; great views, so they tell me. I was staying in the Cavendish. How about you, Simon?"

"Er, I forget, this apartment hotel for the press."

"Classy. So where does Howard Epstein stay on our taxpayer's ticket then? Is that what you were writing about, because you should be."

"Bernstein," he corrects me, which I don't appreciate. "No, I did the one about the escort agency sending all their girls over," he says.

"Yeah, that's that one," I lie again. To be fair I'm interested in what he's got to say here.

"How did that work then?"

He rambles on in far too much detail and with far too much information about who told him what. Then pennies start dropping. I really need to wake up sometimes. The tart in the villa with Foster, she must have been one of them. It all makes sense now, and it's a stroke of genius, to be fair. Follow the money.

This is the thing with these journalists. Ash seems to take what they say and what they think as important. I don't. And this one is far too pleased with himself for my liking. I don't trust the fucker to be honest.

And what is it with journalists always trying to take a pop at the entrepreneur? To be fair, his paper is great for ripping into the muppets and they have a list of who's got county court judgements against them, who's going into admin, which is great gossip; compulsory reading.

On Ash's advice I give him some opinions on the usual things journalists want to know about: politics and money.

Even though I've just flogged the business, I tell him how pissed off I am with this so-called "green agenda" and how it's really getting my goat. I point out that my Hummer has been sprayed green to bolster my credentials.

"But, surely..." he tries to say.

"The only green agenda I think we need to sort out in this country is how green with envy people are and how the government encourages it. It all starts with committees in parliament grilling the private equity boys and ends with some scrote scraping his keys down the side of my wife's Range Rover in Kendals car park."

"But doesn't business have a responsibility to pay a fair share of tax?" he asks.

"Put this in your paper, mate. It's high time the people in this country stopped taxing entrepreneurs altogether. Instead of taking OUR money from OUR pockets, the government should be thanking us for employing people and for spending so much money in the economy. I reckon I must spend at least £2m a year on 'stuff'. That's £350,000 a year in VAT for the government to waste on the National Health Service.

"So I refuse to get involved in a discussion with these nasty, bitter, hateful people who sleep under the blanket of the nanny state that I provide, then have the temerity to question the means by which I provide it. I'd rather they just said "thank you" and went on their way.

"You've got this creepy Jock, what's his name? Ali Darling. Poof's name. I heard him on this slot he's got on the radio saying he wants to support entrepreneurs and back British business. Does he buggery. I tell you what, if he walked into this restaurant now, I'd kick him the bollocks. Trouble is, he'd probably enjoy it. And you can print that."

Ash laughs like I was joking, but Binns smiles and nods. Another converted to the cause of righteousness.

Anyway, he seems to enjoy his steak pudding and chips with gravy – the baby's head. It always gets me about these journalists; don't they get fed at home? He wolfs it all down and then tells me a load of stories about some of the people he's written about. Some other property lad, a few of the council mob. I switch off, to be honest, I just want to make sure he's got the message. I'm sure Ash's fluttering eyelashes and come-to-bed eyes don't harm our cause.

I give him a card and ask him to call me if he's got any questions – they never do – and send him on his way.

Once we bin Binns I get my cheque book out and tell her it straight.

"Ash, I want you to go into business with me."

"Oh."

"Here's ten grand up front now." I push a cheque across the table.

"Oh," this time a little longer. More like "Ohhhhh".

"Work for me, you can have other clients, Foster wants some help flogging his big houses, organise a few events and shit. Armani's got a deal on that he could do with your help. Martinez always needs PR, he says he could use you. He'll put you on retainer."

I don't tell her the rest of what they said they'd like to do to her when I floated the idea with them, but she seems to get the message, as she blushes a bit.

"So, there you are, start up on your own. We'll back you. I don't like Denise, she's not paying you enough. What is it, £30k?" She shuffles like I'm not far off. "Well, it's not enough, I'll double it." I'll get the paperwork sorted, use Bellamy to incorporate a company and set up a shareholders agreement – me and you 50-50 (though to be fair, Martinez and Foster are partners in the newco we're setting up).

"What about it?"

"What about Denise?"

"Her contract is with Chunky's now. She can take her chances. You work for me. It's a different entity. I can put a good word in."

"Okay, Roger. It sounds alright. But I might have a few questions, I'll have to talk to my family about it."

"Yes, well don't ask too many of them, I know how big your families are in Paddyland, love. There's plenty of your type who'd gnaw off their right arm for a job like this. I can't be arsed getting it out for a pitch, I want you to do it."

I realise I've made a good move here. Though it means I'm even less likely to shag her now, but to be honest as long as everyone thinks I might be, it does me no harm. I look over at this bird who I'm part hitting on, part getting into business with. She's got these big blue eyes you could launch ships in, and I snatch a glimpse at her tits. Nothing special, not like Serena. She's weighing up what I've suggested and can't believe her luck.

As we walk to the Hummer (parked outside, another parking ticket but who cares when you're as rich as me?) she looks content. She looks like she's about to say something.

I toss the parking ticket to her. "Here you are, love, you can sort these out as well. Consider it part of the service."

On the journey to Dingle Dell, or wherever it is we're going, me driving the Hummer, I bell a pal of mine, Dave Ecclesthwaite, an investor, a good lad who I've been shooting with a few times.

"Roger! How are you? Did you get your deal done?"

"Sure did, Dave pal. Sold to these Indian lads for £80m. Can't complain, mate. Plenty of time to come shooting with you and the boys now! Must have a chat about this and that. Anyway, I'm on my way up to your neck of the woods, but I'm unarmed!"

Ash looks sideways at me, slightly surprised.

"Yes, pal, got company by the way, my PR adviser, as it goes. So keep it clean."

I nod back at Ash who looks pleased at the attention.

"I'm doing this TV filming lark up your way on some estate."

"Not one we've been shooting grouse on I imagine? Ha, no, Roger, all a bit of a mystery to me when you turn right onto the M65. Listen, I'm with some people at the moment. Give me a call again soon and we'll get together."

"Will do pal."

Click.

"Great lad that, Ash. I need to get these kinds of lads inviting me to their houses, holidaying in Barbados, coming to my charity dos. Do you get it?

"Anyway, where are we going?" I ask her.

"Well, we're meeting the crew at a community centre on an estate near Burnley," she says.

The satnav beeps for us to take twists and turns. One of the instructions seems to be sending us onto a wasteland of smashed-up houses on streets that have been levelled, but where it hasn't updated yet.

I pull over and look around, horrified at the sight all around me. A group of rancid tracksuited men, who could be aged anything from 19 to 90, with bottles of fortified wine or cans of lager stare open-mouthed at the Hummer. Across the rubble a family of Pakistanis rush by, the mother in full head-to-toe Muslim garb, the graffiti on the wall they have to pass saying: "BNP packies out". Some other local scribe has written a backwards swastika and the words "Hale Hitler" which wasn't, I guess, as a result of a fraternal visit from the Altrincham branch of Combat 18. I'm not about to correct their spelling, but it gives you a flavour of the place.

Outside a house two old blokes are hacking away at a battered Escort van, stripping it for parts, like wolves scavenging a carcass. It's propped up on bricks and with the windows out and the bonnet removed, they are literally chopping into it with axes.

They stop what they're doing and stare in awe at the Hummer as we cruise past, squinting to try and peer through the blacked-out windows. I inch forward.

The satnav bleats out a belated instruction. "Turn around where possible."

"Best idea I've heard all day," I say.

Ash laughs, nervously.

We edge towards the end of what used to be a road with the shell of a terraced house, crudely whitewashed, with a badly painted red cross of St George on the side. England's pride. The street opposite is completely boarded up. The satnav downloads a new route and indicates we head in the direction of a low rise compound surrounded by tall steel fences. The sign on the outside says "Community Centre".

The gates are shut, but there are two Volvo estate cars and a white Mercedes van, a clear sign that the TV tossers have set up shop.

We park up at the front entrance and Ash phones Ben to let us in.

Inside the "community centre" Ben and his *Slumdog Entrepreneur* crew have arranged a gaggle of Burnley's finest, *X*

Factor hopefuls thinking this is some kind of talent show. In a way it might be; it's a potential spot on television and a shot at making a few quid.

The slippery fucker sidles up to us. The hoity-toity toff from Cannes has become a faux cockney from some London gangster film. "Oi, oi Roger. You find it alright, my son."

"Yes, yes, whatever. What's the script then, Lock Stock? This the new *Phoenix Nights* or a business programme?"

"What? Er, yes. Right, all these, er, people here have got a business idea they want you to support. You give them advice, you steer them towards ways to make the idea happen. It's not like *Dragon's Den*, you're not just giving money, but you can if you want. They know you are a successful businessman, but that's it."

His mate Giles, another foppish tosser, says: "You aren't to talk to any of them outside of this pitch, we're just going to film what you say to them. At the end of it, you pick the three you want to develop the business and we'll be back next week to check on progress. Alright? One more thing – they don't know the name of the programme – we're not using the *Slumdog Entrepreneur* thing until transmission – we're just using the codename *North Stars*."

So, there I sit, at a table and chair, but with the camera, lights and various shades of telly ponce gathered around making these grunting peasants even more nervous.

First one up is a passably fuckable scrubber in her early twenties. Blonde hair tightly tied back and with a rough version of the look the slappers around Alderley and Hale have perfected, even down to the leopard print, the pushed up tits (I doubt she could afford silicon jubblies) and the tarantula false eyes. I mean, you would. Then she opens her mouth.

"Right. Ooooh. I'm Kaylee. Oooh, and I'm right nervous me."

I give her the look like I would and it seems to relax her a bit. "What's your idea Kaylee?"

"My idea is for a special dance school. I used to like dancing at college. They do a whole load of these new dances in clubs and it's great for fitness and stuff."

I wonder at this a while and ask her nicely, trying to relax her and giving her the flirty eye: "Is there demand to watch people dance up here, Kaylee? That has to be your first market testing move. Where will the dancers go on to earn money with the skills you have coached them in?"

"Have you danced much, Kaylee?"

She hesitates. "I done a bit in clubs and stuff."

"And your friends, are they anything like you?"

She points over at a group of girls who are either texting, chewing gum, holding babies or generally just sat around scratching their arses. All of them look overweight, frighteningly made-up and hard as nails.

She prattles on and on, barely drawing breath. Going on about some dance craze that's sweeping America. My mind drifts to images of fit porn stars and lap dancers with toned bodies writhing around on a sun-kissed beach. I wonder what Kaylee would look like face down being done firmly from behind. Correction, scrub that, bound and gagged so she couldn't speak. I think, yes, she looks alright, yes, definitely I should do her. And then I remember, I'm in a corner of hell called East Lancashire.

I wonder how these people live. How do they carry on from day to day living in a shit tip like this? What dream do they cling to that says: "Tomorrow will be a better day"? What do they eat? What do they do for entertainment? Why the fuck do they even bother?

OK, thanks very much Kaylee, you've given me a few ideas we can work on. We can maybe talk later."

The next lot are a procession of no-hopers and deadbeats with nothing more ambitious than chippies, taxis and buying gold rings.

One bloke, get this, tells me his life story. He was a major league football hooligan; the founder of the Burnley Suicide Squad (I swear I'm not making this shit up). He jumped bail and went to America, got involved in smuggling drugs in Thailand, and spent years 10 in the Bangkok Hilton ("it's not really called that officially," I pointed out). He then came home and has been running a martial arts business. He's developed a new martial art, a mixture of kung fu, t'ai chi, karate and a good old-fashioned technique he said he'd learnt on the football terraces.

"Who, when they have a fight actually stands up with the arms up in the air when all the blood's pumping? No, you go windmilling in". He actually demonstrates for the cameras as well, swirling his arms around at either side.

When the cameras are off I have a quiet word. "So, football lad, eh? You'll know Tosh McGeoghan then?"

He looks at me slightly taken aback. "Yes, I know him; Man U. We had it with his mob up in Glasgow a few years' back. They thought they were better than the rest of the England lads. Yes, how do you know him like?"

"Business, you know," I say, tapping my nose. You can tell this dope has underestimated me. It's the same wherever you go, drop the right names and doors open. It's not who you know, it's who we know.

"Is Tosh still active?"

"Very. At least he was when I spoke to him yesterday."

He looks at me with a long stare and he's weighing up possibilities.

The next few are mostly idiots. Whenever I ask them why they haven't done anything about their ideas they say they can't get any support as they are "the wrong colour in this town."

Still off camera, I ask another what his problem is. "Look around, the Pakis have all the jobs. We're second class citizens in our own town now."

There isn't much to say to all that, to be honest. It's quite obviously a different world to the freewheeling free market cut and thrust of Alderley and Manchester. What would they say if I'd been Martinez (swarthy), or Bobbi Armani (I'm not really sure)?

When it comes to selecting them for the next round and the ideas I'm prepared to back, Ben tells me I need to pick three and to give them a steer. To do this I have an hour to make my choice and say what businesses they can work on until next time.

This is obviously a piece of piss. I ask Ash how it would look and she says to pick a woman for "diversity". Given the door-to-door nail services being suggested, and the slappers asking for ten grand to open a tanning salon, the only real option is dancing Kaylee.

As for the others, I ask the other judge – some beardy local community bloke - what he thinks.

"Well, there are some core challenges in the area of identity and alienation," he says. "Unemployment has hit them hard and there are obviously substance and alcohol issues."

He drones on like this for a while, skirting round the bare facts that these are basically unemployable basket cases just in need of charity and cheap booze and drugs.

"So basically, they're all a bunch of racist savages? But to be honest mate, I don't see much of a market for lynchings. I'm at a loss as to what this 'social cohesion' agenda is all about."

"That's far too simplistic," he says, stroking his beard, looking at me like I'm a simpleton.

"Here's what I'll offer them," I say to Giles. He gets the camera set up and off I go.

"Kaylee, I'll back you to start a new club in this centre, I'll even bring some clientele up from Manchester. You can put a couple of acts on, but to be honest, if you've got it, flaunt it, love. Sort out the lighting, install a pole and invest in

161

a load of baby oil and we'll have a special talent night - lap dancing Lancashire style. I tell you what, here's a name you can have for free: *Peppermint Hippos.*"

She shuffles nervously and smiles. Spreading my joy wherever I go.

"And you, big lad. I'll buy you a minibus – call it Union Jack Taxis – guaranteed whites-only drivers, but you don't have to say it. You and your mates can use it as a taxi service round here. No more excuses for blaming the Asian lads. See how you go. And you can work for me offering giro day loans to the punters around here. Pay on time it's only 20 per cent interest; any later, then you can start your windmilling on 'em."

I look over at Giles and he is smiling so wide I think he's going to burst.

I knew I had what it takes to be a TV star.

Another triumph, and another string added to my ever-growing bow. Why did I ever doubt myself?

May 2008

A report from BDO says that if it wasn't for the rush before April's tax deadline, deal volumes would have collapsed. Scottish and Newcastle breweries is taken over by Heineken and Carlsberg for £10bn. AIG loses $7.8bn. EuroManx Airlines on the Isle of Man goes bust. Private equity giant KKR admits debt for private equity deals has dried up and announces it is moving into infrastructure. Manchester hosts the UEFA Cup Final between Glasgow Rangers and Zenit St Petersburg. Manchester United are to play Chelsea in the European Champions League Final in Moscow. British Land makes a £1.6bn loss.

One of the good things about getting wedged up and having a bit of dosh in the bank is the kind of invites you get. Once word is out, the volume of invites that land on the mat get larger and larger. I might have a tad fewer noughts on my personal statement than I'd hoped for, but not everyone knows that. It is a truth universally acknowledged that wealth begets wealth. Opportunities knock.

I've had them all knocking on my door in the last couple of months. Private wealth managers, stockbrokers, investment advisers and entrepreneurs who just want the comfort of working with me and getting my name attached to a project. I can honestly say I've never had as many decent money making opportunities put my way in my life. It's all I ever wanted.

But the best thing is it gives me the time and freedom to work with who I want, building up businesses I want with other brilliant people.

Take my new business, RC Aviation, which is going to be a real winner. I've signed up a lease deal on an Agusta 109 Mark II helicopter. These beauties sell brand new for £6m. A dealer I got put in touch with sorted one for £400,000. That's no big deal, obviously, but the day-to-day running costs – paying for pilots, getting them serviced - takes money, which is why more people don't have them. The trick is to get those costs paid for by subbing out and lending them out for the lads to "chopper in". It could do with a bit of work, so I'm getting it done inside like a Bentley, which obviously is taking a bit of time, but we'll be set for the summer, all being well. Bobbi Armani says he's signing up when he brings some big hitters over from Italy and Dubai. Whatever.

There are plenty of proper Alderley lads who could do with a lift here and there, whizzing over to the Isle of Man, across to Abersoch and down south to watch their nags at Ascot, Epsom and Newmarket. It certainly adds a touch of class. And Ash is sorting the brochures. And when I'm on TV, I really will have arrived. They'll all want a go.

And that, frankly, is what I need; the perception of stinking wealth, the ticket to the top table. The raw cash might not be there - it might need to be postponed – but I'll get there this year one way or another. At the moment, I just need to make it look like all is well.

This plotting and planning is all a welcome distraction from the inevitable nonsense at the office. Four weeks in to the great Indian takeaway and all was calm. I'd pop in and out, spreading occasional pearls of wisdom a day or so a week. Then, out of nowhere, one day, Bellamy rocks up with two Indians and Denise the PR tart in tow. She's clearly massively pissed off with me for nicking Ash off her, but she's obviously got her claws into these Indians.

"Roger, it gives me great pleasure to introduce you to Sunil and Vinjay Chundapul," he says in what I swear is a slight Indian accent.

One was a skinny little fucker in a blazer three sizes too big for him. The other, his brother, was a fat tit dripping with bling, a beard and a pony tail. Seriously.

They camp in the board room and start calling people in. You'd think they'd want a presentation or something. As it happened, I'd been expecting one and had the whole projection thing lined up.

But instead they start calling in random people from the business who go in for insanely short meetings from which they emerge very pleased, or really long meetings from which they come out confused. Nobody seems to be getting sacked, which isn't that surprising as we cut everything to the bone before we flogged it to squeeze all the costs out. It's like a lottery.

As everyone thinks I know everything, I have to go along with it all. From what I can gather, first of all they get people in and tell them how pleased they are with how it's all going and give them a massive pay rise. During the longer meetings, they start warbling on about how the business is going places, how they want to double in size in a year and start winning business from IBM and Cisco. It all sounds pretty good and increases my chances of hitting the earn-out number, which also buys my silence. I don't really want to go along with it because it sounds bonkers, but it's their train set now.

When it's my turn I pretty much know what to expect, and they offer me an immediate £500,000 one-off payment. Not that it makes that much difference, given I'm holding out for another £4m, but it seems like a sign there's more to come.

Denise and Bellamy sit impassively, both going along with it. He's got print outs and organisational charts in front of him. They've got red ink and scribbles and new lines written on them. He knows I can read upside down and flips up the paper that I was glancing at, so I can't see it. I thought he was meant to be a corporate financier? What does he know about running a business like this? I look at him looking for a flicker of what went before, but he's with these Indians now. He's their bitch, not mine.

Then it occurs to me, where the fuck is Rick in all of this?

Sunil, the one with the bling chips in first: "Well Roger, we are so pleased to own this business. It feels like part of our family. We feel the spirits are with us with this business; we have a very, very good feeling about it. We have great hopes for how it will perform for us, but we will need to make a few changes."

Now this I expected. The changes they wanted to make, however, came as a bit of a shock, to say the least.

"We will be terminating all our relationships with existing suppliers and relocating that function to our business in Chennai. All of the staff will be offered similar roles if they would like to relocate and we will pay relocation expenses."

167

I chuckle to myself at the absolutely ridiculous suggestion that anyone from here will move to India. He then has an even more stupid idea.

"We are also going to look for new premises as the rent here is quite high."

This is all bad news for two reasons. The Russian programmers at Secure Solutions, which I don't think Bellamy knows is mine (I put it through another Isle of Man shell), are the unseen backbone of the business. Without their targeted scare tactics the whole sales solution bit is a much harder sell. Of course I can't really fess up to this, as it's not strictly legal. But maybe they have another plan.

This is for them to do with as they see fit. Sidney has already sat me down and warned me about all of this. I have to go along with it; it's part of my managed exit.

The property is part of the deal. We signed the business up to a 'growth increment' in the annual rent. Upwards-only reviews for 10 years. It was the only way the landlord, Martinez as it happens, could secure us on a long term deal, but he's long since flipped it to some property investment fund run by an American pension mob. He agreed to our rent-free first year and the tidy 'reverse premium' we divvied up amongst us that helped us all to take a few quid off the table. And they can't have that back; it's safely and securely under lock and key in the Isle of Man, guarded by my Icelandic pals.

Anyway, we negotiated a good deal with the bank for plenty of headroom on working capital. Well I say negotiated; we pretty much dictated terms. You could do back then.

Bellamy knows all about this because he was acting for us on the sale. Now he's acting for the buyer and they don't like it. Someone should have spotted it, and it's him. Ha.

Now, hold on a moment," I say, as Bellamy avoids eye contact and pretends to write something down. "The building is part of the deal, guys. Unless you have another use for it, or want to sublet it, there's nothing you can do."

Vinjay, the weedy one, grins at me and shakes his head. "We have a saying in India: happiness is when what you think, what you say, and what you do are in harmony."

I have absolutely no idea what he means. Not a clue. Neither does Bellamy. But he's nodding like a puppy dog. I just look at him in a stunned state with my mouth gaping open. I cannot believe what I am hearing and start to hear voices in my head. Tosh saying, "you shitter, are you going to let these cunts walk all over you?" Then Sidney's wise counsel about being serious and patient.

I don't snap this time. "And is there anything else for your masterplan that you think I should know?"

"Yes, ahem, there are to be some changes to the management structure of the business?" Bellamy has got back into his annoying habit of ending each sentence with a question. "The role of deputy chief executive is to be taken by Dave Ritchie."

You. Have. To. Be. Fucking. Joking.

Dave Ritchie is a no-mark, slippery conniving weasel who Rick brought in because he's a gullible dick. He's one of those blokes that, if you've been to Tenerife, he's been to Elevenerife. He has that chummy habit that Scottish salesmen have where they talk about themselves in the third person and use your name a lot. Except that he gets names wrong all the time.

For the first two months with us he'd address Rick as "Rob" – which was hilarious as Rick was too polite and embarrassed to correct him. He claimed he'd been a professional footballer for St Mirren, but we flushed that out and proved it to be a pack of lies. He said he'd been one of the original line up in Wet Wet Wet and was a big mate of Marti Pellow. The trouble with lies that like in the age of Wikipedia and Google is they eventually catch up with you. He managed to bluff his way out of it, though, claiming he was in dispute with them and the settlement meant his name was taken off in lieu of royalties.

It suited me to have him fiddle his targets over the course of three glorious years while he manipulated his team, followed my orders and motivated people by fear of his underhand tactics and his intimidating accent. But he's a soldier, not a leader. I can't think of anyone less able to lead the business than him. What are they thinking of?

He also plays tennis with Bellamy. Who is now completely avoiding eye contact with me.

"Deputy to what? You don't want me to be chief executive do you? And what does Rick think of all of this?" I ask, guessing the answer before it arrives.

"Richard Thornton-Chambers is to leave the business with immediate effect."

"Who's chief exec?" I ask, but before even waiting for the answer I know what's coming.

"There isn't one, is there? Who's finance director then?"

"I am," says Bellamy, trying to look assertive and strong but looking ridiculous, frankly. He's just a little man who can twizzle a few spreadsheets, who can make a cup of tea and happens to have read a few books by Stephen Covey and that other one, Tom Peters.

I burst out laughing. "Is this a wind up? Sorry, at what point does Jeremy Beadle burst in?"

Denise hands me a press release which outlines the changes, the Bellamy news, Dave Ritchie's promotion and two other details they didn't have the bollocks to say to my face.

"Denise Ripley is to join the board of directors as deputy chairman."

There's even a quote from me.

"I look forward to the future success of the business and fully support the new management team and their plans for global expansion."

There's no chairman. This tart is joining the board as the deputy to the invisible man to keep an eye on a non-existent chief exec.

"And what is my role, exactly?"

"It's kind of business as usual, Roger," says Bellamy, shiftily. "You'll be a ambassador-at-large, representing us in the business community and - you know - opening a few doors."

"Keeping the clients happy, eh?"

There's a lot I could say at this point. Like, the coin flip trick in the completion meeting. What if it had gone the other way? What if I'd been the one who was staying in the executive role, would I be dispensed with, getting the full earn-out? I'm assuming Rick is, or does he have to wait for an earn-out like me? And I realise that we can do fuck all about helping it hit any target, especially as they've torched my cash machine. Did Bellamy have this planned all along? Not shafting me now, but keeping me hanging on, making it impossible for the earn-out targets to be met; giving me a sweetener?

Maybe it's the plan? A question at the end of every sentence like that pikey little runt would add.

Rick would be much more likely to go along with all this ying and yang stuff and follow orders. Why get rid? For the first time I'm genuinely out of the loop and not in control of what is going on here, and I don't like it. I mean, I don't even want to be here, but there's £4m resting on it.

Denise has been staring at me the whole time with barely disguised contempt and with a look like a loon. Her eyes are wide with the stare of the woman who can't quite believe she's actually ended up on the client side of this whole deal after a lifetime of being screamed at and not taken seriously - often by me - but also hit on and flirted with fairly consistently over the years. I'm trying to remember whether I ever did try it on with her. I don't remember doing, but then again, there's a lot that's passed by in a blur over the years. I can't even remember times and dates and even if she was with us or not. I don't notice women unless they're fit and she's a borderline boiler at best. Only now she is in a new and unique position to be inside a real company, not just her PR coven of muppets, and to be actually be taken seriously. She slides an A4 envelope across the table.

"What the fuck is this?" I ask Bellamy, because I can detect his ratty little tricks a mile away.

"A service agreement, just putting down on paper what we need from each other legally," Denise adds, trying to take back control of the conversation so that it doesn't just seem to be between me and Bellend.

I open it, looking at them both as I do, the Indians just nodding and grinning. There's only one bit that really matters: the money, a monthly retainer of a few grand. I think for a minute that I might drop into town and run it by one of the lads at Halliwells, but, as we speak, Manchester is overrun by 250,000 wrecked and incontinent Rangers fans in town for a European Cup final at City's ground. They're hell bent on drinking the city dry and then hosing it down with their tartan piss.

Fuck it. I haven't got time to battle through that lot and anyway, I'm not playing their fucking games. So I sign it there and then and slide it right back over at them.

"Make sure you pay on time as well. All in the interests of getting off to a good start. Legally."

Vinjay finally pipes up: "We'd like to invite you to our home in Chennai so you can meet the rest of the family."

His brother Sunil, looking like a coach driver with his blazer and shiny buttons, has a high-pitched voice with a funny questioning lilt at the end. No wonder him and Bellend hit it off.

172

"When you see the great opportunities for the business, we think you will be impressed."

I can't fucking wait.

So after sucking on that shit for a week or so, forgive me if I'm slightly excited by tonight's gathering of big swinging dicks. I'm at the Zeus Capital conference at Manchester's top chinky, Yang Sing. Zeus are a quality outfit. The lads they draw to a do like this are proper quality; my kind of people.

There's Jon Moulton, the bloke who should have saved Rover, not that you'd bought one of their old rust boxes (but the MG brand might have been worth saving and he'd have turned it into a British Porsche). At least he didn't sell it to Indians. If the mob who've run RC are anything to go by, Jaguar's looking like it'll be going to the dogs as well.

Oh look, there's my favourite Dragon, Theo Paphitis, guarding his kids' inheritance and batting off the legions of muppets. He's here to do a turn on stage as well, telling a few tales off the telly and recounting how he sorted out Ryman and Millwall Football Club. And La Senza (this reminds me to get Serena a load of their naughty night attire, the thought of which gives me a right boner).

Joe Dwek's here, a real big hitter and a mate of Manchester United director Mike Edelson.

Tom Bloxham is knocking about. Another good lad. Likes his hats, which is a bit weird, to be honest. And his trendy flats aren't quite my cup of char, but he's cleaning up in that game.

Foster's driven my Hummer in. He always likes to make an entrance, and the girls at whatever cathouse he's stopped off at think it's his. He's bending the ear of some lawyer about the latest twist in his divorce. He seriously has it in for his ex. I don't catch the full story, but I overhear him say, "piss flaps like cabbage leaves."

"Alright mate," I say to Foster. "How's the battle of the sexes?"

This is one of those conversations that as soon as you start it, you wish you hadn't.

Most of the time he's moaning about his ant infested two-bedroomed flat in the wrong end of Knutsford and the latest mechanical problems with his VW estate car.

But to cheer himself up, the same week his ex is taking his kids to Barbados for half term, he's off to Thailand for one of his sex benders, which he usually - bizarrely - still tries to claim is for the golf. Except with me, worst luck.

"Do you know what Rodge, I think British women are just wrong for me. All these trips to Thailand have spoilt me. I think that's where I need to be."

He looks into the middle distance, shaking his head. Whatever the dirty fucker has been up to over there it's clearly addled his mind. He's probably thinking about a Thai basket, this contraption he told us about after one visit where a girl sits with her fanny poking through a hole. It's then lowered onto him and spun round.

"Women are different over there," he says. He gets out his mobile phone and shows me this picture of a Thai bird in a bikini, skinny, with a pair of tits you could crack eggs on. "I bought her off her parents last year for a grand. Got her a decent-sized pair of norks put in. What do you reckon?"

"To what?"

He looks at me like he's searching for approval or encouragement. "You know…"

"What? Are you thinking of crating her up and shipping her back here?"

"Yes, maybe. Well, it's an idea."

I can't wait to tell Martinez, this is hilarious. "Yes mate, whatever makes you happy. Listen, I've got to be off."

The world is seriously going mad. Unbelievable. But I have to say, the jubblies were pretty good.

Martinez is at the bar talking to a couple of girls who work for Zeus – both tasty – and Ash is there as well. Did I invite her? Must have done.

One of the Zeus lads is well in with a few football lads. Neil Rodford, the football agent, is here with a few of his crew (might see if he can get me a few cast-offs for Wilmslow Wanderers). And on the top table is big Sam Allardyce, the football manager who's made a few quid from this and that.

I need to get Foster off his sex soapbox and get him into some of these football lads.

"Listen Dave," I growl, "we need to step up on this football stuff. There are people here you need to get stuck into; agents and investors, like. Have you got the agreement to buy the land from the football club?"

"Er, yes, we need to talk about that," he's sweating and blustering. "The bank have been going quiet on me. You know what it's like at the moment; they're not doing new lends on land deals. We should be alright on the funding line for the projects in development, but it's looking like we might have to bridge on some of them."

"Some of them?" I snarl at him through my teeth. "Some of them? You mean my new house?" I want to properly yell at him, but raising my voice in here isn't an option. I swear the clap must be eating away at his brain.

"This my new fucking house," I hiss. "Call me tomorrow."

I must be snarling at him with such aggression that he physically wilts. It's good to be scary like this. He looks like he's going to do something about it as well.

"Sorry mate," he says.

"Yes. Just fucking sort it."

I turn round in a fog of dizzy anger, trying to stay smiling, and I run right into this lad from our bank. He wants to know how we've been getting on with the Indians.

Wrong question. "They're alright if you like cretins who talk in riddles and are supported by the biggest bunch of clueless yes-men and a micro-managing cow. Apart from that, great. Why, what do you make of them?"

"They've not been in touch," he says, to my surprise. "We're trying to organise a meeting. Richard isn't returning calls."

No surprise there. I put him in the picture: "Between you and me, pal, Rick's left. It's going to be announced tomorrow. And yes, they are clueless. I don't even know if they've got the money. It all looks very strange to me. They're closing off the biggest profit centre and moving shit to India. Didn't even ask me what I thought. Fucking idiots."

Sidney warned me about this. Letting go, moving on. Looking for the next thing.

I scan the room looking for someone uplifting to talk to. Someone who I do a bit of business with. You can spot the hangers on - the lawyers, the tuppenny ha'penny mortgage payers - by the way they swarm around the real business lads. Lads like me who these lot feed off for their fees. Wankers, all of them. As I talk to the bank lad they're nodding at me over the shoulder of someone less important than me, trying to make eye contact and wishing they could be in my face and chasing a fee.

We have a few swift beers and a bit more chinwag, but before we can get stuck into the nosebag – which in this gaff is seriously top drawer – we have to listen to a few speeches first.

Theo is first up. He rattles off his life history before telling this brilliant story about this lad on the top table. He'd squirreled a pile after selling some company or other. He puts it all in his wife's name and made her go and live in Belgium for a year. It wasn't long before she started getting wind of his nights out around town when she was looking after the nippers and minding his dough.

Next time he's with her he notices something on the bedside table: a tub of superglue. "What's that for?" he asks her. "For you, darling. If I ever hear you've been misbehaving I'll glue your dick to your leg."

With all this hilarity knocking about, you'd think the headline act would have a few jokes up his sleeve.

Trouble was, it was Jon Moulton. He might be a clever bloke, but don't expect to see him doing stand-up comedy any time soon.

I try and follow what he's saying, but it's basically that the banks are fucked. He rambles on for a bit, sending all of us into a bit of a hush.

"I'm living in a world in which nearly everyone in meetings I attend ends up asking, 'Which banks should I put my money in?'

"The frenzy of corporate takeovers and a US house-price bubble built on labyrinthine debt structures is going to end in tears.

"We are in a financial world in which a company is linked to a monoline insurer, which is attached to a credit default swap, which is attached to another insurer. They don't know who's involved and whether they've got problems, and that's frightening.

"The Bank of England has lost the ability to stoke the economy by using interest rates to encourage borrowing. Their principal tool is not working, because banks are too scared to lend to one another."

Honestly? What do I think? He's lost me. This is just the way; once these yanks stop writing mortgages to penniless Mexicans this will all get sorted one way or another. But he's obviously got his own reasons for saying all of this.

I get a text from Tosh just as Moulton's off on another rambling story about financial instruments using charts that make no sense. "Ta 4 info pal. Need more from u. Got planes 4 Moscow."

I'm texting back that this sounds like a perfect deal for me. A real earner to get me back on track. The rest of the talk is all about the up-and-coming trip to Moscow. After a semi-final win in Barcelona, the Man U boys actually managed to get to the final. Playing Chelsea might not have been part of the script, but the alternative was Liverpool. Messy.

Sidney is chartering a private plane with a few of his pals, though I notice he hasn't exactly extended the hand of friendship. Pete Cowgill, Ron Wood and Bryan Robson are doing it private as well. There's talk of week-long trips, going by train. The whole march to Moscow has got everyone excited.

But with a shortfall on the money the Indians are likely to stump, I can't think of these trips as a big jolly, not when there's a fair bit of money to be made.

And the good news: me and Tosh have secured 10 planes all with his name nowhere near it, and all underwritten by RC Aviation. He's got eight out of Manchester on the day and two out of Belfast International; obviously the paddy Man U fans will be as up for this as anyone. For not much outlay we are going to make some serious money and have a massive laugh along the way.

After sending him back a quick, 'no problem' text, Moulton is wrapping things up.

"The firm to watch," he says, "is AIG, the world's biggest insurer."

This is more like it, I've got a couple of mill in a decent bond with them (Coutts sorted it out). Glad he mentioned what they do; sponsoring Man United has obviously done well for them, and everyone knows insurance is a decent game in all weathers. And as for banks, whatever squeeze they've got now, if he does have shit to chuck about he has an angle. I mean - get this - for all his miserable doom-mongering, he's into 'distressed debt'. So the downfall of the economy is because banks create complicated vehicles to lend, and then protect themselves and he's into - er, right - complicated vehicles to lend.

I do a mental tick-off of my investment portfolio. Contracts for differences - check. Icelandic bank – check. AIG

Variable Rate Fund – check. Collateralised debt obligations – check. These were where all the smart money was going. Let's call it a balanced portfolio.

I look at the row in front of me and there's Sidney. He usually has a good wind of these things. What is it with this guy Moulton? Is he just a miserable fucker from Stoke, which would explain a lot, or is he onto something? I catch Sidney's eye, crack a laugh at him and shake my head. He doesn't smile back. In fact he's gone a grey shade of white, even for a well-tanned sun bird like him.

Moulton wraps up his 20-minute motivational lecture on how the world banking system is heading for oblivion with a dismissal of Iceland. Proves how much he knows.

At our table the talk is slow. I'm in one of those situations where I'm stuck talking to one boring fucker, but the other conversations sound much more interesting. A couple of older blokes are talking about this idea to bring in a congestion charge for Manchester. It will cost a fiver a day to get into town in the morning and will pay for bus lanes and trams and shit.

"Sounds like a great idea," I chip in. "What's a few quid to us? Anything that makes it easier to get around and keeps the scrotes and their rust-heaps off the roads."

Sidney sidles off to the corner of his room to make a phone call. I can hear him saying, "Get me out now. Don't delay. I want it into cash in HSBC. No, you can forget Coutts and Royal Bank; get me out of them as well."

I've never seen him like this before, and back at the table he's rattled.

He's been completely taken in by this Moulton bloke. "Only an idiot would have their money in Icelandic and Irish banks anyway," he says. "It's crazy."

Only an idiot like me, he means. I swallow hard and pretend to agree with him. "Bit harsh, Sidney; those boys have some decent assets."

"Roger, it's like this. How can a country of 200,000 fishermen go from owning fifty times what they owned in 2002? All those big houses in Beverley Hills, West Ham United, half of the UK high street, power stations in India, airlines and other banks?"

I'm thinking of Olaf and Eider, the two bulky piss-heads who back us on stuff all the time. They seemed alright to me.

"They're a nation of entrepreneurs, Sidney, call it bigger balls and a need to catch up."

"They're either laundering Russian mafia loot, or worse, they're borrowing and leveraging from the international money markets on the promise of ever-rising asset prices, rising of course because fools like these are paying way over the odds for them. If you've sold to an Icelander in the last year you've taken candy from a baby. If you've dropped your deposit money into their banks, then you're just mad."

I don't say anything. I like Sidney - he's right about a lot of things - but he sometimes seriously believes the last daft thing someone's told him.

"Sidney, if the Russki mafia have been using Iceland as a laundry, then that's pretty good security, to be honest. They've probably got the best-funded banks in the world."

Sidney looks at me with his mouth open, "Roger. No."

"Maybe. Not much though. Worth a tickle."

Which is sort of true. In Sidney's world he could probably afford to spunk £10m. I can't. Not now anyway, but it'll all be alright.

The rest of the night livens up. There's a comedian, a ventriloquist who gets one of the Zeus babes up on stage, puts a mask on her and we all have a good laugh. Then this lad called Mike Finnigan then gets everyone wound up with positivity and excitement, he's a bloke who could get excited about a traffic jam. If I was still running RC he'd have been perfect for the annual sales conference.

Once I chill out, I realise I love nights like these. This is my world. These are my people and if this last week or two has taught me anything, then I definitely prefer Chinese to Indian.

To be honest, Moscow via Belfast sounds like the worst holiday ever. But RC Aviation has a flying start for this first big adventure, getting thousands of football fans out to Russia for the Champions League. Tosh is running things at the Manchester end with me making sure we get a load of paddies in and out.

The deal is this: I get to Belfast on Monday, mooch about, pick up the tickets, hand them out on Monday night, fly everyone out on Tuesday, hotel in Moscow, day out, match, fly home. Hopefully with Man U as winners.

We'd had a meet-up about it, but this isn't laid-back menacing Tosh we're dealing with now. This is five mobile phones on the go, surrounded by his gang of mates. No nonsense, no bullshit, always at it. In his basic office on some grotty industrial estate over Salford way he's got the invasion of Moscow planned to a tee. He never writes anything down, just remembers everything, barks out orders, remembers numbers, amounts, old debts, favours. And it's all in his head.

When I get there he's got lads running around. The way he runs his operation is tighter and leaner than RC Solutions ever was. And he doesn't seem to write anything down.

He introduces me to his mates – no-one has a proper name – Mad Eric, Spunk Bubble, Black Fred, Macca. One's called Hitler; when I ask why I'm told "he was born in Germany". Another's called DD; I know him, he was in the year above us at school, another school mate of Tosh. His nickname came about when his Dad died - DD: Dead Dad – and it stuck from there. He was from Hale or somewhere and Tosh took him under his wing from then on.

He introduces me as Roger The Cash. And just so I don't think I'm important he reminds everyone he used to think I was a shitter. "Should have seen the soft twat in his local coffee bar – 'sorry, sir, no sir, not me sir' – when some rugby cunt with a mouth on him was giving it large." He nods at DD, or was it Hitler – "you know, that one."

Then he swings a fake punch at me, ducking around me. "But we've got to be careful Mr Cash doesn't lose his rag though or he'll knock you out, won't you? The Old Bill felt his collar for rucking outside a titty bar, didn't they? Alderley's main lad, this one."

I get a few nods of approval. Being good at fighting counts for a lot around here.

"We need to send our top boy to Belfast, don't we lads?"

His mates laugh, but I can see a few of them, while not thinking that I'm exactly as he described, realising that I'm able, if not necessarily willing.

"You'll do fine in Belfast, son. Good move, Tosh," says DD, deadpan and stone-faced.

As a parting gift, he hands me a new BlackBerry. Use that. "The number's on the back. Don't text me neither, use the BBM on that instead; you can work it out. OB all over us, pal."

The flight into Belfast City Airport, on a FlyBe crop-duster, is a stark reminder of what I desperately need to leave behind. Private jets and helicopters are the way forward, no more queuing up with the peasants, no more delays, no more sitting with your knees around your chin and a plastic table with inedible food shoved in front of you.

As I gaze out of the window, I reflect on the madness of the last few weeks, of the mood of panic everywhere. How people's sense of risk has gone out of the window. How the seriously wealthy are battening down the hatches. Lads in the Alderley Bar and Grill are returning with tales of banks saying no to stuff they were falling over themselves to back just a year ago. There's a deepening feeling that they're losing their nerve. Thank fuck I've thrown my lot in with the Icelandics – at least they're still jolly and ambitious.

The wind on the plane makes for a very unsteady landing. I can't work out whether we're over sea, or some kind of lake, when the city comes into view as I look out of the plane and spot two gigantic yellow structures, cranes of some description. The plane hits the runway with a bang and a swerve. For fuck's sake, I'm so sick of this cheap shit. Some of the passengers gasp, which makes me think it's not always this bad, at least.

The pilot makes a reference to "side winds over the loch" as he talks calmly over the tannoy, but the sales reps and assorted busy salarymen on the plane barely look up.

As we queue to get off the plane the pilot is thanking the passengers one by one, suspiciously with his hand on the arse of one of the fit trolley-dollies. A big bloke in front of me with a Belfast accent as thick as a pint of Guinness says to the pilot, "So tell me, was that a landing? Or were we shot down?"

Waiting for me as I walk through from baggage claim is a rum-looking, shell-suited paddy holding a card with my name on it. At least there are some trappings of my exalted status.

In the car (a Merc, not new) he tells me my hotel, the Europa, is the most bombed hotel in Europe, and is where Bill Clinton once stayed.

"If you'll be needing anything while you're here, big man, I'm here to watch your back, so I am. You'll be fine around the hotel, but don't be letting on with your name if you stray up the Shankhill."

"I wasn't planning to go very far either way, mate. But why do you say that?"

"Cashmore? It's a Fenian name so it is. Marks you out as a Taig."

"Is it? But I'm English, so I've to stay away from both lots?"

"Just watch your back that's all, my friend."

He takes me on a scenic tour of what he describes as Belfast's city sights. It's a mixture of building sites and council estates. He points out pubs and chippies where bombs went off, where massacres took place and where British soldiers were shot or where they cracked a few heads. It's like Moss Side with murals, to be honest, and I can't wait to get to the hotel and get on with why I'm here.

Without wanting to get myself shot or stabbed I opt to stay in and around the hotel – I've booked out the Bill Clinton suite as well, but couldn't find the cigars – but even around the hotel bar there's fuck all in the way of action. Across the road at this old pub that looks like it's overdosed on ancient bling – the sort of thing some people would consider quaint and olde worlde – there's probably time for a quiet Guinness.

In the hotel, I get set up in the bar on the first floor waiting for some local travel agent to come and collect the travel packs I've brought over to hand out.

A group of six big lads walk in the room, baseball caps pulled down covering their faces. None of them talk to each other and the smallest of them goes to the bar and motions for four out of the rest of them to sit over in the far corner. He whispers something to his mate, the biggest of the lot, and he nods in my direction. Great. This is all I need, cased out by the mob.

The big menacing looking skinhead sits down.

"You Tosh's boy?" He sounds like one of the locals.

I'm not going to quibble with his description. "Er, yes."

"You got what we need?"

"I think so mate. What's your name? I've got a list with 140 names on it for the plane we're taking."

He looks up at his stunted pal at the bar and I look down the list Tosh gave me, a printout from a spreadsheet with the envelopes and travel packages in my briefcase.

His mate comes over and shakes my hand without offering his name.

On his hands I make out the prison tattoos on his knuckles, LOVE and HATE and across his hand "Chelsea, Combat 18."

He sticks his hand into the inside of his parka, a large oversized white with the Stone Island patch on the left arm. I've had a few of their pieces over the years, but it's a bit obviously hooligan these days. He keeps his eyes fixed on mine and puts his hands back on the inside of his coat.

Two more men walk into the bar who they don't recognise. Older blokes in business suits.

His eyes dart around the bar and the pair look at each other. "Are you definitely on your own?"

"Yes."

"What's your name."

"Roger Cashmore."

"Right enough," says the local, raising his eyes, weighing up the significance of it, but not in good way. I'm thinking about what the driver told me. His mate, the little cockney, keeps his eyes on me and says, "you better not be mugging us off, you fucking northern monkey."

"Woah, woah, lads. Why would I be doing that? All I'm doing is passing on the tickets and the travel stuff to some of our clients who Tosh has sorted out with a trip to Moscow. Is there something I should know?"

"Are you staying here?" he asks, looking over at the two suits at the bar who seem oblivious.

"Right, I'm coming up to your room. Bring the case." He nods to his mate. "Make sure we ain't followed."

In the lift he seems to relax, exhaling before he checks his reflection in the mirror and takes off his cap (blue Aquascutum, I notice).

In the suite, he checks out to see if there's anyone else around, which of course there isn't. I'm in total confusion, wondering what the fuck is going on, who these lot are, and why I'm here in a former war zone with a bunch of paranoid psychopaths instead of sitting in a bar in Moscow eating caviar out of some hooker's arse crack.

"Give me your phone," he says.

He scrolls through the last numbers dialled. He reads them out: "Serena, Ash, Martinez, Sidney, Paul Beck, Rob, PC. Who's PC?"

"A bloke I know. What's it to you?"

"Not Old Bill then?"

"Are you taking the piss, mate? This is getting beyond a joke, what's going on here? It's a bloke I know called Pete Cowgill. Ring him if you want, but he's a businessman who will probably be half way to Moscow to the football, where I wish I was, to be honest. Are you going to let me know what's going on? Let me call Tosh at least."

"No, I don't like it. I'll bell him, on your dog. You ain't cushty."

188

He rings Tosh and keeps staring at me. "Oi, it's Evil. I'm in Belfast and I'm with this muggy cunt who says you sent him to see us. Describe him."

He stares at me while he listens to the voice on the other end of the phone. He eventually cracks into a smile and laughs. That must be his name, Evil. I can see why.

"Yes, that sounds like him, ha, ha, ha. 'Ere, your boss wants a word," he says and hands me the phone. Tosh obviously thinks this is hilarious and talks to me in his best business-speak.

"Ah yes, Mr Cash, sounds like you've made contact with our clients there. Listen, these customers need to be handled very delicately. Call me when you've got the money, alright?"

"Okay, I will," I say, staying on-message with a suspicious Evil staring right at me. "How's the rest of the operation going, mate?"

Click. He doesn't reply.

What I want to say is, what the fuck is going on? And why do a bunch a nutters seem to think I'm an undercover copper? Why is my so-called business partner landing me in this situation, and will I ever get to Moscow?

What I do say, I think wisely, is nothing at all. But my new friend does all the talking.

"Hold up, right, this is how it is. I'm on a ban for life from Chelsea and England. But this is the big one. I can't miss the European Cup Final, can I? We're going over 140-handed to have tear-up with these Russians and all. It's all going to be filmed and put on YouTube, proving we're the top firm. It's my life's fuckin' work."

He notices the look on my face.

"I know what you're thinking. I am too old for this shit. But I'm like a brass monkey on the Fleetwood Mac. I need it. I can't stay away. If an alcoholic gets off his nut and needs help, he goes to Alcoholics Anonymous. A druggy gets rehab. There ain't a cure for football hooliganism. But I'm on a banning

189

order. If I get caught even trying to get over there I'll get a lump of bird.

"All the Chelsea travel lot won't touch me and my crew. There's Old Bill crawling all over us. So, we're going from here. We've a few mates who we've been involved with like, some of the Linfield boys. Let's just say they share some of our political objectives. We've got some of the Rangers lot arriving today and I got Tosh Tours to sort us out with a trip. Old Bill just think we're tiddly-aye paddy Man United."

I pipe up, "yes, well that's what I was expecting. Tosh said…"

"Tosh and me go way back, but he understands my position and helps me out. It's business isn't it? Listen, he says you're alright. But this trip is now being 'outsourced' as you business boys say it. We're running the trip; you hand over the tickets and all that, and you get paid, alright?"

What I'm thinking is, I do have the tickets, but I thought I was on this trip as well. Now I'm not so sure. The prospect of flying with this lot fills me with horror. And what if they lose? No, it doesn't even bear thinking about.

He gets out the envelope from his inside coat pocket. There's a plastic carrier bag stacked with paper stuffed up his back, all full of twenties and tenners, online credit card payment receipts and then cheques made out to RC Aviation. We're charging this lot £750 a pop, so I'm here to collect 139 payments for the trip. No wonder he was twitchy with all that money on him.

He sits on the sofa watching the build-up to the match on Sky News, which is showing coverage of the players getting on their planes to Moscow and waving for the press. The regular news features pictures of Russian armed police in armed convoy preparing for the English invasion. His chirruping phone goes off and he jumps from one nonsensical conversation to another.

190

On the screen there's footage of this Obama guy, standing for American president. I look up and nod at the screen. All he says is: "a fucking tree dog as president. And a fucking Muslim mud. Unbelievable."

I'm not about to share my own admiration for American presidents, or tell him the tale I heard earlier about when Bill Clinton came to Belfast, so I concentrate on managing to match up the payments with the travel documents. As I do I get more irritated. Why the fuck am I even doing this? It's the kind of boring, tedious, paper shuffling admin I pay people to do. But it's also a hell of a lot of money. A lot to count, and, thinking on, a fair amount to wash as well. I could get over to Douglas and open an RC Aviation account at the branch of Volcanic over there that pays eight per cent interest on deposit.

Eventually, as darkness falls outside, he leaves with his travel docs for him and his band of stormtroopers. And I contemplate the horrific possibility of what a couple of days in the company of these total psychos could bring. Chucking me out of the plane? Not letting me on the plane? Violence, mayhem, getting caught up in a staged battle with Moscow's neo-Nazis, all filmed for YouTube? Forget it. No, it all seems safer and more comfortable sitting holed up in Belfast waiting for the match in Moscow to be over, so then I can go home with my stories to contribute to theirs. No-one will be any wiser, and I'll have a stronger chance of being alive.

When he's gone and the sense of relief and fear and anger burst out of me in the form of a stream of bile and puke all over the bath, I get myself together enough to have another short conversation with Tosh, which goes something like this:

"What were you doing setting me up like that?"

"I couldn't have sent one of the other lads for that drop, Cash; too moody. Why did you mentioned my name up in Burnley."

"Oh yes, Norman, what was he like, ha?"

191

"Well this fucking in-bred up there called me, said one of my top lads had called it on with his mob, saying we were game on."

"Who? Me? Tosh, you don't think…"

"He thought you were alright, but I put him straight. I told him you were a cunt. And do you know what, you are. Don't go using my name again, right. It's bad publicity and bad for business."

Before I can even say anything, he's back down my throat again.

"Do you know how serious this is. I get a text off him saying him and his pals were going to be passing through Manchester and to text him "row" for a fight and "beer" if we just wanted a drink. I had to ditch the phone. If Five-O get that, I'm away. So it serves you fucking right, after everything I've done for you. Plus, we're partners aren't we? You help me, I help you. Information and opportunity. The Russian book, Dan Kay. The planes, more money."

The small matter of £100,000 makes me want to sleep with all of that under my pillow, and it is a very good day's work.

I sit cooped up in Bill Clinton's suite in the most bombed hotel in Europe ordering from room service, dinner, breakfast, lunch, drinks. I watch the match. Well, I try to. I have no idea what goes on at a football match; I'm always amazed at the things people say and the things they pick up on. 4-4-2, 5-3-1, holding midfielder, who plays where, drop off the front two. I'm sure it means something to them but it's all nonsense to me. At least when United win the penalty shoot-out even I can work out it was because John Terry missed his, but even as I'm watching his crushing disappointment I'm not that pleased, not bothered about a football match. I just think he looks like Rob Cotton from NCC Group, another lad I know.

There's actually only one so-called pal of mine who will know I didn't make it to Moscow, and that's Tosh. But, to be honest, there are pennies dropping all over the place now and frankly he's starting to give me far bigger problems.

June 2008

Barack Obama is selected as the Democrat candidate for the American presidency. Chris Sheffield sells his online and mobile gaming company Million-2-1 to IGT UK, a subsidiary of International Game Technology. Shares in housebuilder Barratts collapse. Dubai World buys property firm Minerva. Barclays looks to raise £4bn from sovereign wealth funds to repair its balance sheet. The FTSE falls to 5500. The government promises Manchester £3bn for public transport if a congestion charge is introduced.

North West Business Insider June 2008

Deals Despatches

Who? RC Solutions

Did what? Was acquired.

When? Just before capital gains tax went up in April

How much? £80m, or so it is claimed.

By who? Chunky's, an Indian conglomerate looking to build a group of businesses in food and technology services.

Who advised? Endean & Bellamy for the vendors, legals by Halliwells.

What's it mean? On the face of it this looks like a good exit for the founders and shareholders of RC Solutions. The business has been on the market for a year and a lengthy auction process looked like delivering the highly-geared business to private equity, with Delphic looking the most likely buyer. That all changed at the last minute with Roger Cashmore, executive chairman of RC Solutions, claiming: "We are delighted to be selling the business to Chunky's and to be working with them on the next phase of their development. An exciting future lies ahead for the international technology solutions marketplace."

What next? A new and inexperienced management team has already been installed, with corporate finance adviser Bellamy assuming the role of finance director, David Ritchie as deputy chief executive and Denise Ripley, MD of Ripsnort

PR taking over as deputy chairman, all reporting directly to India.

However, all is clearly not well. Cashmore has taken an almost invisible backseat role in the business while his close friend and business partner Richard Thornton-Chambers has left the business altogether. It's not unusual for this to happen, but a whole new management team in a short time frame may not provide the required stability, while the Indian owners have relocated a service centre from Manchester to their home country and have only visited the head office once.

Most likely to say: Too many chiefs and not enough Indians.

Least likely to say: Chicken feed.

The texts started at 6 in morning in some nightclub in Banus. Pilled out of my tree, I couldn't even focus. But once I'd sat by the pool in the morning I sobered up pretty quickly.

Sidney: Roger – terrible. Feel for you. Call me.

Ash: OMG. Roger, this is outrageous. X"

Even Tosh has been texting. "Gud show m8. LOL."

People whose numbers I don't even have stored in my phone text me out of the blue.

"Couldn't happen to a nicer idiot."

"What goes around comes around"

Or just for good measure: "Scum"

There's one that just says: "Sorry mate. Grim." From Foster.

I'd actually come over to Banus to get away from the shit storm that was whirling around. The Taurus boys bagged me a place on a lads' trip with some of their hedge fund pals from London. Just the sort of lads I need to be knocking around with who can put me into a couple of opportunities to catch up on the investment strategy. Private plane, villa, long weekend on the lash. The usual. What could possibly go wrong?

But first of all, the week from hell had possibilities. On Monday morning, knocking on towards half past ten, I'm rocking up at RC. First off, my usual car park spot is taken. Some silver BMW X3 in my spot, a chick's car if ever there was one, but there's plenty of other spaces.

The entry code has changed – 6969 was my idea – so I have to get buzzed in.

I walk in and at least half expect to see the place as it used to be when I was running the show, but the big bell in the middle of the sales floor has gone. The lads would ring the fuck out of that bell when they'd made a big sale. The exercise bike that we nearly killed Garner on, gone. Gone too is the big picture of the Porsche which used to keep the guys focused on the riches available to the salesman of the month.

The wall of shame has been ripped down as well, where we'd cut out pictures from nights out, peppered with a few posters from our favourite family newspaper, the *Daily Sport*.

The whiteboard where we used to announce the "muppet of the week" (usually some client who spoke out of line to one of the lads), or "mug of the month" (the customer we actually raped for fees). And the gallows, where we nailed the company logos of the competitors we'd forced to the wall. All gone. All relics from a happy time and a successful era, lobbed in some fucking skip in the name of responsible inclusive capitalism or some such bollocks.

But nothing in its place either. Just a lifeless, soulless atmosphere and stupefied boredom. It's like the centre of Baghdad after Saddam Hussein was fucked off, with all the statues pulled down and the goodies looted (but without the beheadings, the suicide bombs and the mayhem). But it's the passing of one world, and this is the new world order at RC Solutions.

Denise and Bellamy are locked away in my old office. I can see them through blinds at the meeting room table where I used to watch Sky Sports News and occasionally drag one of the lads in for a pep talk, or a bollocking, or a chat about golf because I was bored, whatever I was feeling that day.

The layout of the office has changed; all rows of empty desks and lots of unfamiliar faces, mainly wet-looking blokes.

So I'm sat on the edge of Garner's desk and he starts with a story about Moscow. It's not the first time I've had to rely on TV footage and bluff my way through, pretending I know the layout of the stadium, the madness at the airport coming home where lads were just piling onto planes like they were taxis.

But he's not a happy bunny and pretty quickly he's telling me about how sales have fallen off a cliff, that there have been sackings, and that people are having their desks cleared on a daily basis.

Good lads who'd been around for years just not being there the next day. Geraldine, who'd been showing a bit of promise under Rick, got put on reception and was made to skivvy for Denise. She left yesterday in tears.

The last two targets were both missed and everyone's being sent on sales training courses with some client of hers from Ripsnort, her crappy PR agency with an ever-shrinking client list since Ash robbed the best ones.

All told, Bellamy and Denise Ripley (Twit and Twat, Garner says he calls them) can't make a decision without ringing India, but that the Balti brothers haven't been back since last month when I met them.

"Mate, she's properly off her head. Every time my email pings and it's from her, I have no idea what it's going to be. At least with you it was either sales figures, porn, videos of violent deaths, a bollocking or an invite to a piss-up. With this one it's yet another new rule. And there's no pattern to it. We'll be having a shit week and her priority is to stop people eating food at their desks."

"Where's Wilcox?"

"He's been sent to London to open a new office there."

"What about Ritchie? How's it going with him?"

"Oh, he's a nightmare, we've missed our first two targets by a mile and he just keeps nodding away, saying we have to keep positive. That we've got a 'great groop'."

He says that in a very good impersonation of Ritchie's Jocko accent, to be fair. But he's no idea what's going on.

"It's shit, Roger. They're clueless. They're the worst I've ever seen. They've haven't a clue how to build sales now the pipeline's been closed."

We share a conspiratorial glance. Only a couple of my inner circle quite knew how that piece of business development worked.

Denise and Bellamy emerge from their meeting with Ritchie, who waves over at me with his big witless grin. What lies, what fiction has he been spinning. The other two are looking for me for our planned session. All the heads in the office go down; no-one looks up, no-one shouts over about a piece of business they've creamed.

She offers all the usual pleasantries ("How's your little travel business?") with all the insincerity and patronising crap I'd come to expect.

Grrrr.

My 'little' travel business, my 'little' fucking travel business has just pulled in close on two million quid in hardly anytime at all, bulk-ferrying plane-loads of football fans to Moscow. It has a helicopter being refurbished in Bentley interiors which will transport people with more money than you can ever hope to see to houses you can't afford to spend weekends in places where you're not invited.

On the downside, Denise, it is run in partnership with a certified psychopath and unconvicted murderer who is probably using it as a front for money laundering the proceeds of robberies of my neighbours, using data which I accidently handed him on a plate. But you know, that's the least of my 'little' problems.

I don't say that of course. I grin and say, "fine and dandy, scraping a living."

Bellamy just looks blank and fairly shifty, a bit embarrassed.

Sitting down, she gets her folder out labelled with my name and looks up, "So my dear, what have you got for us?"

"What do you mean?"

"Where's your business development plan and your lead referrals? That's what this meeting is about."

"Is it?"

"Roger, our agreement, which you signed up for, which you signed in this very room, and which we are paying you a huge amount." She massively overemphasises the word 'huge', and I just think what a huge fucking horrible cow she is.

"It clearly stipulates you will provide us with 10 referrals and introductions a week, that you'll host a round table seminar on important issues in the industry with key players every month. Have you done that yet?"

She knows I haven't. And I just shake my head, mumbling vaguely.

"Do you have a copy with you? Or would you like me to read it out to you?"

No-one in my adult life has ever spoken to me like this before. No-one. And I am not about to squirm and defend myself and make excuses in front of these two pair of fucking monkeys. But it is very fucking uncomfortable and I don't want to just throw a hissy fit and storm out. I don't want to give either of them the satisfaction. With all the other shit flying around, I could do with the profile and the regular income. But not on these ridiculous terms.

"Well, let me tell you how I think it's going to work," I say, forcefully, but not losing my rag. Bellamy knows this tone of voice; it's the one I adopted before I nutted him.

"If you want me to give you something for this business, then look out there. Look around. All the good people, the ones you've got left – that's my contribution, that's my pipeline. You want a favour, call me, but ask me nicely. I don't respond well to this micromanagement bullshit you seem to have introduced."

By the time I finish though, my sinews are close to snapping and my knuckles are bursting white just looking at the fucking pair of them. Morons. Cretins. Imbeciles. This is their fucking revenge. This is actually what they want; they actually want me to be their fucking bitch.

And she actually writes down everything I say, nodding and smirking as she does.

Bellamy, the wankstain, smiles as if to confirm what I was thinking, and adds another sting in the tail. "We seem to have a simple misunderstanding here, Roger. Maybe we just need to iron out what we expect of each other. It works both ways, mate."

"Yes." He can tell I'm close to leaning over and sticking the fucking nut on him. He's seen that look before and he shrinks.

"There's also the small matter of company confidentiality, but we'll come to that later," she then chucks in as if it was a loose afterthought. This is why I fucking hate women in business. Snakes with tits.

Before I've got chance to digest where they might be going with this shit, Bellamy opens his ratty little mouth and dares to speak. And that fucking questioning lilt has got worse.

"The owners are in the process of moving to one of their Indian banks. It's not a big problem or anything, as they were planning to move to an Indian bank to consolidate their group facilities. However, they've had to move on it quicker than they anticipated because Caledonian have changed the terms of our facility. Based, apparently, on a conversation they said they had with yourself last month..."

"Don't know what you're talking about," I lie, recalling with crystal clarity the chat I had to the bank lad at the Zeus party.

"Moving forward," says Bellamy. Another of his fucking meaningless phrases, which he inserts into everything. He checks me laughing.

"Moving forward, ahem, communications on confidential company matters will be done by ourselves," he shuffles his papers and I don't hear what he's saying.

Denise pipes up again: "You are not authorised to comment publicly on the strategy of the business to any third party."

At this I really want to explode. I want to point out that it's a bit fucking late for that, you fucking quarter wits. As if you don't know, I've been in the *Sunday Times* Rich List, every bit of trade and local media. I'm the best asset you've got. And what shall I do about the television programme I've made which will make this business a household name and get in front of millions?

Obviously I don't.

"Shall I cancel the TV programme?" I say sarcastically.

They look at each other like it's a serious offer, check themselves, check my expression and realise I'm not actually serious. But before it's all done she has one last patronising sting left in her tail.

"Oh and Roger, my dear, one more thing. Could you ensure that when you are on company business that you maintain a standard of dress consistent with the stated dress code policy. Men must wear smart trousers and jacket, and a shirt and tie."

I look down at my £250 Church's brogues, a two grand hand-made whistle from Shaun Levine the travelling tailor and a shirt made by Frank Rostron. Then I lightly run my finger around the circle of my Breitling.

It's 70 degrees outside and the rest of the world is open-necked and staying cool.

"And when it's hot? Like today?" I say, with a curled lip and a look of utter contempt for them.

"As deputy chairman and group director of HR policy, that will be a matter of discretion as to when I relax the policy."

What a bitch. What twisted vision of work and business this bint must have, crushing people's fun, banning food at desks, limiting breaks, call sheets. Fucking call sheets, not like the freewheeling days when we ruled the world. And it's not even as if they're any good at it.

Another day ruined, but it was about to get worse.

I don't mind people saying shit things about me. In fact, there was a time I used to get a bit pissed off if two months went by and I wasn't on the back page of *EN* magazine or the *Insider*. But these muppets on t'internet can't be bullied like the witless journalists on those magazines could. They can't be tamed. And the old faces you used to be able to have a laugh with have become serious and po-faced and want to win an award by being snotty about you.

So, what started with a few snide comments in various bits of media that I can take or leave got out of control. Which is why Ash comes out with that shite about not reading your media coverage, but weighing it.

But then it got progressively worse. Starting with the fucking car crash of an appearance on TV, which the papers had a field day with.

Daily Telegraph **TV review**

Television producers use all kinds of devices to create the heroes and villains of reality television. The latest trend seems to be warming the nation's hearts through kindly rich people bestowing their generosity on the poor and needy.

Using music as a manipulation technique is pretty old hat, but still effective. On The *X Factor*, the Pavlovian stimulus is usually the guitar bridge from Coldplay's *Fix You*, building up in the background as Louis Walsh holds a talent show hopeful in suspense. The build-up to our introduction to Cheshire bad boy businessman Roger Cashmore was use of Human League's *The Mirror Man* as he boarded a private jet.

Slumdog Entrepreneur follows a not dissimilar format; fish is placed out of water, fish faces challenges that are unusual for a fish, fish triumphs over said challenges whilst being filleted into a juicy portion of telly. Specifically, a rich person goes undercover among poor people, decides which of them are the most deserving, and helps them.

There was no such danger of that happening with the first instalment of *Slumdog Entrepreneur* last night. As hatchet jobs and personality assassinations go, you couldn't quite beat the treatment of not so jolly Roger Cashmore, an IT entrepreneur and property developer from Alderley Edge, a village nestling in Cheshire's footballer belt.

Maybe there is a parallel universe in which loud and bawdy business people with questionable taste are revered and are more kindly thought of than Cashmore. But not here. Our first view of him was as he was about to board his private jet to Cannes to attend a property conference. It got steadily worse, and we then saw him and his perma-tanned friends comparing their £100,000 watches and discussing tax evasion strategies.

Then he's at the poolside of a lavish beachfront hotel with various people talking up his skills, including one woman who runs an escort agency shipping out prostitutes from Cheshire to Cannes for the conference, and describes him as one of her best clients. If you still liked him at this point, what you then saw will have made you foam with rage.

Cashmore, 39, has made a huge fortune from a rather vaguely described IT business, but he seems to be a man without a single moral scruple about business. He extols the virtues of blood diamonds, animal experiments and proudly boasts he'll invest anywhere "except a country ending in 'stan'."

The worst of it is, like a David Brent without the self awareness, he seems to think he's a natural performer.

But when the action switches to east Lancashire, and Cashmore is sent to help out at a rundown community facility, we really get to delve into the dark heart of this utterly dreadful man.

The Lancashire Lifeline project matches reasonably good business propositions with mentors. Some we see have seen money flowing into some imaginative retail offerings. Run by Tony and Margaret Branagan, two kindly Christians in their sixties, who Cashmore seems to ignore completely, he instead takes just two potential recipients. A pretty young single mother called Kaylee with a diploma in business studies who he suggested should effectively turn to prostitution and lap dancing. While Norman, a rather rough and streetwise market trader was offered investment to set up a "whites-only taxi service". Ku Klux Kabs, anyone?

If TV likes its villains, then in Cashmore it had one ready-wrapped with a ribbon. Heroes weren't hard to find though. The quiet dignity and disgust of the local people was evident.

The programme left a feeling of real uplifting bravura, but also raging anger. Here in the darkest and poorest places are people with talent and ideas, while the greedy rich bastard from down the road seemingly has none. Life just isn't fair.

We're better than this: fury of local church charity couple

A local charity is claiming it was misled by TV producers into opening its doors to humiliation and ridicule by a millionaire businessman.

Tony and Margaret Branagan's social enterprise, Renew Lancashire, was the location for a documentary this week in which a millionaire technology and property tycoon from Cheshire humiliated clients of the charity.

Mr Branagan claimed the producers made him promises about the programme and its intentions which were not kept.

"We were told the programme would be a way of getting support and help for some of the people in our community who have business ideas. Instead it became a tawdry game show in which a wholly unsuitable so-called investor just insulted everyone. I feel we were set up."

And another estate resident has slammed Cashmore's offer of support for a whites-only taxi service as a disgrace. Norman Bodell, a martial arts instructor and car mechanic said: "He seemed to think we were nothing better than street scum. And the producers kept trying to trick us into using racist language. If he comes round here again, I'll knock him out."

Residents insist the *Slumdog Entrepreneur* show was one-sided and purposely focused on the negatives. Some accused the broadcaster of encouraging local people to look more menacing than they actually are.

Councillor Jim Iley said: "As someone who has lived around here for the past fourteen years, I am horrified. They chose us as an easy target.

"Constituents tell me of young lads being asked to pull their hoods up "for effect", and working people being edited out simply because they work. I despair if this is true."

Daily Mail

I wanted to go on television to promote my new business idea but was treated like a prostitute by racist and sexist millionaire

A young mum who bared her soul on national TV when she needed help to start a new business has slammed the millionaire businessman who tried to make her take up lap dancing and prostitution.

The documentary *Slumdog Entrepreneur* saw would-be businesses being supposedly matched with a real-life corporate big hitter and being given mentoring and advice. However, Kaylee Keeley claims the programme makers exploited her and made her look cheap.

Kaylee, 24, was outraged when millions of viewers showed Roger Cashmore belittling her attempts to start her own dance studio to take advantage of the Zumba craze that is currently sweeping America. However, Cashmore suggested she and her friends perform saucy dances for him and his millionaire Cheshire pals.

Her anger comes as the community business trust participating in the show claims it was never told the name of the programme would be *Slumdog Entrepreneur* and that they would have never taken part if they knew it intended to portray life on an estate in Lancashire as racist and miserable.

The voiceover of the programme described the estate as 'one of the most deprived places in the country' and noted that 'on average, per person, had one of the highest welfare bills in the country'.

Mrs Keeley, as well as other estate residents and local councillors, has now hit back.

She was filmed holding back tears as Cashmore, who has recently sold his technology solutions business for a reported £50m, laughed at her idea and suggested she strip for a living instead.

"He was just a complete idiot. He had nothing at all to offer me and my business idea. It was a total waste of time. All he wanted to do was show off his cars, watches and private jet and make me feel nothing better than a prostitute.

"I have a business studies diploma and have raised money for a franchise of dance studios, but he didn't even listen to what I was saying."

But she also slammed the television producers for presenting her as a down-at-heel single mum. "I have a baby, but I'm married and I went to college. It just suited them to make us look poor."

Crains Manchester Business

Tax Avoidance Leads To Cut-Price Indian Takeaway

By Simon Binns

A deal announced in April to acquire Manchester-based IT solutions and technology security company RC Solutions by Indian conglomerate Chunky's was sparked by the Government's changes to the capital gains tax regime.

Roger Cashmore and another director sold RC Solutions to Chunky's London LLP Group in a deal which was "said to be worth up to £75m," although it was made clear that an element of this was based on the firm hitting future performance targets.

Crains Manchester Business has learned that the deal was in fact sold for just £16m, according to documents filed at the Indian Stock Exchange. At the time of the sale the business was earning pre-tax profits of £1,611,000 on a £32.4m turnover.

The initial payout to the RC directors — including Cashmore and his business partner Richard Thornton-Chambers — was just £8m, with no mention of any future performance-related further payments.

A lengthy auction took place leading up to the deal. Private equity fund Delphic had announced it had beaten several trade buyers and a management buyout team, and *Crains* understands a deal was on the table ready to sell for the same amount as the Indian buyers who have also purchased several food industry and engineering businesses in Europe.

Cashmore has claimed he is to take over North West Counties Football League Club Wilmslow Wanderers and launch RC Aviation, a helicopter and private jet leasing business.

Cashmore and his fellow directors began talks about selling the business to reduce the potential tax hit shortly after Chancellor Alistair Darling announced the CGT changes in last October's pre-budget report. "Why should the government take more of the money I have earned than I do? The problem with this country is that entrepreneurs have to pay tax at all," he said.

Cashmore is considering moving his new business ventures to the Isle of Man to avoid any further tax penalties.

RC Solutions was advised by Wayne Bellamy of the Manchester office of boutique advisory firm Endean and Bellamy, who is now advising Chunky's on European strategy as the acting deputy chief executive of RC Solutions.

How-Do – **media news from the North West**

Ashling Mahon has launched her own PR and events company Ash and Cash, backed by disgraced tycoon Roger Cashmore. She already has her work cut on a major crisis management project after her business partner and client was featured making a fool of himself on TV programme *Slumdog Entrepreneur*.

Her other clients include RC Aviation, Cashmore's new helicopter leasing company; Cash4Business Fund; The Cashmore Foundation and the Martinez Property Group.

Denise Ripley, of Ripsnort PR and now deputy chairman of RC Solutions said: "We wish Ash luck in her new venture. She'll need it."

In a statement, Chunky's said: "Roger Cashmore has our full support."

2 Comments:

Anonymous:

"What a prick."

Anonymous:

"This will end in tears. Cashmore has not only made a complete twat of himself on national television, but he's sold his business and started getting involved in things he knows nothing about."

So, the week got progressively worse.

Hookers, footballers and millionaire punters: the sleazy world of escort sex in Cheshire's golden triangle

Football star Jesu Bravado is to be quizzed by his club officials after he was secretly filmed romping with pals and prostitutes in his Cheshire mansion.

The five girls were all on the books of Maxine May's high class escort agency Edge Escorts and were hired to party with the players.

The girls spent around six hours partying in the pool, Jacuzzi and changing rooms with Bravado, his team-mate Julio Grande and several other men.

The girls took a series of photos inside the house on mobile phones. One even videoed and snapped South American midfielder Grande naked apart from a pair of boxer shorts. The stars laid on booze for the party as they cavorted with the girls, leaping in and out of the pool in the early hours. Some of the girls went skinny-dipping.

The girls all work through Alderley Edge-based Edge Escorts.

Their website brags: "Edge Escorts is the freshest and fastest-growing agency in the North. We pride ourselves on running an honest and efficient escort service. Whether you want companionship in the privacy of your own home or hotel, or a business or pleasure trip away, we have the right companion for you. You will find all of our escorts to be beautiful, seductive, fun and accommodating.

"We realise that privacy is of the utmost importance. When making a booking with us, any details you provide are kept in the strictest confidence and are only stored until the end of the booking."

Madame May was seen on TV's *Slumdog Entrepreneur* bragging about how she shipped prostitutes to Cannes to service business men attending a property fair in the swanky French resort.

Next week the *News of the World* will exclusively lift the lid on the tycoons and business big-hitters who use the services of the agency, as well as the lengths they go to in order to obtain sleazy paid-for sex services.

A *News of the World* reporter posing as a wealthy visiting businessman has obtained details of the clients of the agency. Our man was told by May that footballers and company bosses use the agency, and that the girls are generally students looking for extra cash or are professional women looking for no-frills sex for money.

Our man was offered full sex with any of the girls on May's books but made his excuses and left.

So, you will not believe the panic this has caused around Alderley. Everyone reckons they're getting blown apart by this tart. There are lads in their houses this weekend sweating, I can tell you. Me included, especially as this slapper was with us in Cannes gobbing off about who her clients are and what they get up to. On TV! And that tart that Foster shipped back to the house, she was one of them, obviously.

It could have been so much worse. I was lying low after the programme had gone out, Serena in tears and throwing a proper wobbly at me. So I'd fucked off to Banus with Chris and Rob from Taurus and their crew. Some bloke calls me saying he's a *News of the World* reporter, asking me if I'd like to comment on the story they're planning to run about me using brasses. Obviously I thought it was a wind-up by Martinez or someone. And before you say, "they're like the pigs in pork pie hats, all cockney accents and gor blimey..." well no, actually, this journo speaks like he went to Eton and is related to the royal family.

Polite as anything, he says: "Obviously you know you were filmed with Maxine May," then reads out what he intends to write.

"May was filmed with Alderley Edge property developer technology tycoon Roger Cashmore, whose racist and foul mouthed rants on the TV show *Slumdog Entrepreneur* left a young woman in tears and provoked anger amongst locals on a rundown estate in Lancashire."

I'm not having this. "Stitched up mate. Here's a fucking story for you: how TV companies twist what they say."

"Yah, yah. Listen, we've obviously got Madame Maxine on camera confirming she was shipping her girls to Cannes for a property trade fair where they entertained regular punters away from their families, including you."

"Not true. Print that, mate, and you're in big trouble." There's a pause on the line before he laughs.

"But we have it all there."

"Mistaken identity, pal. Yes, she was out there, but you can't trash my reputation any more. I never touched her, or any of her skanky hookers. Not my style, pal."

He continues: "Listen, you don't cover your tracks very well. We have transcripts from a website where punters review prostitutes. And there's one regular punter, using the codename 'Hummerman', who posts reviews of his liaisons with these ladies on the Punter Posts web forum.

"Would you like me to relay one to you?"

He reads it out. It's not even well written; how could it possibly be me?

"Always a good service from Edge Escorts, clean girls, fun and experimental. Tanya entered the room just as I had finished my shower, very chatty and open personality. Opted for the talc massage which was wonderful. My turn to please Tanya so teased and probed down below, said yes to EATY and seemed to enjoy the attention. Tanya then returned the favour with some OWO which had me holding on for dear life, and on with the raincoat and some cowgirl, the sight of Tanya bobbing up and down had the desired effect as I could hold on no longer. Chatted and rested – almost a GFE - before round two started. I was convinced the old man wasn't going to play at this point but somehow Tanya made him stand to attention again, reverse cowgirl, 69, doggy and ended up letting go again in missionary. Finished off with FF and with COF. Throughout the hour Tanya had kept eye contact and kissed the whole hour. Just what the doctor ordered."

I just laugh, though obviously I don't point out that I don't do blobs and wouldn't be likely to write about it either. How fucking stupid can you get?

"Obviously we won't be printing that in full as it refers to sex acts too disgusting to describe in a family newspaper. But that entry was written in the name Hummerman, and is it true that you drive a bright green American style 4x4 Hummer?"

"So fucking what? It's not me."

So this fucker needs stopping, obviously.

Do you know what Ash said? Seriously? Yes, that shite about not reading your coverage, but weighing it? No news is bad news. And it's an opportunity. Fuck me, if I didn't own the business with her I'd sack her on the spot, but right now she's probably the only hope I have left. She told me she was on the case and that I needed to get a lawyer. No shit Sherlock.

So the phone is red hot. I've had mates texting taking the piss. Some saying I came across well on the telly, others laughing at the News of the Screws trying to nail me as Cheshire's number one Tom. That needs sorting pretty damn quick.

To be honest, I was still fairly pissed off about the comments on that message board, but this has just led to open season on me and now we've got the gutter press sniffing around. Is that what people are saying about me? And that stuff that Binns printed about the true value of the deal, that starts to make me look really bad. It's one thing to get screwed over on a deal, it's another to have the cat get out of the bag and have everyone know that me and Rick are nowhere near where we should have been.

I can't have all that bad PR causing problems for me with the Taurus boys. Was I good enough for the dosh for the film and games tax schemes, could I afford to chip on their next funding round? The heat is very much on.

If anything, this stuff with the prozzies is actually easier and more straightforward to sort. It's just fucking wrong. How the fuck can they print shit like this?

I can't show my face in Manchester, I'll get slaughtered, and probably papped coming out of San Carlo (that's if they even let me in). But this is when you realise what a safe haven Alderley is. Your neighbours just look out for you. People give you the look that says they know, and it doesn't matter. As long as you can stand your round in the Bubble Room, all is well.

First call I made was straight after the Screws had been on. I belled from the runway in the Lear Jet at Malaga airport to bend the ear of the brief that got me off last time, Freddie Derbyshire. He must think that meeting me is fucking Christmas. Who'd have thought, eh?

He says that suing the papers isn't his thing, but that he reckons I should use some bird who he's heard is good at this kind of rap.

I tell you what, just give me some fucking bloke who can talk common sense. I've had it up to here with fucking bitch business women who talk in riddles and have no grasp of reality. Surely Halliwells have a couple of bruisers who can sue the TV lot, and scare off the press pack?

Bellamy rings and I break the habit of never listening to messages. He leaves a voicemail to say the fucking chicken munchers want me to get my arse over to India to explain it all. Obviously I won't be doing that, but I need to get away and lie low somewhere.

My driver Ray meets me at the private terminal. The Taurus boys are looking bemused, fucked and bombed after the utter mauling their bodies have taken from a weekend of debauchery. Me? I'm so fucking angry and pumped up on rage I can take on the world, hangover and shakes or not. Eventually this will hit me, but I'm steaming.

I'm not best pleased to crash through the doors of my own house, cold and empty with a note from Serena, suggesting that the scumbag journos have been in touch with her already:

Dear Roger,

I don't know how much more of this humiliation I can take. You have really embarrassed me this time and you have a lot of explaining to do. Any right-minded woman in my position would divorce you on the spot, but I don't believe that would be a financially astute thing to do. We're supposed to be moving into our new home this summer. Plus, I want to think things over for a while.

I've gone to California on the trip I told you about. I'll be away for four weeks and think we need to have a serious sit down and talk through all of this when I get home.

S

And in the middle of all of this, with all the shit piling on top of me, my wife heads for fucking Hollywood. We've got the cash flow disaster of the builders stopping work for a week. Foster says his bank have said they can't fund him any more at their end. He says Bobbi Armani is putting together an investment syndicate to fund the option on the land around the football club in Wilmslow, but that the club isn't worth it.

Basically, you can't pick up a paper or turn on the news these days without some crap about the banks in all kinds of shit. And the Paddy ones are in a particularly bad state, especially the one he's in hock to.

223

So I'm basically now paying them out of my back pocket now. What a fucking liberty. We owe the Bogtrotter Bank £4m, but they were cash flowing it, we were going to satisfy the loan, secured against the houses once we'd moved in and obviously sold the old place. I can draw down on one of the Isle of Man accounts, cash in the AIG bonds, but I can't bottle it on the investment I've piled into the Taurus film and computer games fund. I can't even contemplate it, but the only liquid cash source I have right now is from my stake in Tosh Crime Inc, formally known as RC Aviation and unofficially the biggest criminal money laundering operation in Cheshire. The access on the bank cash is three months to get the proper rate of interest so I'd rather juggle what I've got here.

I keep stopping myself and asking the same question. This can't be happening. This simply isn't right. My world is falling apart.

We can't just chuck the keys in and stop, but it's starting to look like a nightmare. It's so near to being finished that Foster even suggests we rent it out or use it as one of his show homes.

So, I'll either have to pay it in one go, or bridge it at some godawful rate of interest; something horrible above base. This is depleting my cash, there's no income while the helicopter's getting tarted up, which means we now need to get the house on the market, All the estate agents are saying the same thing - Stuart Rushton, Stopps, Gascoigne Halman - the market isn't looking too bright at the minute, buyers are sitting on their hands.

Ash comes up to the house and I'm in a right fucking state. Pacing up and down. Martinez is at the door as well, but his car isn't.

I scream and shout at her for a while. Martinez steps in. "Roger, mate, it's not her fault. How can we sort this?"

"You mean, who can we kill? Believe you me, I know someone who would do that." Fuck it though, this is serious. It's been an hour since I called Freddie Derbyshire and he's still not got back to me. I'm just about to ring him and tell him to go and fuck himself when my phone goes.

"Roger, it's Freddie, Amanda Webb is going to ring you."

"Who?" Not another fucking bird after my wedge or trying to wind me up.

"She's a feisty young thing at DNT Solicitors, specialises in this kind of thing, worked with a few high profile celebrities."

Within ten minutes of me ranting and raving and Ash fielding more calls from journalists, I've got this lawyer bird on the phone, sounds young as well, and as much as I always like young skirt around me, this isn't the time, surely Freddie wouldn't have me over by palming me off with a junior on something as serious as this. It takes ten minutes to run her through it and within an hour we've got another guest at this party.

In quick time Ash has set up a website blog page called *Slumdog Lies* with a full rebuttal of everything that turned me over in the programme; taking them head on. She says this is what that nutter from RyanAir does, which seems fair enough. Martinez is making himself useful by making cups of coffee, answering the other calls that are coming through on my mobile, most of them abusive, but some supportive.

To look at, this young lawyer bird is alright facially, blonde, blue eyes. I can't tell if she's fit as she's wearing fucking pyjamas, or some fucking posh bird's version of a shell suit, the scruffy cow. As I explain the basis of the case she has to build she doesn't appear to be listening, and at first I think I've been chucked another clown.

"I don't use prostitutes, the rubbish on the TV programme was a stitch up and that everyone is going to get it. Are you fucking listening?"

"So, let me get this right. Are you saying you never said the comments attributed to you in the TV programme?"

"Yes, I said them, but they made me look bad the way they put them together. Some of it was just a laugh."

"That won't wash. That will be almost impossible to prove libel. It could go to the regulator, but that will take a long time. Suing TV companies over how they made you look is very difficult. Presumably you signed a release form?"

"What? Some piece of paper that said I agreed to go on the programme, yes, I did that, they said it was standard stuff."

"Well, we really have to forget it then. And all of the TV reviews and how you made the other people feel, that's all fair comment I'm afraid."

"But I never said we should call the cab firm 'Ku Klux Kabs': they completely made that up. I want to sue them, all of them, buy their companies, sack them, grind them into the dirt, kill their families, their friends, their friends' families. Then some more people they barely know. Hit them with everything we've got, but we need to stop the News of the fucking World."

Ash is writing it all down and adding it to her website.

"OK. Calm down. So, this story they want to run is completely wrong?"

"Yes."

"They will claim justification. That's their first defence."

"That woman, I have never paid her, her agency, or her whores for sex. It's wrong. That rubbish from that website isn't me. It's just some bloke who drives a Hummer. In fact, there's fucking loads of them round here. It's mistaken identity.

226

"And this scabby-faced slag, she pops up in Cannes, at some party. Foster was talking to her. I thought she was a property agent, or something."

"They will almost certainly claim justification, they may even have evidence from this woman, which they will claim is her word against yours. At the moment, given what happened with the TV programme, you'd be hard-pressed to find a jury that would be sympathetic to you. And if I'm honest, it would be a hard case for us to build."

At this I want to hit the fucking roof, that just because everyone else thinks you're a twat, then they can just make stuff up about you, just like that. It's insane. But I don't, despite being a bag lady with eyeliner, she's alright. I feel calm, reassured, angry and ready for war. She even uses the 'we and us'. As I listen to her I see Ash and Tony working away on my behalf, him on the blower, her writing a release, a statement and building a list to distribute it to.

"But there is no evidence, and if they want to risk ruining my life by claiming something against the word of a prostitute then I'm going to clear them out."

It dawns on me that Foster could probably shed a bit of light on all of this, but he's in Thailand. She's sucking on the end of her pencil, deep in thought, and I'm not sure she's heard a word I've just said. But what she then says starts to make sense and says it all in a manner that I find, well, soothing.

She's only been spread out over my kitchen table for an hour and already she's created a vortex of chaos; post it notes, cuttings from papers, legal pads, bits of paper with cases on them, stained with coffee and all sorts of shite. She then reaches into this woodpile of mess and pulls out a small notebook, scribbles something down and starts to speak.

"There might be another way," she says. "Irrespective of whether you have done this or not, we could apply to the High Court in London for an injunction preventing this newspaper, and any other, from naming you or revealing anything to do with you as a breach of privacy."

"So we don't get a denial, but we stop this. I'll take that. I just want it stopped. How does it work?"

"Let me read it to you."

Her note she's reading from is scribbled on a napkin – fucking mental.

"We'll apply for an interim injunction which restrains a person from publishing information which concerns the applicant and is said to be confidential or private and from publicising or informing others of the existence of the order and the proceedings."

I nod along, making sure I understand what we're about to do.

"We make it about privacy and make them go away for good? Is that right? Can we actually do that?"

"Yes we can," she giggles. "Yes, we bloody well can. So basically, we stop them publishing the story and from even referring to the existence of what we have done," she says, making it all sound so simple.

Ash looks on impressed. "Wow, she says, that's not just an injunction, it's a super injunction."

On the Tuesday morning, after a frenzied 24 hours of non-stop litigation and legal argument, marital breakdown and corporate catastrophe, a courier arrives at the house at eight.

Inside is a one page letter on the familiar RC Solutions headed paper.

Dear Mr Cashmore,

I regret to inform you that your employment with RC Solutions is terminated immediately for the following reasons:

- *Gross misconduct in respect of breach of confidentiality of parent company financial position to our bankers.*
- *Misrepresentation of financial performance.*
- *Failure to comply with the company dress code.*
- *Unauthorised absence.*

It is essential that you return all company equipment you may have at home. Your final day of work will be last Friday. You are not entitled to receive any outstanding benefits.

You are also reminded that your restricted covenants prevent you from working for any competitor for a period of 2 years from the date of this letter.

Thank you for your time at our company and best of luck to you in the future.

Respectfully,

Denise Ripley
Deputy Chairman and group HR director

July 2008

FTSE falls to 5000. The US government takes control of mortgage lenders Freddie Mac and Fannie Mae in a deal costing $200bn.

When your luck is against you, you start to find out who your friends are. Bellamy doesn't return calls. Fuck him. He's dead to me. Anton Wilcox, who always likes to gossip and doesn't have a loyal bone in his body has gone to ground on me. I am now officially at war with my old company.

Amanda Webb seems to have fought off the tabloids for now. All has gone very quiet on that score. The News of the Screws ran some poxy piece with the acne-scarred whore from Alderley that was so bland and tame you'd barely even know it was about sex. They striped up some actor off the telly and repeated the same old crap about the footy players. We seem to have had a result on that score. All I have to worry about from her is a bill.

Bobbi Armani has vanished, which isn't that unusual. More than once I've been sat in some bar somewhere expecting him to rock up, and he just doesn't show. Lays low for a while, then comes back. Nothing is ever mentioned. We even call it, 'doing a Bobbi'.

Honestly, I just don't get him. Even leading up to all the bollocks on the telly and the mauling I got in the papers, he'd been behaving very strangely indeed. Even by his standards his bullshitting had been getting completely out of hand. One day I was by Piccolino in Manchester and he's in that seat by the window with this bloke I've seen around and about, Jimmi Barnes, this lad who's into radio and media and what have you, who Armani says he's backing for some new punt.

I'd been having a sensible coffee across the road in Starbucks with this lad Phil Jones from Brother, the Jap printer mob. He seemed pretty clued-up for a salaryman. But he lost me when he told me the latest thing I should be getting into is some shite called Twitter. It's like sending joke texts to all your mates at once, but you build up a "social following". It'll never catch on. It always surprises me how some supposed sensible people can get so easily taken in by the latest gimmick.

Bamboozled by all of this, Barnes taps on the window and beckons me in. "Come and have a glass of wine," he says.

I pop in, and Armani's on one of his rants about this deal he's doing with Barnes to create the next big thing in media and radio or something.

"So, this guy, right, gets his lawyer on. He wants these warrants. Do we have proof of funds? Do we have proof of funds? Have you seen this watch? Have you seen the latest issue of *EN* magazine – the best deal I ever did. I tell him Roger, 'that man is like my major backer.'"

He means me. Using my name to open doors and do scams. Unbelievable. Is this how low my reputation has slumped?

He keeps taking calls and interrupting Barnes with questions. He says he's making plans to go to Dubai to meet this lad from Bahrain who's got this property deal in Bhutan, and is buying some sheep station in the middle of Australia, and do I want to meet him. My head is spinning with all this nonsense. And that's what it is, nonsense. I think back to all the things he's ever said to us, all the businesses he's claimed he owns.

"I'm hosting a reception with Lord Trafford at his house. Great friend of mine. We met at Sandy Lane."

This I know for a fact is rubbish, he's never even been to Barbados. You'll be talking about some business, a hotel in Abersoch, or an office building near Manchester Airport. "Yes, I own that," he'll say.

Out of the corner of my eye I notice Barnes crouching under the table with a bottle of screw top white wine in a Tesco carrier bag, topping their glasses up and playing up to Bobbi Big Bollocks and his stream of bullshit.

The only reason I'm giving him the time of day is he's part of the Wilmslow Wanderers syndicate – and he reckons he's got some Arab investors into the land. It's probably all bollocks, but these are desperate times. Worryingly he says all is going well on the Wilmslow land deal and that Foster has paid the facility fee to unlock the money, another step on Foster's slow slide into destitution.

Martinez takes my calls, we chat, we swear about people we don't like, bankers for the most part, but he's a hardworking lad with his own business to run as well. He's being a bit coy, but he's obviously ratting another married woman as he's lying low on the fanny front.

The slightly better news is that the trip to Ibiza has done me no harm at all with the Taurus boys, who I reckon can get us out of this scrape. I've joined one of their syndicates to buy some 'contracts for difference' – basically taking out a small loan to make a one-way bet. Always a winner. We all made a nifty £35K on the last punt, so we're rolling into the next, which should become closer to a mill, all going well.

It works like this: Whack £100, 000 into the market, it goes up 10 per cent, and I make £10,000. Big fucking deal. Now if I stick that full £100,000 into a CFD syndicate and it goes up 10 per cent then I make another £100,000. That is what I call a deal.

That's why I love these boys. There's a great fund that's building holiday resorts in the Caribbean that they're getting me into as well and they've let me join another tax scheme, something to do with computer games this time. Basically, it's a tax write-off of any losses. There's also a brilliant fund to invest in South American footballers and what their future transfer values are going to be. Get a share of a decent one and the returns are phenomenal. And if we get our shit together, it could all come in very handy indeed for Wilmslow Wanderers, which we're going to need every bit of help we can with that now Foster's bank have fucked off.

This whole Wilmslow Wanderers thing is starting to bore me, to be honest. What started out as a property deal to split a load of land from some tuppenny ha'penny football club has ended up as a giant pain in the arse. And, as Sidney says, it's hardly consistent with being serious at a time when I have to find things to make me money, not just entertain me.

Me and Foster still own title on the land, but we have a charge over it by a bank which has no money. At the moment it has no potential for new houses, no leisure complex, no boutique hotel. Just shit football. A crooked industry dominated by the greedy and the vain. Now that Foster is desperate he's even entertaining the idea that Armani can actually come up with some cash to develop it properly, except he's gone right off the radar.

All me and Foster need to do is split the title and the registration of the club from the property and the development rights and, as long as we've started it and got the outline permissions, we flip it to Peter Jones and his sons over at Orbit, or someone like that. I mean, genius. What could possibly go wrong with a combination like that? But we would still be left with the obligations of running a football club.

And the lovely Ash is always there, but at least I'm paying her, our fortunes are intertwined and she knows she has a lot riding on rescuing my tattered reputation.

To be fair, her first piece of advice from a PR bird with her own business is pretty good. Do nothing. Lie low. Say nothing. But presumably the client carries on paying the retainer. It's like the other tactic I've heard her using – "we can rebuild a key relationship with a target media, but it will take six months" which means, pay us, and on month four we'll take some ungrateful journalist for lunch, or the football, and she tells her client he's back on message. Money for old rope.

As for me, she says it'll all die down and they'll be talking about someone else before you know it. The plan is to get bigger opportunities in the long term, she says.

236

Ash's big idea is for me and her to hold a big conference, like the Zeus one, but bigger. Call it the Confidence Convention. You keep reading all the negative shit about the economy heading for a recession, that the banks are clamming up, that the oil is running out and it's a classic case of talking it all down. It's bollocks, and this bloke on the BBC, Robert Peston is popping up more and more with his motivational lectures of doom and gloom. We need a big get-together to cheer everyone up.

The plan she's come up with is to get big name speakers from all over. Yanks, lads I know through business. A few of the Alderley boys. Can't fail. Hire a big marquee at Tatton Park. Get everyone there. I'll see if Paul Heathcote will do the grub.

Yes, Sidney, is that serious enough for you? Does that tick your boxes?

All that helping out the scrotes was his idea, but he says I should have been better prepared and not as quick to make a fool of myself on TV. Me? I don't see what I did wrong. I've been stitched up like a kipper.

Ash has a brainwave to get a few people who've been turned over by the media and have made good: Gerald Ratner, Derek Hatton, Shane Warne, me. Lads who know about bouncing back.

The thing you have to do to get the big hitters excited is make it exclusive, charge a grand a seat, and splash out on some top speakers. Ash was full of ideas, talking about getting all sorts shipped in. Some bird called Julie Meyer, who looks hot, but I can't see the lads I need to buy tickets taking an American bird seriously. Then Ash suggests some bird who's made bras - Michelle Mone – fit and that, but like I said, dancing girls and underwear models can wait for the Christmas party. This is serious.

Jon Moulton won't be invited. I mean I'm sure he's serious enough, but we don't want anyone slashing their wrists. I tell Ash to get Theo Paphitis involved. He'd be great. So would Ian 'Beefy' Botham. It's shaping up to be a top idea.

To be fair, as I stayed in his room in Belfast and had a lot of time to think it through, I thought the best we should shoot for would be President Bill Clinton. What's not to like about him? Didn't start any wars. Shagged his assistants and plenty of others. And he managed to stay married to that Hillary one. There's a lesson I could learn there as well. Have a bit of fun, but there's always something to be said for keeping things stable on the home front.

Raise your profile, make money. Slowly but surely, she says, when it suits your agenda, not theirs.

We're going to have it in the first week of October, a couple of weeks before my annual golf trip to the Algarve with the lads, which this year it's the turn of Caledonian to stump for. It was mine in 2005.

Getting everyone together is sort of high risk, profile wise, but people are starting to say the economy is picking up a bit. I mean, the RBS rights issue went okay.

I tell Ash I love it, "I'll get a few of my top contacts to sponsor it; Volcanic Bank and Halliwells are good for a few quid and they need a marketing push now they're in their smart new offices."

I reckon we could ask Tony "Fordy" Ford over at Ford Campbell. He's a lad who knows a good time and is hard-wired into the more entrepreneurial end of the market. The Taurus boys will sponsor it, no problem. Bauer Millet should stick a few American trucks, Hummers and Alfas out at the front, we could get Ron Stratton to chuck a few grand in. All in all, it is all promising to be a stellar line up of the very best that Cheshire is pioneering.

So all told, she's coming up trumps. The events business, eh? How hard can that be?

But there are acquaintances, mates, fair-weather friends, mates and proper friends. And up there, in a league of his own, is Sidney Silver. For all this is my way of showing him that he was fucking wrong about me not being serious.

He's still got the right hump. He has this habit of calling you and reminding you who he is, asking "remember me?"

But I go and see him anyway because I never regret it. He's actually waiting for me when I get there and bouncing around a bit. None of this hiding in wardrobes. He seems properly rattled.

He peers over his glasses and pinches his face close together in a rabbit expression, the one he always does when he's agitated and is thinking.

"What's going on, Roger?"

"Nightmare, Sidney. It's been a nightmare," I shrug, but before I can pile on the excuses, or even dare to start any self-pity he's on me.

"You need to focus. That television thing was stupid, they can't be trusted. I keep telling you, there are opportunities out there to make money. When I was running things in the seventies we didn't have distractions like this, but we had the unions to tackle. They were always cunning and good at wasting your time, always very articulate and always off to tell the newspapers how badly treated they'd been.

"I learnt then, there's no point trying to play your enemies at their game, you have to defeat them with a single devastating crushing blow, a nuclear weapon, based on information, facts and research. We'd keep files on them all, and we never hired anyone with a black mark. Information is power."

"Sidney, you've lost me, pal. I'm not going to have anyone beaten up…"

"Know your enemies, Roger. And keep your friends close and your enemies closer."

"You mean Serena?"

"She's not your enemy. Get a grip, Roger, but you need to protect your asset position and have a true view of it. I don't think you do. You just scratch around with this 40 by 40 idea. But how much do you really know about these Indians? What are you entitled to? Who are their funders? Their advisers? And why's Serena in America, ask yourself that?"

"Having a holiday, as far as I know."

He looks up at me like I'm a total fool for not realising the blindingly obvious.

He puts his head back down and screws his face up as he writes down a few people he'd like me to talk to, and rings a number and makes an appointment.

His expression changes from wise owl to slightly scary bear.

"He's here. Yes, tomorrow."

He's impressive when he's in work mode, doesn't use five words when four will do.

"I think you've lost sight of who can help you and who can't. So I've made an appointment for you to talk to Mel."

He hands me a piece of paper with a postcode and the name Mel on it, but no further clue as to why or who? A real man of mystery.

Then there's Tosh. I try to avoid him as there's a smell of menace around. It's gone nice and quiet for now.

All of Serena's clients have changed their keycodes, so all that data that may have come from me isn't any use any more, and it looks like I might have got away with it.

Luckily, as England were knocked out of the Euro 2008 footy championships, the arse has gone out of the hooligan airways business for the summer. I just get the odd message on the BlackBerry Messenger thing, the odd quip and the drip of money into the RC Aviation bank account, which now has a nearly a million quid in it.

I'm sipping a cappuccino outside the RBG in Alderley, reading some more legal papers and updates from Amanda. There's a glimmer of hope that the News of the Screws might settle as we've gone in hard and they're wriggling on what their sources were.

There's a couple of leathery old witches who keep looking over, their foreheads smoother than a balloon and their faces with more touch ups than a grand master painting. I know Serena's had a little bit of work done, but with some of these others you have to ask yourself if it's still the same woman. I mean, if you buy a bike and you change its wheels, add new handlebars, replace the frame, the seat and eventually the frame, is it still the same bike? It's a fair question.

It's obvious they're talking about me, and not in a good way. I'm about to go over and offer to sign their plastic tits when I sense a shadow at my side.

"Hello Mr Cash."

"Fucking hell pal, don't do that."

"Been a while my friend."

"Yes, Tosh, how's tricks?"

He looks at me and nods, not saying anything, so I break the awkward silence.

"Moscow worked out well, then. Great trip." He still doesn't speak, or offer anything by way of a contribution. So I carry on. "Great result on the pitch, everyone back safely, no-one got arrested or anything, no planes lost!"

He's smiling like he's waiting for the next bit. He leans in, raising his eyebrows over his piggy little eyes, as if to say, 'and go on…'

"Obviously I was a bit gutted that I didn't get to see the game, but it wouldn't have been as much fun on my own. Those Chelsea lads had overbooked and I, er, I, I didn't want to ask one of them to not go, so I volunteered my seat. Probably for the best given the score."

"That's not what I heard," he says. "But it don't matter. Wankers anyway. As long as we got our money. Don't blame you for being a shitter, Mr Cash. Not this time. Not like I was

241

rushing to get over with that lot. They'd probably have lobbed you out over Poland on the way back."

His expression mellows and he cracks what passes for a smile. I've noticed he only ever does that when someone else is uncomfortable. "No, we've got business to do my friend. I need some leads from you."

Here we go. "What kind of leads?" I say, feigning innocence, hoping he might spare my embarrassment at spelling it out.

"Don't be so fucking clever with me. You know what you're doing. And if you don't, and if you even think about coughing anything to the Five-0, then you're right in it up to your neck on conspiracy."

I wasn't thinking of that, but I was hoping he wouldn't bring it up. I hold my hands up to him defensively, as if to say, well 'as if'.

"I need leads like before. Codes and security layouts. You know, another data stick would do us very nicely. I thought we were in business together."

I scratch my nose and can feel the sweat building up at the back of my neck and under my armpits, I even get a whiff of myself through the Hugo Boss scent I'm wearing. It's a rich clammy smell. It sticks in my nose and I realise what it is. The smell of fear. He can smell it a mile off too and he likes to play me along even more.

"And the wankers behind that TV programme, do you want them slotting?"

"What, like you did to Dan Kay on my behalf? No thanks. I mean, he was a dick and all that, but you nearly killed him, Tosh."

"It's the least I could do for my friend and business partner. It's what I'd do for any of my good pals. Mates, United, wife. In that order."

"All I can say is you must have a very understanding wife, Tosh."

"Well, I used to have." He pauses for effect. It would get a laugh in some bar in Rotterdam on a United away trip, but here it's just surreal.

I can do without all this aggro.

"Look, this isn't really what I'm into. I've given you cover for the away trips through my business, but there's nothing in writing. It's a business in my sole name and therefore, legally, it's my money just sitting there. Let me just transfer it into an asset for you, a house or something. It'll take a while, but you need to start making it work for you. And you need security of ownership. If anything happened to me have you thought about how you'd access that capital? What's to stop me just taking it all out?"

"Why would you do that Mr Cash?" Everything he says has menace to it. Every sentence tinged with violence and the quiet threat of destruction.

"Having you look after all that money for me is safer than in a bank. I mean, you read the papers don't you? Don't go moving it around, we know where to make the cash deposits in small notes in different branches every time. It must be piling up quite nicely now, yes?"

"It is, but this is a messy horrible business. There are nicer ways of earning a few quid. Please."

I don't like grovelling. Yet this is another new low. What I've become, a stark and horrible slide from a year that started so promisingly. At least no-one's here to see this one.

I either need to cut him into something more lucrative, up the ante of money making, or this just spirals into something far, far worse. He knows I'm a gateway to even more booty for him.

"What? You mean like translating my book into Russian?" he laughs, dismissively. "That made me about a grand. And they'll be pirate copies all over Russia now, anyway. No respect for copyright law these Russki hooligans. What is the world coming to?

243

"Come up with something better to do, and somewhere for me to start cleaning up so I can go legit, but until you do, then I have to stick to my core business. But, you know the score with the Old Bill all over me. I need to gently ease my way."

I'm trapped. Trapped and gripped by this monster as surely as I was when he'd make me start a fight at school with some other kid over something and nothing. As trapped as when he'd draw me into plans to extort dinner money out of weaker, softer kids, storing the cash he'd nicked in my locker at school. Holding his bag while he headbutted someone or when I'd be striding two places behind him when he was offering out the so-called hardest lad at a neighbouring school.

A light bulb goes off in my head as he's talking about his plans and trotting out some dubious excuse for what he does, like he's some latter day Robin Hood. But sometimes you can solve two problems at once by putting them together. Not always, but you can now. Call it opportunism or strategic thinking, or just getting lucky.

"Tosh mate. How would you like to own your very own football club?"

High above Manchester, off a motorway exit I've only ever driven past, down lanes where only tractors seem to go and down tracks that aren't even on satnav, there's a place where my luck just might be beginning to change.

All there is to see is a farm with a collection of abnormally large satellite dishes where you'd usually see a tank full of liquid shit. There's a car parked outside, a dirty great black Range Rover, which unusually doesn't have personalized plates. You wouldn't get away with that in Alderley. Parked next to it is a smaller white soft top Audi A4, a giveaway chick's motor. Next to it is some other pile of crap, a Ford or something.

It's a brand new refurbished farm house, without a trace of cow shit, cows, horses or even dogs.

A nondescript but passably fit young Doris in a black suit and flat shoes shows me into a kitchen where this older bird sits, obviously ready to make us tea. It's not like an office at all. But in a side room I can hear the hum of technology, key strokes and a bloke's voice quietly speaking on the phone, but not in English.

"Morning love, I'm here to see this geezer Mel Bailey. I'm a pal of Sidney Silver."

The older woman holds out her hand. "Yes, I've been expecting you. I'm Mel, this is Karen, take a seat Mr Cashmore."

There isn't a question. She has little room for humour, but everything she says carries the aura of total certainty to it.

"Are you taking the piss? What's this all about, I thought I was coming to see some ex-copper called Mel who can give me heads up on what my wife might be up to if she divorces me."

"Quite. You can tell us all about what has happened," she says, not trying to justify who she is or what she's about.

We're sat at a big kitchen table and I let it all out.

To start with, I run through the shite with Serena. She's off in America, I show this Mel the note, I tell her I suspect there might be third party involvement (though actually, I don't). I give her heads up on my assets, leaving out the tuck up in the Isle of Man. No-one needs to know about that.

Throughout it all she doesn't take a note, she just stares, her expression a mixture of amusement and authority.

"Right. Mr Cashmore, I am going to tell you three things I have learnt about you today.

"You have personal bank accounts with Caledonian Bank, both here and in the Isle of Man, your balances in both are healthy. As are your accounts with Volcanic Bank on the Isle of Man.

"Two, there are people around you, who you are dealing with, who are not what they seem. You need to be very, very careful."

I nod in that resigned and slightly apologetic way you do. That'll be Tosh then, but how can she know? I thought the whole point of him was that he covered his tracks, that he left no trace.

"And number three, you have in the last hour called three people. Bobbi Armani, Aisling Mahon and Sidney Silver. You left voice mails for 'Armani' and the girl. You spoke to Sidney. You have also texted Tony Martinez saying – "beer in Hale later, pal?"

And she says 'Armani' as you would. Like, is this guy for real? Though to be fair we get that a lot.

"You left a message with Aisling Mahon telling her to call you back as you have some good news about Olaf."

"That's a fucking liberty. You can't do this. How do you know that?"

"Yes I can. And please, language, please. Though I've heard it all before, I am a lady. This is how it works. You need to sharpen up. You are up to your neck in more bad things than you realise. I am going to tell you how much. Apart from Sidney Silver, who I can vouch for personally, I honestly don't think there's a single person in your life who you should trust. Call me suspicious, call me paranoid, but a lifetime in my world it pays to start with 'trust no-one' and work from there. But you're a business man, you know that the only way you can manage something is if you measure it."

"Yes," I say, "I heard that."

"For starters, you are going to protect your password on your mobile phone and change it. Even better, don't use it and certainly don't leave anything on it that you wouldn't want anyone else hearing. If I can access your phone, then others can too."

"Like who? Coppers?"

"Bad people. Journalists, for example."

"You're joking me. Journalists? How does that work?"

"Well, sometimes they do it themselves, sometimes they use so-called private investigators, but it's really because most people don't change the default setting on their passcodes for their voicemails. It's very basic actually. Someone calls your number, checks the voicemail option, gets asked for a security code and depending on the network it's something basic like 1234, or 1111. They then listen to whoever has left you a message. It's what I've just done to all your recent numbers. Plus we have some military-grade surveillance equipment and some good friends in the phone companies."

I sit and listen to this with my mouth wide open. Unbelievable.

My mind's racing now tracing back as to how the *News of the World* found out about the Edge Escorts and how they turned over the football lads. Which phones they might have listened to, which phones and internet connections are in my name.

"Who the f…, I mean. Like, who are you? I just thought Sidney was fixing me up for some private dick ex-copper who was going to work out if Serena's sha…, er, I mean, has third party interest and if I can protect my assets."

She smiles at my rare showing of good manners.

"Thank you. Well, you are half right. But Mr Silver is a good man. He thinks your problems go a bit deeper than that so we're going to provide you with a business risk diagnostic analysis."

"Oh." Sidney eh?

"We can do that and we will, but anyone could find that out. In fact you could, you know, you could just try asking her. That's the first thing we always ask clients in these situations. Just trying talking to each other once in a while. As for who we are, well, I'm Mel and that's all you need to know. We're good. We're fast and we can find anyone, unearth anyone and get to the bottom of any problem that has a data deficit."

"A what?"

"We find things out. Keep up."

"We don't have a website, a brochure or a business card. This is strictly word of mouth. The only direct contact you will have from us is a bank account number where you will transfer our fees. There will be no invoices and there will be no audit trail. But you'll be used to that."

"Very discreet, yes, I've heard of women running discreet business services."

Rather than looking shocked, which is sort of why I said it, she brushes it off. I'm still thinking about the Edge Escorts and their role in this chain of events that got me in this mess with Serena. And what messages I might have got in the past that I would prefer no-one but me to have listened to.

This bird is actually quite clever. She's got a way about her. Posh, bossy, but reassuring. I'm trying to think who she reminds me of. I'll be frank, I didn't know women like this even existed, except on the telly or when they're reading the news. This can't be right.

248

"You don't tell anyone you've been here. Don't tell anyone you've met me, where we are, or anything. I need your word."

"So you're not a private detective, you're a private spook? I get it."

"We're much more than that, Mr Cashmore. We're your guardian angels. Whoever you've been dealing with, whatever you are into, wherever you've been deceived, we can unravel it. If people owe you money, we will find them. We help people and businesses to manage risk. We can't guarantee we'll get your money back, but we know people who can help. We can certainly tell you where it might have gone.

"I will tell you everything you need to know. Give me a month. Leave the country if you want, be completely normal. Don't, whatever you do, do anything out of the ordinary. There's a good chance Mrs Cashmore could have some high street private eye keeping an eye on you and we don't want to attract attention. Certainly don't make any financial transactions for a few weeks."

But that's what I do. I do deals. She can tell what I'm thinking and raises her eyebrows towards me and just says. "For a month, Mr Cashmore."

What was it Sidney said? There are deals to be had and bargains aplenty. You just need to know where to look. And what else was it he said? That I'm just not serious. Well, I feel serious enough at the moment. Seriously pissed off and seriously desperate to make a few more quid and find out who's been having me over.

I weigh it all up, the bullshit, the complications with Chunkys, with my investments, the house, my so-called friends. Getting blanked. Having people whispering behind their copies of *Cheshire Life*.

And what was it that Chinky general once said; 'All warfare is based on deception'. Well, let's have a look at who's who? This is the fightback. Time to work out who is friend and who is foe.

But a thought has gone off in my head. Just an inkling and something that's been gnawing away at me. I call Amanda Webb and ask her about the mobile phone stuff.

"Right, can I just check something with you. I had mobile phones and computers registered to my old company. I had all kinds of people using them, mates and family and whatever. I don't even look at the bills, but what if the press scum were hacking into them and listening to messages? What if that's all they've got? If that's it, not only can they not write a story about me, but they've broken the law to get it. And if they've been doing it to me, who the fuck else have they been on to?"

There's silence on the other end of the phone. And I wonder which Amanda I've just been speaking to. The dizzy bint in her pyjamas, or the sharp legal brain who silenced the beasts of Fleet Street?

"Roger, this is absolutely enormous. I've not been able to prove a case beyond all reasonable doubt, but I have a growing body of evidence to suggest this could be bigger than any of us could possibly imagine. Did you say you have computers and broadband accounts registered to you and that third parties can access them too?"

"Yes, I did," Foster has one, for starters, and I'd bet my last penny that the ratty fucker has been leaving my digital fingerprints all over the dark corners of the internet that he's been whoring around for the last year.

"Roger, let me hit them with that and I'll see what they come back with. Thanks."

I can't believe this mobile thing actually works, so I try it out and call Martinez. It goes to answerphone. I key in the default factory setting and listen. It clicks back and says, "you have 2 new messages. To listen to your messages, press 1."

I press one and it's Martinez's old man in Spain saying, "Hello son. Give your father a call."

I press to listen to the second one and what I hear changes everything.

So, I've got to lie low. I've got to be anonymous and I've got to stay out of the way for a bit. So I head for the Isle of Man. I have to come up with something new. I've got fuck all chance of rescuing it at RC, so it'd be better all round if I just moved. Spain's too far. Too hot and too many gangsters. And Serena wouldn't trust me around the flesh pots of Banus. I wouldn't trust me around them, to be honest.

But what about the tax-free life in the Irish Sea? Close enough to pop back home to Manchester – half an hour from the Airport. Easy access for a trip to the football or a lads' night out. I mean, it's closer than London. Alright, and there's a whole new pool of friends to make and a social scene to dominate with my wit and jokes; they won't have heard them before, and Serena will have a few thick millionaires to trick with her interiors stuff.

And from what I hear, no gangsters, grafters and hooligans. No one calling me a shitter and accusing me of not being serious, but not poking their nose into my business either.

And friends I could do with keeping an eye on who don't betray me. Friends who I can get into business with and not worry that I'm going to get stabbed in the back. I desperately need options.

I mean, they might put cheese on their chips and shit, but it can't be so bad out there. I could even handle having a cat with no tail if I had to.

But the thing about the Isle of Man, right, is it's like stepping back in time. Like some sleepy seaside town would have looked like before it got taken over by chain bars, bling and the thuggish pond life that have made our city centres so unsafe.

As the chopper's still not finished getting done up in all the Bentley gear (and a quick hop over on a private plane isn't worth it for a trip like this) I have to take the scheduled crop duster from Terminal 3.

But unlike the unpleasant experience of queuing up with the great unwashed that I have to endure for public flights (something I don't intend to do again, by the way) piling over to three-legged land is a pleasant enough experience.

I flick through the glossy brochure from the mob who are meeting me at the airport.

Here at Manx Lifestyle Choices, we appreciate that relocating to the Isle of Man is a major move for you and your family and we would like to offer you assistance at every step. The list of "to do's" can seem endless, ranging from the most important – finding the right property to live in or work from, to others such as finding your nearest doctor and dentist or organising your broadband connection and utilities.

We appreciate that the time incurred before and during the move can seem like a major upheaval. We have the local knowledge, availability and experience to make the move far more pleasant and save you considerable time and effort. We also are confident that our enthusiasm and diligence will be the ideal start to your new life here on the Isle of Man.

You kind of know how this is going to work, who they normally deal with, the kinds of places they'll show you for £500 a day. But if I don't show Serena I've gone to the trouble of having this lot show me round, she'll think I've just made it up to keep her sweet. So, it's all part of the masterplan to keep her happy.

Before I get on the plane I call a lad I used to know from round and about, Dougie Barrowman, but he's away in America, his office tells me, which is a shame. Doug was a proper character back in the day, bought the penthouse at the top of Number One Deansgate, ran a tip-top corporate finance business, then started buying up industrial companies. He properly nailed it and now he's doing great things on Craggy Island. Great lad. Shame he's not about for a spot of lunch; I could do with cheering up.

I don't really know Trevor Hemmings well enough to make an impromptu house call but, like Tim Knowles, he's a good normal northern lad who's moved out here. I could do with a social circle with these characters.

I then call this other bloke, some corporate lawyer, Phil Metcalfe, a rugby monster who I've been on golf trips with. He comes on the blower right away and is bang up for some scran, saying he'll book us a table at this gaff on the front.

This driver and a young lad meet me at the airport with a sign with my name on. The young lad is well turned out and posh, no hint of that funny scouse paddy accent they have over here.

The plan is a bit of a whiz around a few hot spots in the morning, before dropping my case at the hotel on the front where I'll be spending the night. Tour in the morning, lunch with Metcalfe, then a few hot spots and houses in the afternoon. And finally, a presentation from the Isle of Man government at some do at their offices.

Smart boy is showing me these villages where we don't pass a single car. An amber light seems to be the sign to slow down, not speed up.

We look at houses, all very nice, but none of them big and grand enough for what we're used to. Tarted up bungalows, mills, farmhouses, all done out with the boards throughout, pale walls, decking, nothing that screams out at you like the classy gaffs in Alderley; no underground cinemas, wine cellars, car ports and wet rooms. All very vanilla. Dull as fuck.

I'm sitting listening to some tax lawyer talking about, you know, tax law, and going out of my mind with boredom. I try and get a hint of life, of fun, of where you might go and get a beer or have a laugh somewhere. He even knows which hotel I'm staying at.

"Yes, how do you know that?"

He looks at the young lad, "there are no secrets on the Isle of Man. It's like a village. What time's your lunch appointment with Phil Metcalfe?"

"Er, you know about that as well?"

"Yes, quite a 'character' isn't he?" and he does that thing that birds sometimes do with his fingers showing the inverted commas around as he says 'character'. I think I'm going to fall asleep with the tedium of it.

"Yes, he called one of the chaps here who he plays rugby with. He's looking forward to seeing you. What time did you say you were meeting?"

I look at my watch and it's 11.30 - only another hour of this - but I lie, hoping even this busy cunt doesn't know my diary that well: "12 o' clock pal, although I've got a few calls to make. But then you probably knew that already."

The tour lad says, "It's only ten minutes away, we can take a drive down to Langness, where Jeremy Clarkson lives. And this afternoon I was wondering if you wanted to take a drive up to the Laxey Wheel?"

"Listen, I'm not being funny mate but, like I say, I've got a few calls to make. I've got the drift; we'll have a look this afternoon. Pick me up at 2.30, alright?"

So, is it just the company so far, the places this shiny corporate salesman has shown me? Or it is that this isn't just a village where everyone knows what you're up to. I mean, we've got that in Alderley. Is it something else, something that obvious. IS IT JUST ME OR IS IT JUST SO FUCKING BORING?

I settle in the window seat of the 'best seafood restaurant in Douglas', which is a bit like a boast from the land of the blind where the one-eyed fella runs things. But from what I remember of Metcalfe, he knows a good time and can root out a 'scene' if one exists.

I hear him before I see him with his big booming voice. Huh huh huh, to some waitress who recognises him and who he shares a laugh with. Everyone else in the restaurant - well, the other two tables that are occupied by old biddies - turns around to have a look. I mean, you can't *not* do, to be fair. He's near as damn it seven foot tall and has a scar across his cheek, big filled-in cauliflower ears like you get with rugby lads and a nose that's had its fair share of breaks.

He greets me like a long last pal, with a massive bear hug, and calls the waitress over to sort us a couple of beers right away. Then he orders: "Oysters, prawns, mixed fish to start; your very best piece of fish with veg and chips for my main, and a bottle of Sancerre please, lovely. And he'll have the same. Huh, huh huh, huh," he roars.

"And can I just say, you look absolutely delightful today, darling. Doesn't she Roger? Isn't she quite the loveliest girl on the whole of the island?"

I nod, sizing her up. She's alright, to be honest, you wouldn't kick her out of bed if she farted. This is obviously his patter. She doesn't look embarrassed, she actually looks flattered. I'll have to try that. I usually just prefer to get them pissed and ask if they sweat much when they fuck. She looks proper dirty as well. Eastern Europeans are. Filth.

"Pole?" I ask.

"She's Czech, mate. Huh huh huh, huh. Her boyfriend did the plumbing at our apartment. Good people."

He's full of stories of golf trips and rugby tours, reminding me handsomely of the banter and loyalty I've been missing for these turbulent and horrible few months. We recall a trip to Majorca where one of the lads took two hookers down to breakfast. The Weetabix of shame. Where a Brazilian monster-whore in Portugal who challenged him to a 'fuck off' saying she would take him on. Crazy times. Even the trip to Banus with the unfamiliar hedge fund crowd was thick with competitive tension over who could do the most drugs, pull the fittest woman or run up the biggest bar bill. Every story was about deals and how much money they'd all made. I mean, I could keep up, but it's hardly relaxing. Just being one of the lads wasn't exactly Hollywood, but it was more fun.

"So pal, you said 'our'. Have you finally settled down?" I ask him.

We've already sunk our first bottle of Sancerre when the starters arrive, so we order another.

He roars with laughter again and bursts into a story about tax-free money, how the girl who brought him over is from here, that her old man is an old school lawyer on the island, so he has to behave himself, that she knows what he's like and needs to keep an eye on him. But that his weekends on rugby trips are as full of drinking and partying on the mainland. It's a good life here.

"How do you manage it? Not being funny like, but you pull some unbelievable tush, mate."

"Be nice to them. Don't think of them as 'tush' for a start. Huh huh huh huh. Hold their hands, smile. Men and women aren't that different. Women enjoy sex just the same as men, just make them feel you're in it for the same reason, mutual satisfaction, not for power or favours. It's not that difficult, Roger."

I'm getting randy and morose listening to his stories and I get him to rattle through some of the women he's been through. And he fills me on what they were like. "Filthy. Shy. Surprisingly dirty. Wild."

We've drained another bottle of Sancerre and he's in full flow. "Anyway, I'm sure a man like you doesn't need sex tips from me. What are you doing here anyway, you thinking of coming to live here?"

I reel off the whole story, which he totally fails to miss out anything as an opportunity for laughter. Chunkys, Bellamy (who he knows), Denise (who amusingly he claims to have shagged), Sidney, Angela's husband, helicopters, the press coverage, the *News of the World,* the deal, the injunction, getting fired off.

"Mate, you should write a book, this is brilliant."

I obviously leave out anything to do with Tosh and the Belfast trip. But another two bottles of wine and a table full of fish later, I'm completely fucked. The driver is at the door of the restaurant and Metcalfe is obviously on a roll from which he cannot be stopped.

"Come and join us pal, we're having a few more." He says no, which means for £500 I got a taxi ride from the airport, a look around some houses and a lecture in trusts from a lawyer, which I've forgotten already.

I cut to the chase with Metcalfe. "Look, where's the action over here? Shall we go and sit in a titty bar for a bit? I've got time to kill before this drinks do at the Isle of Man government at six."

He roars with laughter again. "Roger, there are no massage parlours here, no saunas. Well there are, but they're actually sports massages and actual saunas. No bar has ever got a licence for lap dancing. That's why she brought me over here, keeps me out of the way of temptation. But... huh huh huh huh. This could be our lucky night. I've heard they're doing a few discreet gentlemen's sessions at this hotel along the front."

By now he seems on firing form, talking to everyone, while I'm doing what I always do when I get pissed: I get even more surly and want to stare at tits.

I call Serena and I get the foreign ring tone. Even through the alcoholic haze of destruction from keeping up with a monster like Metcalfe, I work out it must be eight in the morning over there, so I leave her a message, taking on board Metcalfe's guide to life women and everything. "Hello darling, wakey wakey. I hope you're having a nice holiday, hic, I'm planning our future together. Hic. I love you."

I get the bill, at least £200, which I slap down a few fifties and get a load of their Mickey Mouse money in change. We roll into some ale house called the Rovers Return, all full of football stuff, where Metcalfe knows everyone and gets a round in. This time it's a pint of real ale loopy juice they brew themselves.

By the time we're due at the government reception I'm so mortally wankered I can hardly walk. Metcalfe literally props me up as we walk to the government house overlooking some square. The room is full of posh ladies and older blokes in suits. Just as the speeches start, something about welcoming a new breed of entrepreneurs to the community of the island, the room is swaying. My sea legs not being what they were, I find a plant pot to spill my guts into. There's a pause in the speech, something about contributing to the life of the island, and it comes out URRRRRRRRRRRRRRGGGHHHHHHH all over the side of the white wall.

Followed by a roar of "huh huh huh huh huh" from Metcalfe. "I think he must have caught a bad prawn, huh huh huh huh huh."

I wipe my mouth on a red drape that's hanging by the door and edge my way to the back of the room.

Then we're on the street again and heading for this hotel bar with the private dancers that some rugby lads he knows have heard about.

It's dingy and even with the curtains drawn the light streams in. A bird is gyrating on stage to one side while half a dozen lads who greet Metcalfe like a brother are whooping and leering at her. She's nothing special, but then I walk to the side of the dancefloor for a better look and work out why she's only dancing to one side. It's because all down the other side she's limp and partly paralysed and her face looks like she's permanently shocked. She's obviously had some kind of stroke.

The pint of lager that Metcalfe has bought me doesn't do the trick and this time I make it to the toilet and launch another multicoloured yawn all over the cubicle. I don't even return to the room with the spastic stripper and Metcalfe and his pals. Instead, I walk down the sea front with all the early evening joggers and the old dears walking their dogs. And there's me, in a state of utter disgrace. I ask one old woman where the Sefton is and she jumps back from me, the smell of vomit from my shirt and trousers repulsing her while her little dog barks at me.

Bedtime.

In the morning I'm woken by the sound of banging on my door, "Mr Cashmore."

The room is at least tidy, the curtains still open as it was light when I got in. Still fully clothed, I answer the door. My head throbs like never before. Memo to self: never try and match a rugby monster pint for pint, wine for wine, on top of seafood.

There are two geezers in black suits at the door. "Hotel security, sir, we're here to assist you with check out."

"I think I'm going back to bed. It's alright".

"No, Sir, there's a car waiting to take you to the airport. Would you like some assistance, Sir?"

One of the blokes peers over my shoulder at the bathroom, where the bath is splattered with vomit. Otherwise the room is barely touched. I try and piece together the events of the day before.

My suitcase isn't even opened and I've slept in my suit. In the car I get to call Metcalfe. He says he carried me to the hotel as he found me asleep on the promenade.

"You were off your tree, mate, sat on a bench on the front, shouting at these girls asking them for another dance. Huh, huh, huh, huh, huh."

All I can say is: "Uh".

"One of them said to you, "look at the state of you, why don't you go back to your wife and behave yourself?" and you said – huh, huh, huh, huh, 'she's in America getting fucked by darkies'."

I can't even muster an "uh", all I can say is "nooooo."

Once at the airport the driver hands me a letter. Inside is a bill for the repair of a heraldic flag of the House of Keys, which I "fouled", and a curt letter from someone from the Isle of Man government informing me that my invitation to take a place on the "entrepreneurs accelerated relocation programme" has been withdrawn.

Ah, well. Won't be coming back to live here then. Never liked it much anyway.

Even with a raging hangover and a thudding headache, this is a warning shot. I have to get a wriggle on and sort things out for the return of the Queen of Sheba. The new house is nearly finished which has to be good news, as it's all part of the plan to get Serena back onside.

I'd sorted a £400,000 bridging loan, so the work is nearly completed. I can pay it back as soon as I've freed up a load of working capital that's sitting in the bank of Tosh.

Serena's last snagging list was eight pages long, so I've been cracking the whip so it gets sorted once she's back home. Wrong light switches, wrong garden ornaments, the right kind of glass in the orangery, wrong shade of wood for the window frames, (apparently it doesn't match the doors).

One of the benefits of the slump for the building lads is that Foster's crew have fuck all else to do at the moment. He's also knocked the labour costs right down as everyone's short of work.

I've even added a couple of nice touches of my own to make the whole thing look a little bit more permanent, with the Cashmore coat of arms strategically placed in the hallway, engraved on the glass as well as on the gates. It's quality, a Hummer, a Ferrari, a bottle of champagne and - if you look from the right angle - a bare arse. A cheeky touch she's sure to appreciate.

There's been no interest so far in the gaff we're moving out of, but it's early days. If push comes to shove we could always rent it out. United are bound to sign some Johnny Foreigner now they've got the European Cup in the trophy cabinet, and they're always good for the rent.

So basically I'm loading everything on red. Winning Serena round, everything builds up to that, or everything flows from it. Shit or bust, basically. The conference, the lads I can trust, some tasty investment schemes, shoring up my wealth, not halving it, and using whatever the ex-spooks come up with on the gutter press to build a case to rebuild my name as a helicopter tycoon and all-round hard done by victim of media persecution.

Staring over the building site that is now happily becoming the fully-formed work of beauty that will be Cashmore Towers, I realise what a fool I've been, how deluded and occasionally how carried away I've been prone to get. This is it. This is where the lines are drawn. No more trying to prove I'm something I'm not and no more getting led astray.

My phone, which I probably need to upgrade, buzzes into life, the 'Simply The Best' ringtone beeping out and disturbing the builders and grafters, who look up and catch a look at each other.

It's Martinez.

"Now then, fella."

"Tony. What's new?"

"Rodge. Got any plans for late October?"

"Not really. Why?"

"Need to organise a lads' trip, pal."

"Where to? Banus? Portugal?"

"Doesn't matter, but we'll do some golf. Can you sort? I'm off to Spain to see my mum and dad, mate, see you in two weeks. Ha, I'll tell you all about it, long story. Ciao."

Click. With friends like this, eh?

August 2008

Woolworths rejects a bid approach from Malcolm Walker, multimillionaire founder of the Iceland frozen food chain. Plans for the new £3.2m Panacea restaurant and bar in Alderley Edge are announced. 'This is an excellent opportunity to expand the Panacea brand in a unique area with a fast growing social culture. Customers can enjoy our globally-themed menu, well-mixed cocktails and exemplary service in a stylish and upmarket environment,' says boss Joe Akka.

Knowledge is power, or so I hear from Sidney. Funny, I always thought money was, until it starts to look like you don't have as much of it as you thought.

Take my so-called mate Dave Foster, who is seriously on his uppers. Not just with the whores, the clap, the ex and the Happy Meals with his kids and his ant hill in Knutsford. His business is on the brink as well, which means he can't even afford the time or the fare to get up to his nuts in Thai minge to take his mind off it, and possibly bring one back.

This is his dilemma. He has contracts to build houses for rich people. So far, so good. In the old days he'd get a bank to lend him silly amounts of money based on an even sillier valuation. They'd cash flow the development costs. The houses would sell easily and when he did he'd pay the bank back the smaller amount and he'd keep the rest. It was a licence to print money.

Just like my residential buy-to-let portfolio in Salford, the valuations were bent. Dodgy surveyor does dodgy survey, rubber stamped by crooked brief, back hander to muppet at the bank who's targeted on writing as much business as possible. They get letters from estate agents claiming the going rate for a two-bed apartment in this emerging area of City Centre West. It's Salford. You can put lipstick on a pig, you can call it a cat, but it's still a pig.

He's now got three houses he can't sell and he's up to the hilt on borrowings from banks that are beyond their own hilt. In a fit of desperation and rage he even marched up to their offices in Manchester with the site keys, the cheque books, the keys to his office and a shirt off his back. He had the plan to throw them all at them. But there was no-one there. They'd cleared off as well. So now he's dealing with a computer that sends him updates about how much more he owes them.

He could technically sue for breach of contract to two of the intended buyers who've walked away and left him in the shit, but both the blokes went bust. And guess what sector they were both in? Property. Everywhere you look the arse has gone out of the property game. Offices? No-one's leasing, they're all cutting back. Retail? Everyone shops on t'internet now, and the high street is closing before our very eyes. Even Alderley has a few empty units now.

He has two potential lifelines. One is he's gone and spunked £50K on an arrangement fee to set up a facility with Bobbi Armani and his mysterious investor on the football club redevelopment land. But his one sinew of comfort right now is me. That's right. His knight in shining armour. And if all this with Serena goes horribly wrong, it's proper game over.

Men's minds work in strange ways. Ever since Foster's Doris chucked him out it's suited him to weave his own tale that it's a lifestyle choice. The only way he can find to justify himself is that everyone else's marriage is shit as well. As Martinez is better looking and comfortably single, he never particularly rams home that particular line of enquiry as he's a lone wolf. Or was.

Foster is pretty much a dead man walking. I know this, but he doesn't. My bridging loan on our new gaff sees us right, but then I've got to keep the payments and flip it to me and Serena, all being well.

A jowly red-faced runt of a man anyway, all of this has properly messed with his head. I haven't even brought it up with him yet that he was within an inch of being outed as "Hummerman" in the tabloid press. Using my car, my computer and I suspect, my name, to open doors and impress skanky prozzies. What a nice guy I must be, eh? Or maybe I'll just save this one up for a rainy day.

But Foster now needs me and Serena to hold it together. No marriage, no house. No house, no money for him and he's staring down the barrel of bankruptcy.

To be fair, his lads have done a tidy job on the new gaff and though it needs a bit of work on the lawns and stuff, the house is ready to move into. A proper show home. It's stretched me to get there, but all being well, we'll be moving in for the start of the football season. A new lease of life and a fresh start.

Martinez is unusually edgy when I turn up to meet him for a late afternoon sunny livener at the Alderley Bar and Grill. I can't quite make out his expression as he's wearing sunnies. He leaps up from his chair and gives me a proper handshake and a man hug.

"Fella! Good to see you." And he laughs loudly.

"Good holiday?"

There are two birds on the table next to us. A couple of identikit young scrubbers from Macclesfield, or worse, Wythenshawe, out on the pull. You can tell from how they talk and how they look around that they don't belong here, but would love to. They order 'dry white wine' for fuck's sake. They're perfect prey for Martinez, except he doesn't even look over, even though they're both checking us out. Especially as they clocked me cruising outside in the Ferrari, and Martinez has his Maserati key on the table next to his ridiculous Apple iPhone.

One of the slappers gets up to get something from her bag and shows off a midriff and a decent arse. "Look at the arse on that pal. You'd fucking rat one up that in no fucking time, eh?"

"Yes, too right, she's nice," he smiles, but doesn't mean it.

"Come on, let's get stuck into these dirty bitches mate. Serena's away, we'll take them up to mine. What do you reckon? Come on, I'm well up for it."

I only say this because I'm testing him. The old Martinez and the new. Seeing how much he's changed, and why?

He just laughs it off, but it's obvious there's something he's here to tell me. And I think I know what it is.

"So, mate. We going to plan this lads' trip in October? I was thinking Thailand. The minge over there is sen-fucking-sational. There's this multi-storey knocking shop out there in

Pattaya, the Pussycat Hotel. Four Floors of Whores they call it. Absolutely crawling with fanny."

He's shuffling in his seat and looking uncomfortable, playing with his ears and twisting in his seat. So I turn up the sleaze to make it worse for him. "Alright, I know it's a bit far, but I went to Ibiza with these lads from Taurus and a load of London hedge fund boys. We could do that, I'll give the lad a call, he's got it all straightened out over there..."

"I'm bored of all that," he snaps. Something's on his mind and he's struggling to find his moment. "Look, this is what I was going to talk to you about today..."

Before he can say anything Jimmi Barnes rocks up looking rough. He hasn't shaved and he's stinking of stale booze.

"Okay Jim mate, you alright?"

"You lads seen Bobbi?"

"No, not for ages mate, why? What's up?"

"We had a deal to buy a radio station in Majorca for all the expats out there, then link it to a new pop station in Dubai."

You know where this is going. It's got disaster written all over it. I vaguely remember pretending to be interested at one point.

"Yes, I remember it Jim. Nice one, what's happened?"

"It was a mint deal, Rodge. I got a few of the Alderley boys to pile in 10K each, but he said he was bringing in a co-investor, this Arab lad he knows. But he's not been returning calls. They were meant to be putting in a million quid."

He's a nice enough bloke, got some entertaining stories, but he's small fry, to be honest. The fact that Armani has taken him for a few quid is a bit of a surprise, because they were supposed to be mates. He's also given Foster the runaround. It's starting to feel a bit flaky. Even more than you'd expect from him.

"Listen Jim lad, if we hear, we'll get on his case pal."

All this time Martinez has bursting to let rip with the vinegar strokes of his confession, which I know already and haven't hinted at. So I just hit him with it.

"Tony, cut all the bullshit, when were you going to tell me you've been shagging Ash?"

He laughs and wipes his mouth. Clearly unsure as to where I'm going with this. I'm not about to give him the satisfaction of telling him I also know he's got her up the duff. Information I sneaked off his answerphone, a tearful message from her to him telling him about a clear blue line.

"So, you make a lovely couple mate. Chuffed to bits for you. Two of my favourite people getting together. You've not exactly been discreet have you? As far as I'm concerned it's a dream ticket."

His expression is a mixture of relief and surprise and he lets out a rip-roaring guffaw. He'd obviously been building up a little speech he was going to give, thinking they'd kept it a secret. But I wonder how much he's going to let on.

"Mate, I'm in love. She's great, so good for me. How long have you known?"

I tap my nose, and give him a look. "Before you two even met, mate. You don't think I didn't want this to happen, did you? I've known all along," I lie again, and he seems to believe me.

When I heard her voice on his answerphone I was anything but calm.

It was like a rewound video screeching through my head, all the evidence started to pile up around me, Martinez going away for weekends to non-specific locations with unspecific birds. Ash turning up at the Zeus do, with him. Her being known in places I hadn't taken her, like Sam's Chop House. How long has this been going on, under my nose? How many times has she been on the brink of trying to tell me something, but holds back? How Martinez has toned it down lately on the chick front. It all started to make sense.

But more important than anything was the desperate importance I attached to not being made to look a total idiot. In fact, this was a proper piece of 'get real'.

Inside, to be fair, I'm still churning up, but I'm never going to let it show. She was my token bit on the side, for show. True, I was well into the idea of giving her one, who isn't? She's knockout. But it never quite came off, me thinking she was fit, but didn't quite look dirty enough. Or, as they say, she just wasn't that into me.

But as I weighed up the reputational damage that this has done, I had a moment of clarity. Some people think I've been nailing her all this time, but it's always about appearances, not reality. Me? A married man? Surely not. Even Serena suspected, which kept her on the edge, but equally it nearly pushed her too far.

So as I weighed up the balance of forces here, I had a thought, that all of this also neatly plays to my advantage now.

This will also prove to Serena that I wasn't. I mean, how could I? Tony's a mate. What do you mean you didn't know? I was just keeping it quiet. Everyone knew. Not only do I need to tell her that she had a hold of the wrong end of the stick, so to speak, but Ash had her hand on a different stick as well. Gives me an even greater chance of sorting it out with her. The perfect alibi.

Martinez is bluffing about where and when it started. "Well, it started at MIPIM mate. She was shit scared you'd find out and bin her off, but she's really into the business and seeing through everything she's started with you, she's just been worried you'd go mad."

"As if, pal. What do you take me for?" He's always been a good mate. But I have to hand it to him, he's a sneaky fucker. I wonder how long she'll put up him with him when he's had it with doing the same sex with the same bird and temptation catches his eye. I wonder. And when her tits go and her arse drops. We'll see.

"So, why the lads' trip pal? Something else you need to tell me?"

"Er, yes, there is mate. She's expecting. We're getting married, and you know these Irish Catholics. Her old man's only daughter and all that."

There's a routine you have to go through with all this. I've done it so many times with lads in the office who've told me the news and I've had to pretend to be pleased for them. I can't make an exception for this one, even if he is a mate. So I give him the big handshake, tell him it's great news, all that shite.

"Well pal, as long as she sorts out this conference in October we'll be alright. Don't want her popping at that, when's it due. Or do you know what it is yet?"

"Due in February mate, she'll be fine for this. But you know what she's like; she'll be out working away when her waters break. What a girl."

While I'm filling in Martinez on the low key plans for the start of the Wilmslow Wanderers season, he gets his iPhone out – she really has got her claws into him, didn't have him down as a shallow ponce – and sends a quick text, or whatever they do on these toys.

"She's joining us," he smiles. "She's been in Costa, bricking it."

Ash walks gingerly up to us, and I'm straight over to lay it on thick about how pleased I am for the both of them. Funny though, this whole dynamic has changed between us. Mate, mate's bird, also business partner, but she still sort of works for me as I'm the senior partner. But because of Martinez it also means she's got a bit of protection from me, so I can't take out my bad moods on her any more. But business is still business and I need to remind her of that, if anything I need to make it clear that's all our relationship ever was.

After she prattles on about baby shit, patting her belly where this thing is growing inside her and just below her tits which, to be fair, have never looked as good, I switch the chat to matters in hand.

"How's the conference shaping up? We sorted Bill Clinton yet? How are we on numbers? Any press interest?"

"Oh, Roger, let me see, I've been onto Clinton's people, but he's too busy with the election, working for Barack Obama."

I remember what that Chelsea twat said about Obama in Belfast, calling him a "mud," and it's insights like that when you realise where you actually stand in the civilised world. Which side you're on. I'm no angel, but these people are the savages: him, Tosh, all his horrible mates, it's not funny, or dangerous, or exciting. It's horrible.

She's on about getting Clinton to do a video relay of a speech to us. His people are into the idea, she says. He still wants a decent slug of wedge, but if it shifts a few tickets, then it'll be worth it. She says she's fascinated by the US election and just as a measure of how much Martinez has changed and how much he's prepared to go along with her, even he fakes a new-found interest in American politics, any politics in fact.

"It will just be amazing if Obama does it, he's mobilising support using social media, it's fascinating," she says.

"Yes, yes," adds Martinez, showing off. "But don't underestimate John McCain. People like a veteran. He spent years in a Vietnamese prison."

I can't take much more of this: "Yes, so did Gary Glitter but I wouldn't vote for him."

The slappers at the next table who've been looking over and listening in are frozen in shock and are caught out listening in as Martinez looks in their direction out of embarrassment.

One of them turns her face at me: "I think Gary Glitter is disgusting. They should put him in stocks in the middle of

London so the people can really tell him what they think of him. It's sick."

There's a strange conversational silence, which Ash breaks, speaking quietly and conspiratorially so the bints from Benchill can't hear. "We've secured Siggy Siggurdson, the Icelandic entrepreneur who's been buying up hotels, airports, power stations, lots of retailers. He's a great success story."

"And sponsors?" I ask.

She takes a breath and reels off a list: "We've had a long list of no's I'm afraid, Roger. But you know what you always said, it's not 'no' that kills you, it's 'maybe'."

"Did I really?" I say. Sometimes I surprise myself. "So who have we got?"

"Your contacts are good: Halliwells, Volcanic, Caledonian. They have all said yes, haven't they, Roger?

"Yes, course they have."

"Ah ha. Ah ha. If you could just get me the signed order."

"Will do." This is the other thing she doesn't understand. My contacts don't need purchase orders and invoices, they're good for it. Their word is a bond and all that.

"Our new client, Rosebud Telecom, are in as well," she say.

I put her onto this outfit who resell mobile phone contracts, money for old rope, to be honest. Olaf has put his lads at the Volcanic Invoice Finance team into them, and they're funding acquisitions of smaller players.

"And the North West Regional Development Agency are very keen," she adds.

"Good. Well make sure you charge them double. Public sector rates, that's our money anyway, make sure you squeeze everything you can out of those muppets." Fuck me, we might as well, everyone else does. They're like a cash machine, as long as you've got a lawyer with you to make sure you fill the

276

forms in properly. "Tell me they don't want any of their lot to speak, though. Can't risk that."

As she's talking, telling me the rest of the line up which she's very professionally sorted, I look up at a black Porsche Cayenne 4x4 with larger than normal wheels and music pumping out. It's that song you hear all the time at the moment, something about never seeing your face again by some fit black chick. It's been up and down a few times now. As it spins around by the De Trafford Arms I catch sight of the driver and he's checking me out. It's Hitler, Tosh's ratty little mate with his curly bob of hair and some kind of shellsuit top on. Never mind putting gates at the front of your house, or at the end of the street, it's about time Alderley was a gated village altogether. Keep these lot out for good.

When we first had a sniff of getting stuck into a footy club I had a picture in my mind's eye of how we were going to announce it to the world. Flash bulbs, champagne and dancing girls. Fergie wishing his local team well and the legend that is "The" Stuart Hall to do a tannoy announcement. Great bloke, by the way, hilarious.

But the new era for Wilmslow Wanderers had passed by with hardly a whimper. 150 paying punters to see a mixture of failed pros, arrogant kids who think they should have been contenders and a manager who rants and raves on the touchline. We don't even mention it in the programme, and we don't update who the new board is. In fact, we can happily leave this in the shadows until we're ready to flip the land over.

There's hardly a flicker of interest from fans, press, anyone really. All the players will want to know is will they be paid. Everything stays the same for now, which is good.

The only discernable difference is the presence of one of the 'interested consortium' at the first home game of the season. Tosh arrived with his entourage. He showed no interest in the place except a detached scout around, weighing up what can be ripped off. His mates were passing round the charlie and swigging beer from cans in the row of wooden seats at the front of the stand while he sat smartly observing what the possibilities were.

Old blokes who've been coming for years gawped at his crew and wondered who they were. I was just keen to make it plain they weren't mates of mine. But you could tell people were wondering why some overweight bald hooligans were moodily staring out the opposition physio and directors.

A geeky looking gadgy in a blazer comes and says hello to me and one of the old directors. Tosh leans in to say hello, introducing himself with his slow, pretentious business-like accent. If he wasn't such a nutter I'd break out into a fit of giggles.

The football isn't up to much and he spends most of the match telling stories, breaking off to constantly send messages on his BlackBerry.

After the match he sidles up to me in the 'boardroom' (well, a formica-walled side room with some pictures and plaques and a crappy bar at the end).

"So, what do you reckon, mate? Fancy it?"

I just get the Tosh sneer. "It'll do, for starters, but it's a shit hole, Cash. I need some more leads, know what I mean?"

I nod, but clearly this isn't going to keep him in the manner to which he's become accustomed and he wants to stick to what he knows.

Ever since then he's had the boys circling the manor. Turning up at my side. Starting fights in bars around Alderley and Wilmslow. Spooking people out at the football was just the thin end of the wedge, it seems. As if I didn't have a bad enough reputation, people are starting to put me in the same bracket now that they're following me round like a bad smell.

It's a problem that isn't going away any time soon. Either they get bored and move on, or it's a party that has to come to an abrupt end with police involvement. And that brings risks for me too. For all the code of honour bullshit these thugs pledge to each other, I'm not stupid enough to think one of them isn't capable of landing me in the shit. Grassing your mates doesn't count when it's some rich fucker who you've been taking for a fool.

How I solve that problem isn't even something I can lean on these two loyal lovebirds for.

Martinez nods like a puppy dog, encouraging her at every turn, as she tells me she's lined up an interview with some journalist.

"Are you free for coffee to meet David Rhodes, a journalist with the *North West Business Times* magazine? They've been quite good about you, and they seem to take a positive stance towards anyone who gets roughed up in *Crains*."

"Yes, you mean like I did. Thanks for that. I won't be taking Simon fucking Binns for a steak pudding again. Are they the rules for journalists now then? Coffee is the new lunch? They'll be going hungry."

"I've got a story for him. Don't you worry about that," she says.

"Is he going to write an article about us? Help us knock out a few more tickets?"

"We are talking to a few media about a media partnership strategy, Roger."

"See, you've got it sorted love." All told I'm pretty pleased with the progress she's making here. "There you go, piece of piss this event lark."

She looks down into her coffee cup and her face drops. Martinez puts his hand on her shoulder as she lets out a sob. "Roger, she's working really, really hard at this. Give her a bit more credit, will you."

Like I said, a changing dynamic. She dabs her eyes, shuffles and says, "sorry, hormones, you know."

And you wonder why I never like employing women.

"To be honest, ticket sales have been a bit slow, but the NWDA want to invite a key target list which should fill the room."

"How many?"

"We've got 24 bookings, plus sponsors, and the key target invitees. That's 160."

It's pretty shit, to be honest, but I can't say anything or she'll start blubbing and Martinez will get defensive. So all I can say is comforting words of encouragement, which makes me feel weak.

"We'll get there. I'll get some of the lads on the case." Though actually the truth, the dark horrible, fearful and recession-riddled truth, is that there are no lads any more, everyone is skint. Everyone has the drawbridge up.

I hire a stretch limo from Elliots to meet Serena from the airport. She's on a shuttle up from Heathrow that bangs down at 10. I don't exactly expect her to come running into my arms, but either she's tired, or I'm still in the dog house.

She's completely without make up and her hair is tied up. She's wearing a pair of grey sweat pants and a tight vest top. She's still got it. Even looking like this, at this time in the morning, you see lads catching a look at her.

The driver helps her load the cases and trunks of excess baggage into the back. "Quite a shopping trip," I say to her.

She tells me about the flight, the meal, the weather, but she's a bit off with me. I just pretend I'm really interested in everything she's been doing and keep saying I can't wait to hear all about it.

"Roger darling, you do know I've been working don't you?"

"Yes, yes, of course I do. I was telling Sidney all about it the other day, how proud I am of everything you do, and I've been reading your blog, the Learning Journey Journal."

This is also true, I've never thought she was capable of such quality bullshit, but as I've made a living from it, I'm hardly one to quibble. I like it, even if she does overstate the importance of her little business. But you can't argue with 'Never let tactics define strategy' and 'always control the narrative.' I'll remember that.

Funny how women like to reveal a lot about themselves on these websites and what have you, but how they keep it all back from me. Blokes I know would just never do that. She's been saying the trip has given her a new perspective on life. That's she's been learning lessons from strong women, amazing women she's shared insights with. She says it's given her clarity on life choices. I'll be honest, my reaction to that was 'Oh fuck'. But we'll see.

We're slumped in the back of the limo and, as we approach Alderley, I'm telling her with great excitement about Martinez and Ash getting wed, like it was the most obvious thing in the world. "Yes, didn't I tell you he's been seeing her?"

I can see what's going on behind her eyes, she's pleased, and she's mentally crossing off her grievance list me hanging around with a fit piece of tush.

I fill her in on a few bits of gossip around Alderley that she's into, including the fact that we've got invites to the re-opening of Panacea at the old Braz site. All her mates will be there, she'll love it. I tell her how the conference is going. How the helicopter is looking good.

I don't tell her there's been another couple of robberies - she knows this shit hasn't gone away - but I do have some little bonuses to point out.

I tell the driver to keep going past our house and head towards the new place. "I've got a surprise for you."

We pull up to the gates to Cashmore Towers, with the family crest looking resplendent on the heavy iron fortress railings. The swing up to the drive is impressive as the house comes into view. Turrets, mock gothic, bit of Tudor black and white. The lawn is down and there are sprinklers and a few of Foster's lads tidying up, sweeping and planting flowers and stuff, just as she'd wanted it on the drawings.

The large black door has a large balloon tied to the chrome plated knocker, not that any fucker will ever get close enough to knock it without having first been buzzed through.

It's all been done completely to the letter of her plan, and every single one of her snags on the list has been sorted out.

On the polished marble hallway there is a bed of rose petals I got the lads to scatter.

She stops in her tracks and slowly sinks to her knees, scooping up a handful of petals. I can't see her face, but I can tell by the hunch of her shoulders that she's sighing.

"Serena? Are you alright?"

She spins round and stares at me. It's a fierce look. Proper serious. No pity, no anger. Just a scary, serious look. "Roger. This is lovely. Really lovely. Thank you. No really, thank you for being so nice to me." I'm not sure if she means it, so I shrug.

"But what's taken you so long? Why now? It's Tony isn't it? You've lost your partner in crime, going out chasing all those tarts in town. You're just a lost soul, aren't you? Well whatever it is, that's your final warning.

She's got a pen in her hand and she's jabbing it in my general direction. She lowers her hands to her side when she realises quite how aggressive and violent she was starting to come across. She jerks to one side, gathers her thoughts and starts clicking the pen.

"You are nearly 40 years of age, but you behave like a demented teenager. It's got to stop.

"You've given me a life that's opened doors for me, introduced me to people, given me breaks, given me time to pursue my career. But I would swap all of it for a life of dignity and respect. All of it.

"The way you talk about women, the way you treat women, makes me ashamed. That incident with poor Angela and her husband in that strip club, it still makes me shudder."

To be fair, the thought of Angela in her bra and pants had a pretty similar effect on me that night, before it all kicked off, but I tactfully don't say anything. I didn't even know Serena knew, but then it's always a surprise what people know and what they don't.

"Roger, name me one woman who you actually professionally respect?"

Her pen is clicking ten to the dozen now and I'm thinking she's going to split it, or something.

I'm lost for words, again, I splutter out a stream of incoherent sounds that may or may not be words and might possibly make up an actual sentence. "You Serena, I mean like a creative business woman and someone who understands trust. And the dimensions to life and everything."

She stops clicking and looks confused. I look confused, but I gather my thoughts. I'm trying to blank out all thoughts of legs and tits and hair and leopard print and instead focus on the 50 per cent of my assets, 50 per cent of my assets. I can't face losing any more. I will not get done over in a divorce court.

"I've changed Serena, I mean it. I've really changed. There are loads of women I've been working with that I respect. Ash, for one, we're in business together. I've had this lawyer working for me, Amanda Webb. And these other ladies who Sidney's put me onto who I might be doing some business with."

She looks at me with her brow furrowed, not quite believing me, but trying to process it all. Or something. Serena knows.

"And there's Denise Ripley."

Her expression shifts to "really? Serious?"

Okay, maybe not.

"Serena, alright, I've been a dick, I admit that, but I just want it to be right. And I do want a laugh, golf, footy, all those things, but we're all growing up. It's been my release as we've worked hard for all of this."

"Roger, I've been working hard for this home. And I know you have. But we don't have a chance if things don't change.

"I've got something else for you Roger." She puts her hand in her handbag, Prada, I notice, as she puts the pen down on a glass table from DeLighTable (imported form

American, $2k, easy) I notice that it's from Mishcon de Reya. She then fishes out a small tube from her bag.

"What's that?"

"This is superglue Roger. I've been waiting to pick my moment and show you this. If I ever, ever, hear even a rumour that you've been playing away then I swear to God I will glue that wandering cock of yours to your leg. Is that clear?"

"It's clear."

I'm more than a little scared that she's been swapping tips with the girls about techniques to keep lads in check. And while I'm secretly impressed, I'm also shitting myself at the fact that's she's getting advice from a law firm that specialise in the pillage of twatty husbands.

"Crystal clear, sweetheart. Sometimes I just don't realise how lucky I am."

"And one more thing, Roger, I appreciate what you were saying about these women, it's nice to hear. But I have to say, Denise Ripley really is a total fucking bitch."

September 2008

Lehman Brothers goes bust. Bank of America buys Merrill Lynch for $50bn. Gordon Brown forces Lloyds TSB to rescue HBOS. FTSE falls to 5000. Manchester City Football Club gets bought by investors from Abu Dhabi.

For a change and because I'm keen, I'm actually early to meet Mel and her mate (Carol? I forget) to go through their dodgy dossier.

They're outside in their garden, walking around in the grey but warm outdoors that passes for the arse end of another shitty English summer. They're sniffing rose bushes, but are still talking to each other with a copy each of a spiral bound report.

As I watch them, I'm sat in the Hummer listening to Radio 5 and there's some news I can't quite get my head round. Manchester City have been bought out by some Arabs. Their Thai owner bloke turned out to be a proper rogue, and there's all sorts after him. The thought of Tosh, Sidney and all the other United fans helping City every time they fill up their cars makes me smile.

Blokes just don't do things like that do they? They don't ask each other to take a scent of a rose. I can't actually imagine any of the other women I know doing it either. Serena might look at her nails, compare shoes. Stuff like that.

I don't usually get nervous before any kind of business meeting, even when there's money riding on it. I take it in my stride, or just get ballistically, explosively angry when things don't go my way, which until recently hasn't been very often. I don't wait for things from people either; they bring things to me. Waiting on anything from anyone, usually I'm in total control of whatever it is that I'm up to.

Today though I'm a proper mess. There's bound to be more humiliation on the way. I've been properly had over, but the clear implication is I don't know by who and with who.

We sit down in the farmhouse kitchen and they've been baking bread. At least it smells like they have. It has that contented and happy smell of a place well-loved. This time there doesn't seem to be anyone around either.

They both have a copy of the report in front of them and a copy for me. The slow and methodical way Mel talks is both reassuring and attention-grabbing. There's no pretence that what they've found has any kind of gloss or good news.

"Well Mr Cashmore, we've completed the report, which you have a copy of. There's a lot to take in. Karen will summarise the main findings." (Well, I said I was close).

"Thank you, Mel. First, the good news. We could find no evidence whatsoever of any extra-marital relationships that Mrs Serena Cashmore is having. We had her followed in America. We have monitored her email and phone traffic and, by applying some very simple observational techniques, we conclude that she couldn't have possibly found the time.

"I have to say, I was incredibly impressed by how dedicated and hard-working she is. I'm sure you must be very proud and feel very fortunate to be married to such a talented and successful woman."

I can't quite believe they're talking about the same person, but I don't want to interrupt. So I nod along, pausing to politely ask what she's been up to in America.

"For the first week she went out with a group of entrepreneurs from Cambridge, Glasgow and London on something called a Learning Journey. They had back-to-back meetings around Silicon Valley with Google, Symantech, eBay, a design company called Whipsaw, a couple of banks, some venture capital firms and a day at Stanford University."

"Stanford University! Serena? At a fucking University? Ha!" All of this is a mystery to me. Serena blathers on about interiors and computers and security and houses of the future, but to be honest I didn't think it was serious. I thought it was just something to keep her quiet and out of the shops.

"She then stayed on and spent two weeks with her technology partners at VisualVirtual Systems."

"Er, yes, of course, remind me who they are again?"

The two of them look at each other slightly embarrassed, but I sense that all the shame should actually be mine.

Mel sits forward and speaks: "They're the world-leading architectural visualisation software business. They've licensed a new domestic entry level design product from Serena."

I must look spaced out, because I don't know any of this. But I do now. It starts flooding back. "Can I borrow your Russian boys?" And I thought it was to clean someone's pool, tidy a garden, shift a few plant pots, or at a push, knock up a website.

I pretend to let on that I've known all of this and it's actually of no real surprise to me. "Well, that's all good stuff, ladies, I didn't need you to tell me that Mrs C is a good sort. Out of interest, what's a valuation of what this is all worth?"

"She's got 400,000 preference shares in VisualVirtualSystems and the last time we looked they were trading at $11 on NASDAQ. But the option to purchase her business could be far, far more valuable. Their investment bank, Lehman Brothers, have an analyst briefing on it next month. There's a lot riding on that but we're looking at a value of around $15m."

I feel a rush of fluid through my groin. A tingling sensation up my spine and then the pits of my stomach start trying to surge upwards. As I've been watching my wealth slip away, Serena has been the quiet success story.

It's a lot to take in all at once. And I can't work out in the heat of the moment whether this is seriously very good news, or it just puts a very different dimension on any divorce arrangements, which I'm pretty confident I can avoid. I also have to get my head around what I know, and how I know it.

"Listen, just tell me the bad news, will you?"

Karen looks at Mel, who purses her lips and looks back at me. She draws breath.

"Bear with me on this. I'm going to have to back up a little bit and you might wonder where it's all going. But stop me if you don't follow," she smiles, not in a patronising and belittling way, but in a firm and 'in charge' manner. Something I've been getting used to lately.

"In the last ten years we have witnessed a shift in the economic and political power axis in the world. The fall of the Soviet Union, the consolidation of American military muscle, the rise and rise of economies we have previously thought of as 'third world' or even 'developing'.

"The two most important of these have been China and India. We see it every day in the goods they produce and the opening up of markets. The western banking system is close to cracking point. I can't put it any other way. There are all kinds of financial instruments that were designed to offset the risk in our economies that have started to run the other way.

"There has also been the distribution of investment from sovereign wealth funds into western assets. I take it you've heard the news today about the Abu Dhabi investors buying into that football club?"

"Yes, I heard that."

"At the same time the emerging economies have been preparing for this by waging a quiet war for resources. These come in two forms: raw materials and intellectual property. The Chinese are good at pursuing the first one, and the Indians are good at the other. The pursuit of soft power and technology skills."

I follow all of this to a point and feel the need to interrupt. "Mel, that's all well and good, but you're not telling me that this bunch of incompetent chicken munchers who bought my company are part of some global conspiracy. Listen, I've met them, they couldn't run a bath. You cannot be seriously telling me anything different."

"Well, they might not be, and that's your impression. They have a different way of doing business. But the motive behind the purchase of your business was very much in pursuit of that aim. Chunky's are a large conglomerate with long standing links to the Indian military. What they do in food, manufacturing and agriculture is impressive, of that there is no doubt. But what we've also managed to discover is that they wanted to buy businesses with either brand value, international recognition or a core strategic technology function in security and business intelligence.

"The one thing the west has that the developing world doesn't is cultural muscle. Soft power. All the most noticeable brands are American and British. Sport, music and film. All very western. But it's changing. Take *Slumdog Millionaire*."

I wish someone would, I wince inwardly thinking back to the telly nightmare.

"But Mr Cashmore, believe you me, if there was any danger that they really were buying a hi-tech IT security company with the ability to do what they thought you could do, and find the black boxes that will help them to enter the bowels of UK PLC, then there was no way on God's earth that Her Majesty's security service would allow that to happen. As it was, as you know, RC Solutions is a slightly polished up version of a software reseller and a technology protection racket. Why do you think the Americans and the private equity buyers backed off?"

I blush a bit and shuffle in my seat, as she's sort of summed it up quite neatly, but I'm a little pissed off to hear it, especially from someone I'm paying money to.

"I'll give you this Mr Cashmore," she says, smiling, knowingly, "you're obviously quite a salesman."

"So what about Wayne Bellamy and Denise Ripley?"

"We had a technical term for them in the service: 'HUIs'"

"What's that?"

"Harmless Useful Idiots. In a way they're as much the victims in all of this. The promise of wealth and status has seduced them; they're greedy, desperate and they covet what they see around them. It's a British disease. Their job, but they don't realise it, is to help the owners discover the black boxes, the code, the intellectual property in the business.

"The Indians aren't stupid though, they have actually realised pretty quickly that there is none. They're now just stripping it for contacts, data and cash. If the new management team make any kind of success of it they have a new business. But to be honest, the Indians don't have a flicker of interest in what happens next, they're just waiting for the whole thing to implode and they'll blame the old colonials for arrogance and incompetence."

"Anything else I should be worried about?"

They run through where my risks are and where I'm especially vulnerable. I'd be lying if I said any of it was a surprise. The paddy banks are up shit creek without a paddle; they even trot out the usual bollocks about AIG being a bit exposed if any more American banks go pop. Then they give the same smart-arsed line about the Icelandics that Jon Moulton was going on about a couple of months back.

A few pointers they've managed to dig up on the lads prick my ears up: Rick, happily retired to his castle in Italy; Foster, underwater on debt, messy personal life. Martinez; business is a bit stretched, but he should be alright.

"Do you mind if we reveal the personal details we've discovered? Are you sure you won't be offended?"

"No, carry on. We can compare notes," I smile at the pair of them.

"I'm glad to learn that Mr Martinez is settling down. Now Aisling Mahon is an interesting young lady. Fiercely loyal to you, she did a very good job keeping you out of the papers and working with Amanda Webb, another young woman who's going to go very far. She's done a fantastic job with that injunction on the newspapers. I wondered how long it would be before someone started working out how these awful journalists were getting all their scoops."

"Yes; dogs, scumbags. We sorted them out," I say.

294

"Obviously you know Miss Mahon well and work closely with her. You're going to miss her when she's on maternity leave, aren't you?"

I shrug. No-one's irreplaceable. "Listen," I say, "I know you must think I'm a total head in the sand, and I didn't spot some of this, but I do know that Bobbi Armani isn't all there. I mean, that's clearly not his real name and he's obviously potless. But out of interest, what's his story?"

They smile at me, and I get at least some comfort that I've got something right.

"Bobbi Armani's real name is Yusuf Ahmed. He's not Italian, he's of Pakistani heritage. He lives in a rented house in Macclesfield. All his cars we observed him driving are leased." To show they've done their homework there's photographs of him in full flow with all kinds of dupes.

"He has a car valeting business which doesn't do very well but it throws off enough cash, classic black economy, and he has a couple of student houses in Fallowfield. He has run up a £1.5m personal overdraft with Caledonia Bank as one of their entrepreneurial heroes. They threw away the rule book and started backing people they thought would make them look good, allow them to take risks."

"Yes, I knew it, and does he think he's getting anything out of me for the Wilmslow Wanderers deal? And what about all his kings and sheikhs and stuff."

"Mr Cashmore, the trouble with the world now is that it's full of very strange people with lots of money. He's landed a new role as the UK agent for a Bahrain-based investment house called Gulf Investment Services; it's run by a character called Nanda Mani. They've got offers to buy land in Bhutan, New Zealand, Australia and India. We understand they have a requirement to buy a football club in Italy. They own a small private fleet of aeroplanes and have offices in Zug in Switzerland. They are, at the moment, represented by reputable lawyers and accountants in all these jurisdictions.

"On Mr Mani, we have found an unpaid council tax bill, some parking fines and a small claim by a court in Bristol from when he was a student over rent arrears. There's also some questions about his background in India, but it's a hard place to get information from, as you know. So yes, your friend seems to have landed a job with the last of the great international playboys."

"Is this for real? Nanda Mani? Sounds a bit too much like No Money to me." I can't quite believe what she's telling me. It also sounds like he was half way telling the truth; either that or he's just being reeled in by another bullshitter like him, but on a bigger scale.

All this is whirring around in my head as we're talking. Pleasantries, holidays, weather, shit like that. They walk me to my car and we feel a few drops of rain. There's one more thing I could do with knowing.

"I accepted a caution for a punch up I had, which you said you knew about. Was there any other police intelligence on me I need to know about?"

"No."

"Have you come up with the name Thomas McGeoghan in all of this?"

They look at each other and shake their heads. "Well, obviously I've heard of him, he's that Teflon gang man, right? But why do you ask?" Karen says.

"Who is he?" says Mel, like someone's farted.

"Doesn't matter, he's just a kid I was at school with who I could do with avoiding."

They seem non-plussed as if they wouldn't even contemplate me and him in the same world.

I sit at the wheel of the Hummer. Chucking the dossier on the passenger seat, I flick through the perfectly written pages they've given me, skimming it for detail. Scanning it for any other names I might have missed. Any other contacts.

Sometimes it isn't what they leave in, it's what's been left out, something that's been missed, something that's off the radar.

I flick on the radio and there's that bloke Peston talking even more excitedly than usual.

There's chaos as the American markets are panicking about these Mexicans who are behind with their mortgages, except it's led to a chain reaction that has left all the banks holding the keys.

There's another desperate text from Foster who says he's worried that the £50k he pawned everything to advance to Armani has disappeared. There's no sign of Bobbi Bullshit anywhere.

My phone rings and it's the lad from the estate agency who's meant to be flogging our house. I thought he must have died he's been that quiet.

"Mr Cashmore, we have some interest in your house." He sounds out of breath and a bit excited.

"Go on."

"Yes, yes, it's not a sale, but we've an urgent need for immediate occupancy if you can agree letting this weekend.

"What's the rent?"

"Ten grand a month, up front for a year, contract for two years."

"A footballer or an Astra Zeneca scientist?"

"Ha. The former, he's an African superstar, Flomo Ballo, just signed for City. We're rushed off our feet, they're buying all kinds and we're finding homes for them. He picked your house out first. Can you be ready for handover this weekend? He's holed up with his friends and family in the Radisson in town and the club are quite keen to get them into Cheshire and out of the city."

"Consider it done pal."

Serena likes nothing better than a project and before I've even got back to Alderley she's on the case, moving stuff into our new drum. We've had a blast in the old place, but this is the move we've been waiting for. It might come to shit, we might all be dead tomorrow and if the news is as bad as we keep hearing, but at least we'll be safe.

I have a vague idea that's full of risk and might just work, and get out the BlackBerry Messenger and ask Tosh if he'd like to come round for tea.

"Do you know where my house is?" I ask.

Comes the answer: "No".

Good. First bit of the plan comes clear. "Meet you at the usual table at Costa on Friday."

A sh has sorted out for me to meet this other journalist, David Rhodes, some character from the *North West Business Times* magazine. She gives me the word to behave myself this time. To butter him up a bit, to tell him what a good job he did writing about property, to give him a couple of exclusives and not to swear. Shouldn't be too difficult.

We're using the meeting room in the office of Ash and Cash, our PR agency. It's round the arse end of Canal Street, near the court house, and the streets are crawling with scallies drinking wife beater and Buckfast. Outside, a skanky junkie with a proper bust-up face, wiry legs, short denim cropped shorts and a vest top comes up to me: "Are you looking for business?"

I decide to humour her. "Why do you do this, love? Why don't you move to Alderley Edge, you can have a massive house and a choice of a different restaurant every night of the week?"

Just as she's about to hurl some abuse at me a lad in a chinos and a cord jacket, sporting a backpack, arrives in the same doorway as me and smiles. "Hi Roger. David Rhodes," he says, offering me his hand. "What was that all about?" he nods in the direction of the tom who's now swaying up the road, shouting at people.

"Oh her...she said she wanted to discuss business, but not the kind that you write about, pal."

Luckily Ash has tidied up the meeting room, brought my laptop, and I'm in good order to impress this kid. I've slapped on my best whistle and my tight shirt that shows off my twanging biceps after a good session in the new gym.

In the meeting room, Ash brings him a glass of water. And I come straight out with it: "Right pal, you're not going to stitch me up like that twat Simon Binns are you?"

I nod in the direction of the bin on the floor where I got Ash to get the latest copy of that *Crains* paper, and after we'd scanned it for all the latest parade of losers that we've stitched up and hung out to dry, it's positioned strategically in the bin so he can see what I think of his rivals.

He laughs and insists he isn't. "No, no, no. We're just trying to get a range of different business personalities in the magazine. We want to get your opinions on different key issues of the moment and to put your side of the story on all your recent deals, and things that have, er, happened to you."

I look at Ash and she seems alright about it. She nods. "Roger won't be talking about his ongoing litigation with the television company, and his portrayal on *Slumdog Entrepreneur*. That's off limits. Everything else is fine. Ask away."

He gets his notebook out and asks the first question: "Do you feel the economic climate is getting tougher, and what measures are you introducing as a result?"

"Listen, mate. You can tell there's a recession coming; my missus was telling the woman who does our juices this morning that she's worked out we've spent more weekends at the place in Abersoch than the villa in Majorca this year." Ash laughs out loud, and speaks loudly over me, saying, "undoubtedly there are difficult economic decisions to make, but Roger feels there is also room for opportunity and risk, if you are prepared to work hard, don't you Roger?"

"So, yes, pal. No problem. Next question."

"What's your view of the proposal to introduce a congestion charge to drive into Manchester city centre?"

Ash has primed me on this one, but I'm going to surprise him. "Most business people don't use public transport, because it's smelly, you have to travel with other members of public and it's shit. It means they drive. If you made it better, they'd use it more often and leave their cars at home. But the people you need to get off the roads you can only do by penalising them. I want to drive freely into the centre of Manchester without crashing into white van man or Dolly Daydream putting on her lippy at the lights in her Mini." Just two examples of people I've clipped recently, or who've raged at me as I've cut them up at lights.

He writes it down, and Ash tries to butt in again. "What Roger is saying is that he is against the introduction of another tax on business in the present economic climate."

"Yes, Ash, I am, but actually I would also quite like the idiots off the roads. So no, I'm also in favour of it."

This is what I've been reading up on about Bill Clinton, holding conflicting viewpoints at the same time and convincing one lot of people they're voting for one thing, when you are actually doing another. Triangulation.

Ash then says: "Roger doesn't have a vote on this. It's only for residents of Greater Manchester, so I don't think it's fair to quote him. And his principal businesses are in Cheshire as well."

The Rhodes lad nods and asks a few questions about property schemes that he's heard might be running out of money. Some big tower on Whitworth Street, a shopping centre in Stockport, the casino next to City's ground. It's all falling apart and there's a lot of panic about.

I haven't told Ash what I'm up to, but I have a better idea about what to send this lad away with. He can get ten-a-penny opinions off any old muppet. What I've pulled together is a nice portion of the report that Mel and Karen gave me. All the references to them taken off. Just names, dates, times, pictures, links. It should serve me well. He reads it, taking a couple of careful notes.

"Trust me mate, this is good. If you need any more, let me know."

The move to the new house goes smoothly, as it does when Serena's giving orders to various companies who need her endorsement in this line of work. The footballer rocks up with his family, his brothers, his mates. None of them seem to be carrying anything more than a few carrier bags. But there are a lot of them. I count 15 in total. It's like one of those news reports with a rag bag army of child soldiers; all menace and steely killer stares.

We don't get two words out of Ballo as he's got his enormous DJ headphones on. But this lad from his agency does all the running around. A dirty great furniture wagon parks on the lawn at the front, because there's nowhere else to go and they offload about 20 mattresses, but no beds, into the house.

There goes the neighbourhood.

Our new house is cushty. Everything's so new it's like living in a five star hotel. Serena's stressed about a couple more house robberies. The usual form: violence, intimidation, fake accents, and they're looking for cars, watches and cash. Everyone's upping the security, and we're no different.

I spent a couple of hours learning how it all works with the technician from the security installation company. We have two panic rooms with industrial-strength doors, power supplies and a different access and escape route.

I still haven't let on that I know how loaded she is, but I have started listening to what she's doing a bit more closely. She thinks it's because I'm a much nicer guy, which is sort of true, but I've also got a firmer vested interest in the success of her business.

She's also taken a proper shine to Ash and they've started chinwagging and becoming friends. Martinez, loved up and stupid, thinks this is great. I just think it's weird.

We're all planning a big night out together at the re-opened Braz, except it's going to be Panacea Alderley, a real chance for Martinez to relive some of his magic Manchester nights on the pull. Or maybe not.

Over wine in our orangery the happy couple are sitting there, telling a story that they were at Richard Hughes' 40th where Spandau Ballet were the main act, the point of the tale not that some band or other were playing, but they were there. Everyone was there. Of course they fucking were. Everyone except me. Why not?

"What are you doing for your 40th, Roger?" asks Martinez.

"I was thinking of having a big surprise party. Eh, Serena?"

She looks shocked for a minute. "Just kidding." No, we're just going to celebrate quietly at home, get a proper chef to come in and do us a big slap-up dinner, all the trimmings. "Something civilised and serious."

"Speaking of serious, Roger, how's the conference coming along?" Serena asks, nodding in Ash's direction.

"I can ask Allen Blue if you want, the founder of LinkedIn." Serena's name dropping some of these American big hitters she's been hanging around with, but I've stopped listening as I stare up at the TV screen in the corner, showing that Peston bloke on the BBC World News with a serious expression and that funny rambling voice.

In the background is a graph going down, a massive number with a billion after it and the logo of AIG.

"Quick, turn it up. I've got a load of dough in this lot."

As he's talking, the picture goes to America and there's all these Yanks carrying boxes out of an office, blokes in tears. It's Lehman Brothers, the bank that were doing a load of work on Serena's thing. Obviously no-one knows I know this, but I sense the look of dread on her face and ask: "What's up?"

She picks up her phone and she's trying to call someone. "Come on, come on."

To be honest it's the other news that's making me as sweaty under my collar as AIG. I'm onto the lad at the bank that put me into it, and I'm obviously not the first idiot to be calling him today.

"Get me out," I scream.

"I'd love to, and I'd advise you to, but it's not that simple," he says, like he's rehearsed the line before. "AIG have shut the variable rate fund and while the American treasury are restructuring it and trying to work out which assets it can sell."

I can hear Serena asking where the analyst's report is.

My guy meanwhile reels off a load of nonsense from another statement. All sorts of shit about notional exposure, yadder yadder, super senior credit default swap portfolio, derivatives written for financial institutions, guff guff guff, regulatory capital relief, blah blah blah risk mitigation.

With all this whizzing around in my head it's hard to concentrate on getting work done. Even a trip down to Chester to see the chopper in all its glory is a blur of stress and tension. The chopper looks boss. It has a Bentley-style control panel, red leather seats and it's painted black, just as I like it.

The pilot fires up the bird and we lift off. It's a class ride, flying straight over the Cheshire plain, following the route of the M56 roughly towards Tatton, then peeling off to do a triumphant flypast, right over the Edge, hovering over our house, then down the High Street.

I ask the pilot if he can put us down somewhere for a spot of lunch. "We need to secure landing permission,"

"How much is that?"

"Usually a few hundred at a hotel."

"Forget it, I only want a sarnie." This is starting to be more hassle than it's worth.

All told I'm up the air for an hour and the charges are horrendous, stupid, but as soon as we've got the helipad built in the grounds in Alderley, at least it won't cost me an arm and a leg and I can have lads come round to borrow a ride.

The only customer I've booked so far has been Sidney, who took a few pals up to Scotland for a round of golf. Other than that, nothing.

After a bit of pottering at home, a quick chat to Serena who's been lucky that the Lehman's bloke handling her deal has pitched up at Goldmans or somewhere, so we're going to be alright.

For a celebration I figure it's time to take a little trip to Macclesfield, but this time by road. On a street near the town centre with rows of nondescript terraced houses, I find the one I'm looking for and knock on the door.

I remember a walk of shame down these streets once. A fat lass I'd picked up at the Braz, bounced around on it for an hour. Sweated a lot. Betty, that was it. Sweaty Betty. Big knickers.

"Evening Bobbi." Armani looks at me in a state of surprise as he clocks me through the curtains.

"Surprised to see me?" I smile. The house is as basic as you could find. He's blustering about and muttering something about house-sitting for a cousin. But I just keep smiling, flattering him with expressions of surprise that he's not been about for a bit, that he needs to come for a ride in the chopper sometime, and talking about stuff, bringing him up to date with the gossip about Martinez and Ash. I let on that me and Sidney Silver are keen to come in with him and Jimmi Barnes on the radio and TV deal. I'm talking to him like nothing has happened, that he isn't a con man from a different continent than the one he claims, and that I'm pleased we're doing a bit of business together on the Wilmslow land.

"Just a formality mate, but to get the rights to the land, you need a firm and declared interest in the existing use. I've got the documents drafted up that assign ownership of Wilmslow Wanderers Football Club (2008) to you, with the provision for a charge over it from any funders you may have."

He doesn't hesitate to sign, slipping from slightly shifty to uber confident. "This could be the beginning of something amazing, Roger," he says, and starts to reel off some plans for loaning footballers from this team in Italy that an associate of his is buying.

"Sounds great, Bob mate," I say. "You know, we should do more business together." All encouragement and bravado.

He's sat on his threadbare sofa, wearing fake designer jeans, a smart white fitted shirt and socks with a hole in the toe. I even remember him blagging the shirt from this lad who'd set up a new bespoke service a couple of years ago. He leans forward as if to let me into a secret.

"I'm the northern European agent for Gulf Investment Services," he whispers.

"Tell me more, mate," I say, pretending to look surprised, intrigued and excited all at the same time.

"We have funds to invest. We could be the largest provider of capital for property and business expansion," he says, with total conviction, but with the look of a double glazing salesman thrust into the world of used cars.

I need to let him know I believe him, that I think this is legitimate, and that he should trust me. "I could have a few deals for you, pal; let me have a meeting with this mate of yours. We can chopper in."

He gives me one last story before I leave. He's going to be racing at Silverstone in the next Formula Three Grand Prix event. "I can get you box tickets, Roger, no problem."

By the time we say our goodbyes I've stopped listening to him. I just leave him with a little parting comment – "Dave Foster says hello. Give him a ring mate."

It's a crash back to reality for him and a reminder that I know it's all bollocks.

I turn on the radio in the car and the grim reaper Peston is back on. This time the whirlwind of chaos has come closer to home. Lloyds Bank have been told to stump up £12bn to rescue HBOS, which was a gnat's fart from going completely tits up. The FTSE has dropped below 5000 for the first time in yonks, unemployment has gone up again and the Bank of England have printed a load more money to prop up the economy.

I'm not in the mood to suck up to Tosh, kiss his arse, or give him too much rope to twist round my neck. The Champions League hasn't kicked in yet and it hasn't been worth getting trips together to ferry louts to bully foreigners.

He's at Costa before me again, even though I arrived 20 minutes early this time. I don't even order a coffee, I just show him a piece of paper with an address, a four-digit number and a date. And then I take it back. Later I will totally destroy it, chew it up, spit it out and flush it down the bog.

He's laughing about Panacea burning down the night before. More strange goings on. "Now THAT was nothing to do with me," he says, cracking a smile I don't share. Whatever we may have once had has gone, but he doesn't care.

He tries a matey attempt at chat. "See you at the next home game. I'm quite enjoying real football, Mr Cash. Thinking of getting my own sheepskin coat measured up."

The club secretary at Wilmslow has already been on to me asking me about the impromptu visits by the Salford scumbags. They've insisted on running the security at the club, though there's no need for any. All the trophies have been taken away and put into storage. DD has insisted on his 18 year-old son playing at centre forward for the next game and they've been helping themselves to the bar. The part-time staff have walked out as a result of the new atmosphere of intimidation.

"Yes, see you there. Sounds great," I say, chuckling at the introduction I'll be able to make to the new 'official owner'.

Two nights later and I'm sat in the bushes next to the shed of my old house waiting, waiting, waiting until, as expected - and true to form - two figures dressed in black skip over the side wall of one of Alderley's most prestigious addresses. Armed with holdalls and balaclava masks, they know what they're doing and they've clearly done it before.

The lights are all off in the house except for one downstairs room, the kitchen. The two men walk round to the back door with a key pad entry and press in four numbers. The door opens without making a sound. The taller of the two leads the other in. It seems like ages - but in reality it's only about three minutes - before there's an almighty scream and a commotion. Lights all over the house go on and there's shouting.

Taking the remote control locking device from my hand I press the lock to my old back door, now the abode of Africa's finest footballing superstar and his extended family. At the back door I can just about make out the image of one of the two masked men, the smaller one, frantically trying to open it, but he can't. Inside, the silhouettes of the African army, the wild and unschooled newly wealthy, protective and angry soldiers are racing around the house in a state of high excitement.

The head of their house is away in Brighton playing for Manchester City, the rest, lounging around, listening to music, eating, shagging, whatever it is they do.

There's screaming and banging, thud after thud. More screams and a bit more banging. Then there's silence. One of the Africans tries the door, but it's locked. I press the button again. Another tries it with a bit more force and it opens. In whatever language they speak I can still work out one is joshing the other for not trying hard enough.

There are raised voices and they drag out two bodies feet first, bumping them down the steps. One is either dead or unconscious, the other is slowly moving his arms around, one mask is on the other is off. I'm waiting, waiting, waiting, please, please please. Let it be Tosh.

The three oldest African lads are standing over bodies, arguing. One of them goes into the house and comes back with a bowl – I remember that bowl, I puked up in it enough times – and it's filled with water. He chucks it over the conscious one who groans. One of the lads whips off the mask and stares into his face, holding him up by his hair. It's Hitler, the truly horrible one, named after the most evil fucker the world ever knew, and without either the sense or the intelligence to do anything about a nickname that's stuck with him. Die you horrible bastard, die.

The other body on the floor, the taller one, gets a kick to the ribs and a shakedown.

In a foreign country, away from anything like the reality they grew up with, these proud men have done what they always do, they've defended their home. They don't want the police involved, they'll know how it could soon be twisted in this fucked up country where burglars have rights, where black people are stopped in the street and searched, as they have been every time they walk into Wilmslow or Alderley. How they're refused service in restaurants, little knowing that they're all part of an enterprise that's becoming a global industry – Ballo PLC – a global challenger brand.

The one who looks like he's in charge stands over the two of them, looking like he has a plan. "Go now. Go now. Never come back. Next time we kill you. Go."

I feel like standing up and applauding. Go on, son. On the head. I'm just willing the other one to be Tosh, but it isn't, he's too tall. He takes off his mask and rubs his bald head. I can see that it's DD. I'm just wondering now if this is either going to put them off, make them more determined, or realise that my intelligence isn't to be relied upon and to move on.

October 2008

Carnage.

The chopper airlifts me from Cashmore Towers to Tatton Park, where the compere without compare, the one and only Vince Miller is warming up the expectant guests with a heartfelt speech and then welcoming me onto the stage to open the Confidence Convention.

Vince is telling a few of his gags, getting the crowd up, all ready for a special day. We have a few TV camera lads filming the chopper coming into view as it circles and lands. Then they cut to me leaping across the lawn at the front of Tatton to the main auditorium, where the crowd greets me as I run into the room to that rock tune that's everywhere at the moment. My sex is on fire.

The roaring helicopter blades twirl around me. An exhilarating waft of air creates the sense of motion and action all around me as I take a quick breath and adjust my headset, with the microphone on a wire thing wrapped round my head so I can use my hands to make my points.

Everyone is on their feet. Chanting along with my punchlines, just like all the yanks who are going mad for this Obama guy who I've been watching obsessively on YouTube.

"Ladies and gentleman, I've heard there's a recession on its way, but I've decided I'm not going to take part.

"There's no need for it.

"There's no demand for it.

"There are people out there with plans and schemes that deserve to be backed. It's time for banks to grow a pair of balls and back British business.

"Are you with me?"

"Yes! We are."

"Can we beat the blues, people?"

"Yes we can!"

"Can we stop Gordon Brown taxing us to death?"

"YES WE CAN!"

"Can we show that Cheshire is the number one place in the world to do business?"

"YES WE CAN!"

My seat in the front row - marked 'reserved VIP' - is alongside all the top lads we've got over to speak. The video link to Clinton kicks in and the last great American president gives us a lesson in leadership, fighting back and resilience.

I've done a bit of public speaking before – company conferences and all that - and the lads usually lap it up, rolling about laughing at my jokes. They say I'm a natural, and for all the way the telly lot stitched me up with spiteful editing, I actually did pretty well, or so Ash, Serena and Martinez reckoned.

Right, as I say, that's the plan. The reality is things are looking a little bit shaky, to say the least. First off, Clinton pulled out. Ash says he can't even commit to the video link as the election is getting too close to call and he's needed.

My plan B is we get someone to edit a video together and get an actor to voice the first bit.

The other plan is to get a bloke in Arab gear to stand up there and gabble away in Arabic. We'll then have a translator to read out a speech about how the balance of power in the world is changing and that Manchester City are going to reign supreme in football. I mean, who'll know? No-one's ever seen this sheikh who runs the gaff, so why not? Ash isn't convinced, but we're running out of ideas.

To be honest, it's putting a brave face on it. The AIG shit has properly fucked me off. Wiped out a big chunk of wealth and it sounds like I'm not the only mug who was sold that particular turkey. Jeremy Clarkson has been shafted, but as usual he makes a joke out of it. I don't; I just need to keep it quiet.

Sidney calls and he's a bit smug. "You got out of AIG didn't you?" I ask him, knowing he did because he was actually

316

listening to Jon Moulton rather than misunderstanding what was going on.

"Yes Roger, I told you to as well. Didn't you?"

"No I didn't, I'm wiped out. But the American government are bailing it out, we should get something."

"How's the rest of the portfolio?"

"Balanced," I say, lying.

Truth is, I'm starting to brick it about the Icelandics now. As soon as the drawdown on the money from the Isle of Man lands one day later this week – three months after asking – without penalties, then I'm going to stick it somewhere safer still. Under the mattress? Not with Tosh and his band of merry men stalking the patch. Into a supermarket bank? They don't seem to be lending it to hillbillies or Mexicans or scrotes who are maxing out on credit cards. I saw that Terry Leahy bloke from Tesco on the TV and, though you wouldn't want to have a pint with him, he's done alright flogging stuff to the general public. Word on the street is that there's one on the way to Alderley; about time too.

Sidney's still got me in with the syndicate that the Taurus boys have been creaming it with. That's the good thing about market turmoil. The hedge fund lads know how to zig when everyone else zags, they have these computers that play the market like maestros with these CFD things. We've got an option on a movement of the FTSE for the day of the conference, so it's shaping up to be a big day all round.

After me we'll have speaker after speaker giving the punters some inspiration, some charisma and a few laughs. I practice it in front of the mirror and study how Obama, Clinton, Thatcher and Churchill do it.

By Monday morning, at the final site meeting with the lads slapping the marquee up, the caterers sorting out the grub (Heathcote had another booking, worse luck) something was telling me that all wasn't right. The weather was pretty shit as well.

317

Ash is sat around with the crew, telling them what to do. I never knew you needed so many people just to put a few chairs out for an event, and who are all these hairy-arsed blokes twiddling knobs at the big desks they have. It's only a few microphones and a stage, why do they need to drive the Starship fucking Enterprise? What do we pay them all for?

And that's all I've basically been doing since I stopped earning. Paying. Signing cheques, moving money around. There's only Tosh who actually earns for me, and I can't actually think that's worth dipping into, but with this conference, the house, the legal fees, the chopper, more legal fees and being asked to top up the client account with Taurus to join the next syndicate, it's a drain. I daren't even look at the bank balance.

I'm watching the crew put up the TV screens in the client business suite, like a private airport lounge, but at a conference – another great idea of mine. One's being tuned to Sky News and the big graphics show a massive RBS logo with the words BANKING CRISIS splashed above it. That Jocko chancellor with the eyebrows, Alistair Darling, is on the screen looking whiter than a sheet.

"Turn it up, turn it up."

Everyone stops what they're doing and gawps at the screen. Just when everyone was thinking the world's financial system had stabilised, that the Yanks chucking a few hundred billion at AIG and letting Lehmans go to the dogs had flushed out the shite, more shit was on the way.

He's talking in a calm but strained voice. The government have whacked billions in to prop up RBS. They've nationalised it, basically. Lloyds is being bailed out too; the strain of having to patch up the basket case of shitty property loans, over-leveraged private equity deals and ridiculous loans to fucking idiots like Armani has broken them. The trail along the bottom of the screen reads like a roll call of my investment portfolio.

The updates on the financial markets look terrible as well. The FTSE keeps falling. All those little signs with red and green, and the up and down arrows? Well, they're all red and the arrows are all pointing down.

I look over at Ash, her face drawn and tired, but still shining. What is with some women? They just shine and smile even with all the shit we chuck at them. Most women at RC looked perpetually terrified, on edge and tense. They smile, but you catch the expression when they turn away and see that awkward stressed, exhausted look. Not Ash; she radiates. Even pregnant, even working her arse off, and even taming Martinez hasn't finished her off.

To be fair, she's done a decent job filling up the conference; there were 220 registered by close of play last Friday, which should at least look respectable. Not as many as we'd hoped, but she keeps saying it's about building a movement. We start well and build up.

Then her phone goes. She takes the call, turns away, looks up at me, nods towards the screen which is a burst of colour and large letters. "Caledonian Bank on the brink". Ash has her free hand in her hair. She clicks off the phone and stares at me. "That was the marketing team at Caledonian." I know this isn't a courtesy call, or a request for more tickets. "They want all their branding, all their people, removed from the event. As far as they're concerned it can't happen. They're on the brink of a rescue and can't be seen anywhere near an event like this right now."

"It'll cost them." I'm snarling, the sweat's rising in me, my stomach's turning.

"They've paid; that's not the problem. It's the bodies. They were bringing 30 guests. They were bringing them here personally; all their top entrepreneurs and property clients," her voice is close to cracking.

Usually at this point I run about, bang a few tables, chuck a calculator at a hapless salesman and tell them to "Just

Fucking Sort It." But that isn't going to cut it here. It's me and her. And she's my business partner and my best mate's pregnant bird.

"Roger, we need to round up the other sponsors, can you check with Volcanic and Halliwells?"

I'm on the blower, trying to track down the lad at Halliwells I did the deal with but his phone is giving out a foreign ring tone. Golf? Or he may be at his place in Spain. I call the marketing department and speak to some young bird who says she doesn't know anything about it.

"Sometimes the partners do their own sponsorships out of their departmental budgets, nothing to do with us," she says.

I mention his name and there's a pause. "He left three months ago, I'm afraid."

When I call Olaf at Volcanic's office in London, he picks up on the second ring.

"Roger, this is so shit. I'm so sorry, my friend." He sounds like he's crying.

"What is it pal?"

"The whole thing. It's turned to shit, Roger."

"Listen mate, I'm calling about the conference. How many tickets do you want?"

There's silence on the line. That's never good.

"Roger, I'd clean forgotten." More silence. "The bank is going down, Roger. All of it. Kaput. Over."

All I can hear is the guttural, distraught wail of a towering Icelandic beast of a man, who in that flash of a moment realises he should have stuck to fishing.

"Olaf, Olaf, what the fuck do you mean it's over?"

"It's over, I'm so sorry," he says.

"Yes, but the governments are all piling in pal, my money will be alright, all protected and being sent over. It was due to hit my UK account today."

"All assets were frozen Roger, all the banks here have gone, all depositors' money has gone. Our government doesn't have anywhere close to the resources to rescue the bank like the Americans have."

I'm shouting at this point. I'm not even sure what I'm saying, just lots of fucks and cunts. "What about the Russians?"

"Roger, that was just an urban myth, and if there was Russian mafia money laundered through Iceland, do you think they're going to bail out people like you as an act of charity? Roger, I'm so sorry." Click.

I'm spinning around at this point, whirling around. My mouth dry, my arse going, my guts churning. This is an absolute and total disaster. The worst. Arma–fucking-geddon.

Some bird in a headset carrying a clipboard, with a bloke holding a load of technical equipment, comes up to me and says something about rehearsals that I can hardly hear. I spin round and fall over a table, kicking over a chair.

"FUCK OFF. I DON'T FUCKING CARE. DO YOU HEAR ME? THIS IS FUCKING OVER."

Ash comes running over looking mental. I take back everything I said about calm.

"I hope you are here to tell me some fucking good news, sweetheart."

"No I'm not, Roger."

"What's the hell's the matter?"

I just look at her with pleading eyes, my breath shortening and my heart pounding. I stop and try a brief interlude of calm, hoping for something, anything, to arrest this unfolding madness.

"I've just been on the phone to one of the other sponsors, Rosebud Telecom. They can't make it tomorrow," she says.

I'm not even surprised now.

"They have to be at an emergency analysts meeting in the City tomorrow. Their share price has collapsed, and they've also got some banking problem, they've had a credit line with another Icelandic bank and the government have frozen it under anti-terrorism legislation."

"Ash, this can't happen. Cancel everything. Sack everyone. Stand them down, all of them. I haven't the time or the energy. Much bigger shit has exploded."

Her phone rings and she answers it, sounding cheerful. "Thanks, that's great. Lovely."

"Who was that?"

"Mike Finnigan, the motivational guy. Just confirming tomorrow. Says he's really looking forward to it. Are you sure you want to cancel?"

"Yes, Ash, I do. I am finished with it. This would just be the final humiliation."

I leave Ash to break the bad news that the show has been canned and to let the dwindling band of people who were planning to waste their day listening to people talk shite while the world's economy, and more particularly, my personal fortunes collapsed around me.

I don't know why I would imagine for a moment that James and Chris from Taurus would be capable of bringing me good news in the midst of all of this shit. But at least I had the good sense to draw down some spondulicks from my client account with them to pay off the builders, and settle the bridging loan. I call James anyway.

"Roger, what's happening? Chaos, isn't it?"

"You boys need to prove your worth now. What's the latest on our syndicate? I desperately need some good news..."

"We've placed an option on the close of market today. But the FTSE has tanked, it's the biggest drop in a decade in a single day."

"Speak to me in fucking English, James, what am I looking at?"

I can hear him tapping a few things on a keyboard. "£4 million mate."

"Yowzer." After all this shit, after all streams of bad news, after looking into the abyss, the dark chasm of utter destruction, this. Yes! Thank fuck for that. "When I can get cleared funds? I'm desperate."

"Roger, it's a four mill loss mate. I'll check the details, but you'll need to settle your account at close of business tomorrow."

Ah.

How has this happened? I was almost expecting him to say that. In for a penny, in for a few million quid.

Before I can even think about what to do next, the phone pips with a text, I look at it, thinking it's going to be a mistake, a crank, or worse, Tosh. It's Sidney: "Come over now".

I'm driving along the lanes of Cheshire in the Ferrari, passing other people who probably have no idea what any of this means; no idea what abyss the world is facing. I have to turn the radio off because Peston is starting to make me want to drive the car into the next oncoming lorry. If the banks have no money, then it's over. Nothing can be safe. Cash machines will be turned off. Loans will be called in. Businesses will close. You could already feel the life draining out of people anyway. But the sound of these quivering jocks on the news, Brown and Darling, makes you think that everything's being bailed out. Where the fuck have they found the money to do this?

I park up and run to Sidney's office, buzzing the door for dear life. Val, Pam, or Pat, or whatever her name is, is looking a bit flustered.

"Oh, hello, Mr Cashmore, you're the first here, he's in his office."

I brush past her, mutter that I don't care and find Sidney, as per usual, watching the world financial news on Sky and smoking one of his big cigars. "Ah come in, Roger. Have you been following all of this?"

He actually looks pleased with himself. "Sidney, it's a nightmare, I'm absolutely screwed. AIG last month, the Icelandics, Caledonian are going down. And now the stock market has wiped me out for £4m with Taurus, with that CDF thing you got me into. I've just had to cancel the event; that's been a disaster. The Indians are coming after me for the cash we took out on the property. Sidney, sorry if I'm not smiling. Serena will properly have me out on my arse this time."

"Yes, that's what happens when the tide goes out. Some are unlucky, some play the market well. Like me. And some will get completely caught out, stuck with nothing left. I told you it was all going to end badly didn't I?" His grin is starting to properly send me doolally. He is obviously now completely deranged. He thinks this is a game.

I try and wake him up from whatever world he's landed in. "Have you spoken to the Taurus boys? We're stuffed."

"Keep watching," he smiles, nodding at the TV.

I'm lost by all of this. Totally lost.

"Did you honestly think I'd let those pair of chancers manage our risk in the stock market? I've been selling short positions on the financial stocks. I'm making plenty as the market drops."

"What about me, Sidney? I've got to find four gorillas and my tuck up money's been wiped out. In Iceland. Frozen. You know what I mean."

Sidney's on his feet, wearing one of his crisp white shirts with his trademark silver cufflinks. He's got new glasses on which he keeps pushing up his nose, like he didn't have the patience to have fitted properly.

"Roger, sit down, shut up and listen. You and Serena don't have children. You can live comfortably and well with everything you've got. £10m will see you through a good life towards retirement without ever having to worry."

He twirls his hand around in a circular motion, sinking into his chair and leaning back.

"There will be bumps along the way, but you don't need to do what you're doing and aim so high," he pauses for effect and watches my reaction, which is silence. I'm wrung out. Done. I run my fingers along my forehead and rub my temples, scratching my hairline.

"Roger. Spending and consuming is boring. You can't retire at your age, any more than I can at mine. It'll soon lose its attraction. You need some excitement in your life, not silly football teams and all these holidays. You're getting too old for that. When I hit 70 I started thinking about what I was going to do with what I'd piled up. Either I sit on it and watch it grow, but for what reason? I've decided I want to make some more, but I want it to do good, without ever trusting the government to waste it. I don't like paying tax, as you know."

"But Sidney, I'm completely fucking wiped out." I keep thinking he's not listening, but I decide to stop interrupting him as he often veers off on these flights of fancy, these long stories that you don't think are going anywhere.

"Do you see all this? It's called 'creative destruction'? A cleansing of all that's bad. The banking system is rotten. It needs replacing with something that works. We need to root out opportunities. I wish I had your health, your energy and I wish I knew as much about the internet as you and Serena. But I do have the money."

What I want him to say - what I always want him to say - is what he thinks I should do and that he's got a few quid to bail me out.

"I've set up a trust that will pay out a million a year, but only to people who'll make it grow. But there's more. And this is my plan.

"You have built and lost a fortune. You might get some of it back, but I want to support entrepreneurs. I have been backing one of the best and smartest I've ever met and that investment has come good this week. It's given me an appetite for more."

"Who's that?"

"You have to ask? Roger, it's Serena, don't you see it? Her business has been bought by a Silicon Valley software company. It's peanuts for them, but it's an incredible return for me."

There's a tap on the door and the old bird is there with a silver tray. On it is an ice bucket with a bottle of Krug, and four glasses. "Come in Pat," says Sidney, rising to meet her, the old charmer.

He sinks back into his chair and starts off on one of his big speeches again.

"These banks have become stupid and greedy. There's going to be a reset. I've decided you're going to be my new business partner. I don't know why but I like you. I want to knock some sense into you and turn all that energy and those ideas into something useful. You haven't taken the hint that you should grow up a bit, you shoot yourself in the foot, but hopefully today has taught you a lesson."

"So I work for *you* now?" Already in my head I'm working out how to spin this, what I'll say, how I need to keep schtum about the horror of the fortune flushed down the bog in Iceland, the disaster of the conference. But what the fuck will anyone believe from me?

"You're a good salesman, but you cut too many corners. I think there's a big opportunity out there. Businesses will be under water with debt, there'll be properties that have bigger loans on them than the land is worth. But if the government is taking control of banks they can't be responsible for them closing businesses down. There'll be zombie companies who can't invest. There are property assets that the banks and the government will have to take a haircut on their values. It will mean they won't be able to lend, but business must go on, it must. There's another thing in our favour, my friend," he says. His face is all lit up; he's beaming like a beacon and is now on his feet and jumping from foot to foot.

"There are going to be people out of work, good people who want a challenge. This is the start of a better way, Roger."

My BlackBerry starts buzzing in my pocket. It's Ash. She's bound to be panicking over at Tatton. "I have to get this, Sidney. She'll be having kittens, and having that baby early..."

Ash is trying to be calm and professional but I can hear the panic in her voice. Be cool, I keep telling myself; be cool. Be like Sidney. I'm doing that thing where I try and listen to the conversation in the room I'm in as well as the voice on the

327

phone (this is usually easy when you pick up the gist of what the voice on the phone is saying). Ash is prattling along about how many people we've had to stiff on the Confidence Convention.

"Just tell them to submit their invoices to us. We're making arrangements. Don't worry about your own position, we'll sort it all out. Listen, I'm with Sidney, it'll be sweet. Trust me."

We're finishing off, and she seems a little calmer, when the door buzzes and Sidney starts hopping even more. I hadn't even thought to ask him who the other champagne glasses were for, or to question Val, or Pam, or Pat, when they said I was the first to get here.

"That was that young Irish girl, right?" says Sidney. "She's good; Mel rates her very highly. She can help a lot of these companies, who need to sort their PR out, get an edge. This can start to look very good indeed for us, Roger." As he's talking I'm still curious as to who else is going to walk through the door to this little gathering.

Standing the door, smiling, beaming and with her arms open to greet a long lost friend is the corporate wing of MI5, Mel Bailey, and following her in to the room, with a glow I've never seen on her before, is Serena.

This is going to get really interesting.

November 2008

Barack Obama is elected as the 44th President of the USA. FTSE falls to below 4000. Barclays is bailed out by Arabs from Qatar and Abu Dhabi. The UK government nationalises even more of RBS and Lloyds as the rest are backed by a massive capital injection. The government's Asset Protection Scheme is extended to depositors in Icelandic Banks. The International Monetary Fund (IMF) approves a $2.1 billion dollars loan for Iceland.

The phone call I was dreading, the phone call I was avoiding, but the phone call I was nevertheless expecting came just as I'd dropped off Serena at the airport for another one of her US trips, hopefully this would be the one that was to toast the deal with for the yanks.

"Mr Cash. Been a while. Thought you might have shown your arse. You not gone bankrupt then? I've been hearing all sorts."

"Ah, Tosh. I thought you must have retired on all the business I've been pushing your way."

Silence. The kind of silence that says he knows that I know that he knows. It's awkward, but I have to come across as cheerful and naïve at best. There's always the possibility that I'm just a dopey dupe, which is how he feels quite comfortable in marking me.

Ever since we were kids at school he's thought he could rag me over. The fact that I made a few quid, despite being a clueless shitter who wasn't as hard as him, or his fucked-up, psychopathic crew, was a constant source of bewilderment to him.

But even though I'm bricking it, I know I have to confront this problem if I'm going to make it go away. I had a moment of clarity. A moment where you realise all of your demons need to be confronted, but using that element of surprise. Making them go away, not kicking the can down the road. Appealing to your opponent's weakest point; the thing they hold most dear and the way that they see the world. You see, to this horrible bastard I'm just a means to an end, a figure of fun. Someone who he can make fun of; a useful idiot. I know where he's coming from. In my day I've used enough people in the same way.

Him not getting a shoeing from a mob of discharged child soldiers from some African war zone was a major disappointment, granted, but it has seriously upped the ante for me.

"I'm just heading into Alderley now, why don't we have a quick one in Costa?"

"No. You come to me this time. I fucking hate that place."

On a fine sunny day in May his grimy industrial unit in the arse end of Salford – his global HQ - was bad enough. On a drizzly November day it's not only a dog to find, but Salford's poor and desperate look up at the green Hummer crawling through the desolate streets of their bomb-ravaged hovel like I'm the invading army in some post-apocalyptic nightmare.

Tosh's X5 is parked outside but, thankfully, there's no sign of anyone else around.

The office of RC Aviation (though it has no sign to identify it as such) is deserted and sparse. It's also freezing, with just a single electric heater bellowing out warm air. Tosh is wearing a CP Company Mille Miglia parka with the zip pulled up to the top. He's well padded and I wonder if he's wearing a bullet proof vest. There's no sneering warmth to him this time; he's edgy and pissed off and when he speaks the vapours of air emit the usual nasty odour of stale puke and bad ale.

"Funny times, eh?"

So, in answer to his leading question, I play the pity card.

"Honestly, mate? I'm properly on my arse. Times are tough." Humility like this would hurt, but it's just that moment of weakness that he'll seize on.

"You haven't dipped into the dough from the Euro trips have you? That's my fucking pension, pal."

"No, it's safe." It isn't, of course, as I've had to burn through it to bail out the convention while everything else has been flushed down the same hole in the Isle of Man, with no sign of getting it back.

"And what about the football club? Me and the lads are having a few laughs down there."

I tell him I've transferred over the football club land ownership to Bobbi Armani, that there's a little squabble over detail that may have to wait. After all, how can you contest the ownership of something with someone who doesn't actually, legally, exist?

That morning the first copies of the latest issue of the *North West Business Times* have started dropping into the office receptions all around the region. For those that open the polythene bag there is that one story they like to trot out in order to enter some awards ceremony, creating the illusion that this is what they do every month.

In there, David Rhodes has held nothing back on holding up his investigative powers of journalism in unmasking the conman that is Bobbi Armani. 'International Man of Mystery' says the headline, picturing him with top coppers, business lads, the Duke of Westminster and some MP he claimed he was giving some money to. It's a brutal, precise character assassination. All handed to him on a plate - not that there's any acknowledgement of that - but he knows his sources are good and he's checked out the details in order to join up all the dots, up to and including the ludicrous story about Nanda Mani.

Rhodes, with an eye on bigger prizes, has also tipped off his mate at the *Mail on Sunday*, in return for a mention and a few hundred quid. And while a tasteful business magazine in the north of England may concentrate on the scams, the unfiled accounts and the unpaid debts, the defender of British values had a couple of other priorities in mind.

"How 'Paki Joe' conned the New Labour top brass" – screams their unsubtle headline, picking up on his ethnic fiction and how he blagged his way onto some government committee and was pictured with Gordon Brown. It quoted an old school friend who, when presented with the news that this was an Italian entrepreneur, guffawed loudly and put them right. "He's not Bobbi Armani, he's Paki Joe from Macc". But it's not racist, apparently, because it's alright when they say it themselves.

If he hasn't gone yet, he soon will. If he has any pride he'll never show his face in Alderley, Wilmslow and Hale ever again. Hopefully to fuck off to some place that welcomes all this bullshit and bravado with open arms. Somewhere like Dubai with his new best mate Nanda Mani.

"What's new?" I ask him.

He doesn't invite me to sit, but I pull over one of the rickety swivel chairs, which has a wheel missing.

"I'm getting grief all over. I lost a couple of lads. DD and Hitler are out of action. Word gets out and you have other firms trying to take the piss. I'm short-handed and need to keep the money rolling in."

He looks cornered and edgy. The only thing that will wind him down is something simple. To run him through my plan, my desperate act of a man on the edge. It has to be the last throw of the dice for a man scraping the bottom of the barrel of life. A plan from someone in an even worse position than him.

"I haven't got any leads for you; I'm all run out. That last one I gave you was the only one she's done."

He looks at me sternly. I try not to look in any way like I have any idea what happened, or try and contemplate the chain of events that it has started and the problems it has caused him.

I fill the awkward silence. "Tosh, I help you. You help me. I've got an idea. I need cash quick. I've got shit I don't need, Serena's away and I've got pretty fucking good insurance. If you promise not to batter me, I think we could have a plan."

334

He gives me the gormless impatient look, but I can tell he's biting. He laughs at the suggestion that he could have me in a compromising position in my own house and has a chance to inflict a measurable amount of physical harm.

"I just need to tweak the security system to get you in, sort out the CCTV and leave the safe open. Let's do it tonight while Serena's away. I'll meet you at the Edge at nine."

He nods, sneering at me and the fact that I've succumbed to his will. He's enjoying the power. Which gives me the afternoon to get everything lined up and ready.

I'll show him who's a shitter.

The texts have been flying in about Bobbi Armani. I've deliberately not said a word, even to Ash, even to Martinez and definitely not to Foster. Each of them sounds shocked. Each of them claim they always knew there was something not quite right about him.

I just play it straight. And to be honest, the chances of him rearing his head after this are zero. He's strung that many people along that it's game over.

Just for fun I try his mobile and it goes straight to answerphone. I try the code and the dopey fucker hasn't changed his factory settings. It's a long parade of birds, bullshitters like Jimmi Barnes and – get this – one from Denise Ripley with an edgy tone, insisting she ring him immediately. The dark horse. And I reward myself with a wry smile, thinking of what yarns Bobbi Bullshit may have spun her.

By nine o'clock at night, and on a drizzly cold November, not even the doggers are in the National Trust car park at the top of Alderley Edge. Shagging some stranger in a car while perverts peer through the window was never my idea of fun. It never ceases to amaze me what people will get up to. At that moment, as if by magic, Foster calls.

"Mate."

"Have you seen this about Armani? That twat owes me £50K, he piled in on the Wilmslow deal and cleared me out. Roger, this is serious."

"Patience, mate. It'll be alright. Do you seriously think he has any right over title to the land in Wilmslow anymore?"

"What do you mean?"

"According to the Land Registry, the freehold of the football ground lies with owners of the club and no-one filed anything to contradict that. He may emerge and try to make out he has title over it, but who's going to believe him?"

There's a silence on the line. "So it's ours?" he asks.

"Sort of. Just a few other loose ends to tie-up, but let's just say there's a realignment of equity positions to sort out."

Predictably, Tosh is there before me, parked up in a faraway corner in his black BMW X5, staring out of the window. I'd already scoped out the area for CCTV; there's none. I take Serena's sleek black Range Rover Vogue - more discreet than the Ferrari or the Hummer and less likely to be noticed by anyone.

"Hi, pal. Get in the back and keep your head down. You never know who's watching once we get into Alderley. Camera'd up to fuck." A phrase I'm sure he's used before, a lament for these changing times.

I draw through the gates, up the rise of the drive, then down again to the underground three-car garage where my

Ferrari and Hummer are tucked up safe for the night. Serena's Vogue lives in the bay closest to the house, next to a safe discreet entrance into the wine cellar, games room and safety room, all carefully planned by Serena and the architects.

My heart is racing, and were it not for the warm heated environment of a luxury car I'd be sweating like a rapist. Just like I was, I recall, when all this started cranking up with Mr Psycho who is checking the place out.

I use my remote key to draw down the steel reinforced garage doors and Tosh is looking around quizzically. He's obviously seen his fair share of alarm systems, security doors, codes and the like, but he's taking nothing for granted here.

I stick my face into the iris scanner which unlocks the door. Another of Serena's little touches and a nifty bit of tech from America.

"How am I supposed to get out?"

"Your exit will be through the orangery," I say and he looks at me like I'm speaking Swahili. "I mean the conservatory, at the back. We can make it look like that's where you came in as well."

I don't intend to give him a guided tour and, with my pulse racing sky high, I take the first right turning into the basement living room, pushing through the heavy spring-loaded reinforced and steel-framed door. To the untrained eye it looks like a smallish living room, curtains drawn, but there are no windows, only one door in or out, a small ventilation portal, two sofas (both trusty brown leather Firebirds from Arighi Bianchi, nothing flash) and a wall-mounted flat screen plasma TV. In a hidden panel behind the door is our safe, which I open, taking my driving gloves off to emphasise to him that I'm doing it to ensure there's no trace of him here.

I take out a yellow David M Robinson box containing a diamond necklace; Serena's last Christmas present. I casually toss him the Ferrari car keys. "You can have that," I say. "I never drive it much anyway. Worth more to me nicked anyway."

Also in there are six watches; two are Serena's, four are mine and there's about five grand in cash.

He's eyeing it all up and shoving it in his reusable black cotton Co-op Fairtrade bag, the irony of which isn't lost on me.

"There's about half a mill there, Tosh."

"It'll do for starters," he says, always looking to get ahead of me, pushing me out of my comfort zone.

I'm properly quaking at this point and he probably thinks it's because I can sense he's going to have to give me a kicking to make it look realistic. "Wait here, I'll go and get some tape and a few more bits for you."

This was the moment of no return.

I wait for the door to click shut behind me and then press the lock button on my remote keypad. Safe rooms, the latest executive toy for the paranoid rich, can work either way, especially when you change the lock mechanism. They're also encased in Kevlar panels, which means you can't get any kind of mobile signal, and especially if you're on some crappy network like his BBM is. In this case, a bit of engineering with the locks means the room isn't just safe for those inside it; it's a cell. And he's now locked in it.

This is now past the point of no return. Over the edge.

Before he properly suspects anything's up, I take a left turn back to the garage, enter the code to get into the independent power supply for the safe room and flick on the air supply. In quick order I then attach a long super-strength hose with a clip to the tailpipe of the Hummer. When I fire up the engine he won't be able to hear anything because of the sound-proofing, but he might also find it hard to breathe in a few minutes.

In another of the sweet ironies of modern life, the Hummer H3 won't win any awards for low carbon emissions,

338

but when you remove the catalytic converter and route the hose into the air conditioning system of an enclosed space then, basically, anything living in there has about 10 minutes, tops. Less if they're in pitch black and totally disorientated. So just as he's suspecting I'm taking my time getting down to him and he's finding the air just a little bit thin, he tries the door and realises it's firmly shut.

Obviously I lied to him about disabling the CCTV. Instead I had the hidden camera in the saferoom fixed on a wide shot of the room so I can see his panic. First he's trying to use brute force to kick the door, which is good because that will quicken his heart rate, increase his lung capacity and the speed at which the carbon monoxide enters his system.

Then he realises there's no windows – just walls, just reinforced thick walls, none of your plasterboard shite that he's probably kicked through when he's enforced some drug debt at some bedsit in Salford. Welcome to Alderley, mate. We do things properly here.

Now, here's the thing, topping yourself by carbon monoxide isn't as easy as it used to be. Fucking greenies and the move to unleaded fuel and cleaner engines. Thank fuck this horrible bastard drives a BMW X5 as well. Once I'd worked out he was completely secure with no way of getting out, I had to work out the best way of getting his body out and into his car.

Because there's no way I'm leaving him there, tempting as it is to get him stuffed as a trophy, I've actually no wish to ever see him again.

Do you know where I got the idea for this genius plan? I got a gas mask from this Army surplus shop in Manchester. It was meant to be a joke, a party piece to add the punchline to a joke Serena didn't find funny. Me and Bellamy were stocking up on a load of gear for a paintballing trip we were planning to celebrate the deal. As usual, I went a bit over the top with all the clobber.

After an hour, which is more than enough and after I've watched him writhe and mouth various pleading obscenities at no-one in particular, I turn off the engine, turn the lights back on and watch his still form collapsed on the floor in the safe room. His tomb, his death chamber, will be personally and secretly known forever as the Tosh McGeoghan Suite.

Now this is the bit in the film where the almost-dead axe murderer rises up in a last desperate gasp, a lurch with a concealed weapon. But his lifeless corpse is quite dead. It's just going to be an effort to drag him along and into the back seat of the Ranger.

Slipping on the gas mask, turning the door slowly, I grab him by his ankles and drag him the short distance to the garage, carefully propping up the body. I leave the door wide open, wedged open by a toolbox, whip the hose out and take it with me, reconfiguring the air conditioning unit to pump sweet fresh air back into the room so no-one will ever be any the wiser.

The drive to the Edge takes only a few minutes and I draw up into the corner of the deserted car park where I slot along next to the abandoned X5. It's no mean feat to move his body into the driver's seat, re-rig the hose to the tail pipe of his car, turn on the ignition and pray the stingy fucker hasn't run out of diesel.

As a parting gift to the crime scene investigators I chuck in loads of random estate agents details, a copy of a gay contact magazine and a printout of a fake profile I created for him on a dogging website. For good measure I leave gay sex magazines, calling cards for rent boys, an anal probe and a jar of pineapple joy jelly. All stuff we used to leave on Gary Garner's desk for a wind up.

December 2008

Woolworths goes into administration. Manchester votes decisively against plans for a congestion charge in the city centre. The American car industry is bailed out by the government. The Irish banks are rescued by a government and European programme. Bonuses at Goldman Sachs are cut. UK house prices fall everywhere, except in Cheshire.

The roaring log fire lights up the baubles on the Christmas tree. Serena gleams by the tree as she holds court telling our guests, our friends, the story of how we've braved the storms of the financial crisis.

Ash, with bulging belly, glows with pre-birth warmth, while Tony Martinez holds her glass of sparkling mineral water while she adjusts and plumps a cushion to sit on one of our shiny white sofas.

Sidney and his missus are sharing a moment. Is it Val (not Pam or Pat, that's the old girl who pours the tea at his office) or is it Doris? I forget. Anyway, she's a golden oldie, definitely a proper looker in her prime. She tells the story of when Sidney chatted her up in the Hotel du Cap in Antibes in 1961 and took her around the hot spots of Cannes.

"We know Cannes well, don't we?" I glance over at Ash and Tony, and they share a moment and blush. The scene of their first bunk-up.

But Sidney, the wise old wizard of Alderley – the grandest of them all - has seen a few recessions before and isn't for losing his nerve now. Sidney has that spring in his step of a man on the move, a man whose time is now. A man for the fight, not just the easy money that we've all been creaming, a man who is going to make a lot of money out of turning companies around and troubleshooting.

Serena has that well-woman shine of someone who's getting lots of sex. As well she might. A drunken promise to start a family led to an appointment for a reverse vasectomy, which now means I've started producing seeds. Who knows where that might lead, but I am at least starting to enjoy shagging her again – and she seems well into it as well.

The op hurt even more than the first time I had my nads tied, but the main priority now is keeping her happy. No more games and no more stringing her along.

It's been a tough year for the hard-working entrepreneurs of Cheshire, but the mood is already lifting.

Recessions never last forever. The government bail-out has calmed a few nerves.

Foster's life has taken a turn for the better. He's shipped over his Thai bride and she's keeping him serviced after a hard day's grafting. He's even knocked the brassing on the head and his ex is letting him see the kids more often. He's moved into one of his show homes for Christmas, which seems to have impressed Ting Tong. He knows he owes me for getting him out of the shit with the *News of the World* – a scandal of his making.

Business is doing well since Manchester City's Arab owners started splashing the petro dinars on every Brazilian fancy Dan and chucking millions at journeymen squad players. They might have no class, but they have taste and they all want to move to Alderley.

Foster's also looking after Sidney's portfolio of property investments and he's underwritten a new development aimed squarely at the footballer bling. City basically spoffed their wad into the face of the resi property market, as well as all the other hangers-on and providers of useless services to people with more money than sense. Serena would be at the front of the queue normally, but she's onto bigger and better things and she's got a few clueless mates fannying about in the curtains and sofas end of the game.

Our new stressed fund is inundated with enquiries. Sidney reckons the banks will be too shit-scared to put businesses under the cosh now that the government own them. He's worked out their tipping point and says they'll be more than willing to 'take a haircut' at knockdown prices. With Mel and Karen doing the due diligence, it's a sure-fire winner. I always thought there was something between these two, and so a Cashmore family Christmas features its first lesbian floor show. The old house had one before, but that was when Serena was away and it's not something we talk about any more. That was then, and this is now.

To make up the numbers we've invited Amanda Webb, who Serena has adopted as her new best mate. She's raking it in; acting for celebrities who want to keep out of the papers (Serena's clients, for the most part). She pops up on telly all the time as this expert on media law and privacy. For Serena, it's all a classic case of network-selling. Amanda's husband, some bloke called Steve, hovers in the background, muttering shit like, "wow, it's a different world". He does something in recruitment. I can't see it lasting.

I chink my glass to call everyone to order, just as the iPod shuffles on to the next festive tune, *Driving Home for Christmas* by that bloke with the gravelly voice.

I propose a toast, it's my 40th birthday party, after all. Firstly, to my beautiful wife Serena, the love of my life. I start to say it and it's like I'm taking the piss, but I catch her eye for a moment and realise - do you know what? – this is real. I get a lump in my throat and realise my voice is going to crack, so I take a breath.

Martinez laughs and then raises his glass to propose a toast.

"Friends," he says.

"Real friends," I chuck in for good measure. They say you never really make real friends in Alderley, but we have.

It's also a reminder of the old saying – "no good deed goes unpunished" - one of Sidney's favourites. Why make the effort? Why stick your neck out for muppets. Well, actually, maybe you should sometimes. You get payback.

A few timely reminders to all the key clients that there might be a better way than RC Solutions for protecting their data results in a spate of cancelled direct debits, which sends their business into freefall.

My spies over there are dwindling thanks to redundancies, lads leaving to get better jobs and to even start out in vaguely competing businesses to chip away at the wreck that Bellamy and that witch Denise are watching sink while they witlessly bullshit away their dreams.

The monster they created in Dave Ritchie has been an ever-present in the local media, speaking at events and even getting on the local news to boast about the secret of his digital triumphs to come, and how taking his team on away days up mountains is the sure sign of success.

Truth is, the Indians have long gone, bored with it, and no longer knowing what they can get from it. They're just not interested and the whole place is on the brink of administration, just as I was told by the spooks up on the moors that day, whose wisdom was proved right at every turn.

As a nice little early Christmas present Gary Garner came round with a bottle of wine for Serena and obviously for a bit of career advice from me. He showed me this poem he'd penned as a massive 'Fuck You' at his leaving do.

A poem by Gary Garner

We were the best in the business, the cream of the net
We sold technology solutions to hold off the dark threat

There was no team on earth that could sell tech like us
The place was alive with an incredible buzz

But it's all gone sour, become a wreck
What was once the finest team in tech

We were bought by some Indians, but we weren't chicken feed
Something was going on, and it smelt like greed

A new team arrived with a new set of rules
Deep down we knew they were nothing but fools

They fiddled away like at the burning of Rome,
While one by one we all found a new home

Some went to Dubai, some went to Spain
Others to London to dull all the pain

I have to say it broke my heart
To see our team all ripped apart

But who do I blame for this tale of woe?
For torching the place without a fair go.

You could fault Cashmore or Chambers for taking the cash,
But blaming them would be far too rash

Seems the business was built on foundations of sand
It suited us while we lived the life and made a few grand

So now I will name the guilty three
Who destroyed a dream on a reckless spree

Bellamy the midget with his nervous tic
Denise Ripley and her black broomstick,

And Dave Ritchie, the kilt-wearing jock
I wouldn't give them the cheese off the end of my cock

I never knew I had such talent under my roof. One day I will unleash all this genius in the right direction.

I think I'll suggest that Serena takes him on at Secure Solutions, which we sold into her Ambient Technology Solutions as a security subsidiary. With Mel giving strategic advice, they can conquer the world. As Serena keeps saying, you have to iterate to survive in the modern digital economy, whatever that means.

The Isle of Man Icelandic money has gone. Wiped out. We get updates from the campaign group looking after our interests, but what are the British government going to do about a bunch of tax dodgers like us bellyaching that our dough has gone?

AIG have written and said we might get some money back this month, or next year. Jeremy Clarkson, the *Top Gear* bloke, has been in the papers again, moaning about how much he lost.

The helicopter is stuck in a shed at an airfield somewhere near Chester. No need for that anymore, who wants to be seen doing that when the world is falling apart? I binned off the pilot and wished him good luck. The last I heard he was ferrying about some Arab in Dubai.

Local gossip soon faded over the strange case of the police finding the body of a Salford man in the car park up at the Edge.

Within a day or two, the Old Bill were more than happy to pervert the course of the coroner's official report by leaving out none of the gory details of what they think happened.

The papers gleefully lap it up – 'Gay Sex Secrets of the Violent Crime Boss'. On the basis that the dead can't sue, they declare open season on him and dance all over his grave.

They paint him as some kind of maniac: the instability, the violence, the tempers, all ignoring their own incompetent and failed attempts to ever bring a successful case against him. Part of me admires his boldness, his daring. But then he couldn't stop himself. It was him or me.

Even his mates can't bring themselves to turn out for his send off. There are new sheriffs in town, new bad guys, worse maniacs, but none of them close enough to me to give me any grief. I'm just another victim of their dead mate.

What started as the year when I was going to make my 40 by 40 has turned into the year my arse went, but it was always a goal rather than a dream. The dream lives on, just not the means to achieve it.

As I was saying to Serena when I picked her up from the airport on her last trip back to meet the Yanks who've made her - us - wildly rich; we could always look to make 50 by 50. And anyway, at the rate she's going she'll hit that number before anyone.

I was also just saying to her that I could do with a little business all of my own, something to keep me out of mischief, something to keep me out of the car showrooms, the clothes shops and the jewellers.

It might even lose money, but as I'm sure I heard somebody once say: hey, I'd only spend it on shite.

THE END

ACKNOWLEDGEMENTS

There are many people to thank, too many really.

All of the business observations were as a result of my 12 years as editor of Insider. While there, I'd particularly like to thank Lisa Allen and Neil Tague for their constant support and encouragement and for their rather special world views.

The process of writing the completed book was made possible by editor Joanne Lake, by proper writer Dave Chadwick and with the invaluable help of the angel on my shoulder, my wife Rachel Taylor.

Stuart Wilkin of TH Media has been consistently enthusiastic for the project. And as well as being a great hand at Scrabble, Steve Kuncewicz is a pretty good lawyer too.

I was delighted to be a finalist in Pulp Idol 2014 at the Writing on the Wall Festival and for the encouragement I was given by Mike Morris, the festival director.

I'd also like to thank Frank McKenna of Downtown, Ian Currie and Ian Battersby of Seneca, John Fox of Liberty Pensions and Andrew Spinoza of SKV Communications for being such great people to work with over the last couple of years.

Research wise I am grateful to many people. For being a good sport about locating an early scene in his restaurant, I thank Marcello De Stefano of San Carlo; for the Alderley observations, I couldn't have done it without Steve Hoyles, Nick Carter and Alec Craig; Andy Shaw of the FA gave me insights into the world of football; and my time talking with Eliza Manningham-Buller, the former head of MI5, was particularly useful.

Finally, I can only reiterate that while the backdrop of the story was very real, all the characters are entirely fictional.

Michael Taylor, Marple, 2015